Godmersham Park

ALSO BY GILL HORNBY

The Hive
All Together Now
Miss Austen

Godmersham Park

A Novel of the Austen family

GILL HORNBY

PEGASUS BOOKS
NEW YORK LONDON

GODMERSHAM PARK

Pegasus Books, Ltd.
148 West 37th Street, 13th Floor
New York, NY 10018

Copyright © 2022 by Gill Hornby

First Pegasus Books cloth edition November 2022

ISBN: 978-1-63936-258-5

10 9 8 7 6 5 4 3 2 1

Printed in the United States of America
Distributed by Simon & Schuster
www.pegasusbooks.com

To Robert

Note to reader

This novel is based on a true story. The characters at Godmersham Park are all real; the events are taken from those diligently recorded by Fanny Austen in her daily journal. The rest is imagined.

Friendship is certainly the finest balm for the pangs of disappointed love.

Jane Austen, *Northanger Abbey*

DRAMATIS PERSONAE

The Godmersham Family

EDWARD AUSTEN, third son of Rev. and Mrs George Austen and Master of Godmersham

ELIZABETH AUSTEN, née Bridges, his wife and mother of:

FRANCES AUSTEN, known as Fanny, the eldest child of the family,

and eight younger siblings

The Godmersham Household

MR JOHNCOCK, the Butler

MRS SALKELD, the Housekeeper

SACKREE, known to the children as 'CAKEY', the Head Nurse

NURSE, the Under Nurse

COOK, the Cook

DANIEL, the Coachman

SALLY and REBECCA, the Maids

ANNE SHARP, the Governess

and ten others

The Visitors

HARRIOT BRIDGES, younger sister of Elizabeth Austen

HENRY AUSTEN, younger brother of Edward Austen

CASSANDRA, MRS GEORGE AUSTEN, widow of the Rev. George Austen

CASSANDRA AUSTEN, eldest daughter of the Rev. and Mrs George Austen

JANE AUSTEN, her younger sister

ACT ONE

CHAPTER I

At half past six, in the bleak, icy evening of 21 January in the year 1804, Anne Sharp arrived on the threshold of Godmersham Park.

She was not afraid. Though an urban creature suddenly transplanted in Kent, an indulged only child forced to earn her own living, she felt almost nothing. It is not that she was fearless by nature, nor, it must be said, a stranger to that evil: self-pity. But by then, so much had occurred, so altered were her circumstances and sudden her decline, that there was naught left to fear.

The footman admitted her, and then vanished. A maid appeared, muttered that she would find Madam but did not take Anne's cloak. She was neither a guest deserving of especial courtesy, nor a servant to be treated as a friend. Left alone, in that impressive square hall – bathed at that hour in extravagant candlelight – she considered drawing nearer to the excellent fire, but resisted. One must not appear forward or impertinent or grasping. First impressions are wont to linger and, as yet, she knew nothing of these people and what might offend them. So she stood still and patient upon the black-and-white chequered floor, like a small pawn on a fine chessboard.

She looked at the great, grand doors beyond which, she must assume, lay equally grand rooms. What a perfect house for private theatricals! She wondered if the family already put on such evenings and, if not, whether she might ever enjoy the power to suggest such a thing. And then, to her left, one set was opened, and there came the tap of silk slipper and crackle of taffeta.

'You must be Miss Sharp.'

Elizabeth Austen, Anne's first-ever mistress, came floating across the floor's gleam and extended a pale, elegant hand. By her side trotted her likeness, in childish form. Both were fair of complexion, slender and conventionally handsome – with the glow of those benefits accrued through a life of pure privilege, though without the quirks and exceptions that make for real beauty. Their blue eyes followed Anne as she dipped into a curtsey and returned to their level.

'How do you do, madam.' Anne caught two flickers of satisfaction with her poise and the manner of her speaking.

Mrs Austen politely enquired after the journey. Politely, Miss Sharp gave the briefest reply. She was loath to appear dull, and quite well aware that the journeys of others are inherently tedious. Only had she been waylaid by highwaymen and tied to a tree might then she have mentioned it.

'And this is Fanny.' The new charge stepped forward and bobbed, her eyes drinking in every inch of this stranger. The new governess studied her in her turn. The child seemed tall – was she not but twelve years of age? Anne had once been the same. Her father had taught her to attack it with confidence: stand up, he would urge. Inhabit your own frame. Never feel shame for the woman you are destined to be.

'Good evening.' Anne reached both hands for Fanny's, in a gesture she hoped was warm and yet not too familiar. 'I am delighted to meet you.'

'And we are delighted to have you here, at last.' Mrs Austen guided Miss Sharp towards the stairs sweeping up at the rear of the hall. 'There has been much excitement about your arrival.' She stopped at the foot and bade Anne upwards. 'You must be tired. Fanny will show you to your room and we will send up some supper. Let us save our interview for the morrow. Shall we say before breakfast? Nine o'clock in the parlour.'

As they went up, Fanny chattered while Anne took in her surroundings. Godmersham did not disappoint. It was – still is, no doubt will forever be – a beauty of a house. With a pang, Anne thought of her dear Agnes, and the maid's dark thoughts on country folk. 'You don't know where you'll fetch up . . . They'll have you in a pie there . . . Drown you for a witch, you mark my words . . . Believe me, I had a cousin . . .' Agnes *always* had a cousin.

It seemed that Anne had fetched up in a place of great spaciousness, with intricately carved plasterwork and the finest silk drapes. There was nothing in the air of the ancestors whose portraits queued up the walls to suggest a fondness for witch-drowning. She would write to Agnes that very evening and reassure her.

They came out on the first floor. Across the passage, in front of them, she spied a chamber of perfect proportions, with long windows that must look over the park. It seemed unoccupied. Might that be . . . ? But Fanny had turned left, they took more stairs up to the attic and Anne was reminded of her station.

The atmosphere below had been tranquil. Up here, though, everything changed. A baby cried; a nurse rushed through a door. Boys – Anne assumed they were boys: war was being waged and the French roundly abused – made an unholy row at the end of the corridor. Anne was used to a quiet house – a roost she alone ruled. But that was behind her. She must now adapt.

'And how many brothers and sisters do you have, Fanny?' The volume was such that the quantity not easy to estimate.

'There are eight of us at the moment.' Fanny led Anne along. 'Mama won't stop there, though. There is sure to be another along soon. We can generally expect one every eighteen months or so.' As if, Anne thought, Mrs Austen were some champion breeder kept out in the farmyard.

'How splendid! And are they all brothers?' Anne's tone was casual, but this was a matter of some consequence. She did not yet know for how long she might be expected to earn her own living. But if this position were to last only until Fanny's sixteenth year, then she could hope for no long-term security at Godmersham Park.

'Four boys after me, then two little sisters and another baby boy. But they are still in the nursery.' Anne felt a lurch of disappointment. It was unlikely that the education of *sons* would be entrusted to a mere governess. 'They are perfectly adorable,' Fanny continued. 'You will meet them in the morning.' She opened the door at the end of the corridor. 'Here we are.'

This room – her new home, her refuge – seemed pleasant enough to Anne at first sight. It did not, of course, compare to the suite of rooms to which she was accustomed, but she had no more need for space and its freedoms. Her old life – those days once so large, rich and colourful – was behind her, for now. A small corner would be all she required, into which she could shrink and think and reflect. Where her intellect might hope to flourish, though her body and her time must henceforth be enslaved.

It was longer than it was wide, with a window set high in the wall. Anne crossed over, lifted the curtain to study the view and her eyes met with the deepest night she had ever beheld. The cry of a solitary owl pierced though the silence. She shivered. A view with no neighbours, no lovers, no great commerce that never dared sleep: where was its beauty? The county of Kent was a mystery to her. Why would one live here, so far from the world?

Anne turned back to the interior and found it, on the whole, reassuring. There was no dressing room, of course, but a small, shelved alcove for her meagre new wardrobe and one set of drawers. The walls were papered with a trellis pattern of a powdery blue which she judged inoffensive. Though it glowed rather than roared, the modest fire dealt with the worst of the wintry chill. Above its plain, white surround hung the room's only ornament. Moving in closer, Anne at once recognised the depiction of Christ sharing his Parable of the Lamp. She reached into her memory and retrieved the concluding words of the text: *For nothing is secret that shall not be made manifest; neither anything hid that shall not be known and come abroad.* She shivered again.

The presence of a small bureau cheered her, though. She would have somewhere to write on her long, solitary evenings. There was a small bookcase which she would very soon fill. And, one on each side of the window, there were two beds! Her spirits rose at the prospect that she might, on occasion, be permitted a guest. And they soared at the thought of Agnes beside her one day.

She looked at Fanny and smiled. 'Thank you, my dear. It is a charming room.'

'I am so pleased you think it so.' The child beamed in return. 'I do hope we will be happy here.' She moved to the bed on the right and sat down on it. And then came disappointment-the-second. 'Mama has said you should have a week or two, to recover from your journey, and only then shall I start sleeping with you. Would you mind if this one is mine?'

At length, Fanny went down to the library to be with her parents. A silent footman delivered Anne's trunk; a silent maid brought supper and then dealt with her things. Anne thought of Agnes, packing her possessions with loving care. She watched this nameless young girl – Anne made several attempts, but the maid would not engage – taking them out again, and eyeing them covetously. Of course, she handled the plain, simple dark gowns with contempt. One could not blame her. The one good silk – rosy pink, Brussels lace trim; Agnes, convinced Anne's fortunes must change, had insisted on packing it – did attract notice. The silver brush and combs, *AS* engraved upon them, brought a lift to both brows. And her best handkerchief, embroidered so beautifully by her devoted mama, seemed to come in for particular scrutiny. Anne resolved to launder that item herself. Small things were prone to go missing in larger households.

And then she was alone: weak with exhaustion from the events of her day, yet tormented by sleeplessness. The shock of this new situation hit her with force and, in its wake, emotion engulfed her at last. The Kentish silence roared in her ears; her guts twisted with sickness for a home which no longer existed. She buried her wet face in her pillow and questions raced through her mind.

How did she get here, so alone and among strangers?

CHAPTER II

Anne had first heard of the position the previous summer.

The sun had been bright then, and the air was clear. Though dressed in mourning and with a heart still heavy from the loss of her mother, masculine heads turned as she stepped into the office in Mount Street. Anne paid them no heed. She thought only of the difficult interview ahead.

The clerk gave her the coolest of welcomes and ushered her into the chamber.

'Miss Sharp.' Mr Jameson bowed stiffly and sat down at his desk. Agnes – Anne's maid and, on this day, her chaperone – he ignored altogether. She took a seat at the back of the room.

'Thank you for seeing me, Mr Jameson.' Though he

had long been her family's man of business, Anne had never had occasion to meet with him herself. She sat down and faced him, determined to appear poised and in control. 'First of all, if I may, I *must* ask—'

He at once interrupted. 'A Mr and Mrs Edward Austen of Godmersham Park, in Kent, are seeking a governess for their eldest daughter.' Mr Jameson leaned back in his large leather chair and contemplated his equally large stomach. 'An associate of mine, connected to the family, has asked if I know of a suitable candidate.'

This unexpected beginning left Anne quite baffled. They had much to discuss, and of a most pressing nature. Why must men waste one's valuable time on mere gossip? And, it went without saying, there was no possible *governess* in her circle of acquaintance.

Mr Jameson shuffled some papers. 'And you could start at once which would solve the imminent problem of your accommodation.'

Despite the July warmth of the chamber, Anne felt suddenly cold. 'Sir, I do not quite understand you. I am not seeking *employment*. Moreover, we have a house – a home, indeed – in which we are perfectly content. I fear you have been most horribly misled. We plan to go on as we are, thank you.'

'I am afraid, madam, that arrangement will no longer be possible.' He studied the ceiling and avoided Anne's eye. 'The lease will close at the end of the year. It requires vacant new possession.'

Agnes gasped.

'Mr Jameson! What can you mean?' Anne's voice was rising; her poise slipped away. 'This is the most ridiculous notion which I must condemn in the strongest of terms.' Were there financial problems of which she was not yet aware? Surely not. These past few years, her dear father had worked so very hard that he was away almost constantly. 'Perhaps I might accept that, in future, something smaller would be more manageable. But to be rushed out like this, in a manner unseemly—' An impartial listener might think Anne rather grand at this point – even pompous, indeed. In her defence, she had been raised to believe herself a woman of some privilege and was yet to acquire and command the required mannerisms of a woman who had none.

She took a deep breath, gathered her wits and endeavoured to steer the conversation back on to the course she had planned. 'I am come here this morning to ask if you have had any communication with my father. I have heard nothing since the day after my dear mother's funeral and, naturally, my concern is acute.' Her voice cracked. 'I fear his letters to me are somehow going astray. And if his business in Brussels is to delay his return, then I must now discuss my annual allowance and its best possible investment.'

Mr Jameson held up his hand and looked her full in the face. 'I speak on instruction.' The tone was now firm. 'You will move out by Christmas. From January forward, you may expect an annual allowance of thirty-five pounds.'

The shocked silence was broken by a cry of '*No!*' from the back of the room, followed by Agnes's weeping.

'*Thirty-five—*' The might of that insignificant sum crashed through her defences. 'But – are you asking me to believe that *I* am being cast off? By *my own father*? Mr Jameson!' Such was the strength of her security in her father's devotion, she laughed at the very idea. 'What is this game you are playing? When Mr Sharp hears of it, I can assure you, he will be *greatly* offended. Take this as my warning: I intend to write and tell him at once.'

But Jameson was grave: he raised both bushy brows, protruded his fat bottom lip. And in that moment, Anne felt the shield of her comfortable life break into frag-ments and crumble to dust. They sat in silence for some minutes, and then Anne cleared her throat. "Surely, I am, at the very least, due some explanation? I am struggling to understand what lies behind such a *change* . . .'

'You are indeed. Unfortunately, I am not at liberty to provide one.' He hesitated then and ran one swollen finger along the bevelled edge of his desk. 'My client has asked that you be gently reminded of the alternatives which you have, in the past, been so *obstinate* as to refuse.' When he smiled, he appeared more reptile than human. 'Indeed, I myself am – am – still *available*.'

'*There's* a surprise.' This came from the back of the room. Agnes had never mastered the art of the *sotto voce*.

Jameson ignored her. 'I would like here to mention that I am not entirely averse to the idea of . . .' He paused here, eyes flicking to the insubordinate chaperone, and restarted: 'Though you may no longer be in what we might call your *prime*, I am, nevertheless, willing to overlook—' He stopped again, took a damp cough. 'Perhaps, Miss Sharp, you might like to reconsider our earlier—'

How dare he? 'No!' Anne spoke too much in anger, but was sorely provoked. 'Forgive me' – she lowered her voice again – 'but that is out of the question. *I would rather teach.*'

'Then that settles the matter.'

And at once, Anne regretted her words. Of course she would not be a governess! The thought was fantastical. But for the first time in its life, Anne's pretty nose sensed the acrid fumes of true danger. Her body remained perfectly still, while her mind wrestled the options.

She would simply . . . But – *thirty-five pounds per annum*! What *could* she do while her father's strange mood persisted? She would not be reduced to begging from this villain Jameson. She could not be a burden upon her dearest friends . . . And yet there were things, Anne had to admit, of which she had become unreasonably fond: the odd, comfortable conveyance; decent food in her stomach; a sound roof over her head. Oh, the shame! The shame of it all. Why would her darling papa inflict such a cruelty?

Yet still, she could not accept that she faced true

disaster. After all, she had not been cast off with nothing. There was not enough to form her own establishment, certainly. But, then again, nor would she starve. It seemed the amount had been perfectly calculated to both protect her from harm, while forcing her into employment . . . Surely, this was some ploy, or a challenge? Yes! It must be a challenge: a testing of her mettle. In which case, Anne would meet it. And so, her manner now quite businesslike, she announced: 'I quite agree.'

Agnes let out a low moan.

'Very well.' Jameson looked satisfied. 'There will be no further appeal. The gentleman in question considers his offer most generous. And there will be no other provisions, beyond your mother's possessions.' He inflicted the last wound with relish. 'Lastly, I would like you to know that the discovery of the position was my own work entirely. My client has not been involved.'

'And, please, permit *me* to remind *you*, sir, that I am all that remains of my dear father's family.' Anne stood. 'I cannot know what provoked this bizarre situation but have faith that it will prove only temporary. He will change his mind, Mr Jameson. He must. For I am all that he has.'

CHAPTER III

On her first morning in Godmersham, Anne dressed with particular care: she washed with plain soap – the scented would not be appropriate; brushed her hair fifty times, rather than the customary one hundred – it would not do to gleam – and buried its rich brown under a workaday cap. Her dress was a cambric in a dull grey which had never much suited her. On top, she tied a white apron and then studied herself in the glass.

She had known little of the qualities required in a governess until the moment she found she was to become one. Once the die had been cast, the hot tears shed and dried and the bitter fate accepted, she and Agnes began to research the subject. Anne was a determined creature, unaccustomed to failure, and, once committed, then determined it must be done well. Their greatest aid, it turned out, was *The Lady's Magazine* and its sisters. Anne had always eschewed these feminine periodicals, preferring a political treatise or diverting novel. She had presumed them to be trite, pandering as they did to women whose focus was home and the menfolk. But, suddenly – apparently – this was her world. The regular features on the travails of home education taught her all she now knew.

She and Agnes had pored over them, and made lists of requirements. Naturally, they included gentility and a sound education. Anne satisfied on that score. Equal importance was given to the woman's appearance. One wanted, they learned, a governess who was clean and well presented. That, too, was no challenge – Anne had been brought up to elegance. However – and this was the point that caused Agnes alarm – one should always opt for the plain. Of course, not so ugly as to frighten the children; that would be regrettable. But stern warnings were issued: a good-looking woman under one's roof led to all sorts of trouble. The men could never be safe with them! Those poor, vulnerable creatures – that is, the menfolk – would be left with no option but to be led meekly astray.

'Oh, Anny!' Agnes wailed. 'It's no good, what with your beauty. She'll send you packing at once.'

Anne now looked at herself and wondered if dear Agnes would be pleased or dismayed by her new, indifferent looks. Recent trials had left her much thinner than she had been in happier times. The dress fit badly and hung off her figure without showing its shape. Her eyes were dull. She was too pale. Anne's features were still even and prettily positioned – eyes on the large side, nose on the small; lips that fell naturally into a neat little bow. There was little to be done about them. But, at least, new lines were scored across her forehead and her skin had lost that dimpled softness which others had once so admired.

Of course, Anne's age helped rather than hindered. It was almost wonderful to behold how, at thirty-one years of age, the mere withdrawal of effort could lead to such a collapse – like a well-tended garden that runs quickly to seed at the first hint of negligence. It was not for nothing that these were called the Years of Great Danger.

She angled her face this way and that, spun her trim body from one side to the other and admired her new self. Her past beauty had brought her nothing but trouble and she did not mourn it. Indeed, she rejoiced. The reflection in the glass was of the most perfect candidate. No small child would be provoked into screaming; no adult male tempted toward the high road to ruin. She was delighted to declare herself all but invisible. With confidence, Anne went downstairs.

Once in the hall, though, that confidence wavered. Behind which of these many grand doors was the parlour? There was no way of knowing. She could hardly just pick one and open it: what if she were to disturb the Master, or see something she should not?

At last came a woman whom Anne surmised was the housekeeper, Mrs Salkeld. Anne smiled, introduced herself and, with a small, modest laugh, explained her predicament. The woman was as friendly as the servants, which is to say not friendly at all. There was no smile in return – indeed, no facial expression. The only animation was provided by the cat fussing at her feet, pressing into her skirts and, at last, raising its fur and its back in hostility to Anne.

Seemingly satisfied that the correct tone had been set, Mrs Salkeld gestured towards the room nearest the front door. Anne knocked and entered. The interview began.

'And I gather this is your first such position, Miss Sharp? May I ask why it is that you now seek employment?' This being a Sunday, Mrs Austen's morning dress was a sober claret.

'Yes, of course. I lost my mother last spring.' By the tilt of Mrs Austen's head, Anne deduced her employer sought more information. 'Consumption, sadly. A most horrible affliction. She had borne it well for several years and we had hopes that she might continue to do so. The decline came on suddenly.' Yet more? The popular fascination with Sickness and Death never ceased to amaze Anne, though she was not minded to provide further detail. 'The end, when it came, was merciful. And her death has resulted in something of a change in my circumstances.'

"I am sorry for that. I am told your background is one of unimpeachable respectability. Some Church connection, I believe?'

Anne was taken aback. How could Mrs Austen have got that idea? They had lived *near* a church, certainly; Anne could see the spire from her window. Though, as far as she could remember, neither she nor her mother had ever been through its door.

'My mother was an excellent woman,' she said vaguely.

'And your father?'

This was an unnecessary question, and Mrs Austen should have known better than to ask it, for behind every well-bred governess there was an absence of man: be he dead, be he cruel or, simply, feckless. If it were not for the casual dereliction of the odd gentleman's duty, there would be no women to teach well-bred daughters at all.

Avoiding Mrs Austen's gaze, Anne spoke the words into her lap. 'I fear I never really knew him.' And as she spoke, it dawned that the words were not entirely untrue.

'Indeed.' Mrs Austen seemed to find comfort in Anne's sorry situation. The ideal governess has as few ties as possible. 'And so to the matter in hand. I must first tell you that I take a serious interest in the education of all of my children – the boys *and* the girls. Now, my sons are all, or soon will be, off at school, so dear Fanny will be your sole pupil.'

It was as Anne had already suspected. She took a deep breath. 'If I may, madam, I would like to confirm my commitment to the task.' This seemed to please Mrs Austen. 'Though I did not expect to find myself in this position – and fate has, somewhat, forced my hand – I must reassure you that I now embrace the idea of it with whole-hearted enthusiasm. I would go so far as to say: *passion.*'

Perhaps that last, powerful word might be considered a trifle out of place in the context of their interview. Certainly, it caused Mrs Austen to flinch. But Anne would not retract it. She was simply a creature of the most passionate nature. She felt intensely; where she loved, there she loved absolutely. This had already caused her some conflict and drama. She fully accepted that, one day, it might bring on her undoing. Yet she would not change it, could not see why one would even live in this world without ecstasy or misery or genuine feeling. Insentience, in Anne's view, belonged in the grave.

'Teaching is, I see now, the most delightful of all prospects. And, from what I learned of Fanny yesterday evening, there is a lively intellect there with which to engage. To train the young mind, cause it to grow and to flourish! What greater privilege—' She broke off; had gone too far. The Mistress appeared now to be highly alarmed.

'Miss Sharp!' Mrs Austen's eyebrows were raised and her smile sharp and brittle. 'You are *not* here to turn my daughter into a *bluestocking.*'

'Oh, but of course—' Though Anne could think of little else finer.

'A smattering of knowledge for the stuff of good conversation . . . Passable French . . . Your French *is* good, I take it? Well, that is something. Fanny's mind must be developed to the point at which she can demonstrate a sound understanding of any subject that might arise when she is out in society. And, in the future, she will need to oversee the education of her own family with confidence. An aptitude for music would be pleasing . . . Then etiquette, deportment and regular dance classes will give her that *finish*.' Here, Mrs Austen laughed prettily. 'No man wants a *professor*, after all!'

'But—' How, Anne wanted to say, could Fanny's future be impaired by a sound education? And what if events came not as predicted? Then Fanny would need all the independence of thought that her mind could allow.

Instead, Anne shrank down into her seat. 'Of course, I understand perfectly well what is required.'

The conversation moved on to the grubby particulars. Anne would receive thirty-five pounds per annum – that sum again! It seemed to be the universal valuation of her worth. Her food was included, her laundry was not – that was to be arranged between herself and the laundress. The cost of materials for lessons would be met by the family. Ink, paper, books &c. for her personal use would come from Anne's own pocket. All meals would be taken up in the schoolroom, although in some instances she *might* be invited to join the family downstairs. These occasions were not likely to be frequent. Lessons would begin on the morrow.

Anne smiled her acceptance and prepared to rise out of her seat, but Mrs Austen had not yet finished.

Anne would also be expected to be available to look after the boys or the babies whenever required, on all days of the week. She would not enjoy set hours of freedom, though when the household had no demands of her, she might enjoy liberal use both of the grounds and the attic. Mrs Austen very much hoped that, at all times, Anne would present with a cheerful good nature. She then concluded: 'No doubt today, Miss Sharp, you are still tired from your journey, so we do not expect you to join us at church. You may say your own prayers in your room, after which Fanny will show you the park.'

Mrs Austen stood then and smiled, and Anne did the same. They felt equal relief to have that behind them. It was Anne's first time in such a situation, so naturally it was awkward to her, but, she felt, for her mistress, too. For, however often one does it – however diligently one is prepared for it – dealing with staff is an uncomfortable business.

'It remains only for me to say that I do hope you will be happy with us, Miss Sharp.' That should have been enough. But Mrs Austen was, at heart, a very kind woman and, though she had gone to great lengths to suppress it, her natural kindness could not help but break through: 'You must consider yourself part of our family.'

CHAPTER IV

'Do you like it, Miss Sharp? We think it the *dearest* old place in the world.'

Fanny and Anne were standing together out on the drive, their backs to the park and gazing up and along the Great House. She having arrived in the darkness, this was Anne's first clear view of it.

'It is lovely, of course. Am I right in thinking much of it modern?' Certainly, the pavilions which stretched out to either side – graceful arms in extension – seemed a recent addition. Anne took comfort in that. It suggested the family's social and financial journey was set fair in an upwards direction. Since she was to work for them, this was more preferable than down.

'The middle section is the original.'

Anne studied the high, solid, red-brick façade and judged it as handsome – approved the quantity of generously large windows, with their dressings of white stone relief – but could no longer bear to stand still in rapt admiration. Was it always so cold out here? She burrowed into her cloak, and they began to walk along the front, straight into a wind fierce and determined on biting.

She peered around her hood at the panorama to her right. Although no expert on country estates – she had never ventured beyond Chelsea – even Anne could see that Godmersham Park was a fine one. There was something about its confident air, the way it spread, rolled out and took up the whole of the view, that informed her Godmersham thought itself excellent. And she would have been happy to take it at its own estimation, return to her books and her fire – perhaps venture out again sometime in the spring? But her charge was insistent that she should see everything.

First, Fanny decreed, they *must* take in the kitchen garden, so Anne meekly followed along. Not that she could pretend any interest in the provenance of, say, a turnip – only caring that the turnip should arrive, preferably cooked, on her plate – but, as she was soon to understand, that was not the way with true country people, nor even wealthy gentlemen like Mr Edward Austen. Their lives and their calendars revolved around their crops. Their roots were in the earth, just like their vegetables – always one foot in the clod.

In short, Anne had landed in alien country, among people with quite alien ways. But she was doing her best, affecting enthusiasm – 'Oh yes, *charming*'; 'Most *fetching*, indeed' – when, suddenly, the alienation was taken to extremes. She stopped in alarm. 'Fanny! My goodness!' Although they were still on the path, within reach of the house and domesticity, a large herd of deer bore down upon them. 'Should we not *run*?'

'Poor Miss Sharp!' Fanny laughed. 'Do not be afraid.'

It was not the does that had disturbed her – at once, Anne trusted them to be sweet and harmonious creatures. But among them, charging the atmosphere with his very presence, stood one huge and long-antlered buck. He stared, with a menace quite open; revelled in his size and superior strength. Snorted his threat – or was it, perhaps, his anticipation of triumph? He was all too aware that, in any battle between them, he would assuredly win.

'You are perfectly safe here. There *is* a ha-ha, it is just very discreet. See the ditch there between us and them? Papa says a fence would be a block on the view. This way, we are more part of nature.'

Anne adopted the relaxed air of one who also – but of course! – viewed nature as friend and not mortal enemy. 'Ah, yes. Indeed.' Before scuttling through the gate in the wall of the garden, and taking a moment to recompose. 'Tell me, Fanny, have you been here all of your short life? You were born here?'

'We moved here six years ago, when Papa inherited the house and the parklands.' They had crossed the lawn and were now in the sheltered enclosure of a formal walled garden. Fanny gestured at rows of brown stumps. 'This is Mama's rose garden.' The housekeeper's cat peered out from a bed and narrowed his mean, yellow eyes.

'So your father inherited on the death of his father?' People, families, held more interest for Anne than plants out of their season.

'Oh no! My grandfather on Papa's side is just a retired rector from Hampshire. Papa was adopted, in a way, by the Knights. They had no children, you see, so they sort of borrowed my father and Mrs Knight handed all this to Papa when her own husband died. We are all quite *devoted* to Mrs Knight, you know.'

Understandably so, thought Anne; churlish to be otherwise on receipt of such grand generosity.

'She is part of our family. And, Miss Sharp, soon you will see that our family is *very* large,' Fanny cheerfully continued. They were now, as promised, among what might be the turnips, and Anne found them as captivating as she had expected. 'Mama is herself one of *twelve*! And they all live here in Kent, so we tend to see *them* rather often. Sadly, we see *less* of the Austens, though there are *lots* of them, too – five uncles, two aunts and two grandparents. And of those, it is my Uncle *Henry* who visits us *regularly* – to our *very* great pleasure. No doubt he will be joining us soon, and *then*, Miss Sharp, you *too* will have the pleasure of meeting him!' She smiled, as might a noble in the act of some great benefaction.

They were now arrived at the stables, which apparently demanded a full tour and, as personal introductions were required for each beast within, seemed to take some considerable time. As was only natural, a particular fuss, involving a carrot and much petting, had to be made of Fanny's own pony. On inspecting the stalls, Anne noticed them all to be more spacious than the average London poor dwelling. The family coach and the chair, which had carried her from the stage stop the previous evening, were modern and grand. The horses shone with good health, the vehicles with polish: everything gleamed. Anne had been much impressed, so far, with what she had seen of the mansion, but the luxury of these quarters left her quite stunned.

At last, they emerged on to the formal gardens to the west of the house. 'And what about you, Miss Sharp?' They were crossing more lawn, made glassy with cold. 'Tell me of your family. Or am I being too inquisitive?'

From here, the whole estate was spread out before them; all the tropes of the pastoral landscape contained in one sweep.

'I am here to teach you, Fanny, and broaden your interests,' replied Anne, with her gaze on the vista. 'Please, never stifle your curiosity when you are with *me*. A mind which enquires is a mind that can grow.'

She saw hills to both north and south, dotted with

coppicing. One boasted a small Gothic seat; the other was adorned by – was that a temple, or folly? She could not quite make it out. It was the sort of thing, certainly, created in an idle moment by one with more money than pressing expenditure.

A Norman church steeple peered out over the brow of a long and brick wall. There was a string of pictur-esque cottages, housing, no doubt, the less picturesque poor, and a small river, spanned by a stone hump-backed bridge. In short, it was much like one of those more amateur watercolours at which Anne had once glanced, then dismissed at the Summer Exhibition.

'But you and I are quite different.' Her voice started to falter. 'I am all alone in the world now. Apart from Agnes, that is.'

Suddenly, she was struck by the blow of the contrast between them. And – oh! – what a contrast it was. Anne's small, solitary self against this huge tribe of Austens.

'I have no siblings, no parents. No relations, even – or not that I know of.'

And as for their patriarch . . . Born the son of a parson, and now master of this whole estate? Mr Edward Austen was as a boy from a fairy tale. And she could not help but feel that they were travelling along the same road, he and Anne, but in quite opposite directions.

'Oh dear!' She held out her hand. Yes – it had started to rain.

CHAPTER V

'I was eleven or twelve years of age.' Mr Austen was in full and confident flow at the head of the table. 'And there arrived at our rectory the newly married Mr and Mrs Knight. Now' – while his tone was conversational, the content inclined more to the monologue – 'why 'twas *I* upon whom they alighted, out of *all* of my family, I shall never quite know –'

'I *believe* it was your great personal beauty, Papa,' Fanny kindly reminded him.

'Oh,' Mr Austen demurred, with great modesty. 'I do not know about *that*.'

'But it was, Papa!' Fanny wriggled in her seat, beyond delighted to be able to help out the recall of a superior grown-up. 'Truly. You have told me so, often, yourself!'

'Well – er . . .' Mr Austen was momentarily discomfited; his wife smiling into her soup. 'Nevertheless. To continue . . .'

This was the evening of Anne's first full day of employment, and yet already she was seated at the family dinner. The occasion was Fanny's thirteenth birthday. It was not a grand affair – just the parents, the four eldest children and a young local aunt. And, thus far, the entertainment appeared to be Mr Austen's recitation of anecdotes they all already knew well.

'– and, in a quite remarkable turn of events, they took me away with them.'

Fanny turned towards Anne, and whispered: '*We* think it rather funny: to select a small boy as your honeymoon companion.'

Anne, too, thought it odd, but was wary of showing any sort of reaction. She had no doubt Mrs Austen thought the privilege of a family dinner had been granted far too soon for comfort. It was clear from the anxious glances in Anne's direction – judging her manners, checking her behaviour. Much better that Anne endure a solitary few weeks at least, dining in her room, contemplating the depth and extent of the boundaries between them. But it had been Fanny's express wish that her new governess should be included.

'It was some years later when the dear Knights returned with the idea of formal adoption. Sadly, not blessed with their *own* progeny, they asked my dear parents if they might spare *me*. Of course, my dear father was horrified—'

' "What about the boy's education?" ' supplied one of the children.

' "And what of his Latin?" ' another chimed in.

Anne sensed Mr Austen's regret at the spoiling of his story. 'Quite.' He took centre stage again. 'But my more practical mother—'

'Said, "I think, my dear, we should let the boy go!" ' Fanny recited with triumph.

'And are we not all grateful for that?' Mrs Austen interrupted, performing that awkward, wifely manoeuvre of appearing delighted with the anecdote while simultaneously dispatching it. 'Now then, Fanny. What game shall we play after dinner?'

And while those games were discussed, Anne considered the fascinating figure of Edward Austen – that boy from the fairy tale, now adult and so very prosperous. It appeared he was a gentleman of great warmth, certainly, and not inconsiderable charm – though this was mere observation. He had not, in fact, talked to the governess beyond the courtesies of simple introduction. But he seemed to be solicitous to his wife, affectionate with his children, radiant with that comfortable happiness brought by extraordinary good fortune. His evident pleasure in his own lot brought with it no arrogance, but instead only a boyish simplicity, which made it hard to begrudge.

Alas, he was not a man wide open to wifely manoeuvre. No sooner had charades been suggested than conversation had, once again, to surrender to anecdote.

'The marmot, indeed, is an animal that one finds in these mountains.' Mr Austen was now sharing the high points of his Grand Tour. 'I saw it before it was skinned and, I may tell you, was by no means prejudiced in its favour.' A small boy – perhaps it was George – began, in his boredom, to kick at the table. 'A remarkably unpleasant specimen. Quite unlike our own native mammals, which seem to be altogether superior. Nor does it bring benefit to the agricultural practices most common in the region.'

Anne thought it a shame to find in Edward Austen yet another beneficiary of the Grand Tour, for it was a custom of which she did not approve. Though its express purpose was to improve the character and broaden the mind, she had yet to meet a young man made more interesting by the experience. In her view, the Tour's only true benefit – to the Tourer himself, his sex and his circle – was the purchase of an inexhaustible supply of conversational matter and, with that, dining-room dominance for the rest of their days.

The kicking became louder; the boy yet more restless. Anne waited to hear some sort of parental rebuke. Instead, the mother, placid and unruffled as ever, gave the merest glance of regret to the obstinate kicker, while the father continued with the thrust of his story.

'Mind, as I learned from my extensive Alpine sojourn, the marmot does have one significant advantage and that is—'

'Dear Edward!' Fanny's young aunt, Miss Harriot Bridges, cut in. 'You do know that *I* find you *fascinating*, to the most *desperate* degree. I long to hear more, particularly about our own native mammals. *Too* riveting.' She shuddered with excitement. 'But I wonder, do the *children* want to hear any more about the agriculture in wherever or those' – she waved one pretty hand – 'other things.'

Anne was quite riveted by this bold interjection; Mr Austen was simply astonished: 'The marmots?' He looked to his family for a clamouring defence. 'No more of the *marmots*?' He was thunderstruck. 'And I have yet to get on to—'

'Fanny's promised to buy me a cricket ball!' burst in one boy or another.

'I didn't *promise* exactly,' Fanny demurred.

And the marmot was lost.

After dinner, the family was to adjourn to the library. It was not made explicit whether Anne should join them or not; she received no direction. So, once again, she stood hesitant in the hall, uncertain whether to follow or just disappear. It was the rather fascinating, bold aunt who came to her rescue.

'Do come with us, Miss Sharp.' Miss Harriot Bridges was the younger sister of Mrs Austen. A pretty young woman of about twenty years, she issued a warm, dimpled smile and guided Anne towards the library. Her figure was plump, her stature petite; she was dressed in a fine, pale muslin which seemed to bless her milky complexion. 'It is a pleasure to have a new face at Godmersham. All they ever get here is babies and more babies. I confess I can't help but prefer the company of those who have a *few* teeth and a *smattering* of language.'

'Oh dear.' These were the first words Anne had spoken for some hours. Her voice was enfeebled and her confidence wounded. Put next to this embodiment of high-spirited youth – a little exemplar of excellent breeding – she suddenly felt uncommonly tall, thin and drab. She cleared her throat. 'I am very much afraid, Miss Bridges, that there's not much to be said on the subject.'

'Come now,' Harriot replied. 'I can see at once that you are a woman of secrets. Let us coze by the fire, and I shan't stop till you've *spilled* them.'

Of all Godmersham's many fine rooms, the panelled library was by far the finest: the length of a ballroom, with two roaring fires, an enormous table in the middle for the spreading of papers and shelving on all sides, well stocked with books. Anne longed to go over and examine their spines and see what they had there. Might even she look, or would that create the suspicion of a bluestocking tendency? Before Anne could decide, Harriot had thrust her into the depths of the sofa.

'Now,' she began. 'Tell me at once, Miss Sharp: why on *earth* are you here?'

'Why, to teach Fanny, of course,' Anne returned as she gathered her long limbs into a more decorous arrangement. 'I gather Mrs Austen preferred not to send her to school.'

'Yes, yes.' Harriot dismissed that as an answer. 'Although I must say' – she lowered her voice – 'I do think it a slight affectation on my sister's part. Of course, I know that it is the *thing* these days – I hear they have a governess at Eastwell; no doubt that provoked her. Perhaps you know the lady already? I imagine you all as one happy band, sallying forth into all the best houses. Sharing your stories. *Making notes.* Yes?'

Anne scotched that idea, but could not help smiling at it.

'*We* went to school, after all – my sister and I – and seem to have come out unscathed. Certainly, our manners and accomplishments have not yet provoked any adverse opinion.' Harriot gave a pert grin. 'And poor Fanny needs friends of her own age. She seems rather *marooned* to me, between those two doting parents and that *multitude* of little boy savages.' She dropped her voice again. 'She is in danger of becoming her mama's little creature. I did *tell* Mrs Austen to furnish her with a sister much sooner, but did she listen?'

On the other side of the room, a game of charades was begun. Anne longed to be invited to join it, but Harriot was settling down into her cushion. 'So why are *you* here in particular? That's what I'm after. No woman chooses it, after all. And I've read a great many novels, Miss Sharp. I know all about the wild adventures of the *good-looking governess*, such as yourself.'

'Indeed?' Try as she might, Anne could not recall any such character in the fiction that she had read. Clearly, she and Miss Harriot Bridges enjoyed quite different tastes.

'Yes! You are running away from *something*.' Harriot looked at Anne, musing. 'You are not at all what I expected. I had *steeled* myself for a vision of great *plainness* but, Miss Sharp, you are really rather pretty. You must have been prettier still when you were more of my age. At your *peak*, as it were. You certainly have an *air* about you, though I have yet to quite place it.' Her eyes then lit up. 'But perhaps you are running *towards* something? Yes!' She clapped her hands. 'That must be *it*! I have no doubt that the next news I have of you will be that you have scandalously *eloped*!'

Despite all of the above, Anne found that she could not help but to warm to Miss Harriot Bridges on this first acquaintance. She actually chose to converse with the governess, at least. Anne already knew not to expect this degree of consideration from others among Harriot's class. And she had a spirit about her, which Anne immediately attributed to her unmarried status. Perhaps

Mrs Austen had once been the same, but now that her life had worked out in its perfect sequence – marriage; estate; child after child – Elizabeth seemed to Anne a little dulled by complacence.

No doubt, Harriot would, in the end, turn out like her sister, but at the moment, Anne thought her in an optimal state: she was single, so unquashed by a husband; neither dwindled into a wife, nor yet beset by worry or rank disappointment. She seemed to enjoy status and wealth and the traditional good looks of the rest of the family. There was no reason to doubt that, one day, she would come to be settled. In the meantime, she could enjoy being simply herself.

Mrs Austen was now at the piano, the children were dancing and the atmosphere so gay that Harriot could resist it no longer. The dreary governess was abandoned, her secrets forgotten. Anne sat alone for some moments, benign and impassive, for all the world as if her feet were not twitching to dance, her voice not yearning to sing, her own spirits reluctant to soar with the joy of the evening.

Then she rose, dropped a small curtsey in her employers' direction, and quietly withdrew.

❧

Once back in her room, Anne found it difficult to work. Before her arrival, she had set herself the task of improving her Greek, the aim being to raise her relationship with Aeschylus to a higher and more intimate plain. Though she might have the time, certainly – indeed, with these many hours ahead in which to enjoy the freedom of the attic, she might become fluent in most tongues, ancient *and* modern – the inclination was absent. The texts remained on their shelves, while her mind digested the events of the evening.

She had been introduced to all of the Austens now, but – apart from the boys, who had appeared only together in one, masculine clump – they had come at her as individuals. That evening represented her first opportunity to examine them as a collective. For thirty years, Anne had lived within a small family of irregular shape and – until its collapse – considered it the height of good fortune. This had led her to a prejudice against those, like the Austens, of the regular, large and conventional type. A full set of parents and too many siblings could only lead to a diluted experience. But she was forced to admit to being pleasantly surprised.

Anne's previous anxiety that Fanny might be spoiled could now be laid aside. The occasion had not erred on the side of the lavish. The birthday present from her mama was a pretty sandalwood box for the storing of toothpicks which, while obviously absurd, was hardly immoderate in the context of the family's wealth. They had all enjoyed an excellent syllabub, otherwise dinner, though good, was not out of the ordinary. The table was not exactly over-burdened with guests or sycophants.

In the quiet of the Godmersham attic, she reflected on the birthdays she had enjoyed as a child. In stark contrast to Fanny's, her own had been wildly extravagant.

Had they known the blessing of more children, then perhaps her own parents' love might have been tempered into the more reasonable fondness for which, in time, most parents settle. But in the absence of others, with Anne their sole focus, the feelings her mother (in particular) had for her were inflated to a point too like passion. The day of her birth was seen as a moment of miracle, and its annual celebration resembled the feast day of one of the more notable saints. Anne neither demanded nor needed all this attention. But she did enjoy parties, and her own were the best.

CHAPTER VI

For Anne's thirteenth birthday, her mother had ordered a gown designed for a girl far more senior. It was clearly expensive, had flounces galore, and a neck cut too low. Her hair was curled in papers for the very first time. She felt quite absurd.

But having been a famous beauty once in her own youth – as she so often recounted, at the merest hint of opportunity and quite ample length – Margaret Sharp valued her daughter's looks above all other virtues. And at the sight of Anne dressed up for the evening, the customary tears sprang to the eyes.

'Oh, my love! Such a picture.' Her mama swept across the room and took Anne's face in her hands. 'Forgive me. I *am* silly.' There followed much fussing with a handkerchief and dabbing of eyes. 'It is just that you do so remind me – I was wearing a similar shade, and *Lord Norton* himself said he had never before beheld such – Oh, but no matter. My days of glory are sadly – *You* are our future.'

Agnes, at the table, was arranging the flowers with mounting irritation. 'Handsome is' – she thrust a carnation into the vase with some violence – 'as handsome does.'

'It is not altogether comfortable.' Anne wriggled and tried to pull up the dress to cover her chest. 'I don't feel myself in it.' In truth, she hated it – standing like a mannequin, pretending at womanhood.

'Do stop squirming like that, Anny.' Her mother smoothed down the silk and patted her hair. 'And please remember your posture, my love.' She gave a sharp poke at Anne's shoulders. 'If you are to be a success then at all times you must stand like a flagpole. Up now! Flagpole! There. I cannot wait to show you to your dear papa.' She glanced at the clock on the mantel, and her eyes danced with excitement. 'He will be here soon. I must dress before his arrival. I have strong competition now, do I not, Agnes?'

'I'm off to the kitchen,' Agnes replied and limped from the room.

They dined early, as was their custom on this great occasion. It left the space of the evening for their own entertainment at home, before they set off for Drury Lane – the last and best treat of the day. The same guests gathered as gathered every year: the four Mercer girls, with whom Anne took her lessons, and, for the first time, it was decided that her father's close friend,

Mr Jameson, would join them – though Anne had not been consulted. As ever, they dined very well.

'The most excellent pastry I have tasted in all of my days,' her papa pronounced at the end of the meal. 'These past weeks I have travelled from one indifferent table and on to another. It is a joy to be returned to yours, my sweet love.'

The details of Mr Sharp's professional activities were a mystery to Anne, but one which she was not minded to solve. She already had too many interests for the hours in her day. All she did know was that this 'business' meant that he was almost constantly absent. He worked very hard and Anne and her mother wanted for nothing – apart from his company. But there were compensations. His returns, when they came, were often unexpected and brought a thrill, even ecstasy – emotions not often found in more common domesticity. And Anne long ago decided that her parents were the happiest couple in the world.

'Now for the drama!' Anne's papa rubbed his hands, flicked back his coat tails as he sat in his chair. The girls fussed around, clearing the space at the end of the drawing room and making sure their audience was comfortable. Georgina, the youngest of the Mercers, handed out programmes.

Mr Jameson read his with some disappointment. 'Ah, dear,' he said, with a shake of his head. 'This is one of those what-they-call *tragedies*, I do believe. Is it not,

Sharp? Those miserable sorts of fellows always leave me quite cold.' He settled his ample form into the chair, as if preparing to nap.

Mr Sharp guffawed. 'There speaks the philistine! I believe Othello had much cause to feel miserable.'

'If you say so, my dear boy, though I know not the first thing about him. No doubt he is the author of his own misfortune. These fellows generally are – always well born and then make such a hash of it. Quite tries one's patience. Much more amusing if they could *just* see the *best* in things and give us some *jokes*.'

'We will have none of that here, Jameson. Pay no heed to that rabble-of-one down in the pit, my dears. Players, I beg you: play on!'

Mr Jameson's behaviour was well known to err on the side of offensive but, for once, he was not without some justification. Three young girls might well be expected to indulge in something more sparkling, but they were in a serious phase, Anne and the Mercers. They fancied themselves a group of intense intellectuals and their pretend games did not involve damsels and princes, but soirees and salons.

So, to demonstrate what they imagined to be their superiority of mind, they had chosen to enact some scenes from *Othello*. Henrietta, the loveliest Mercer girl, played Desdemona; Catherine took Iago – a challenge for one so sweet and kind. And Anne, with her ribbons and ringlets, gave her might to the Moor:

'Then you must speak
Of one that loved not wisely but too well.'

She strode about the drawing room, relishing her moment. Her audience was – mostly – entranced. Even Mr Jameson was showing some sort of interest, though Anne could not help notice that his eyes were firmly fixed on her newly exposed embonpoint. She paused to wrench up her neckline and then carried on.

'I took by the throat the circumcised dog . . .'

Anne drew a dagger from her skirts. Her mother hissed: 'Flagpole!'

'And smote him thus.'

Mrs Sharp sat up erect and hissed again: 'Posture, Anny!' She lightly tapped at her own elegant shoulder. *'Flagpole!'*

Anne left Othello behind for a moment to plead with her mother. 'Mama, *please*. I am playing *a man*.' She got back into position and rediscovered her emotion:

'I kiss'd thee ere I kill'd thee.'

'But why? Why *must* she take the britches part?' Mrs Sharp wondered aloud.

'No way but this . . .'

'I *never* took a britches part, did I, my dear?' she said to her husband.

Anne was now gasping for air, in a manner most tragic.

'I was simply *always* the heroine.' She patted her hair and smiled prettily. 'Cannot think why.'

'Killing myself, to die upon a kiss.'

Anne fell to the floor and died horribly.

Agnes leaped to her feet and clapped with enthusiasm, while the others sat and applauded. Flushed and triumphant, the three girls collected themselves, linked up, took their bows, sure that the whole piece was magnificent.

Now upright, still rapturous, Anne was disconcerted to find Mr Jameson still stared at her, and her alone. 'I must admit to being impressed.' He pursed his fat lips and looked her up and down. 'May I congratulate you, dear Margaret, on your daughter's appearance this evening? A fine figure developing – she appears more mature than her years. Almost ready to go off to market, I should say.' He gave a nasty sort of chuckle of the type Anne had never before heard. 'You'll have no trouble finding takers there, Johnny.'

To this gross opinion, her dear papa offered no sort of rebuke. 'Ah, but she reminds me of her mother. It brings to mind the first time I saw you, Margaret my love. What age were you then – in your fifteenth year, or thereabouts? I recall little beyond the way you ignited the stage.'

'Perhaps not quite that.' Her mother smiled. 'Young enough to be impressed by the attentions of such a mature gentleman.' She stroked his face. 'I remember – it was Millamant in *The Way of the World*.'

'She has that certain quality – that irresistible charm.' Mr Sharp took his wife's hand and she duly melted. 'I can see her name too at the top of the programme. Why not, indeed? It did her mama here no harm, eh?'

'Dearest.' Mrs Sharp looked fondly at her husband. 'So *sweet,* your ambitions, but I must support Jameson. Such an angel as ours will make a *fine* match.'

'And the sooner the better,' said Jameson.

Anne listened to the talk about her future with innocent disinterest. Of the two options suggested, then obviously she much preferred that of her father – a fine match, indeed! Truly, her mama did say the funniest things. But she very much intended to live life exactly as she pleased.

The family said goodnight to the Mercers and prepared to go out. Her father's busy life and frequent travel meant that it was not often that the three of them went abroad in public. Indeed, for Anne, it happened too rarely. She was as much looking forward to the particular treat of them being together in the coach as she was to the play.

'May I sit between you?' Anne begged as Agnes fastened her cloak.

One arm around his wife, one around his daughter, Mr Sharp drew them in, both close against him. 'We three,' he murmured, 'we are a fortress,' planting a kiss on each brow. 'We three together and against the whole world.'

Anny's face was pressed against his chest, her face buried in his jacket, the cloth of it steeped in his favourite cologne. She breathed in nutmeg and lime, a small hint of lavender. Love. Happiness. Home.

CHAPTER VII

'What are you busy with there, my dear?' Anne faced
the wall of the Godmersham attic room, her voice muf-
fled through the stuff of her nightgown. She was, at that
moment, indecorously pulling it on at one end, while
removing her dress at the other. 'You have been writing
for some time.'

'My journal, Miss Sharp.' Fanny's young voice was
aflame with self-importance. 'Every evening, I make sure
to fill in the events of my day. I have *never* yet failed.'

'That is impressive.' Anne stuck her head through the
opening, stepped out of her frock and turned around.
'For how long have you kept it?'

'All the way since Christmas!' Fanny, already dressed
for her bed, turned around from the desk and smiled
proudly. It was now the first week of February. 'I confess

it is not very detailed.' Fanny leaned back in her chair, to clear Anne's view. 'It is a *very* small pocket book. Just a line for each day, really: two pages to a week. See, for today I have written: *Aunt Harriot left. She gave me 2/6. Mama went to Canterbury with her. Tonight I sleep with Miss Sharp for the first time since she has been here.*'

Anne had worried enough about the workings of sharing a room with her charge: how to dress and undress while preserving her modesty; the use of the chamber pot; the removal of all privacy of feeling and thought. And to all that, she must now add a new fear: these diurnal details might be recorded for posterity! She picked up her hairbrush and asked into the glass: 'And you intend to continue?'

'Oh, *yes.*' The young, clear face puckered with that now familiar, earnest expression. Fanny was earnest about most things, Anne was discovering, possibly a little too earnest for a child of her age. '*Mama* says I must keep it for the whole of my lifetime, and take it with me to my *own* home, so my *own* children can enjoy reading it when *they* are grown.'

There it was again, thought Anne: that solid confidence in the inevitable pleasantness of the girl's future. 'I am sure they will love it,' she replied as she put on her nightcap. 'Shall we now say our prayers?'

Each took up position by her side of the bed, and fell to her knees. Head respectfully lowered, Anne offered the usual obsequies in a celestial direction, then looked up through her lashes. Was that enough? She saw Fanny's eyes were screwed shut still, her lips moving like those of one in a trance: she seemed in full flow. Anne adjusted her position, again tilted her head. With so many souls in her family, Fanny could be praying for some hours . . .

To her shame, Anne's mind drifted away from the Almighty and proceeded to nibble at the corners of her many pressing concerns. Was she permitted to read past Fanny's bedtime, or was she now to keep the hours of a thirteen-year-old girl? If the latter, then she faced many dark hours of boredom, but to endanger the girl's beauty sleep would be considered the most heinous crime. Or perhaps Fanny might expect them to chatter, after the candle was snuffed, like schoolgirls in a dormitory. That might prove wearing . . .

'Amen,' pronounced Fanny.

'Amen,' echoed Anne with relief. She was now stiffening with cold.

They climbed into their beds.

'I hope you *approve* of my keeping a journal, Miss Sharp? *Mama* thinks it highly appropriate for a girl of my age.'

It seemed that chattering was, indeed, on the agenda. 'Oh, very much so. Naturally, we will be working on the arts of composition during the course of our lessons. But the more practical writing skills are equally useful. After all, over the course of your lifetime, you will write many more letters, for example, than elegies or odes. Shall I blow out the candle?'

'Oh, Miss Sharp, *please* can we talk just a little bit longer? It is our *very* first night!' Fanny snuggled down on her side, and faced Anne. 'I know *very* well how to write letters. You say *thank you* for whatever it is the person has given you and how *very* delighted you are. Then you *enormously* hope to see the person again soon. And then, you thank them once more for the thing!'

'Not even a word on the weather?' Anne smiled. 'That approach certainly has the benefit of economy.'

'You think it *incorrect?*' In one quick, violent movement, Fanny was up on her elbow, her face shot through with horror.

'Oh, no! Not incorrect, my dear. But I wonder if we cannot do a *little* better, now you are a young miss and no longer a child.' Anne leaned over to snuff out the candle between them. 'Let us revisit the subject in the schoolroom tomorrow.'

Anne's first task as governess was to turn the designated attic room into a suitable place for learning. Hitherto, Fanny had been taught only in the nursery and by her mother in the parlour and, though her handwriting was passable and her reading quite adequate, the previous standards of her education did not meet Anne's own. So she decorated the walls with maps of England and Europe, and various illustrations that might give stimulation – a chart of our monarchs, Garrick as Hamlet and so on. She rearranged the table and chairs so that she and her pupil could sit facing each other, rather than side by side – the reason being that she could hold Fanny's eye, and thus her attention.

But she and Mrs Austen were in constant dispute – polite, discreet, always through smiles and yet nevertheless vicious – on the subject of how many hours a day Anne might expect with her charge. The timetable was that work began at ten in the morning and lessons continued until one o'clock. Then, after a walk or a visit, the afternoons would be spent in lighter pursuits – drawing or needle-work; dancing lessons when the master came. However, in the Godmersham world there was always something that was more important. Birthdays, for example – and given Godmersham's large population, the birthdays came often – were always an excuse for a holiday.

On top of that it turned out that Fanny was, as Harriot had perceived, her mama's little creature. So she was taken out all the time, accompanying her mother on endless calls, drinking tea and bearing witness to adult conversations: being groomed for a copy-cat future, when she should rightly be learning to be just herself. These interruptions to learning Anne found irksome enough.

Still more problematic was the conflict over what constituted learning at all. Anne longed to take this young, malleable intellect, exercise and stretch it – fill it to the brim with new and challenging ideas – but already she faced a Sisyphean struggle. On top of Mrs Austen's aversion to the bluestocking ideal, it seemed there was yet another force of resistance working against her: Fanny's young mind was as malleable as granite.

Anne had taken the precaution of bringing books with her – the ones she herself had used as a pupil – as she had heard that the ordering of new works could prove contentious with employers. There were more amusing ways to squander one's funds than on the education of daughters. And so on that day, the staples of reading and arithmetic behind them, she was introducing her pupil to the glories of Renaissance Art.

'Oh yes, Miss Sharp. I should say it is *good*.' Fanny wrinkled her nose at a plate of the Sistine Chapel. 'Thank you so much for showing me.' One momentary study, and she sat back in her chair.

'Do you have no further questions or thoughts, Fanny?' Anne raised an eyebrow. 'It is, after all, one of the most magnificent works ever created by man.'

'Is it?' Fanny put her head on one side. 'Then I am *most* grateful to know all about it.'

'Perhaps one day,' Anne persisted, 'you might go to Rome and see these glories with your own eyes. In which case' – she was clutching at straws now – 'your companions, or *husband*, would be gratified to discover you are already well versed in—'

Fanny put her fingers to her lips to stifle a giggle. 'Oh dear, Miss Sharp. I do not think so. You see, I have no wish to ever leave dear old *England* at all.' She leaned in confidentially. 'Nor even Kent!'

Anne sighed, took the book, turned the pages, alighted upon *The Birth of Venus*, and turned it back again. 'Now this, by Botticelli—'

'Oh! Miss Sharp!' Scandalised, Fanny covered her eyes. 'Surely that is *ungodly!*'

'Forgive me, my dear.' Defeated, Anne closed the book. 'I am sorry if you found that inappropriate. Put it out of your mind.' And please, she silently begged, do not tell your mama. She rose, crossed the room and hid the apparently offensive material back on her shelf, while Fanny explained her position.

'I *think* I prefer Art to be properly *pious*. Not just your paintings, Miss Sharp, but books, too. They should at least *try* to be spiritually improving, do you not agree? Every day, I do *try* to pick up some work of that sort.' She gave a beatific smile. 'I like to call it: *reading my goodness.*'

Anne bit her lip, collected herself and sat back down at the table. 'Now, we still have one hour left to us. Let us talk about the writing of a letter.' Surely here, she was on safe ground. 'Last night, I had the idea that you might pick one of your many relatives and embark on a correspondence. What think you of that?'

'I think it the most lovely idea! Well *done*, Miss Sharp,' Fanny replied in an encouraging tone. 'I have a cousin,

Anna, of my age . . . Or perhaps I should select one of the grown-ups?' Her attitude towards grown-ups was akin to that of the Greeks towards gods. 'Uncle Henry, perhaps? I *adore* Uncle Henry. No, I think an *aunt* altogether more *suitable.*' She leaped out of her chair. 'My Aunt Jane wrote such a dear little letter when I was born. Let me find it! I keep it in my Box of Great Secrets.'

Anne smiled as Fanny rummaged around in the cupboard. 'You must have many Great Secrets, my dear, to require a whole box?'

'Oh, no, Miss Sharp. I have none at all.' She stooped to the lowest shelf. 'But I believe a young lady *should* have something of that sort, do you not? It adds to one's *mystery.*' She emerged from the cupboard in triumph. 'Here! I have found it.' She sat down again, and read it aloud.

My dear Neice,

As I am prevented by the great distance between Rowling and Steventon from superintending your Education Myself, the care of which will probably devolve on your Father and Mother, I think it is my particular Duty to prevent your feeling as much as possible the want of my personal instructions, by addressing to you on paper my Opinions and Admonitions on the conduct of Young Women, which you will find expressed in the following pages.

I am, my dear Neice,

Your affectionate Aunt
'The Author'.

Fanny looked up. 'And then there were a few stories and so on attached, but I believe Papa has kept those for safekeeping.'

'Well, that,' pronounced Anne, 'is the most delightful of letters, and how lucky you are to have received it.' She chose, just this once, to overlook the poor spelling. For listening to those winning few words had set forth a strange trickle of warmth somewhere within her: this aunt wrote with a smile. 'I believe we have found the ideal correspondent.

'So, let us begin.'

CHAPTER VIII

A country house, peopled by those who have known only contentment – whose natures are forced, by their own happy lot, to be nothing but even – is a temperate island. There is little of importance to be done, and yet all are busy. Time ticks by, its hours consumed by a rigorous timetable of pleasure: now they breakfast, now they learn (though just a little, and in a leisurely fashion). Then they walk, perhaps pay a visit? Goodness – the day has quite run away with one – dinner approaches! They must dress, they must eat, then which is it to be – music or cards? Exhausted, they fall into their soft and deep beds and sleep soundly. Whatever storms are brewing out in the world, no great waves ever reach them. They feel only a ripple, lapping gently at their shores.

Greatly assisted by this pleasant environment, Anne's first weeks at Godmersham Park passed as well as she could have hoped. Though she had feared some discomforts, she experienced none. There were no whistling draughts, nor ice in her basin. She had struck up a warm friendship with Cook – a kind soul, with a talent for baking – and was more than well fed.

Her own progress pleased her. She felt herself to have been reasonably effective in the schoolroom; had mastered the art of passing unnoticed up stairs and down corridors, between attic and park, avoiding all contact with Mrs Salkeld. Her demeanour, her behaviours, ran neither hot nor too cold. There seemed reason to believe her old tendencies for drama were quite under control. Anne's own, true self remained happily invisible beneath the cloak of her position.

Moreover, that hidden self, which only she knew, was, Anne was sure of it, new and improved. The act of earning her own living was a source of great pride and she cherished it. Through the episodes of tedium, those long periods of solitude, that pride was her sustenance. She was a Professional Woman. During her long history of resistance to the idea of being dependent upon husband, Anne had never once queried her dependence upon father. This, she could admit, was something of an anomaly and it had now been corrected. The trifle of those thirty-five pounds per annum she considered too little to count. She lived – more or less – independent of all men. A dutiful governess? A woman of courage. For a short while, at least.

Then, quite out of the blue, this new persona was threatened. Two great events pierced through the defences – charged over the beaches of that peaceful territory – and struck at Anne's new equilibrium.

One was that Cook left. The other, that Mr Henry Austen arrived.

❧

The revelation of Henry Austen came to Anne gradually – in fragments, and stages. He was like a sprite in the garden: she knew he was there, but could only catch glimpses, find small crumbs of evidence, before seeing him full in the life.

In the days building up to his arrival, Anne noticed anticipation charge through the household. Fanny could not quite settle to her lessons, and for the first time required the odd, gentle reproach. The boys – given a new sense of purpose by the prospect of blood sports and slaughter with their dear and kind uncle – ran from gunroom to stables and back to the attic, collecting and polishing the instruments of torture required. Even Sackree, the nurse, whose whole world was those Austen babies, could not be immune.

'Not much of a day out there,' she grumbled as she hoisted a baby on to her shoulder and looked out of the window at the bleak, gunmetal sky. 'We're in for snow, shouldn't wonder.' Sackree never went out of the nursery, as far as Anne had yet witnessed, but was as obsessed with the weather as any poor tiller of soil. 'Still' – her dear face cracked into a smile – 'Mr Henry will be here soon. The cold doesn't matter while we've got him with us. He always brightens us up, eh?'

Most significant of all, on the very morning of this feted appearance, Mrs Elizabeth Austen summoned Mr Hall, her hairdresser. Anne watched him arrive in the family chair, driven by Daniel, the coachman, and it set her to wondering: what sort of brother-in-law could merit such level of toilet? It was clear that this Mr Henry was a Godmersham favourite, and Anne was intrigued.

But, as Sackree predicted, it did snow, quite heavily – the greens and browns of the view to which Anne had slowly become accustomed, lay shrouded and virginal. Lacking both the correct boots and the outerwear – as well as the spirit – she was not tempted to explore it. The Great Guest was now in residence, and consuming the attentions of the whole household. The children were out all the time, with their sledges and snowballs. Anne stuck to the attic.

❧

On perhaps the third afternoon of the visit, she was alone in her room and occupied with the dullest of all chores – that, is the darning of stockings. Anne had not long left home, yet already the heels were worn through and large holes were threatening. She and Agnes had always done their mending together, chatting non-stop all the while, and the novelty of doing it alone had occasioned a dull throb of dissatisfaction. This pulsed and deepened when it dawned that, given her new financial restrictions, she could not buy herself new ones for many months yet to come. Soon, her poor feet would be treading on hard knots and lumps. The thought set her off on to the path of the greater worry. Any economy would only get her so far; it would not turn her small income into a large one. How was she to manage at all, as well as send money to Agnes? There was only so much joy to be found in the earning of a pittance. Her spirits were at something of a low ebb when there came a knock at her door.

'Miss Bridges!' Anne jumped out of her chair, dropping the offending stockings into its seat, and gave a quick curtsey. 'What a surprise!' Harriot had not visited her before now. Nor indeed had any adult, other than the maid.

'Miss Sharp. I am simply *so* bored that I am *forced* to come and call on *you*.' Anne whipped the darning away and offered Harriot the one armchair, which she duly accepted. '*Everyone* is out and I have *no one* to talk to. There's nothing for it, I told myself, but to visit the governess or I should simply just *die*. Not that my sister would notice.' She looked around the room with mild interest. 'So this is where they put you, is it?'

'Yes, a charming room,' Anne cut in hurriedly before Harriot could condemn it and embarrass them both. 'Has the family gone out?' Though she had not been bidden, Anne took the liberty of sitting down on her desk chair. It was her room, after all.

'Apparently so. And without *me*, is the point. I must say Mrs Austen can be most inconsiderate at times. Especially when a *certain gentleman* is here.' Harriot blushed then and remembered herself. 'Oh! Forgive me, I speak out of turn.' Then she relaxed and leaned forward. 'Somehow, I see you as something like a confessional. I feel I can say *anything*. For whom could you possibly tell? You have *nobody*!' she exclaimed with delight.

Anne was hardly incurious on the subject of human relations – who, but the ineffably dull, ever can be? – and could see the potential for amusement in playing priest to this penitent. But were she to appear eager, then she would ruin it. They needed some guard between them. To continue with darning might seem disrespectful, so she reached for her workbag and retrieved the embroidery which she had too long ignored. Her lowered eyes, her busy fingers, her working needle all gave Harriot the encouragement she needed.

'It never *occurs* to my sister that I *too* might enjoy the company of . . . the certain gentleman. After all, I am the *single woman* around here.' She spat out the phrase with contempt, and it occurred to Anne that Harriot was more ambivalent about her own status than earlier presumed. Perhaps, in fact, she was longing to dwindle into marriage, headlong? Most women did, to Anne's continual surprise. 'There are only so many men I can meet with, *sans* chaperone.' Harriot twisted her idle hands. 'Mr Austen is never around. Always off counting his cows or whatever it is these men choose to busy themselves with. And, anyway: *Edward* . . .' She collected herself before going too far, even for her. 'But can she not see it would be *good* for me, to enjoy the stimulating company of a Man of the World?'

'Though if the gentleman in question is unmarried himself . . .' Anne carefully measured her silk to disguise this trespass on to ground that was none of her business.

'But he is not! That is what *most* infuriates!'

'And his wife is here with him?' Anne rummaged for her scissors.

'Oh, no. She *never* comes. My sister and she do not enjoy the *warmest* of . . . And, well, between you and me, it is a rather *odd* marriage. No issue, nor sign of it. *She* is much older than *he* is, of course. I believe the Henry Austens lead *quite* separate—' Harriot stood up and walked over to the bookcase. 'What a curious collection you have here, Miss Sharp! I have been reading the spines while I chattered on, and so far I have not recognised *one*. Oh! *Evelina*. Now, that is one of *my* favourites, too. But why all this drama? Who *ever* reads a play? I am beginning to think you, dear Sharpy, something of a funny old stick.'

On she went, while Anne sat and stitched. This bible

was too new! Hers was quite *tattered* by worship, and she so much younger! Mary Wollstonecraft . . . Wollstone-craft . . . But was she not a radical? Miss Bridges was *sure* she had heard it so.

Anne was provoked into speech. 'Her ideas are new, that I would accept. But the concept of educating our daughters is not, in fact, a radical one. Of course girls should be educated. It is for the sober season of life that education should lay up its rich resources, as Wollstone-craft herself says. When admirers fall away and flatterers become dumb.'

'Yes, yes. I'm sure you are right,' Miss Bridges agreed.

Anne looked up, surprised and delighted to find an ally, and one so unlikely. The discussions they might have now!

Then she saw that, in fact, Harriot was no longer listening – had possibly not even heard. Instead, her gaze was fixed at the window, her eye caught by something out in the park. 'Ah! At last, they return.' She ran to the glass, checked her face in full and in profile. Patting her hair, she crossed to the door. 'What a *relief*! I shall go down and meet them.'

And with that she was gone.

❧

After that tantalising conversation, there was a long, pain-ful wait before Anne was to discover any more crumbs.

The adults of the household were suddenly caught up in a whirl of events. There was a ball in Ashford – after which, to her fury, Miss Bridges was deposited back with her mother; a trip to Canterbury; Anne heard with some envy they had been to the play. How she missed the theatre! Yet another Austen brother arrived, with a young lady. There was a proposal in the air, which sent Sackree into paroxysms of vicarious joy, while Anne silently prayed for the safety of yet another poor female soul. All this came to her in her attic outpost, in the form of hearsay and rumour, via children and maids. The nursery staff were like a small village set away from society, into which gossip from the capital arrived long after the event.

Anne was often called to spend the late afternoon in the nursery with Sackree, helping with the cherubim. She never objected, for it was warmer than her own room, where the fire was lit only for the times when Fanny was in it. Also, the news always reached there hours, sometimes days, before Anne's room and her interest was piqued. And that is where she was on that cold afternoon when Fanny burst in with her sensational report.

'Sackree! You must spare Nurse! We need her downstairs! It's Uncle Henry! He has been attacked by a buck!'

With injuries sustained in both arm and hand, any field sports were now out of the question. Quite naturally, this new restriction occasioned in the Great Guest both restlessness and boredom. And that is how Henry Austen found his way up to the schoolroom.

CHAPTER IX

'Oh, *when* do you think I shall hear from Aunt Jane?'
Fanny wondered for the tenth time that morning.

'I am sure she is working on the perfect reply,' Anne
assured her, yet again. 'Now, back to our lesson.' Anne,
who was trying once again to chip away at the granite-
like substance within Fanny's head, reached for her copy
of William Cowper's *The Task*, and placed it down on
the table.

Fanny studied it with mild interest. 'Am I to copy this
out in my best handwriting, and perhaps illuminate it? I
do *rather* enjoy that.'

'Not today. The idea is—'

'Then am I to *learn* it, in order to recite in the drawing
room? That will please all the grown-ups.' She flicked
through page after page. 'Ah, it is very *long*.'

'We can do both those things, if you would like. But first we are going to read it together – *truly* learn it: what is Cowper trying to tell us here, for example. And how does he use language to—'

'Oh.' Fanny's young face, so recently eager, suddenly fell. 'Miss Sharp . . .' She paused. '*We* . . .' Anne disliked the use of this pronoun, so beloved of monarchs, and over-obedient children who parrot the speech of their parents. '*We* think the more usual practice is that you tell me about it, so I have a general sort of knowledge of what goes on.'

Some might think, from this exchange, of Fanny Austen as the most impertinent young miss in the world. To speak back to her teacher! Other governesses might reach for the smelling salts. But Anne had already strongly encouraged that she voice her own opinions in all of their lessons – though, she had also cautioned, there was no need to mention this to her mama. It was Anne's fervent belief that a little challenge of authority – inconsequential and mild – would only create an independence of mind. It was how she herself had been raised.

Fanny went on: 'There may be something already pre-pared on the subject in my Mangnall.' She rose and took herself to the bookcase, retrieved the text and returned to her seat. 'We do like our Mangnall. Let me see.'

Anne's heart duly sank. Richmal Mangnall's *Historical and Miscellaneous Questions for the Use of Young People* she thought the most ludicrous work, with the potential to

68

make simple the minds of a whole generation. In the best houses, however, it was considered the height of fashion. Mrs Austen had used it when teaching Fanny herself before Anne's arrival. The idea was that the pupil learned both question and answer by rote, to the point of easy recitation. It roamed around countries and continents:

What is whalebone?

A sort of gristle found inside the whale in long, flat pieces three or four yards long; it supplies the place of teeth.

And what is whalebone used for?

To stiffen stays, umbrellas and whips.

It leaped between present and past:

Are not umbrellas of great antiquity?

Yes; the Greeks, Romans and all eastern nations used them to keep off the sun.

And rarely passed on an opportunity for a pious aside:

Is it not a mark of the kindness of the Creator that leopards go in search of prey during the night?

Yes, for in the day when man is abroad these savage beasts usually sleep in their dens.

How such an approach was supposed to foster ideas or promote thought was beyond Anne's understanding. Even if the only ambition of this schoolroom was to produce a young lady capable of sound conversation with the best sort of gentleman, it was unclear how this knowledge might help. 'Indeed, sir, I think you will find that *ombrello* in Italian, signifies a little shade . . .'

'I am sure there must be something in here somewhere.' Fanny flicked through the pages. 'Or perhaps we might prepare something? So, Miss Sharp, you say: "What is the subject of *The Task* by William Cowper?" And I answer—'

'Fanny.' Anne spoke firmly. 'I doubt very much that this poem is included in Mangnall, and if it were it would be reduced almost to nothing. When the understanding is not exercised, then the memory is employed to no great purpose. There is no better way to understand any work than to read it oneself. Were we to just skim the opening, you could come away with the idea that it is no more than a hymn to the sofa – and to say, to even think such a thing is the true mark of a fool.

'We can stop as we go on, and discuss our responses and if there is ever anything at all that you don't under-stand, you must ask me. Let us just try. I think you might even enjoy it.'

Anne had put much thought and work into her approach to this lesson, preparing in her solitary even-ings, so she greeted its immediate interruption with no little bitterness.

'Uncle Henry!' At once, Cowper was down and Fanny was up, out of her seat and into his arms.

'What have we here then?' Henry Austen boomed, as if on stage at the Drury. 'The weather is against me, I can do nothing useful with this wretched hand of mine, so I am come here to learn! Miss Sharp, I believe?'

'Yes, sir.' Anne rose and curtseyed.

'I am delighted to meet you, in the light of Jameson's most favourable reference.'

To hear that name, polluting the pure air of this schoolroom! So sudden was Anne's shock, she could not disguise it.

'Pray, do not be alarmed! 'Tis I who approached Jameson on my brother's behalf. Governess, I thought to myself, now who could know a good governess? Of course, my mind leaped at once to our mutual friend. Capital fellow, Jameson!'

Dread flooded through her. If Henry knew Jameson, then what had he heard about Anne? Was she the stuff of gentlemen's gossip? It may be that he knew even more of the cause of her father's behaviour than she knew herself. The thought of it sickened her.

'Uncle Henry is acquainted with *everybody*.' Fanny beamed up at him.

'Not quite everybody, Frances my dear. Let me cite Miss Sharp as just one example. We can now rectify that.' He strode to the side of the room, picked up another chair, brought it back to the table and took his seat. His movements were large, loud and yet graceful – as if he were putting on a performance for them. Or for Anne. 'Miss Sharp, I find myself to have become uncommonly stupid. It may be that buck knocked all sense out of my head. Improve me at once!'

Anne continued to stand – frozen, struck dumb. Even now, with his tall and strong frame folded on to a chair, Mr Henry Austen somehow consumed all of the room. His volume, his force, his extraordinary, masculine confidence – and, yes, she did note the classic good features, bright hazel eyes and thick head of hair – were quite overwhelming. It seemed there was no remnant of space for her poor, insignificant form.

'Pray, Miss Sharp.' He beckoned her into her place, as if she were his to command. As if this were not her own province. 'Let us begin. Now, what is it today, hmm? Fordyce's *Sermons to Young Women*, I should not wonder. That is your sort of thing, Miss Sharp, I presume?'

'Certainly not, indeed.' It came out too strong. But, truly, the impertinence of this gentleman was sorely vexing. Anne added a 'sir', rather meekly, as she sat down, and caught how his face creased with amusement.

'Is that so? You care nothing for the moral instruction of my niece?' He shook his head, and turned down his smile. 'Then I am sorry to hear it.'

'We are about to start *The Task*, Uncle Henry. By' – she looked down at the page – 'by William Cowper.'

'Are we now?' He creased again and, for no other reason than that he was a gentleman, proceeded to furnish them with his own knowledge and opinions. 'Excellent! And what can I tell you about Cowper?' Though no such request had been issued. 'Well, the first thing that comes to mind is that he is a great favourite of your dear Aunt Jane.'

The very author of that delicious letter! It was almost

too much. There and then Anne elected Aunt Jane her favourite Austen.

'And as for the poem itself, all you need to know is that it is a hymn to the sofa!' He took the book from Fanny's hands and placed it face down on the table. 'There! We are done.'

Fanny gasped in confusion. 'Miss Sharp told me earlier to think *that* was the—' Anne's heart skipped a beat; Fanny came to her senses. 'Well, now I know not *what* to think.'

Under this malign influence, Fanny was starting to show off for the first time. How Anne wished this intruder would leave them alone, and let them proceed.

'Well, if you *must* penetrate further . . . There may be a little bit more to it than that, I accept.' Henry leaned back in his chair, folded hands behind head and stretched long legs beneath table. Anne's delicate feet, unprotected by thin, silken slippers, felt the sharp shock of contact. She wrenched them quickly away. '*God made the country, And man made the town.* That's the general sort of tone of it. What think you of that then, Miss Bluestocking Austen? Would you agree?'

'Oh, very much so!' Fanny returned. 'I am quite sure that God Himself made Godmersham. It is there in the name!'

Anne had become an unacknowledged presence: a spectre at her own lesson. Was she now a mere woman who must suffer such insults with no powers of defence, simply because he was dressed in fine clothing and her own garb was plain? Fury rose in her breast. Her cold heart grew colder, chilled with dislike. What greater sophistry than to reduce an epic to a mere quote? Like his brother, Mr Henry Austen was clearly yet another man who mistook the privilege of his superior education as evidence of a God-given, superior intellect. And of all the inequalities to despise in her unequal world, Anne despised that one the most.

She gathered her wits and her strength, prepared to draw up the confidence with which she might assert some authority. And then the door was flung open and they were again interrupted.

'Fanny! Fanny! The mare is in foal!' shouted one of the small boys at the top of his voice.

'Ha!' Henry Austen slapped the table. 'I say, what splendid excitement. This I must see.'

'Oh, Miss Sharp,' Fanny pleaded. 'I beg you, *please* can I go?'

'Of course, my dear child,' said the man who had no powers of permission. 'Forgive us, but Cowper can keep, can he not? The horse waits for no man!' And the door closed behind them.

They never did study Cowper, Fanny and Anne.

CHAPTER X

It was the ambition of this governess that her Godmer-sham schoolroom should follow the model of her own schooling in London – whether Mrs Austen desired it or no. After all, the fine education from which Anne had so benefited had come about by accident rather than parental design. Though it may well be regrettable, nonetheless it is true that not every parent knows what is best for its child. And when that occurs, it falls to another – some superior, external judge – to take matters in hand. And in Anne's case, that wise judge had been Agnes.

Each morning, rain or shine, it was their practice that Anny would be taken by Agnes out into the gardens of Montague Square, so that her mama might enjoy time to herself. (It was not known what Mrs Sharp accomplished with this freedom: she never paid calls; nor did she receive them.) And each morning, Anne met there with the Mercer girls.

The children played while their nurses sat side by side on the bench. Anne loved the games she played with her friends, but she adored the times when they were exhorted to rest for a few minutes. For then, she could listen to the adults' conversation, and had already discovered that, when those around you thought you were not listening, you could learn all sorts of things that you would never be told. And one morning, when Anne was a quick-witted girl of around five years in age, she picked up the following:

'So,' Nurse Mercer began. 'All arranged then. That spinster aunt. Mr Mercer's poor sister. One of those clever sorts. Looks like something the cat dragged in. Nose in a book. You get many like that round at Number Twenty-two? Plague of 'em round ours. Anyway. She's coming to live with us.'

'No!' Agnes was all outrage. She was often, Anne noticed, outraged by things that seemed to be none of her business. 'Just like that – bold as brass! I call that an imposition, I do. You were consulted, I hope?'

'My idea.' Nurse Mercer folded her arms. 'They're my girls, after all.'

'Your girls,' Agnes conceded. 'Though I'm not sure I follow your logic.'

'She's coming to teach them. Says she's happy to stay and do the job lot. So that's a relief.'

'Is it?' Agnes still seemed rather puzzled.

'It stops him packing them off to school for months with no end and I did *not* like that idea. Little lambs.'

'Little lambs,' agreed Agnes. Then her hands flew to her face. '*School . . . !* Why, that never occurred to me! You don't think my lot might send my Anny away?'

'Can't rule it out. There's no saying what they get up to. Here.' Nurse Mercer grabbed Agnes's arm. 'Why doesn't your Anny just come and join in with us? She'll stay home, then. You can bring her round every morning and we can sit in my room putting the world to rights. Very pleasant, I'm sure.'

'Nurse, you're a wonder.' Agnes felt better at once.

'Reckon they'll agree?'

Agnes chuckled. 'Agree? I'm not planning on *asking*. I'll just tell them it's happening and happen it will.'

When it came to matters of maternal devotion, Margaret Sharp stood second to no woman. She would chuck Anny's chin, stroke her soft curls; had been known to sit looking at picture books, small child in her lap, for up to twenty full minutes per day. As a particular present, her husband had commissioned Reynolds to take Anny's likeness and, as one might expect from its cost, the result was lovelier yet than reality. The besotted mama could sit gazing at it for hours at a time, emitting sighs, gasps and, in her regular moments of dramatic emotion, a plump but becoming tear.

The fashion among parents of the day was for an active

involvement in the lives of their children and Mrs Sharp did like to think herself fashionable. On the other hand, she tired all too easily, and felt it wise to conserve any energies in case some emergency struck. So, on the day Anny was returned by her wet nurse, Agnes took charge. 'This child's salvation, me' was a phrase baby Anny often heard in her carriage, while being pushed in the park. 'Don't know why he didn't just buy her a pug and have done with it.'

The Mercer girls, too, were growing up under an absence of parental supervision. Their mother had died in childbirth seven years before and the father offered scant compensation. As a Man of Letters of some distinction, he found great contentment in his widower status. There was now no person who dared voice her opinion on how he might best spend his time. He was free to live in his own head, that head free to live in its library, and need only rarely emerge. So while he was not physically absent like Anny's papa, he could not be described as quite present.

If it were not for their nurses, who knows what might have become of those girls? It was thanks to the wisdom of these excellent women – wiser by far than their hapless employers – that these five precious childhoods were saved.

❧

From the earliest age, the Mercer girls recognised Anny as kith, for they too were intelligent, with minds that were curious and imaginations rich and their schoolroom – adapted from what was once the parlour – became a source of great joy. Every day, furniture was overturned, precious objects became props and old curtains flung about as the History of England was learned through re-enactment.

'*I go from a corruptible to an incorruptible Crown, where no disturbance can be,*' Anny cried as King Charles on his scaffold. '*Remember.*'

Laura chopped off her head. Hetty, as queen, wrung her hands over in France. So affecting was the scene that lessons were abandoned for the rest of the day.

And every month, they would each learn by heart one of the Sonnets for what were known as 'Public Recitals'. Anny's mama never came once – though she did want to, very much indeed – and nor, it goes without saying, did the public. Mr Mercer did struggle down from the library on his sister's command, but he was not the easiest audience for keen little girls. His standards were high, his threshold was low and the number of times he shuddered and winced became the measure of a performer's success. Needless to say, the nurses thought it all splendid.

The situation proved satisfactory to all parties. Aunt Mercer's magnificent mind had, at last, been rewarded with some occupation. She had no interest in interfering in the running of the household, preferring to spend her free time in museums or at lectures and, though the nurses thought her most odd – 'She is a one and no mistake'; 'Call that a hat? More like a pigeon' – they were greatly relieved. All the girls thrived, of course – how could they not? But Hettie and Anne flourished in particular.

These two were the eldest in the class, and the closest in age – Anne was the junior by less than a year – and equals in beauty, though they gave that no thought. They were also the cleverest. And by the sharing of interests and their long conversations, the daily exchange of books and ideas, the confiding of secrets, each found in the other the ideal, fertile conditions to grow into their true selves.

On occasion, when they could not bear to be separated at the end of the day, the nurses would agree to let Anne stay at the Mercers' house. And one such night, when the candles were snuffed, they whispered their feelings: the world had never known a friendship so deep as this one. They could be sisters. No, they were closer than sisters: twin halves of one soul! They must never be parted.

And there in the darkness, they solemnly pledged to defy all convention and be together for the rest of their lives.

CHAPTER XI

'Miss Sharp!' Fanny burst into the Godmersham attic. 'Look!' She brandished a letter. 'All that time, I was expecting to hear by the *morning* post, and it came by the *evening*.'

They both studied the paper, weighed up its width and its quality, ran their eyes over it to judge the length of what was written upon it. 'In my *mind's eye*, I had seen myself receiving it at breakfast and reading it there, just as Mama does. I mean, like a proper *young lady*.' She worried at her lip. 'But now *is* just as *good*, is it not?'

'I should say it is a fine time for the reading of letters,' Anne reassured her. 'A lovely end to the day. And remember, my dear, if this is to be a full correspondence, you can look forward to more in the future . . .'

Fanny breathed out. 'You are so right. I am beginning

to *think*, Miss Sharp, that you are in the habit of being right on *all matters*. So, what happens now?'

Anne was becoming a little concerned by her pupil's over-keen sense of deference. If they went on like this, Fanny would soon be incapable of putting one foot in front of the other without appealing for guidance. 'I suggest that you read it?'

'Oh,' Fanny gave a little laugh. 'Of course! Shall we do so together?'

'No, my dear,' replied Anne, though she was not un-intrigued. 'This is to you.'

Fortunately, Fanny – who was one of the world's greatest sharers – chose to read it out loud:

My dear Fanny,

Your letter occasioned such joy among all in your Bath family – but in me, in particular. I cannot imagine what I have done to deserve such an honour – and nor can your <u>superior</u> aunt, my dear sister. When the post came for <u>me</u>, there was a danger that <u>she</u> might drop dead from sheer <u>jealousy</u>, but I quickly revived her with my shrewd observation – Cassandra is harder to spell and consumes too much ink. God bless my short, simple name!

We all marvelled at hearing your Godmersham news, and you have the advantage of me. How can <u>my</u> dull existence compare with the revelation that <u>you</u> have a new governess? It is clear she is a woman of substance for your pen was clear and the contents quite perfect. If you are so kind as to reply to me *now, please do us the favour of addressing the following concerns. We all long to know what books you are reading – in particular, which poets? Your grandfather desires that you acquire a sound basis in Shakespeare and, as always – he cannot be helped – issues a plea on behalf of the Classics. Is your Miss S. – among her other perfections – strong in the Classics? If so, then she is truly a paragon.*

As you know, your Grandmama has been most unwell and the worry and fear has kept us at home more than is usual. But I am here to report she is now well on the mend, and her spirits returned to their usual height. It cannot be long before we return to the social round. Though I am <u>relieved</u> that the illness is over, I cannot <u>rejoice</u> at being turned out of doors. The streets of Bath are made so dirty by this dreadful wet weather – it keeps one in a perpetual state of inelegance.

We all look forward to hearing from you again, and pray you send our love to all of the Godmersham family.

Your fond Aunt,
Jane Austen.

Each expressed their delight in tones of great rapture and agreed it to be one of the greatest – possibly the best – letter yet to be written. Fanny read it twice more, so as to be thoroughly sure, before disappearing down to the library to share it anew. Anne, at last, was able to pick up her own pen, and then Sally came in.

The sullen maid of Anne's first evening had warmed into a garrulous creature and now, while Anne sat alone working, Sally would work alongside her. Her clear philosophy was that, while the hands toiled at tidying and cleaning, the tongue should not idle.

'What is it you're up to there, miss?' She was sifting through Fanny's drawers and refolding the inexpertly folded. 'Another letter, is it? You do write a lot of letters and no mistake.' She came and looked over Anne's shoulder. Anne covered her page. 'Don't worry about that, miss. All scribbles to me.'

'You cannot read or write, Sally?' Anne felt that glorious, prickling anticipation of a new project. 'Would you like me to teach you? When is your afternoon off? I am sure I could spare a few hours every week.' She was quite magnificent in her own generosity.

'Ta, miss, but I'm right as I am.' Sally went back to her work. 'My afternoons off are my afternoons off, thanking you very much. I go out on the gad, then, with Becky.'

Anne picked up her pen again, crushed. Suddenly intrigued, she put it back down. 'You must be most expert *gadders* to find any gadding to be had in Godmersham, surely?' The village did not even have a shop, let alone a High Street. Anne had found no amusements beyond solitary walks. How does one even begin to gad in a field?

'You'd be surprised, miss. There's some new lads down at the tithe barn.' Sally gave a little shriek. 'Ooh, but we do like a laugh with them.'

'And Mrs Salkeld does not object?' Anne herself could never be so brave as to incur the wrath of the housekeeper.

Sally shrugged her thin shoulders. 'If she does, she daren't say so. We're still young, miss. Got to enjoy yourself, haven't you? It's only a job, after all. If they stopped me, I'd tell them to stick it.'

Anne paused to reflect on their relative positions. She was certainly paid more, but Sally – with her uniform and its upkeep provided – had fewer expenses. Sally enjoyed hours off in the day and the companionship of life in the servants' hall; Anne belonged neither to staff nor family, was almost always on duty and, when not, entirely alone. It appeared that a maid could make an exhibition of herself abroad and it was tolerated, yet if a governess were to attract even the eye of a gentleman, she would face instant dismissal. The comparison provided food for thought on the question of privilege and the cost of its benefits.

'So. All these letters, then. Lots of people thinking about you there, back in London?'

Anne suspended her pen over the page. 'This one is to Agnes. I must finish it today.'

'Wish I had a sister.' Sally moved over to the dressing table and set to work there. 'Eight brothers, me – all of 'em younger. My ma won't let Pa touch her no more. Sleeps with a rolling pin.' She looked over and grinned. 'I hope he tries it, and she gives him a good battering.' There followed an alarming demonstration with the silver head of Anne's hairbrush. 'Take that, you old drunkard!'

'Agnes was my nurse as a baby, and then stayed on as

maid,' Anne said quickly to turn the subject away from conjugal assault. 'But we are close as sisters.'

'Your maid! Well, the Lord love us. There's a strange carry-on. Write to your maid! Never heard the like of it. And you so refined, miss.'

'Oh, Sally! Though my home was indeed very spacious and comfortable, it was hardly on this sort of scale. We were few, Agnes worked for us for many years and it felt quite natural that we should treat her as part of the family. She ate with us at table, for example—'

'No!' Her mouth formed a neat circle. 'Imagine me in that dining room! I wouldn't know where to put myself. Anyway, they're all lively as ditch water.'

'They seem to me the kindest of employers,' Anne reproached with some force.

'Kind enough, to be fair to them. But a stuffy old lot. Apart from that Mr Henry.' She gave a fond smile. 'Here, did you know he gave Cook a six-shilling tip when she left us? Oh, she was charmed. Don't you think that was charming?'

Having made up her mind about Henry Austen, Anne was not open to testimonials that spoke of his good character. She made no reply and got back to her letter.

'I wonder what New Cook will be like then? They say she's a real dragon.' Sally shuddered. 'My ma says they're always old cows, pardon-my-language, and we just got lucky the once. She'll never be as kind as Real Cook, tell you that for a fact.'

Although Anne had become very fond of the old cook and was sad to see her go, she saw no reason to dread this new incumbent. 'Why ever not?' She was still too naïve to suspect an amiable cook of being anything other than the norm. 'One should not always expect the worst of people.' She reached over and took Sally's hand. 'Especially those you do not yet know.'

At last, Sally left her alone and Anne could return to her letter. It was a difficult one; she could not dash it off. For Agnes had taken it into her head that she would hunt down Anne's father. *He can't go around hiding for ever, and once I get my hands on him, Anny, there's no accounting for what I might do to him. Could smote him thus even, I'm in that much of a rage. He deserves a good smoting.* Much of Agnes's colourful language had been picked up at their theatrical evenings. Anne sighed.

Perhaps Agnes was right? It was not as though the thought had not occurred to Anne before. Indeed, she had constantly wrestled with the issue since that morning in Jameson's office. It still kept her awake at night. Oh, why had her papa cast her off so?

This was not just a question of money, though she would not deny its importance. An insecure future was the most terrifying of prospects. But beyond that, his behaviour struck at her very foundations. All of her life, she had treasured and trusted in the idea of her family. This peculiar episode – and she must still believe it an episode – remained inexplicable.

Despite all that, Anne stood firm. She now wrote to Agnes, in very strong terms, that there must be no search: no hunting and, certainly, no smiting. Not in Anne's name. When her father wanted her, then he would find her. She would much rather earn her own living, meagre though it might be, than beg at his feet.

Anne still had her pride, even if Agnes did not.

CHAPTER XII

Some weeks later, Anne sat alone in the schoolroom, looked again at her dinner and sighed deeply. If the dish had a name, then she did not know it. Was it a soup or a stew? Though it had the properties of each, it provided the comforts of neither. The broth was pure grease; the meat was all gristle: the whole was stone cold. She picked up her spoon and steeled herself to make one last attempt but recoiled in the instant. It simply could not be done.

This deprivation had now gone on for nearly a month, and her stomach growled and head felt quite light. If she could only get her hands on a good slice of bread – Anne thought of it, how it would swell up inside her and fill up the space. Her mouth watered. Unfortunately, under the new regime, she was now barred from entry to the kitchen. In a triumph of Sally's cynicism and a blow to Anne's faith, this new cook was a dragon indeed.

There was a sharp tap on the door, a pretty head poked through the crack and then – 'Sharpy!' – the remainder of Miss Harriot Bridges stepped in. 'I *thought* I might find you *skulking* up here and avoiding us.'

Anne lacked the energy – and the will – to jump up and curtsey. Miss Bridges took no offence, and drew up the desk chair.

'We are all *insufferably* dull in the library this evening, so I fancied I might find diversion with you. What is that you are reading?' She peered at the book in Anne's lap. '*Greek?*' shrieked Miss Bridges. 'Oh but my dear, you are *utterly* priceless.' A tinkle of mirth. 'There we are! I am diverted already. Now, tell me: what is your news?'

Anne could think of nothing besides her near-starvation. She looked through the window at the sky. 'Well, the evenings are getting lighter, I suppose. And it was a fine enough day.'

'Oh, *Sharpy*! You do not have to talk to *me* about the *weather*, of all things. We are such *friends*. Though, if you insist, I agree: the spring is most welcome. But chilly in here, is it not? You choose to keep it much *fresher* than the library. No doubt to keep that great mind alert, am I right?' She tapped at her temple. 'Very clever of you, I am sure. The library is like *toast*. I fear it makes us all sleepy. Perhaps that explains why we are so very *dull*.'

The mention of toast made Anne almost hallucinate, but then Sally came in, to take down the dinner things.

'Miss Bridges!' Sally dropped into a curtsey. 'Please do excuse me.' She shot Anne a look of icy suspicion – an improvement of sorts. Lately, she had ignored Anne altogether.

The new cook's dislike of the governess had been instant, and its ramifications profound. Not only were her meals now close to intolerable, but it appeared Miss Sharp was now the official Enemy of the Kitchen. She had no idea what she had done to earn this distinction – most likely the hostility was more for the governess in general, rather than her in particular. And yet it was absolute. The burgeoning warmth of her friendship with Sally Williams was, to her great sadness, a thing of the past.

And it was unfortunate that the maid had stumbled in at this moment. Anne could predict what she would say when she went back downstairs: 'So you'll never guess who *she* had tucked away in her room? Only a *member of the family*. Reporting on *us* up to *them*, I shouldn't wonder. Who does she think she is, then? That's what I'd like to know.'

Sally picked up the tray and looked down at it. 'No appetite tonight, miss?' Only Anne could see the cold smirk. 'That is a shame.'

Miss Bridges chimed in. 'Funnily enough, I was rather the same. I must have left quite almost *half* of the lamb and barely *touched* that good posset. Well, failed to *finish* it, certainly. I wonder if we are both sickening?' 'Oh!' She started in alarm. 'I do hope we have not caught those germs from the babies!'

'I am sure that is not it,' Anne consoled. All the little children were poorly that week and, in her concern, Sackree had stopped all unnecessary persons from going into the nursery. Anne lamented the absence of that extra companionship, as well as the warmth of the room.

'Oh, by the way,' Harriot ran on. 'While you are both with me: Fanny is sleeping with *me* tonight. A little *treat* for the dear girl – just so you are aware.'

'You are a very kind aunt,' Anne replied, while regretting that she would not see a good fire until the following evening.

Sally left then, but Miss Bridges did not.

'Well, if you refuse to share *your* news, I must give you mine. So.' She folded her hands in her lap. 'We had the ball at Ashford last night, of course. You are *so* wise to miss it. I wore my blue and they *say* it was rather a success – did you get a glimpse or were you hiding as usual? Anyway. It is not an *interesting* year, I fear. Thin *pickings*, if you get my meaning. Oh, I danced *all night*, of course. I am not saying there was no man to ask one. But nobody *new*, is the problem. And I am *so* bored of all the gentlemen around here. Even *were* one to propose, I should turn him down flat.'

She got up, wandered over to the chest and began to examine Anne's personal things. Anne thought of

Fanny's words to her the previous evening: '*Poor* Mama and Papa. They say they are *so* tired of balls now. But they simply *have* to keep going for Aunt Harriot's sake. We are *so* keen to match her – quite at our *wits' end*.'

Miss Bridges looked up. 'Perhaps that is not *entirely* true. I suppose it all depends on one's *desperation* at the moment of asking.' Then a new thought struck and she turned back to Anne. 'Do tell me, Sharpy. Did *you* ever receive a proposal? I mean, when you were younger, of course, and . . .' She left her speech hanging.

Anne looked up at her, her head so full of reasons not to answer the question that she could not pick just the one.

'Oh! *Please* do not say that you did but the gentleman *died*. Oh, Sharpy, I do put my foot in it.' She rushed to Anne's side. 'That is the *very worst* that can happen. To get *so close* and then, *nothing* – no better off than if you were never engaged! The heart *breaks* just to think—'

'Miss Bridges,' Anne consoled, 'please do not distress yourself. Nobody died.'

'That *is* a relief. But oh dear, yes – just as I thought. Poor Sharpy!' Harriot placed a kind hand on Anne's spin-sterish shoulder. 'Men are such fools. If only they talked, *truly* talked like we do, you and I. Then they would see what a funny little treasure you are. But enough of all that. I must return downstairs; they will wonder what I am getting up to. And I fear it is too chilly in here for me to sit very long.'

Harriot walked to the door. Anne rose and curtseyed and bid her goodnight. And, as the light tread of silk slipper tapped its retreat down the passage, the schoolroom began spinning.

Anne fainted away to the floor.

CHAPTER XIII

'Every good gift and every perfect gift is from above, and cometh down from the Father of lights, with whom is no variableness, neither shadow of turning.'

The mellow voice of the Reverend Whitfield flowed across the village heads there assembled, poured into their ears, bathing not only the superior souls of the God-mersham family, boxed into a separate compartment as befitted their station, but even those of the servants and farmhands pressed closely together further back. The entire congregation was soothed.

It was a sparkling morning in the middle of May. The air outside was green, new life burst in the hedge-rows and the barometer was set fair for the rest of the week. Anne sat – between Fanny, her sweet face illu-minated with faith, and Mrs Austen, again with child and yet more languid and docile – watched the motes dance in the shafts of warm sunlight and considered what, if anything, He had given to her, in particular. And she was forced to admit that, after a fallow and rather frugal period, during which He had been somewhat remiss, He had lately indulged her with some compensations.

There were the joys of Godmersham itself, and its county. For the first time in her life, Anne was in a position to witness the seasons turn in their natural, miraculous way rather than the traditions of society's calendar. The fields – brown and fallow when first she came – were now rich with growth and presented a constant tableau of simple, human industry. She found, somewhat to her surprise, that she lived among beauty and thanked God for it.

Next, there was friendship. The chance combination of Fanny and Anne was proving a happy one, and the now regular letters from dear Aunt Jane added one more shared delight. In April, Mr and Mrs Austen had both been away, Anne was entrusted with Fanny's sole care and this brought with it twin benefits: strengthening the bond between teacher and pupil, and entailing that Anne took all her meals with the children. For a whole month she had eaten very well and was herself strengthened. Unfortunately, the earlier punitive rations had led to ill health and fits of fainting which had proved hard to conceal from the household. But she was now fully recovered and, most importantly, Mrs Austen had chosen to forgive her. She issued a quick prayer to stay well.

The vicar himself, Mr Whitfield, was becoming a true friend, whose intelligence she valued and whose house-keeper made a fine plum cake. Anne and Fanny often walked down to the vicarage when the weather was clement, where Anne could talk and, most importantly, eat her way to contentment.

And his services had, too, proved something of a rev-elation to Anne. Her excellent education had naturally included biblical study and the tenets of most world reli-gions, yet, throughout her childhood, church attendance had been sporadic, at best. Very occasionally, her mother had taken her to St Paul's, Covent Garden, but only for the quieter services. All the main festivals were passed at home and in secular pursuit. When Grace was said before meals, it was never when her father was present, and always Agnes who said it. And she tended to focus on the presence of particular foodstuffs – 'Lord, thank you for bringing pears back to the market this morning and not before time might I add' – bringing a regrettable, heathenish tone to her prayer.

So while Anne was intellectually equipped to instruct Fanny in religious matters, religious practice was some-thing of a novelty and, to her surprise, rather pleasant. Previously, Anne had been sceptical about the arts of the sermon – considering them no more than ill-written solil-oquys, poorly performed – but she was grateful for those given by Mr Whitfield. No matter how deep the subject, his thoughts upon it never strayed far from the shallows; however wretched the universal condition of man, he alone remained blithe and untroubled. His words were brief, and he dispatched them at speed.

Mr Whitfield now turned at the altar to begin that morning's gospel.

'*Verily, verily I say unto you, Whatsoever ye shall ask the Father in my name, He will give it you. Hitherto have ye asked nothing in my name: ask, and ye shall receive, that your joy may be full . . .*'

Taking Him at his word, Anne raised her face to the altar, and began. She asked that He look after Agnes, temper her passions and lead her to good judgement – though both were unlikely. She prayed for the continued good health of her father and, with a dash of piety here, that he might be at peace with his own conscience and soon come to his senses. She issued a plea for Cook's blackened soul and, indeed, Sally's, which was darkening to a match.

And lastly, if she still had His ear, she found the return of Mr Henry Austen a great irritation. He had arrived the previous evening and so far Anne had only had to endure a brief, polite greeting. But, having taken so firmly against him, she would dearly love to be spared any further engagement.

The congregation emerged into the bright, yellow light, paid its respects to the parson and dispersed into the day. Although it was but a short walk back to the house, Mrs Austen, cautious of the heat in her delicate condition, chose to travel by chair. Mr Henry Austen helped her up in solicitous fashion, and then turned back to Fanny and Anne.

'Ladies.' Though the service had not been long, he seethed with the restless energy of a lion only recently released from a particularly tight cage. 'Let us walk back together.'

'Yes *please*, Uncle Henry.' Fanny giggled when he offered his arm.

'Miss Sharp?' He proffered his other elbow; Anne swiftly declined.

'What an excellent day!' He took a long draught of fresh air as they emerged from the churchyard and came out on to the lane. 'But then does not Godmersham exist in a state of perpetual summer?'

'Oh yes, Uncle Henry. Except . . .' Where possible, Fanny would always defer to her elders. 'Perhaps I am mistaken but the last time you were with us, were we not buried in snow?'

'I have forgotten it already. When I am in town – toiling at my desk, scraping my living – as I count the raindrops which cling to my window, I always think of you here, bathed in the sun's golden rays. Kent, of course, famously enjoys . . .'

And now Mr Henry was taking it upon himself to explain the vagaries of national geography. May God grant Anne patience. They had arrived at the door set into the brick wall to the estate, were assailed by the scent of new blossom. There was only the rich beauty of the Lime Walk to endure and then she would shake herself free of him.

'. . . the proximity of the sea. And being the closest county to France—'

Fanny shuddered. 'Well, *I* wish we were not. Uncle Henry, do you think the French will invade us? It is getting terribly frightening. Papa says—'

'Ha! They may well try it, but once they catch sight of the East Kent Volunteers, they will turn on their perfidious heels before you can say *Bonaparte*.' All the bravado, thought Anne, of a gentleman who risks his life every day in battle with rich clients and banknotes.

'*I* do not fear them,' Mr Henry continued. 'All this talk of war is good for my business. That peace was nearly the ruin of me!'

Now Anne was appalled!

He did not, of course, notice. 'As I know well, from my years serving in the Oxfords: try as they might, and they certainly have, still the French can never beat *us*.'

That was surprising – it was not easy to imagine this sleek sybarite suffering a life in the barracks. But Anne graciously withdrew her silent hostility on that singular point, while retaining it in all other particulars.

Mr Henry stopped. 'But why do we not go and see for ourselves? Your papa is even now training his corps up at the top of the park. Let us all go and watch! It will quite put your young mind at rest.'

Anne had no intention of wasting her morning in this particular company. But of course Fanny had other ideas. 'Oh, let us! Yes, please,' she exclaimed. 'Please, do say you will come, Anny. Oh!' She clapped her hand over her mouth.

'Anny, is it now?' His eyes did that creasing and Anne felt herself blush.

'Oh, Miss Sharp, I am sorry!' Fanny said, pleading. 'Uncle Henry, *please* say nothing to Mama. It is our little secret. Miss Sharp is very strict on the point. I am only permitted to use it when we are *entirely* alone.'

He stopped still and adopted a serious tone. 'Well, now. Not tell your mama, you say.' He rubbed his strong chin. 'You ask me to withhold information that may well be of great interest to your excellent parents.' He shook his fine head in dismay. The sun caught the red and gold strands in his hair. 'This is not an entirely un-serious matter, young ladies. Let me take a few moments while I consider it in depth.' He started to pace up and down.

While Anne presumed he was merely having his sport with her – how she loathed this sort of quiz-zing! As an only child, she had never suffered enough to become truly inured – she was not wholly uncon-cerned. The ideal governess should never become too intimate with her charges. Mrs Austen was hardly one of those absent mothers who lived remote from their children; indeed, quite the opposite: she relished her position at the centre of their young worlds. It would be unfortunate now to offend her, when all had been going so well. Fanny clutched at her hand. Mr Henry continued to pace.

Some minutes elapsed before he stopped and faced them. 'I have made my decision.' He was suddenly all smiles, his voice, at last, gentle. 'And I have decided that, as it is a pleasing little name, and rather befits your pleasing little governess' – he bowed towards Anne – 'then your secret is safe and I shall never speak of it again. But only, *Miss Sharp*, if you promise to accompany us up on to the hill to observe our fine troops preparing for battle.'

Pleasing little governess . . . All this attention was wholly unwelcome; his familiarity quite beyond inappropriate. Was he so weak, so concerned with his own popularity, that he must court one such as her? Like Napoleon himself, he was determined to conquer. Anne expressed a gratitude that she could not muster, smiled through a loathing quite beyond her control, and politely agreed.

The preparations for invasion were not exactly what Anne had imagined. She thought of the nation in general, made jittery with panic by the failure of the Peace and the doom-laden news reports, and utterly reliant on these coastal defences.

Yet here, both on the field and around it, the atmosphere was merry. Onlookers were gathered in the park to enjoy the entertainment: picnics laid out; ale much consumed; patriotic songs chorused with a triumphant lust. Skylarks danced through a piercing blue sky. Perhaps the nerves of the capital might be assuaged if it could witness the confidence with which Kent viewed its terrible threat.

And possibly the sight of the volunteers from the villages of Godmersham and Molash – now marching over the brow, then marching back again – might also calm London's nerves? Anne watched on and doubted it. She had the advantage of recognising many of the future heroes of battle here assembled: the pigman, the cowhand, those lads from the tithe barn around whom Sally liked to gad. Anne was, furthermore, a little bemused that the training seemed to involve no sort of weaponry. Was the plan simply to *march* at the French then, in the hopes that they turned tail? Her own worries multiplied.

'Are they not *splendid*?' gasped Fanny. 'Do look at Papa in his uniform! I can barely *speak* simply for staring at him!'

Captain Austen, as he was known in this company, had gone to much effort with his red coat and sash over blue britches. Emblems of an oak bough and a crescent adorned his black hat. Anne could see, even from a distance, that great thought and care had gone into the tailoring and general presentation. The enemy would be intimidated by the elegance alone.

'The very picture of chivalry,' Henry Austen agreed. 'Bonaparte will quail just at the sight!'

Startled by the sound of her own thoughts being echoed, Anne turned towards him and – was she mistaken, or did Mr Henry just *wink* at her, over Fanny's young head? This was simply too much.

'Miss Sharp!' Fanny exclaimed. 'Are you quite well?' And in an aside to her uncle, for which Anne was not thankful, she added, 'Poor Miss Sharp does suffer so with her poor head.'

'Forgive me, sir,' Anne curtseyed. 'I am finding the sun a little strong up here this morning.' She sounded suitably feeble. 'If you can spare me, perhaps I ought to return.'

❧

Her 'poor head' was a convenient excuse for Anne to leave any situation that proved to be awkward. She was so often laid low that nobody doubted her word when she claimed to be sickening. However, it was also the cause of great personal distress. It was not just the violence of the condition itself, though that was, indeed, horrible: the invisible knives that stabbed at her eyes in the day; the agony somewhere behind them which stalked her by night and, on occasion, brought her to screaming.

It was also the matter of its great inconvenience. She now needed her health while she needed to work. The ideal governess should never fall ill. Yet, to her shame, her 'heads' were generally brought on by her own emotional state. And that she found to be beyond her control.

Anne had been born very robust. Naught but a mild cold ever disturbed her and so she continued until one critical point in her fifteenth year. On that day, as usual, Anne breezed with happiness into the schoolroom. But there was no sign of Hettie! Aunt Mercer explained the girl was still in her room, and before she could finish her sentence, Anne was bounding up the stairs, two steps at a time.

'Dearest! You are ill!' She rushed in without knocking, to find Hettie sitting calmly in front of the glass while a stranger was dressing her hair.

'Anny!' Hettie smiled. 'Tonight I am to go to my first ball! My godmother is chaperone. Is it not too exciting for words?'

'A *ball*?' Anne fell on the bed in a wild state of shock. 'But what on earth *for*?'

Hettie giggled. 'To dance, I suppose! Why do you think that dreary master comes to us week after week? At last, I shall get proper practice. And with proper *gentlemen*, too!'

Anne was appalled at her friend, at the ridiculous world and its absurd designs. They were at last arriving at the age at which Aunt Mercer had promised them lectures and meetings: a place at the feet of those whose ideas they loved to discuss. And now Hettie's head was to be turned in the direction of dances and gentlemen! What could she possibly want with mere *gentlemen*? They had never before talked of the species. They loved each other. They had taken a pledge! Surely, the Mercers could not have been plotting this the whole time? Dear God forbid that her Hettie was ever complicit. For if so, then this was the most monstrous betrayal.

The pain in her eye began as Anne dragged herself back down the stairs. Agnes was summoned to nurse her. There were two empty chairs at lessons the next day. Hettie was too tired and happy to even think of appearing and Anny was too weak to move.

As time went on and Anne's problems multiplied, the headaches came thick and fast. The announcement of Hettie's engagement brought them on in a cluster. The weeks that Hettie spent buying her trousseau, Anne was up and awake in the middle of every night, screaming with pain, and the days she spent sobbing. The servants ran from one house to the other with notes, some written in passion – *I can never share you. If I cannot have you entirely, I do not want you at all!*; the others – *Dearest, I beg you, do not take on so* – were contented and mild.

Then came that terrible summer of 1792, when her mother could not stop crying, and neither Anne nor Agnes could understand why. And after that, it was one cluster after another.

Anne knew that it was wrong of her to suggest to Mr Henry that her head was poor on that day, when she was perfectly fine. Any more suggestions of illness would sorely try her employer's patience. She was foolish to risk appearing any more frail than she was. But then, he was so very vexing.

She prayed that life at Godmersham remained generally calm and she would stay well from now on.

CHAPTER XIV

Despite the warmth of the days, Anne endeavoured to keep to her room for as much of them as was bearable: the risk of another encounter with Henry Austen was simply too dangerous. Sadly, it was close to impossible. On their first acquaintance, she had felt the presence of Mr Austen occupy so much of her schoolroom. On this visit, it struck her that in fact he took over the whole of Godmersham Park.

At certain times, when the coast should rightly be clear, she would tread lightly and swiftly down the back stairs on her way out to take air. And each time, without fail, he found and attacked her with friendliness. Whether in the back hall, behind the garden gate as she opened it or by the stables – even, on one mortifying occasion, far away on the Canterbury Road – Anne could not escape. She did no more than greet then rebuff him, and hurry away.

However, once a week, she had an appointment downstairs which she simply had to attend: Fanny's dance classes with Mr Philpot took place in the drawing room, and Anne acted as chaperone.

These hours were never her happiest. Much as Anne loved all dancing, she generally found the masters of it both priggish and absurd. Mr Philpot's obsequiousness when with Mrs Austen achieved levels which approached the medieval. She was sure that on one occasion he had even walked backwards from her presence. And the fact that he was, no doubt, paid more per hour than the governess per month did not help to win her affections.

On this afternoon, Anne was sitting at the piano, providing the musical accompaniment. Mr Philpot was teaching his pupil how to enter a room, as he had been doing now for some weeks. Anne doubted that, in her entire adult life, Fanny would ever walk through as many doors – in such varieties of manner or to create so myriad effects – as those for which she was being so diligently prepared.

The master tapped his cane on the floor. 'Let us try that again,' he commanded in his affected fashion. 'And this time—' He opened the door to let Fanny through, gave a gasp and plunged into a deep, almost balletic bow. 'Mr Austen. You do us *such honour*.'

'And this is where I find you!' Henry strode in. 'I hope I do not interrupt something of consequence?'

Mr Philpot began to explain; Mr Austen cut him off. 'I have come in search of a fishing companion. Fanny, your dear mama has refused me. I should be as mournful as a catfish were I to find myself alone on the riverbank.'

Mr Philpot rubbed his hands together. 'Mr *Austen*.' He dipped his head in deep supplication. 'Please do permit me to issue the most *respectful* appeal. There is still a full ten minutes left of our lesson.'

'Excellent!' Mr Austen gave the master an extremely hearty slap on the shoulder. Its intent was no doubt amiable. Nevertheless, Anne peered around her music, mildly curious as to whether the effete Mr Philpot maintained an upright position, or was now sprawled out on the floor. 'Then let us call it five minutes and we have a deal! I shall go and gather our equipment.' Henry turned to leave, then turned back again. 'Miss Sharp! Are you by any chance an angler?'

'Sadly not, sir.'

'Hm. I am most sorry to hear it. Would that be by an absence of opportunity or lack of desire?'

Anne admitted only to the former though, of course, it was both.

'Then you will come with us and I shall teach you! We will meet in the hall in five minutes. Indeed, sir, you have already squandered one of those. Four minutes now remain to you. Pray, use them wisely.' With a bow and a flourish, he left. And Mr Philpot now had the air of a catfish.

⁂

Anne stood on the banks of the Stour, a study in reluctance. A little downstream, in front of the bathing house, were Fanny, her uncle and also, unexpectedly, Fanny's mama. Although she had refused the pleasure earlier, once word reached Mrs Austen that the governess was to be included, she experienced a sudden change of heart.

Anne could not be sure – the decision might have been unrelated, and innocent – but she feared it did not bode well. Was she now under surveillance? For it was not unreasonable to suppose that Henry Austen's attentions to herself had been noticed. He may even have made some careless mention of their encounters! She quailed at the thought. Even the mildest suspicion that she had herself been complicit – that she had made any small effort to attract such a gentleman's eye – would put her in jeopardy. She must be on guard.

So she had positioned herself at a distance which she hoped would be taken as most deferential and prayed there to be ignored both by man and by fish.

She turned her head slightly, towards the pretty stone bridge, so that her bonnet hid her face from the party.

Her rod hung from her limp hands and rarely troubled the surface of the water. She heard herself humming a pretty tune, and was forced to admit that that outing was not entirely unpleasant. The slant of the afternoon sun was such that she could count every speckle upon the fat backs of each trout. She smiled down upon them and wished all safe progress.

'Come now, Miss Sharp.' Her persecutor strode up. 'Though tricks do need to be learned, effort is still required – even from a novice like yourself. Please. Allow me.' He took the rod from her hand. 'It is all in the casting.'

There followed a display of athleticism with narcissist overtones – it seemed Henry Austen was rarely unconscious of the figure he struck. Anne obediently watched, and contained her great irritation. 'Ha! Here comes a catch . . . Look at that . . . The most perfect fellow . . . The mouth waters to watch him . . . Now. First, one must attract . . . He must not pass by . . . Then comes a little teasing . . .'

He sounded so much like her mother during Anne's marriageable years, she could not help smiling.

'Miss Sharp,' he chided, though his eyes did that creasing, 'I beg of you. Fishing is a serious matter and I request that you treat it as such.' He turned back to his quarry. 'No! Hang it! We lost him! He was ours for the taking and now—'

Anne watched with delight as the trout swam on its

way; Henry Austen's distress, though, seemed genuine. How he hated to lose! His great masculine pride wounded by the flick of a fish tail.

'That was a lesson in the perils of even a moment's distraction, Miss Sharp, but perhaps this time—'

'Sir.' She dropped a mollifying curtsey. 'Forgive me.' And, using the words which had so often caused despair in her mother, added: 'I fear my heart is simply not in it.'

And before he could stop her, Anne trotted down the bank to take her leave of the ladies. Once out of sight, she gathered her skirts and ran across the fields, back to the house and her refuge.

❧

Those who had known Anne of old might have warned Henry Austen that she would not comply. She was well known for letting good catches go. Some would go so far to say – lips pursed, head shaking with sorrow but no sympathy – that is why she found herself a governess now. The girl had had her chances; she should have hooked them in when she had them in front of her.

Anne would dispute this version of events, and insist that, in the stream of gentlemen who called at her door, there was not one to tempt her: minnows, each one of them. Minnows to a man.

In fact, that was not quite true of the first to propose to her. At the time, even as he was wedged into a chair, physically incapable of getting down on one knee, Mr Jameson appeared to Anne more like a whale. At first, she could not understand what was happening. Why had her parents both left the room, leaving her alone with this ogre? As he outlined his case, she thought he was speaking of some business arrangement, rather than holy matrimony.

'And so, in the bringing together of these differences, we would find each would prove not, I pray, a conflict but, indeed, a complement to the other and with some work and diligence thus find some successes perhaps and mutual benefits . . .'

Anne wanted to laugh. She managed a polite, but emphatic refusal.

The whale lumbered off. Her parents returned. '*Well?*' her mother demanded.

'Oh, Mama!' Anne collapsed back into her chair and let rip her mirth. 'You will never believe it. He asked for my hand!'

'I am already aware,' Mrs Sharp replied crossly. 'But did you accept? Anny, *please*. This is no laughing matter.'

'Forgive me, Mama.' Anne sat up and collected herself. 'I thought you too would find it amusing. And of course I did not! I am sixteen years of age, and he is so old and, quite frankly, repellent.'

'Oh, *Anny*.' Mrs Sharp sank into the sofa and wrung her hands. 'I did hope that you might, just this once, see some sense.'

'Well, fancy, my dear.' Her father chuckled. 'That our beautiful, bright daughter might refuse a big, fat booby like Jameson. And when she is so famously biddable! Are girls not a mystery?' He sat by the fire and cracked opened his newspaper.

'Johnny! This is a serious matter, and no time for jokes. Do you not find it awkward? How will you face Mr Jameson, next time you meet?'

'Jameson?' Mr Sharp looked up and laughed harder. 'Pray, madam, do not mistake Jameson for a person of feeling. I dare say he has forgotten it already. As should we all.'

After that debacle, more gentlemen called, none of whom Anne had met before they showed up at her door. All had some sort of association with her papa – through his business at first, then through his club. Even had she been tempted – Anne had no intention of marrying any man, ever – they all had some defect that would give even the desperate pause for thought: shaking hands and bloodshot eyes which denoted an over-fondness for the drink; fair declaration of debts incurred at the tables, which his father would settle on her acceptance; a beloved, dead wife and nine motherless children. The nadir came with the one who announced, in his defence, that they need hardly see each other, such were his obligations at the family's plantations. If one did not go down there oneself and show them the whip-hand . . .

He was dismissed with cold fury.

'*Well?*' Mrs Sharp came in as soon as he left.

'Mama! How could you? Surely, by now, you know my views well?' Anne demanded. 'You have heard them often enough. And what is my father thinking of, sending round these quite terrible men?'

'*He sends them because I have begged him to!*' her mother cried. 'They come *at my request*! Oh, Anny.' Yet again, Mrs Sharp sank back into the sofa. This time, she wept. 'What is to become of you?'

'I am sorry, dearest.' Anne went to her, sat down on the floor at her feet and laid her head in her mother's lap. 'This *conventional* thing: I just cannot do it! You know that. Papa knows it better! He has no truck with convention. I merely follow his lead.'

'Then you will come to regret it. You think you can live as an unconventional woman? You will be no more than a laughing stock.'

Anne sat back on her heels and implored her, 'Please, Mama, let me alone. I promise that, one day, if I do happen to find myself deeply in love as do you and Papa, of course then—'

'Love!' her mother cried out in anguish. 'You cannot trust *love*. Nor can you live off it!'

'But can I not *hope*?' Anne returned. 'Forgive me, but I refuse to just *settle*. And anyway' – she hid her head in her mother's lap – 'I do not know why, but I have never seen myself as part of some *regular* family. Wife . . . mother . . . those roles simply do not appeal. I enjoy my life as it is, with you and Agnes and my friends and Papa, of course. I am thinking that, as Papa has said often, I might try my hand at the stage, perhaps? As you did, dear Mama. Or even *write* for the stage! I am working on an idea at the moment. Perhaps you might still know some people?'

Mrs Sharp ignored every word her daughter had said. 'And when I am *dead*?' she was wailing. 'What *then*?'

'Then I shall be very sad.' Anne smiled up and reached for her hand. 'So very sad. And no dim-witted husband could provide any imaginable comfort. Please, do not distress yourself, Mama. I promise you, all will be well.'

'You will learn.' Mrs Sharp dabbed at her eyes. 'You will learn the most painful of lessons.'

Anne sighed, with some irritation. Being the possessor of the more superior intellect – the beneficiary of the best education – she had no faith there was anything her mother could teach her. 'What *lesson*, Mama?'

'The one' – her mother blew her nose, delicately – 'all women must learn, sooner or later. The world is not thy friend, Anny, my dear. Nor is the world's law.'

CHAPTER XV

My dear Fanny,

You would be astonished to know quite how you divert us with your excellent letters. We sit with them for hours – singly or together – and extract every last drop – wring them bone dry! Our discussions have ranged from the teeth of the baby to the weather where you are, taking in all other sundries – until we alight once again on our favoured conclusion – that is, what an <u>excellent</u> Austen you turn out to be.

Your answer to the question of <u>Classics</u> was just as it ought, and your Grandpapa is accepting. Your Mama is quite right – mothers are, on the whole – French is more useful than Latin in this modern age. You are more likely to encounter a <u>Frenchman</u> at dinner than a senator of Rome – <u>they</u> are rarely invited into the best houses. No doubt – given the high standards of your

splendid Miss S. – you are already fluent and rudely ahead of
your poor ignorant <u>aunts</u>. Sadly, <u>we</u> had the misfortune of
being sent off to school – absurd institutions whose sole aim is
the <u>prevention</u> of all learning. I fear you shall think us most
<u>ignorant</u> when next we meet.

And, dear Aunt Jane, when will that be? I hear you cry at
even this distance. Alas – not this summer, for our plans are
now made. We have surrendered the lease now on Sydney
Place – which caused me no heartache – and soon set off on our
travels in quite the other direction. 'Tis Lyme which has won
the honour of our company this year – even now, it is
celebrating and preparing our welcome – and your Uncle Henry
and Aunt Eliza will meet us there. You do not need <u>me</u> to tell
you how much joy <u>they</u> will bring with them.

Still, this glorious weather prompts our thoughts to turn
often to Godmersham. But of course Kent acquits itself well in
all seasons. How I wish the same could be said for poor
Bath . . .

> *Yours ever,*
> *Aunt Jane.*

❧

On this sunny morning, with her conscience clear and the
grounds to herself, Anne prepared for a day of pure pleasure. Of course, she could not include her dinner in that:
with the whole family out celebrating Elizabeth Austen's

birthday, her rations would be yet worse than usual. In compensation, she rashly decided, just this once, to stage a shocking rebellion. After all, if there was nobody to see her, then there was no need to play the drab governess. The servants might notice, of course, but then she had no goodwill there to squander. So she laid aside the dull grey and donned her good pink.

She moved before the glass for the affixing of her bonnet and saw, somewhat to her shock, an approximation of her old self. The Brussels trim at her bosom shed light upon her face; her cheeks were now rose from the fresh Kentish air and her eyes had recovered their brightness. Oh dear, she thought: not exactly invisible. But then, as there was no family here, there was no person to offend. 'Through Eden,' she declared to herself, 'I shall now make my solitary way.' And prompted by those words, she plucked her Milton from the shelf and slipped out through the front door and into the glory of that summer day. With every step from the house, her whole being lightened. She had no duties to perform. There were no children to instruct or protect; no prying eyes which might, at any moment, narrow in judgement. She passed by a stable lad sweeping dung from the drive and sang out 'Good morning!' in a confident, clear, almost musical voice so little used lately that it took her quite by surprise.

Out into the lane she skipped, passed the cottages, bestowed a broad smile on an invalid man who sat by his door, picked up her skirts on the hump-backed bridge crossing the river, and took to the fields. For once, she was not required to shrink against walls or into corners, or temper the fires that raged in her breast. She did not need to pretend to meekness when, in truth, she was bold. For on this one blessed day, Miss Sharp was released. All the long hours until dinner – which, no doubt, would be served with a large portion of reality – she would not be the governess, but simply Anne. Flinging her arms wide, lifting her face to the sky, she danced in a circle and laughed out her relief.

And then, with a start, she saw that she was not alone. An old woman in garish dress, carrying a basket of favours, approached and pressed a sprig of white heather into Anne's hand.

In the days when her life had been fortunate, Anne had enjoyed having her fortune foretold. When out with her friends at the Pleasure Garden, they never refused it. Good or bad, each prophecy was met with girlish amusement.

Now, while this teller begged her, Anne could think of no reason against. After all, what was the worst she could hear? She would die an old maid, and never know wealth – and of that she was quite well aware. She offered her palm.

'I see love.' The poor woman had not a tooth in her head. 'A great love, and long lasting.'

'Indeed?' Anne was sceptical. 'And would this love perhaps be with a tall and dark stranger?'

The woman puzzled at the lines. ''Tis an odd one.'

She squinted and held Anne's hand up to the sun. 'It's a passion, that I can see. Oh, it's a passion. But as to the lover – I can't rightly say.'

Anne smiled. Then perhaps, in time, she would gain such power within the household as to be permitted her own pet – like Mrs Salkeld the housekeeper, with her cat. Now, *there* was a passion. 'Tell me. Can you read anything at all on the subject of money?' Money was what mattered. Love, after all, she could manage without.

'Forgive me, miss.' The woman shook her head. 'You're a puzzle and no mistake. You'll live to a good age, of that I am sure. But that's it. Love and old bones is all I can give you.'

Anne had no penny on her person, so she offered a good handkerchief. It was not her best one – that she had unfortunately mislaid. Such was her pity for the future she had seen, the woman refused it.

The temple was set high on the hill, framed by the woods. Anne had run up the fine grassy walk and was now taking a moment to sit on the stone steps, recover her breath and drink in the vista. From here, she could see across the whole of the park: lush now and verdant; pulsating with life. Below her, the shimmering river meandered the way from its source to the sea; on the opposite ridge, the copse, first brown and bare, then white with snow, was dressed anew in its summer's best finery. At the end of the thin thread of village, arranged to mimic the bends in the river, stood the church: a monument to all this God-given beauty. And in the centre of everything, strong, solid – and, Anne wondered, perhaps just a little smug? – sat the Great House.

Anne appraised it from this distance and found her feelings towards Godmersham riven with conflict. It was a handsome place, certainly of pleasing proportions. She commended it for its lack of unnecessary embellishment: there were no pretensions to stateliness, at least. It was simply a home, built for the growth and enjoyment of one fortunate family – albeit on a most generous scale.

But, although she now lived here and had no other refuge, it was not Anne's home and nor could it ever be: it would always be a big part of her, but she could never be even a small part of it. Every night that she spent here, every day that she worked, she would be an outsider, until she was no longer wanted. And then where was she to rest these bones as they aged? Perhaps Agnes was right and she should find her father . . .

Anne's pride faltered. Her staunch resolve started to tremble. She had been here almost half of a year! Long months of hard duty, every day bringing some new, small degradation: a diet rich in nothing but humble pie. Oh, how she hungered for freedom!

At once, she collected herself. How absurd to squander her one day of pleasure in misery and moping. Leaving her Milton on the steps – she was in no sort of mood for him – she stood and brushed her skirts, dusting away all her worries. This, she said aloud in her firm governess voice, would not do. It was not often that one had the pleasures of hours to oneself and a temple in need of exploring.

Anne turned and could not help but giggle at the sheer absurdity of the edifice before her. It was in the Doric style, with a portico entrance of fluted columns: a little piece of civic Athenian majesty dropped into a field in the Garden of England. How money turns men to fools! She mounted the steps and went in.

The chamber was square, built of stone, adorned by a frieze and, to her surprise, quite simply enchanting. Anne was transported at once. After months of suppression, the forces of imagination stirred within her again. Long dulled by drudgery, her restless spirit now fought for expression; that strong voice of old now demanded a hearing. This was a place made for fantasy and she could not resist it. She stepped out of her own life and into another:

My father had a daughter lov'd a man,
As it might be, perhaps, were I a woman,
I should your lordship.

Her performance as Viola, at but fifteen years of age, had been perhaps her greatest moment. A few lines swam back towards her:

She never told her love,
But let concealment, like a worm i' the bud,
Feed on her damask cheek.

Then she recalled the whole and began reciting with passion, the stone walls absorbing her every strong word.

'*Was this not love indeed?*' she cried to the emptiness.

Anne heard a firm tread. A barbarian at the door of her temple! She stepped back into the shadows. It was not the fortune teller, of that Anne was certain. The foot was a heavy and masculine one; its step confident and unhurried. She stayed silent until the intruder receded and, for safety, passed the remainder of the day in the depths of the woods.

That evening's solitary dinner in the schoolroom was as poor as expected but, though Anne was hungry, she felt sustained by the joys of her day. The family was still out, the household was peaceful and Maria Edgeworth propped in her lap. There then came a loud boom.

'*In solitude, What happiness*' – Henry Austen stood at the open door – '*who can enjoy alone, Or, all enjoying, what contentment find?*' He strode into the room. 'Or so says the poet.' He held up her Milton. 'Forgive me if I disturb you. I believe this belongs to you, Miss Sharp? I came across it on the steps of the temple.'

Anne jumped up and curtseyed. 'Sir!' What was he doing here? 'You are not with the family party? '

He walked to the table to put the book down. 'Though the prospect was tempting, somewhere deep within I roused the strength to resist.'

Was he the barbarian outside her temple? Then may God strike her dead. He would not resist making fun of her. She braced against the incoming onslaught. But his eye had been caught by the sight of her plate.

'Miss Sharp, please forgive my impertinence.' He looked down with horror at the sluggish brown matter. 'Am I to understand this is your dinner for the evening?'

Humiliated, Anne dropped her eyes to the floor.

'But this bears no resemblance to the meal I was served. Is it a dish you had particularly requested?'

Of course, there were many poor souls who were desperate enough to consume it – but to actually *request* such a meal? Surely, Henry Austen could not be so obtuse.

'Miss Sharp? Please be so kind as to answer the question.'

'It is not, sir.'

'That does not surprise me. Mrs Salkeld would not feed *that* to her cat. May I ask, does it present a fair example of the food you are generally given?'

'It does, sir.' She paused, for an instant. 'But only when I dine alone and not with the children. Then, we enjoy the same and I eat very well.'

She had not before seen Henry Austen in so serious a mood, nor previously heard the sombre voice with which now he demanded: 'Please, Miss Sharp. I bid you now. Come with me.'

Anne felt most uncomfortable. Surely, he would not drag her down to the kitchen and stage some sort of trial? She imagined the ritual degradation of Cook in front of the servants, the strings of her apron ceremoniously torn from her shoulders. Below stairs would unite against her in hatred. She would not – she could not – follow.

'Must I command you, Miss Sharp?' His words rang out down the corridor.

The heads of Sackree and Nurse, with their mouths hanging open, peered around their doors. He was causing a scene in the sanctity of the attic! At once, Anne did as he bade her.

❧

Down in the library, Anne sat in its most comfortable chair. The late-afternoon sun poured through the long window, illuminating the pink silk she still wore; warming her hair which was, for the first time at Godmersham, uncovered by cap. Naturally, she should not have been there with a gentleman: alone. And, of course, her dress was quite inappropriate for her position.

Henry Austen had not led them down to the kitchen. Instead, when they were met downstairs by Mrs Salkeld, the housekeeper, he had requested a fine supper, and she had responded at once! What came was more befitting to

a queen than a governess. Anne now gave all her attention to bread, cheese and pickles, and an exquisite ham
pie, while Henry held forth. So delicious was the food,
Anne considered his company a small price to pay.

He talked of his father, the parson, whom he revered,
and the family rectory, now in the hands of his eldest
brother. He spoke with pride of his two sailor brothers
and the action they faced in the coming hostilities. Henry
Austen was not unkind, Anne decided. Indeed, he was
congenial enough. And if it were to turn out that he had
been the barbarian, then she might not mind it particularly.

'I feel sure you would find friendship with both of my
sisters, should the chance befall you,' Henry was now
saying. 'It is a sadness to me that their invitations to Godmersham are not more frequent – I often worry that their
lives lack a degree of excitement. But there: it is not my
place to suggest it. I must simply be grateful that the door
is so often opened to me.'

Having watched Mr Henry stride the Great House as if
he was its owner, Anne was interested to learn that, like her,
he too found it difficult to feel quite at home there. Though
Edward Austen had inherited, it can only have occurred
by some process of random selection, for he was the third
child of eight. And surely, in a family, the good fortune of
one should come to the benefit of all. But more interesting
still was the dessert she had started: a smooth custard and
compote which now rolled round on her tongue.

'Cassandra, the eldest,' Mr Henry continued, 'has

always been the more serious of the two, and more so since the death of her fiancé, which hit as hard as one might expect. Jane, though, the younger, I am particularly close to and I do hope you will make her acquaintance. I suspect you would get on excessively well.'

Such was Anne's sense of comfort, and so full was her stomach, that she forgot not only who she was, but also quite where. And thus she spoke up: 'I do hope for it. I have already elected her my favourite Austen.'

Henry let out a loud bark of laughter.

'Forgive me!' Anne gasped.

Smiling, he held up an elegant hand. 'Please. Not yet another apology! I would much rather hear your reasons for dear Jane's election to this covetable position, and why the rest of us are found to be wanting?'

'Oh, I have two reasons. The first point in her favour is that your sister writes excellent letters to her dear niece. The second – and, to me, most important – is our shared, high regard for the poetry of William Cowper.' Anne went back to her plate.

'Dash it! This is both a wound and an injustice! For I, too, admire the man greatly.'

'Indeed?' Anne was now bold. 'And yet you mocked him that day in my schoolroom.'

He fell back in surrender. 'Now 'tis I who am forced to apologise. As my dear father has long chided, and still chides to this day: I am too swift to seek the humour in every moment, and too slow to seriousness. I am sorry to have mocked Cowper, and even sorrier still if you felt yourself mocked. It was not my intention.' His eyes crinkled. 'Henceforth, I strive towards one, sole ambition: to knock Jane off that pedestal.'

'Then I wish you good luck, sir,' Anne replied primly, and returned to the cheese.

CHAPTER XVI

Come September, and Anne was on leave and back in London. She paid the cab and asked the driver to deposit her bags on the steps of Number 37, Montague Square. Before going in to the Mercers, and falling under Agnes's control, she first wanted to stand alone for a few minutes, outside her old family home, and remember.

The new residents of Number 22 had made some improvements. It wore a brilliant white coat; late-summer flowers spilled from the boxes perched at the windows. It was under new management and, Anne was forced to admit, seemed to be thriving. Though, surely, she had to believe, somehow deep in its fabric the house must retain some memory of her own family's life there: a wearing of the wood where their feet had once trod; a slight dent on the wall where the Reynolds had hung; particles, even, of the air they had breathed, caught in the pores of its walls.

At the end of a warm day – with the sun sinking down yet the sky still pale – candles were lit, but the shutters not closed. Anne could see straight into the drawing room. She watched the people within, as she might watch a scene from a play through a proscenium arch. The lady of the house, who looked to be the same age as Anne, sat by the fireside threading a needle; a gentleman read his newspaper by the light coming in at the window. The carved head of a rocking horse at the back of the room suggested young children.

Anne tried to picture her own family, as they might have presented to strangers out there on the walk. But the only image she could conjure was of her and Agnes, vigilant beside the corpse of her mother. Waiting with dread, and yet a strange longing, for the undertaker to come and take her away. Watching her father plant one last, tender kiss on that brow.

So houses, too, have their own seasons, Anne realised. The Sharps' reign there had ended with a particularly harsh winter; the new people were in the joys of their spring. It was too painful to stand there. Anne walked back to Number 37, rang the bell and was assaulted with love from Agnes and Nurse Mercer. And, oh, the relief to be back in such tender, familiar surroundings! Oh, the delight in being free to act her own self!

After much clucking and comment – 'Little lamb!

Seems like they're running you ragged'; 'What colour do you call that? She was a good, decent, pale when she left me, you know. Don't you start getting all brown, Anny. They're all brown in the country, Nurse. Terrifying sight, my cousin says. Foreign' – Anne was released and allowed into the parlour.

Number 37, Anne saw, was changed: now in the depths of its own winter, it was the very model of an eccentric establishment. When their own house was let go, Agnes had tried to find a new place and obtained a few interviews, but, sadly, no offers. Lame from birth, she put it down to her leg – nobody wants a maid hobbling about the place – though Anne suspected that her strong personality might also have proved an obstruction.

It was striking to Anne, too, that for one with so many 'cousins' so often mentioned, Agnes could find no family willing to take her. Fortunately, Nurse Mercer was kind and had given Agnes a modest room – Anne was never quite sure if Mr Mercer had agreed or even knew of the arrangement. Unfortunately, even she was not so wily as to get Agnes a wage, too, and so Anne was supporting her. Still, they seemed very happy together. She was grateful for that, while nagged by the worry that they spent the whole day reminiscing about the young lives of their lambs. The thought made her heart ache a little.

The four daughters had married and left, yet the schoolroom had not been dismantled. The dressing-up box gaped open in the corner, as if any moment a child might plunge in for a rummage. Three mature women now sat around the same table at which the little girls used to study so keenly. But there was no sign of Mr Mercer.

'We don't see much of *him*, Nurse, do we now?' Agnes said brightly. 'Likes to eat on his own. He is an odd one . . . We do *try*.'

'Oh, we do,' Nurse Mercer assured Anne. 'Take our-selves up for a nice little chat, just about this and that, you know. Cheer him up a bit. But he's not a one for chatting, is he, Nurse?'

They still never used Christian names. Instead – like old and retired generals – each still insisted on address-ing the other by the historical terms of their profes-sional rank.

'Don't know why, Nurse, I'm sure. They all say *he's* the clever one, but it falls down to *us* to do all the talking.'

Poor Mr Mercer, thought Anne. The library he had once used a refuge from all those motherless girls, now a bleak prison.

❧

At last, she and Agnes were alone in the bedroom that Anne knew so painfully well. She sat down on the bed she had once shared with dear Hettie; plumped the pillow on which their young, silken heads had once lain while they pledged their devotion; arranged her personal effects before the glass on the pretty dressing table, where Hettie had sat as a bride. Anne could not help but remember that day: Hettie biting her lip with nervous anticipation, dewy eyes dancing with joy; Anne trying so hard not to cry. They had not met again.

'I'll sleep with you, shall I?' Agnes sat down on the bed, proceeding to ease off her shoes and rub at her feet. 'Oof, that's better.' She lay down on the mattress to test it. 'Not bad. Better than the one they've given me down in that back room. Kills me, it does. Wake up in all sorts of contortions. Still,' she went on, having, in Anne's view, grumbled sufficiently, 'mustn't grumble, eh? They've been kind enough just taking me in. Now, tell me everything about these here Austens. You don't tell me enough in those letters of yours. Too busy, I suppose, to think of me these days.'

'Agnes!' Anne protested. 'I write as often as possible!'

'Well. That's as maybe. But you don't give me all of it. For instance, you wrote that they've all gone on holiday but where have they gone? I've got a right to know that, surely to heavens.'

'Why, they are beside the sea at Ramsgate for a few weeks. I believe it is considered wise for Mrs Austen to enjoy the bathing and air, before her confinement.'

'There! That didn't hurt, did it? Ramsgate, you say. Had a niece who . . .' And on she went, while Anne unpacked and undressed. 'Still, if it's brought you home,

I'm not complaining. Only a few weeks, though. Don't put yourselves out . . .' Anne was only listening with half of one ear, when she heard: 'This Mr Henry Austen. You tell me you hate him, but you never stop mentioning him. Very intriguing, I'm sure. Can't make head nor tail of it. Said to Nurse, I said, it sounds like a story out of one of your novels.'

'Oh, dearest,' Anne said into the glass. 'It is nothing of the sort. It just so happens that he irritates me particularly, and yet I cannot seem to rid myself of the man.' She did her hair as quickly as possible, hoping that Agnes's eagle eyes did not spot the cheap brush. The silver one, *AS* engraved on it, had – like her best handkerchief – lately gone missing.

While she got into bed, Anne described her problems with Cook, and how her food had been excellent since his intervention. That she was grateful while, at the same time, resenting the matter was only resolved when Henry took charge.

'Cooks!' Agnes scoffed. 'No better than they should be. Glad he put *her* in her place. Mind you, I can see if he mixes with Jameson, he can't be all good, can he? Best way to judge a man is the company he keeps.'

'Indeed.' Anne put her book down. 'One of the many reasons I have not to trust him.' She snuffed out the candle. 'Hush now, dearest, and let us sleep. I have had a long journey.' She turned away from Agnes, on to her side, stared into the darkness and thought of her father.

He was out there. She was sure he was out there. But then if that were true, why – *why?* – would he not come to her?

❧

Every morning of her visit, Anne faced the same quarrel.

'What's the name of his club, can you remember?' Agnes asked over the first breakfast. 'All we have to do is loiter around it, and he'll soon turn up. Then—'

'I never knew it, I am afraid.' Anne calmly spread jam on a muffin. 'He simply called it "the club". I have no intention of loitering around all of them.'

Anne spent the day alone at a museum.

'Twelve years ago,' announced Agnes the following morning. 'I've been thinking. Twelve years when all of a sudden he didn't come home so much. So what was all that about? *There* is your mystery. I remember saying to the Mistress—'

'He was simply working much harder.' Anne went to St Martin-in-the-Fields and passed a pleasant afternoon in a pew, listening to the organ.

'Today,' Nurse Mercer declared, 'why don't we all—?'

'Thank you, Nurse, but I am busy.' Anne spoke very firmly.

'You might listen to me first, madam,' Nurse Mercer retorted. 'I'm off to see Hettie and *was* going to suggest we all go together.'

Anne could think of no respectable reason why she should refuse.

⁓

Lady Caterham's welcome was gracious, of course: her hair was well dressed; her clothing was fine and manners impeccable. Still, Anne was struck by her coolness. Though she did not mind on her own account – indeed, Anne had hardly expected a return to their warmth – it pained her to witness Hettie's treatment of Nurse Mercer.

'Hettie, my darling.' Nurse Mercer rushed towards this grand lady, seeing only the small child she had mothered.

'Oh, Nurse.' Lady Caterham offered her cheek for the briefest of kisses. 'Please try and remember to use Henrietta when you are here. Sir James does prefer it.'

'Sorry, I'm sure.' Nurse Mercer settled down in a chair, and bade Agnes sit next to her. 'And will we be seeing Sir James this afternoon? Don't think I clapped eyes on him since the day you were wed.'

'Sadly, not.' Hettie rang the bell and a maid came in with the tea. 'But little James will be down from the nursery shortly. I presumed you would welcome the opportunity to see him.' This was met with much anticipatory clucking.

Anne knew little of such Mayfair establishments, but surely, even a mansion must have the odd intimate little corner. The drawing room in which Her Ladyship had chosen to see them was so vast, and its seating so formal, as to obstruct good conversation. The party was forced to call out to each other, as if masters of ceremony at an assembly. Clearly, the nurses, from whom words generally flowed, found it inhibiting; too nervous even to take a bite of a cake. Anne had never before seen them resist.

An awkwardness descended. Ice started to form. Anne reprised, yet again, her now familiar role: Silent Governess in the Company of Her Betters. No remarks were addressed to her. The facts of her pitiable life were, apparently, a matter of bad taste, to which it would be impolite to refer. She shifted in her seat. If only she could simply get up and leave.

At last, the baby came in and the tension was broken. Now on home ground, the nurses set to with a thorough, professional examination and pronounced him a peach.

'Indeed. He is perfect,' Lady Caterham agreed. They were the right words, of course, yet spoken with no motherly passion. She did not, Anne noticed, hold him herself. 'Sir James is delighted. He longed very much for a son.' With a wave of her hand, the child was dispatched back to his nursery.

'The men do love their boys.' Nurse Mercer, relaxed now, thrust a fork in a cake. 'What with their titles and what-not.' She spoke with her mouth full. 'Still, a little girl for you next, eh? We like a little girl, don't we, Nurse?'

'There will not be another,' Hettie cut in. 'Blessed as we are with a son, we now have no need for it.'

The nurses were shocked into silence once more. Why would anyone *not* want more babies? Anne was more interested in the practicalities behind such an announcement. She was not aware that these matters were so easily controlled. Perhaps, like Sally's mother, Lady Caterham slept with her rolling pin?

'Done well for herself, the lamb,' Nurse Mercer declared, once they were out in the freedom of Eaton Square. 'My little Hettie, now Her Ladyship. Don't think I'll ever get over it. She wants for nothing.'

Nothing at all, Anne said to herself. Nothing but passion or love or, as far as could be seen, even the merest affection. Was that not the very definition of poverty? She did not begrudge Hettie the life, but nor could she envy it. In Henrietta – now Lady Caterham – Anne could see naught but an insentient beauty in a luxurious grave.

❧

On Anne's last evening in London, she took the nurses on an outing to Drury Lane. It was a thrill for them all to catch Mrs Siddons, though the play was a trite comedy and the form did not become her. The production was woeful, in Anne's opinion, but she kept her criticism private. She did not want to ruin the treat, after all.

'That wig was fetching, I thought,' Agnes opined as they pressed through the crowd spilling on to the street.

'And a *very* good frock,' Nurse Mercer put in. 'The embroidery! Made my fingers hurt just to—'

As they entered the throng in the foyer, Anne reached for both of them – they had best keep together – when her senses were assailed. A potpourri of scents hung like a cloud over the crush. From within the sweet notes of perfume and the rank, unwashed clothes, something called out to her. She stopped. Sniffed the air. Caught nutmeg and lime; a suggestion of lavender. Her mind tumbled backwards: the happy thrill of homecomings; her small head nestling into a broad shoulder; the terror, the joy, of being spun through the air, up close to the ceiling. *Was he here?*

Anne cast around, eyes searching wildly. The back of that gentleman's head! Now abandoning the nurses, she pushed into the street – desperate for a mere glimpse of her father.

But it was no good. She had lost him. And immediately doubted that he had ever been there.

CHAPTER XVII

'Sharpy! Thank *heavens* you have returned.' Miss Bridges flung herself into the chair with dramatic exhaustion. Anne had been in her room all of five minutes. 'I can hereby report that you are now one of those *darling* little treasures without whom the family has no choice but to *crumble*. The house is at sixes and sevens. Never again can you leave us! We simply would not survive.'

Clearly, Harriot did not bother herself with the niceties of the journeys of others and Anne rather approved. It made for a far superior welcome, though Anne believed none of it. 'Is that so? Surely, they were in Ramsgate until very recently. Fanny wrote often and made no mention of any difficulties.'

'True,' Miss Bridges conceded, pulling herself into a more acceptable seated position. 'It did sound pleasant enough, if' – she covered her hand with her mouth – '*frightfully* dull. *But.* Now the chaos is upon them. My sister is grown so heavy she can barely *move*. The children are all simply *impossible*. Even Mr Austen is not quite himself. I was summoned a *whole week ago* to divert little Fanny. The poor girl is *so* anxious about her Mama, she has been in my bed *every night*. Tossing and turning. Endless questions. I declare she has run me quite *ragged*.'

'And yet you look very well,' Anne replied. 'But I am sorry that you have suffered and thank you for telling me. I shall endeavour to keep her fully occupied from now on.'

'Does it not show in my face?' Harriot peered in the glass. 'Perhaps I *may* have come out unscathed. Though I feel old as the *Ark* in my bones.' She licked a finger and dabbed at a curl. 'But *poor* Fanny. Truly. One *can* understand. Nine babies! It is foolish to pretend there is no risk involved. Trying one's luck, rather.' She sighed. 'I do hope my sister finds some *restraint* in the future. We cannot go on forever like this.'

This was the fundamental flaw in the institution of marriage. She who endures a union of chilly dislike, as did poor Hettie, could reasonably expect to live on into a cheerless old age. Meanwhile, the likes of Elizabeth Austen, blessed with true love and a real, mutual attraction, might well not survive to her fortieth year. Anne marvelled that the curious species of the eager young bride was still not yet extinct. Will they not learn? Surely, financial insecurity was a small price to pay.

❦

On their reunion, governess and pupil fell upon each other with warmth. Each had bought gifts for the other; from Fanny, a small figurine of a mermaid; from Anne, a slice of Bond Street soap.

Anne was not sure quite what to do with her mermaid. She knew that Fanny would like her to keep it out on display, and did not want to offend the dear girl by hiding it. On the other hand, Anne's dearest personal possessions seemed to have developed something of a tendency to 'go missing' in Godmersham. 'Grow legs' was another neat euphemism she liked to use, when considering the mysteries of her handkerchief and silver-backed hairbrush. The more obvious term – 'theft' – she tried to avoid, for to say it out loud would lead to no end of trouble. She studied the mermaid. It could not have cost the child more than a sixpence. It did not speak of a past, more comfortable life in a way that might be provoking. And surely, the worst thing of all would be to offend her dear Fanny. She put it in pride of place on her bookshelf and prayed that it stayed there.

At once, they were back into their old routine to which Anne added yet more activities. She had learned from experience that the only way to keep down one's dark thoughts was to not give them time to surface. At the suggestion of the Reverend Whitfield – dear Mr Whitfield – Anne had begun to use her spare time teaching the children of the village. Now, naturally, it occurred to take Fanny with her: good works were a wholesome diversion of which Anne's mistress could only approve. So two afternoons a week, she and Fanny went down to the small school in the lane.

The pupils were taught little more than the skills that might come useful in service, and Fanny took on the needlework classes with an earnest dedication, determined to pass on all she had learned. Phrases such as 'When darning, *we* hold the garment just *so*' and 'Here, *we* would judge blanket stitch as *perfectly* adequate' were showered like blessings upon the rapt little girls, who sat silent and stunned in this exotic presence. On the other side of the schoolroom, Anne taught reading and writing to those who showed interest. The maid Sally's two youngest brothers, who had all her natural intelligence but their own standards of discipline, proved to be excellent pupils.

As the days shortened and Mrs Austen grew still heavier, Fanny's anxiety increased. She was jumpy in lessons, one ear always cocked for signs of change in domestic activity. When each night they both knelt by their beds, Fanny's prayers became longer and longer. Her concentration was furious, her expression one of despair. It would be unseemly to be the first to jump under the covers, but Anne did feel the cold in her nightgown. And neither found any respite in sleep for it was then that Fanny's torment was truly exposed. She would cry out as if in real pain.

But Fanny did have one source of joy during this difficult time, and for that Anne was grateful. One among Fanny's many kind female relatives must somehow have sensed from afar that the child was disturbed. She knew, too, that Fanny's passion for animals rivalled that of St Francis. And lo was delivered a sweet pair of canaries.

Their splendid cage – the Versailles of the ornithological universe – was set up in the back hall, near the foot of the stairs so that the birds could 'look out at their friends in the garden'. Fanny fell madly in love with them. Her weekly pocket money, with which she was normally so cautious, went liberally now on sandpaper and seed. She spent hours by their side, talking, confiding, informing them of their extraordinary beauty. And, in truth, they brought a much-needed pleasure to the whole household. As winter dug in its heels, it gladdened the eye to catch that bright yellow flash. They looked like the summer, Anne always thought: they were the colour of hope.

As Mrs Austen's time drew close, Fanny spent as much time by her side as she was permitted. So often alone, Anne increased her hours spent down in the school and, afterwards, would walk along to the vicarage and take tea with Mr Whitfield.

Anne had often been told that a parson's life was the busiest in a parish, and that of the parson's wife busier still. Yet the lives of the inhabitants of the Godmersham vicarage seemed to contradict all she had heard.

On the few occasions they had met, Mrs Whitfield had come across as a sensitive and intelligent woman and Anne would dearly like to see more of her. They could be fine friends. Sadly, she was one of those women who suffered some unnamed and untreated – never described nor explained – complaint that kept her in bed for weeks at a time. This rendered her incapable of fulfilling the many parson's wife's duties, and upon whose shoulders that burden then fell, Anne did not know. Though she was certain it was not upon those of Mr Whitfield.

No matter when or how often she called, Anne had not once found a vicarage that was bustling.

'Miss Sharp, Miss Sharp, do come in,' Mr Whitfield greeted her this afternoon. 'You catch me in the middle of wondering what I could possibly find to do with myself before dinner.'

Anne took her seat. 'No sheep to herd yet again today, Reverend?'

'I count often enough, and can find not one lost soul among them.' He sliced the plum cake and passed Anne a piece.

'Then happy their shepherd!'

'Indeed.' Mr Whitfield then helped himself. 'Blessed indeed to have a parish so pure.' He ate for a moment, savoured, digested. 'I am also fortunate to be governed by a higher authority. I can trust in St Peter to judge any sins of omission.'

Anne put down her plate. 'Mr Whitfield, it cannot be true that there is no crime at all in the village. Petty theft, at least, surely?'

'Ah, we have our fair share of poachers and so on, of course. Cottagers who let their pigs feed in the orchards. Oh, yes.' He chuckled, taking more cake. 'A great scandal brewing about those acorns – threatening to rock the Godmersham world to its very foundations! But in truth crimes of that nature offend Mr Austen's eyes much more than my own. Would God mind that a poor man favours feeding his family over watching them starve?'

'But, surely – Exodus, chapter twenty, verse one?'

'Indeed, indeed.' He leaned forward and whispered, as if a conspirator, 'But I fear our modern world is a little more nuanced than any Old Testament prophet could have possibly foreseen. Is it not?'

Although she had not planned it, Anne confided to him then about her missing possessions.

'Hmm.' Mr Whitfield frowned. 'So just the two objects you say?'

'There is also a collar of particularly fine lace, though that may have got caught up in the linens on laundry day.'

He folded his hands over the dome of his stomach.

'But I take it you have no right to suspect any person in particular? You are, surely, not suggesting the presence of some servant with a grievance against you? I would struggle to believe it!' He chuckled. 'One might find such a caricature in the pages of a novel, but in the Great House? Quite absurd.'

Anne was far too ashamed to admit that she had not one friend below stairs. Such a revelation would do more than rock the Godmersham world: it would disturb Mr Whitfield's whole universe. Here was a man so good as to be blind to the badness in others. She would not disabuse him.

&

On her return to her room, Anne was surprised to find Miss Bridges sitting alone in the chair: idle, drooping.

'Ah. Back at last.' She did not smile. There were no affected high spirits. Not even one 'Sharpy'. 'I am come to say goodbye. My sister is to move into the hall chamber.' She spoke as if Mrs Austen were on her way to the scaffold. 'Her leg is dangerously swollen. Dr Scudamore has been called for. I am to return to my mother. Aunt Fatty is now on her way.'

'Aunt Fatty?' The more elevated the class, the coarser the pet name.

'Our family's safe pair of hands. She attends all the Bridges ladies.' Miss Bridges rose and took both of Anne's hands. 'So I shall see you when it is all over. Mama will be on her knees until we have word of a happy delivery.' Her face was pale. Seriousness did not become her. 'Do look after dear Fanny for me.'

The days shortened yet further, and Aunt Fatty patrolled the hall chamber like a highly trained guard dog. Fanny's visits were limited and her anxiety increased. Mrs Austen's leg became more swollen and angry. Fanny now teetered on the edge of hysterics.

In a gesture that Anne found almost unbearably touching, for he too was acutely concerned, Father took Daughter shopping in Canterbury. He sat in attendance while the jeweller bored holes in her ears; helped in the selection of a new, trimmed pelisse; bought her a long tippet, made of black beaver, fit for a lady. Fanny was thrilled and diverted up until their return – when she found there was no change in her mother and, on top of that, her own ears rather sore.

For five more long days, Sackree and Anne had full charge of the children. Days spent in walks to the Serpentine, runs around Bentigh; treasure hunts at the temple or the high Gothic seat. And, when the wintry chill got too deep in their bones, hour upon hour of Hide-a-Hoop up in the attic.

At last, on the night of 13 November, little Louisa was safely delivered. Mother and baby were well. The household could breathe again. Until the next time, when the odds would have lengthened yet further.

CHAPTER XVIII

Like the Court and the capital, the countryside enjoyed its own calendar. Anne's first year at Godmersham had been marked by a sequence of significant days and each of these sacredly followed some custom enjoyed by the ancients – though only the more benign practices had been kept on. Anything unpleasant – violence, for example, or human sacrifice – was, wisely, ignored.

The agricultural cycle began with the Blessing of the Plough. Mr Whitfield seemed more sober out in that field than he ever was in front of the altar but then, as Anne knew, he suffered a strong dislike of the cold. The Feast of Candlemas was a fillip for all: it signified that soon, they would be dining by natural light. And with Lady Day, they knew that they had survived the first quarter of the year and they could open the Spruce beer.

On May Day, Anne and Fanny had walked around Godmersham, enjoying the sight of the cottage doors decorated with fresh green sprays. By the maypole, they clapped as the villagers danced to the pipers and drums. There was a return to sobriety at Rogation-tide: Mr Whitfield out blessing both fields and live-stock; the congregation following like pilgrims at the beating of the bounds. The Gospel was read and the Almighty beseeched to let the crops grow up strong. And if the Almighty had listened and the yield was a good one, then on Harvest Supper, they were mostly blind drunk.

And now – Martinmas behind them, Stir-up Sunday accomplished – they were coming to the end. The Year of Our Lord 1804 was into the gloom of its dog days. Soon, would come the celebrations of a whole new beginning. On Twelfth Night, they would all mark the end of that Advent. Field sports will start up again. And, with field sports, would come Henry Austen.

Christmas was first, though, to which Anne also looked forward. She had made little tokens for all of the children – small animals, stuffed with old stockings; cloth books for little Lizzie and Marianne, who were still in the nursery but on whom Anne had her eye as pupils some-time in the future. For the Austen schoolboys, she had spent precious pennies on whistles, which, she realised, she might live to regret.

And for Fanny, she was making a little silk purse, which

she was now stitching in the schoolroom, while Miss Harriot Bridges talked at her.

'I am delighted to hear that you are to spend Christmas downstairs with the family. Clever little Fanny for *luring* you out of the schoolroom, for once. You are too fond of your own company, Sharpy, my dear. Quite the *hermit*.'

Anne bade her to hold up the blue silks so that she could choose those best suited for the cornflower she had designed. It would not hurt Harriot to turn her hand to one useful thing, just occasionally, she thought.

'You will find it a charming affair, I believe – children and games and so on. Perfectly *wholesome*. A little different from ours at Goodnestone, but then each family makes of the day what it will, does it not? How did you used to celebrate when you were at home? Christmas, *à la Sharp*, so to speak? Tell me *everything*. I am *intrigued*.'

'We did celebrate when I was a child.' Anne spoke through the thread in her mouth while she searched for her thimble. 'I remember paper decorations and a good pudding and little dances. From then on, though' – she peered through the eye of her needle – 'it became very quiet. My father always happened to be away on business at that time of year, so it was just my mother and myself and we did not really mark it.'

'*Away?* Every *year?* Ah, he was a travelling preacher, perhaps?'

'No, not that.' Anne was reluctant to embark on an outline of that which she knew of her father's activities, for that would lead on to the vast areas of which she knew nothing. She pinned the pattern on to the purse.

'Then that is most *odd*.' Harriot sighed and stood up. 'Another piece in the Great Sharpian Puzzle. Much as I would like it, there is no time to *probe*. Daniel is taking me home in the coach shortly.'

Anne rose to bid her farewell.

'Do not *despair*, my dear. I shall be back for Twelfth Night. I *believe*' – Harriot smoothed down her skirts and affected disinterest – 'some other may be joining us then, I remember not who. Not of the *slightest* concern to me, I am sure. Kent is quite gay enough on its own, thank you – we have no need of Londoners. I simply cannot care whether he comes, or does not.' She waved her long fingers. 'Must fly! Farewell, my dear friend.'

Anne's first Godmersham Christmas was, indeed, charming and she was touched to be included in all of it. On the Eve, the Yule log was set ablaze in the hearth, they all sang at the door to the parlour and the children received lottery tickets and oranges as gifts from their papa.

The Day itself, Anne dined with the family. On this occasion, there were no divisions at table, no expectation that she should sit mute. The children, perhaps touched by their presents, enveloped her with warmth and at one point, she was quite startled – what was that mysterious noise? – to hear her own laughter! There in the drawing room! At once, she retracted back into her shell, like an endangered tortoise, awaiting a sharp blow of recrimination – the raising of eyebrows, or pursing of lips. None came. By the time they played Blind Man's Buff, she reached a point of such wild liberation as to laugh almost constantly and joined in with the singing of carols at the top of her voice.

Dear little Charles had curled up in her lap and fallen deeply asleep, so she carried him up all those stairs – his soft, fair hair nestled into her neck; hot, sweet, milky breath in her ear – and, with some reluctance, passed him to Sackree. Back in her chamber and waiting for Fanny, she was perfectly spent – her body, long starved of fun, struggling to digest those hours of unadulterated pleasure – and now in the mood for reflection. And had not Harriot Bridges said something wise the other day, with which, for once, Anne could agree? It seemed to be so. In its moments of celebration, each family did reveal its true self. The Austens, she saw, were entirely contented unto themselves. There were no unsettling cross-currents of feeling, no signs of individual rancour or preference. They were all bound together by custom, tradition and an even, simple affection: united in their felicity.

So what of her own family? What was revealed of the Sharps when they were together? Anne closed her eyes and prised open the vaults in her mind where the memories were stored. There, she selected all she retained of the last Christmas they had enjoyed as a family: turned the day over, spread it before her; proceeded to examine it, as might a constable with a mysterious corpse. It must show some clues . . .

The year was '88 – Anne was sure of that much. So she was about to turn sixteen years of age: the peak of her happiness. It was a few years before her mama's unexplained Summer of Crying; Hettie was yet to betray her with dances and suitors; her own health still robust.

Her father had stayed the night with them – she could see him at breakfast, in his silk dressing-gown – and perhaps this was remarkable? For from this year on, his absences were more common; his presence diurnal. Soon after dinner – much as he loathed it. What would he not give to stay with his ladies? – by some *force majeure*, he was taken away.

It was her papa's very nature to make any gathering festive, and all present to feel wanted. So at ease was he always in his own, handsome person that the whole company was eased. His warmth was infectious, spread by humour and compliments and touch – a tap on the arm, a palm on the back – always casual but intimate. So often, in her youth, Anne turned towards him and saw that he studied her with an unaffected admiration. When their eyes met, he would smile and wrinkle his nose and she knew herself special. How many others had had that experience? she wondered now. It was not something you would notice, unless it was happening to you.

There was a good ham for breakfast that year; beef in the evening, then bullet pudding. Her mother had played; Anne and her papa had both sung. He had a talent for harmony that showed off the soprano.

And then the presents! Anne remembered they were so very extravagant that her mother had chided him. 'A silver-backed hairbrush for Anne, and an engraved one at that! Dearest, what were you thinking?' Though when she opened her own, there were no such complaints. She pulled at the ribbons on the package to reveal a rich velvet cloak, in the deepest leaf green.

'Oh my love!' she cried then. 'It is heaven!'

'That colour shows off your eyes, my sweet.' There was much passionate embracing, but Anne was quite accustomed to that. Her parents' relationship was an unusually tactile one.

Her mama put the cloak on, fastened it at her long slender neck. The clasp alone – pearls set in gold – was itself worth a fortune. To Anne's eyes, she looked like a duchess.

'Confound it!' her father exclaimed. 'I was so precise with my measurements, and yet look! She has made it too long. That hem will trail in the mud and it will be ruined on its first outing. No! I shall not stand for it. Let me take it back and I will have it altered at once.'

Though her mother protested – surely Agnes was

capable of such a small job – her papa would not hear of it. His darling must have perfection. It would be returned at the end of the week. He would make it a priority.

Had Anne ever seen that cloak again? Search as she might through her packet of memories, she could not recall it. Though as she thought about it now, after that Christmas, her mama's sorties from the house had become less and less frequent. Suddenly, she declared herself too old for parties, too tired to dance. The beautiful girl, who had once lit up the stage of the best London theatres, was transformed into a middle-aged homebody who sat by her fireside and, from time to time, sighed.

So what was the cause of this tragic effect? To her shame, Anne had never once thought to enquire. Only now, in her small Kentish bedroom – with time, distance and death between her and her family – could she catch some glint of a truth in the murk of her past. Though it brought pain to admit it, there was but one explanation for her mother's decline. The same one that had brought her to Godmersham Park: the character of her once-trusted father.

The fickleness of man.

ACT TWO

CHAPTER XIX

My dear Fanny,

Your account of the family Christmas filled us all with vicarious joy. Our own was perforce a much quieter affair – Green Park Buildings, alas, is no Godmersham, and the town cannot compete with the country. We had not grown our own goose – he was a stranger to us up till the moment we ate him, which felt impolite, but can pronounce him delicious despite it – and our Yule log was no more than a twig. Still, we were happy and grateful that both your dear grandparents were hearty enough to attend every service. Do you know, dear Fanny, that our church here is the very same in which your G'papa and G'mama were wed, all those years ago? 'Tis a charming thought. To <u>us</u>, that is your Aunt Cass. and myself, Bath still appears foreign and strange, but to <u>them</u> it is as if they are completing a circle.

Your Grandpapa is a little frail at the moment, but then after all we are in January – and who or what can bloom in this darkness? He will mend very soon, I am sure of it. And a few more words from you, my dear niece, will brighten our days, so please do reply soon. Send our best love to all of your family, and one special kiss to little Louisa, whom we do long to meet.

Your fondest
Aunt Jane.
PS. Your Aunt Cassandra did so enjoy her especial mention in your most recent letter. I do believe it softened the blow of our correspondence. Her jealousy abated for almost an hour!

Though there was not much to it, Anne read the little letter again and again. As she wanted for all other company, it was the only human connection she could currently enjoy: the words of a stranger, issued from the nib of a pen. For it appeared that in the last week of the old year and the first of the new, all Godmersham domestic routine was suspended. Anne had expected a return to the schoolroom once Christmas was over, but the celebrations came thick and fast and interrupted her schedule.

On 27 December, Mrs Austen had announced yet another holiday.

'It is Mama's wedding day,' Fanny was aglow with

excitement. 'Of course we must celebrate. Did your own mama not do the same?'

'Not once, I am sure of it,' Anne replied. Was it not a little vulgar to make a fuss of such a thing? She had to presume not, as Mrs Austen would never be caught in the act of vulgarity.

There had been yet more dancing that evening, another day off to recover, followed by a boy's birthday. Anne was included in none of it. Immediately after that, crowds of family descended and all lessons were cancelled for at least another week. The governess's very existence was completely forgotten.

Anne could hardly ignore the fact of the party gathered downstairs. Evidence assaulted her night after night. Loud voices and dance tunes escaped from the drawing room and ran through the hall; charged up the stairs, two steps at a time; finding no person at home in any grand chamber, they thrust up still further: burst into Anne's room. And then how they tormented her! She must listen to all of it – could detect her friend Mr Whitfield's mild tones in the mix – and yet not get a glimpse of a body behind even one of those happy voices. Not even Henry.

Her own disappointment was, Anne saw now, something of an humiliation. Having passed Christmas in dread of Henry's arrival, cleaving to the solid conviction that she did not want to see him – determined to act polite but aloof when in his presence – the fact that he came nowhere near her should, surely, come as relief.

And yet she felt thoroughly thwarted! What a perverse creature she was.

She stalked the attic, disgruntled. For the first time in her life, Anne was in no mood for reading or writing. Nor could she bear to work with a needle – though the fingers were occupied, the restless mind was not soothed.

Absence of occupation is not rest,
A mind that is vacant is a mind distressed.

Dear Cowper: such wisdom in all matters. In desperation, she went to the nursery.

'Well, you are in a funny mood and no mistake.' Sackree cast a sharp eye over her.

Anne sighed, picked up a shawl that was drying on the fireguard, folded and smoothed it. 'This enforced idleness, Cakey – it does not agree with me.'

'Oh, that's it, is it?' Sackree looked unconvinced. 'Can't take being a lady of leisure? Believe that, you can believe I'm a Dutchman. I know a nose out of joint when I see one.'

'Oh, Cakey, it is not that *at all*. Allow me to help you in here today. I would truly welcome something useful to do.'

'No, thank you.' Sackree opened the door. 'I'll not have you in the nursery in this sort of mood. That face'd curdle the milk. Hop it.' She signalled to exit with a twitch of her head. 'I know what's ailing you, madam, and there

164

isn't a cure. Best thing for it is to dress up warm now and get out in that park.'

The outdoors was not tempting at the cusp of the years and Anne did not embrace the idea. Among the more obvious deterrents, she loathed all the clothing required. Her new thick, worsted cloak was the colour of dried cow dung, her boots so heavy as to cause envy in the breast of any farm labourer. While she still did not mourn her past beauty, she could not quite enjoy looking so spectacularly plain.

At the foot of the stairs, Anne bid a good afternoon to the canaries and exchanged a few further pleasantries, then noticed the afternoon post laid out on the table. With the household so crowded, the letters were many and had been neatly arranged into piles by the footman. Mr Henry, Anne could not help but notice, had received more than anyone. Glancing quickly around, to check that she was alone, Anne bent over and counted: six. Six correspondents, in just one afternoon. How wide was his world; how full must his life be! She heard the click of a door, saw Mrs Salkeld peer out at her. Anne picked up her one letter, tucked it into her cloak and went out to the garden.

She stood to fasten her bonnet and scoped the landscape. The sun had been hiding for days; there was still snow on the ground and, judging from that heavy, white sky, a real threat of more. The hills would be icy, and Anne feared getting stuck up there. Would anyone notice?

Keeping to the side of the house and out of the wind, Anne walked to the left past the dining room windows – Mrs Salkeld's cat, on the sill, shot her a quick hiss of venom – across the lawn and into the walled garden. The bitter chill lifted and she was able to slow her pace on the path through the flower beds. Out of season, of course, they had nothing to show for themselves and no effect on her temper.

She was in the far corner, near a young fruit tree, when first she heard voices. Being not in the best clothes nor the best mood for polite company, Anne moved swiftly to cover herself. Spindly, bare branches offered little protection.

'Who is that *lurking*?' Anne heard a shrill laugh. 'Is that you, Sharpy? *Sharpy*?'

Miss Bridges hung from one arm; another fine lady, whom Anne did not know, clung to the other: each leaning into the strong figure of Henry. All three together stood like a fashion plate – a demonstration that cold weather need not, after all, lead to inelegance. The solution, it seemed, lay in rich velvets, and furs.

Anne emerged from the tree and gave a small wave. Henry inclined his head and shot her a look of what she thought might be sympathy, and if so she resented it. The unknown lady –was this Henry's wife, Anne wondered? – glanced over the beds, and studied the drab governess as she might some primitive and mundane museum exhibit – a trowel from the Iron Age, or earthenware pot. Whoever she might be, Anne chose to dislike her at once.

She waved again, strode off to the kitchen garden, shut the gate firmly and marched to the seat. Why was she shaking so? Her knees knocked at each other. Of course, it must be the temperature, though it did not feel as bad as all that. She pressed her hands to her legs to ward off the tremor. One quick glance at her letter, then she would go in.

Having heard from Agnes the previous day, Anne did think it a little unusual she should write again. Nothing had happened in Montague Square for so many years. Was there news? Anne very much doubted it. Anne started to read, and saw there was not. Instead, Nurse had sought some remedy for Mr Mercer – whose condition was described with such unsparing detail as to make Anne feel quite queasy – and she had heard of a new apothecary from an unusual source. Here there came a diversion about the coal merchant, his wife and her own bowel disorder, after which Agnes continued over the page.

The new apothecary, it transpired, having found himself popular with people of fashion, was set up in a new place on the edges of Mayfair and Nurse had said: Nurse – she said – why not go there together and make it a day? And what with the weather lately being so . . .

Anne sighed. Living under the same roof as a Man of Letters meant that Agnes had at her disposal unlimited free paper. Or, rather, she could steal all she liked and Mr Mercer would never notice. Anne, on the other hand, must pay for her own, and this made for an unequal correspondence. *Why must you be so mealy-mouthed?* Agnes often demanded.

A noise caught Anne's ear: the voices of the fashionable trio drifting over the hedge! They were now on the path, just feet away, though out of vision. Anne dared not move, prayed the gate did not open. It seemed they were at the end of their stroll, and drawing it to a close. Once sure she was safe, she read on.

The nurses had arrived at the shop, and been delighted by the bell at its door. Everything was so modern in there, Anne would not believe it. And all his bottles and boxes! He must have a cure for every mortal disease. Agnes said to Nurse: Nurse – she said – pay these prices and you'll live for ever . . .

How many more pages of this were there? Anne flipped the paper and counted yet another two sheets – worth a small fortune. A firm word was called for.

. . . didn't even register! Daft as a brush, Nurse said to me later. I just saw the hat and thought: Oh, there's the Master and fancy seeing him here. Of course, I saw to that hat often enough as to know every square inch of it. I'd spot it a mile off. So, penny dropping, well then I just panicked. I grabbed Nurse. I pointed. Nurse said: Nurse – she said – well, Lord above us! Look, Nurse! It's him!

In her shock, Anne let out a cry. That cry was clearly heard out in the grounds. She clapped a hand over her mouth. The voices had stopped. Her whole body trembled. She did not dare breathe. Until she heard their steps retreat to the house and the garden door close. She finished reading the letter then, and proceeded to quietly collapse.

So her father was out there, living his old life – brazen head dressed in that familiar top hat – and he lived it around Mayfair. And, for some reason unknown, be it on a whim or through malice, he wished to live that life without his precious daughter. His beloved only child! For all of Anne's pride – rejoice though she might in her own independence – the vile force of rejection struck at her heart with the weight of a hammer. He did not have to provide for her, but to spurn her entirely? She gasped, struggled to breathe. It was too much to bear.

Anne was bent double – face pressed into harsh worsted – when she saw the polished tips of two boots just a few feet away.

'Miss Sharp?' Henry Austen asked softly. 'Miss Sharp, are you unwell? Please forgive the intrusion, but I would be only too pleased if you would allow me to assist.'

Anne raised her face, then fought to stand up and curtsey. 'Sir.' She cast around for his companions.

'Do not fret. The ladies are gone in.' With an urgent step, he moved forward and reached for her elbow. 'Please stay seated until you are recovered.' From somewhere about his person, he produced a large linen handkerchief and offered it to her. 'Do you suffer from the headache?'

Anne shook her head, mopped at her inexplicably wet cheeks. 'No, sir. Thank you, sir. It is just' – she gulped –'I have lately received some news from home . . .'

Henry sat down beside her. 'And this news is bad, I surmise?'

'Something of a shock, sir.' Anne spoke quietly.

'And must you leave here at once?'

'No, sir. That is—' She turned to him. 'No. It is only a few weeks since my last visit. And there is nothing I could do.'

'Might it help if I went to Mrs Austen on your behalf?'

'No!' Anne was firm now. 'Thank you, sir.' She would not tolerate his interference into her own, private affairs! It would be nothing short of disaster were Mrs Austen to get wind of this. The ideal governess had as few ties as possible. If Anne abandoned Godmersham now, they might well replace her. Besides that, she could not afford it. The journey would come out of her pocket, and her pocket was empty. And most important of all, she had told him she did not wish to go.

Henry did not press her further. Instead, they sat silent, together, for some time. Then he rose and offered his hand.

'Come now, Miss Sharp. You must not catch a chill.' He pulled her up, and offered his arm for support. 'Let us get you back in.' Stunned still by shock, she consented to lean on that strong and firm shoulder – felt some sensation, not entirely unpleasant – until they reached the gate, when she pulled away and put distance between them.

At the garden door, he stopped and said quietly: 'I will find some cover, some means, for you to get back to London. Please, do not worry now.' He opened the door for her.

'Mr Austen,' she urged, as she entered. 'I beg you, sir: *no*.' She wanted none of his kindness.

But the last words he uttered were: 'Leave it to me.'

⤛

Anne shed her hideous bonnet and that unflattering cloak, threw off those ridiculous boots, slipped into silk shoes, and felt the first tell-tale twitch in her eye. She staggered up to the attic, where the humdrum, ordinary sounds coming from the nursery assaulted her nerves and set them a-jangle. Now back in her room, the pale wintry light of the late afternoon was nigh on intolerable. She ran to the glass and checked her appearance: tear-stained, it seemed, and white-blue from cold but also – yes – starting to swell to the shape of the moon. These were the signs. For the next week or two, in the midnight hours when the household was sleeping, she would come under attack.

As a general preparing for battle, she went to the

window, drew the curtains, but did not light a candle. Now in the darkness, Anne took off her dress, unhooked her stays, unpinned her hair and let it fall where it would. In a warm, flannel nightgown, a shawl at her neck and rug over her knees, she curled up in her one chair. There was nothing to do now, but wait.

With her eyes closed, Anne let her thoughts rage. Agnes had discovered no further clues: the apothecary denied all knowledge of a customer named Sharp, and claimed no memory of the gentleman the nurses had seen. Anne feared they would now set off through London's streets in the manner of spies and could hardly bear it. First thing on the morrow, she would write and demand they do nothing. The next move – whether it be to seek him or choose all forgetting – must be hers alone.

The door opened and brought in the fierce glare of soft candlelight. Anne covered her face with her hands. She could hear that this was Sally with her dinner.

'All in the dark?' Sally thumped the tray down on the table. The smell of good food made Anne want to retch. 'Ill *again*, are we?' There was no sympathy. 'Want me to go off and tell *them*?'

'Please, I would rather you mentioned it to no one. No doubt, it will have passed by the morning. I will not require anything tonight, thank you.'

When the pain shook her awake, the household was slumbering. Anne found she was still in her chair, and freezing with cold. It felt as it always did: a giant fist reaching into her brain, repeatedly squeezing some muscle behind her left eye. She rocked back and forth as it climbed to its peak and her own nervous energy grew feverish. The agony crested its wave as she marched up and down, tried hard not to cry out.

And then, after one long and bitter half-hour, all pain suddenly fled. No trace remained. Then followed a state of relief that bordered on ecstasy – as if Anne had touched Death, yet Death had turned her away. She climbed into her bed and the deepest of sleeps. Tomorrow or the next day, it would come again.

CHAPTER XX

Though there was never a good time to deal with such an affliction, that January was better than most. The household was busily *en fête*, enjoying all the dinners and sports of the season; Anne's days remained clear and calm, and, though increasingly tired, she was well able to function. Governess and pupil spent their mornings together – reading or sewing – but formal lessons were still not required. And at night, Fanny mostly slept with her aunt, so Anne's pain need not disturb her.

One January afternoon – a day so bleak even those queer folk who long dwelled in the country deemed it unfit for walking – Anne was passing through the hall, on her way to say hello to the birds and check on the post table, when she heard uproar. The noise – shrieking and

remonstrating and triumphant laughter – was coming
from the library. Intrigued, she crept to the door.

'You are *wicked*!' Harriot Bridges protested. '*Never* shall
I play *anything* with you *ever* again!'

'Miss Bridges.' The voice of Henry Austen came
through to her. 'Do not take on so! It is merely a game –
and one for which I happen to have the most remarkable
skill.'

'More the luck of *the devil*, sir! I believe—' Harriot
stopped. 'Who is that out there?' she called. 'Miss Sharp,
is that you? Then come here and save me *at once*, before
this rogue makes me bankrupt.'

Anne paused, adopted a suitably meek air as if donning
a costume, entered the library and hovered close to the
threshold. The scene was inviting – flames dancing in
both fireplaces; flickering candles fighting the twilight.
On the sofa was Mrs Austen talking with a gentleman,
little William playing with soldiers on the rug by her feet.
The party of three – Henry, Harriot and that mysterious
fine lady – were gathered around the green baize of the
card table, in front of the window.

Henry was all friendliness. 'Miss Sharp, please do join
the Misses Bridges and myself.'

So this was not his wife after all, then. Anne felt at once
more relaxed.

'We are playing Speculation,' Henry went on. 'Do you
by any chance know it?'

Know it? Anne was a Grand Master. It was too much

to resist. 'I *think* I have played before, sir. I am happy to perhaps stay for one hand.'

'Brava! The table is getting a little heated in current company. We could do with some mild blood. Take a seat. Shall I be dealer?'

'Not again!' Miss Bridges took the pack from him. 'I am sure that is where you gain your advantage. It is *my* turn to deal.'

Each was allocated their chips, and the first hands were dealt. At the first turn-out, only one player showed a good card: it was Anne's knave of hearts. Henry stared glumly at his five of clubs.

'Bad start,' he murmured, his eye on the next turn, to see which was the trump suit. 'Hearts?' He was starting to get cross already, narrowed his eyes in Anne's direction. She remembered the riverbank, and how he hated to lose. 'Miss Sharp, I'd like to bid for your knave.'

This was the height of folly, in Anne's opinion – a knave was not worth it, at this stage of play. And at once, she saw through Henry's methods. He was born lucky, had known nothing but luck and so could be sure that luck never would fail him. He could bid all that he liked, wildly and often; enjoy flirting with bankruptcy and trust to his fortune.

Anne was not blessed with such magic. She knew by now – had learned it the hard way – that all she could trust was her brain. 'Oh,' she replied. 'Must you, sir? Already I am grown rather fond of it.' She looked down at her card with affection, as if to say: I am but a poor orphan in this dark and cruel world. I have so little in life, save for this knave . . .

'I bid you three!' he declared, and pushed his chip towards her.

Anne wrinkled her nose.

'Dash it – five then!' Though Henry laughed, she could tell he was piqued.

Two hands later, and she turned up the king. The same charade was repeated. Following his pattern, the ladies too were buying and selling: raucous auctions took place at every turn. He has led them astray, Anne thought to herself: I will not follow. Anne said and spent nothing – while her mind whirred with probabilities – until they approached the end of the pack. And then she struck:

'Oh dear, perhaps I, too, should spend something or I shall ruin the game . . . Miss Bridges, may I offer you four, blind, for your pack?' As Harriot was now close to broke, she accepted with delight.

'At last she awakes!' Henry Austen exclaimed. 'Though I am sorry for you, Miss Sharp. The wrong move, I fear at this stage.' They continued to turn up the cards as he carried on with his speech. 'At the end of the game, please let me give you a short course in how best to – *Dash it, again!*' That came out in a shout.

Anne had turned over her winner and, as if unaware it had any significance, adopted a nonchalant air.

'Miss Sharp, you have beaten us!' Henry explained to

Anne, as she calmly gathered the chips in. 'A classic case of beginner's luck, if ever I saw one.' He chuckled, and yet seemed unamused. 'My dear madam, I cannot tell you how many errors you committed on your way there. I fear 'twas a victory that should never have happened. Cards – such fickle creatures.' He shook his head. 'I beg you, do stay for another hand and you will see where you went wrong.'

Anne let Henry have the fourth game, simply because she feared for his health – he was quite close to apoplexy. After the sixth, she made her excuses, withdrew, blew a kiss to the caged birds and ran back to the attic. Once in her chamber, she shut the door firmly, leaned her shoulder against it to prevent anyone entry. Throwing back her head then, she let out a great laugh.

CHAPTER XXI

For the whole fortnight of her attacks, this neat arrangement held fast. The nights were torrid, the days perfectly calm. Anne became a card-table regular. Her success delighted Miss Bridges: 'Oh, *do* come and watch my dear friend! Though one *sees* just this meek little mouse, beneath is a *genius*!' It increased her stature within the party, augmented her worth by a princely twelve shillings. Henry Austen's reactions careered about madly – sometimes amusement, more often a broiling frustration – but he never appeared bored. And as the social pace slowed, Anne's clusters of headaches began to subside. There was only Fanny's birthday to mark, then Godmersham would return to normality. And, as before, Fanny was insistent that Anne be included in all celebrations.

The day was to begin at ten o'clock with a family breakfast, with brioches and a creamy hot chocolate. Fanny had dressed Anne's hair in a style they both hoped was still fashionable – curls in front of the ears, the length swept up into a chignon – though, of course, neither was expert in these affairs. The governess had strenuously protested while it was done – insisted she would not have permitted it on any other day – but was quietly delighted with the result. Checking her reflection, Anne wondered if anyone in the parlour would notice.

The two held hands as they skipped down the stairs and into the hall. Fanny was gleeful in her excitement; Anne feeling lighter and younger than she had for some weeks. A day of pleasure, conversation and games awaited them. First, they had to visit the canaries who would very much like, Fanny thought, to wish her the best for the day. Then they burst into the parlour, where all adults were already assembled. Their faces were grave.

Mr Austen, at the head of the table, was holding a letter. Mr Henry stood, pale, by his side. Mrs Austen dabbed at her face with a napkin.

'Papa?' Fanny asked, fearful of that which she was about to be told.

'My dear child.' Her father rose, came towards her and took both hands in his. 'I have just heard from your Aunt Cassandra in Bath. It is your Grandpapa Austen. Two days since.' His voice cracked. 'He did not suffer and is now at peace. As good a man who has ever lived, he is assured of his place with the Almighty.'

'*Poor* girl,' Harriot spoke into the silence. 'And on her *birthday*. Fanny, come and sit here' – she tapped the empty chair next to her – 'next to your *aunt*.'

'I must to Bath at once to comfort my mother and sisters.' Henry turned on his heels and swept out of the room.

❧

At the end of their melancholy meal, Fanny and Anne emerged into the hall, and caught Henry in the last acts of departure.

'My dear child.' He held out his arms and Fanny fell into them. He stroked her young head. 'Think of your grandfather as he makes his way to the eternal. The finest of men.' He pulled back and looked into her face. 'The very best of us. Never forget that it is from him that we have all come. 'Tis a memory to honour.'

Fanny kissed him goodbye, and he turned towards Anne.

'Sir.' She fell into a curtsey. 'Please allow me to offer the sincerest condolence. I know how very much you revered your dear father.'

'Thank you, Miss Sharp.' Entirely because his usual

countenance was one of such unalloyed optimism, the pathos of his sorrow was greatly affecting. A tear formed in his eye. Soon it would drop. Anne longed to reach up and brush it away. 'I bid you farewell.' As Mr Johncock, the butler, opened the door and Daniel appeared in the chair, he stopped and turned back to her. 'And please do not worry – I have not forgotten my promise.'

'Promise?' Fanny asked into the silence he left in his wake. 'What promise, Anny?'

The governess started to fuss at her hairstyle, which seemed, suddenly, silly. 'Oh, nothing to signify.' Her mind cast about for some plausible excuse. 'Your uncle thinks he may know a surgeon with a special interest in the headache. He hopes for an opportunity to consult with the gentleman on my behalf.'

It was all she could think of, and Fanny seemed satisfied.

❧

That afternoon, Miss Bridges' threshold for boredom was apparently broached once again, and she resorted to seeking company in the attic. Anne was writing at her desk. She had started on a play, in which the heroine is cast off by her father. She had not yet decided how the adventure might end.

'It is the most *terrible* shame.' Too unhappy to sit, instead Harriot paced up and down. 'Really, *very* unfortunate.'

'A sad loss. He appears to have been a quite remarkable man,' Anne replied.

'*Indeed,*' Harriot said with great fervour. Now at the window, she leaned on the sill, chin propped up on elbows. 'Exceptional, even. What is it about him, exactly . . . ? Wait – *was*?' She turned around and stared at Anne. 'Oh! *You* speak of Grandfather Austen . . .'

'Why, of course! Who—' Then Anne understood. Penny dropped, as Agnes would say.

At once, Miss Bridges set to work covering her tracks. 'Yes. Absolutely.' The usual eulogies flowed out in a torrent – 'Most distinguished . . . Much missed . . . Fine mind . . . Fondest of . . . ' – before turning back to the view and finally confessing: 'In fact, I was referring earlier to the enforced departure of Mr *Henry*. All told, it was the most *delightful* of visits. How we laughed! And, by rights, we should yet be enjoying ourselves still.'

Was Harriot Bridges *enamoured* of Henry? Anne studied her back, assessed the droop in her shoulders, counted each heavy sigh. It would seem that she might be and in that case – oh, the calamity! The state of Henry's marriage was immaterial. All talk of separate lives, the absence of issue and the fact that – as Anne had noticed and marked down as damning – he only rarely mentioned her name: these amounted to nothing. Though he seemed to enjoy independence to an unusual degree, the fact still remained: Henry had a wife. Harriot must somehow control her emotions. Any further indulgence could only end badly.

'Well,' Anne began, and continued in a voice heavy with meaning. 'He was in any case due *home*, very soon. His *wife* must be expecting him.'

'Hm?' Harriot turned back to Anne, and her tone changed abruptly. 'Yes, of course. I do *know* all that. There is no need to *lecture* me, Sharpy.' She sat down in the chair. 'But we *had* arranged that he would start teaching me drawing. He is a remarkable artist, you know. And that *is* disappointing.' She sighed heavily again. 'I care most *frightfully* about art – did you know? – and would *so* welcome the chance to improve my skill.'

The idea that this couple could have been sequestered together, bent over the same piece of paper . . . 'Then perhaps it is as well that he left,' Anne said tartly.

'You have disappointed me today, Miss Sharp.' Harriot rose out of her chair. 'I came up here in search of my sympathetic *friend*.' She walked to the door. 'Instead, I find you turned into *my mother*.'

Anne watched her leave, and reflected on the devilish, mercurial creature that was Henry Austen. Such a charisma as his was a weapon, against which no woman – or man, or child, for that matter – had the strength to prevail. He would do well to sheathe it, to draw and strike only at times of maximum import. But, of course, he could never rest, or resist; he was always *en garde*. Any person who strayed into his sights was a victim and each must be slain.

Even Anne. Henry had so often offended her, given such cause for resentment, that her defences against him should be secure. Yet after skirmishing with his humour and – yes – odd moments of tenderness, even she was now weakened to a state in which she could not completely dislike him.

But to love such a man? One would be a fool . . .

CHAPTER XXII

Godmersham Park went into deep mourning. The loss of a patriarch so dearly beloved is a serious moment. It is a time to reflect, to share the stored memories and consider all that is still to be missed. But when the deceased has enjoyed such a long and good life, when he has been graced with peace at its end and escaped any suffering, then the grief of his loved ones is tempered. And so it was with the family of the Reverend George Austen. Though his death brought a profound sense of sadness, there was no tragic injustice that might inspire anger; it had not been expected, but nor was it a shock. The mood of the household was simply sombre, and quiet.

One afternoon in the middle of February, Anne was in the drawing room with Mrs Austen and some of the children. All the visitors having now left and all other parties postponed for the period of mourning, Mrs Austen was forced to be content in the society of her family. In truth, this came as no hardship to this fondest of mothers. Indeed, it seemed to Anne that she blossomed. And while their needles worked and the infants played at their feet, the relationship between mistress and governess started to strengthen.

They met almost daily now, and talked about the weather, or children, the places they had seen and times they had enjoyed: the little nothings that make up a life. And each conversation was as one stone which, when put with those already hewn by the conversations before – and the possibilities of all those they would share in the future – created a bridge. A new ease of communication suddenly sprang up between them and at last they could reach out and touch, across the social divide.

'It is nearly time, I believe, for another lottery,' Mrs Austen was saying. 'I do *think*, Miss Sharp, you yourself should buy a ticket on this occasion. Godmersham is proving to be one of the luckier households, but we have won nothing lately.' She reached into the work basket. 'I feel in my bones we are due a little windfall.'

Anne demurred. The lottery was no game of skill, to which she could bring her good brain, but simply of luck. The minute chance of returns could not possibly justify the capital outlay a ticket would require. She had heard it cost over a shilling! If it turned into a habit, then that could be ruinous.

'Oh, come now, Miss Sharp. Do not be a puritan! The cost is hardly *grotesque* and the wins are delightful. This time last year, little George here won a prize of five pounds!'

Anne had already heard – it was the stuff of legend up in the attic – and she thought it an obscene sum to give to a young boy. A governess earned half that per month! It surprised her that such respectable parents would think it right to encourage their children to play. Though one could call it innocent, and so place it precisely on the tip of the thin end, nevertheless it was still on the gambling wedge.

They were all at work making clothes for the babies due in the village. Anne was carefully stitching a bonnet for a tiny newborn and thought of the difference five pounds would make to that family. To ward off despair, she changed the subject.

'Fanny, how is the shawl coming along?' She looked across and noticed her pupil in difficulties. 'Ah! Tied up in knots again, I see.'

'Oh, Miss Sharp.' Fanny dropped her work into her lap with sinking shoulders. 'I fear I shall never *quite* take to knitting. I've got into the most *frightful* muddle.'

'Of course you will, my dear.' She reached out her hands. 'Pass it to me. I'll sort it out and then we can go on together. You'll soon master it.'

'Thank you!' Fanny jumped up. 'Mama, you have never met anyone like Miss Sharp for *unpicking* a thing. She has the nimblest fingers of anyone in the wide world.' She ran for the door. 'I might just feed my birds . . .'

'To go back to the lottery,' Mrs Austen went on, 'I *do* wish you might try it—'

From somewhere out in the house came a scream fit to curdle the blood, then a loud, steady keening. The children ran through the door. Anne and Elizabeth had to carefully lay down their work before they could follow. Once in the hall, they found mass hysteria.

'That *beastly* cat!' Fanny was clutching the dead bird to her chest. Tears flowed down her cheeks. 'I hate it! *I hate it!* Oh, Mama!' she shrieked. 'Oh, *why* did you ever let it into the *house?*'

The smaller children gathered to take a good look at the corpse, and the blood on the base of Versailles. Mrs Austen had her arms around Fanny, pressing the child's head to her bosom, when Mrs Salkeld, the housekeeper, appeared at the scene of the crime.

'Ah, Mrs Salkeld,' Mrs Austen began. 'I fear that something unpleasant has occurred. Perhaps . . .' For the first time, Anne saw that even the Mistress found the woman forbidding. 'Perhaps we could step into your room, where I might have a word?'

The two disappeared, leaving Anne with all those distraught children. She secured the cage – it would be doubly unfortunate if, having tasted one triumph, the murderous cat returned for another – and sent a delegation to the attic to find a suitable box. Within minutes, she had moved Fanny on to the matter of a funeral and fitting tribute. Once Fanny's mind was engaged and imagination fired up, the sobs began to subside.

But the period of lament, which was to produce many a long and emotional outburst, went on for some time. And it was to divert young minds and give them some prospect of excitement that Anne finally agreed to play on the lottery.

❧

The gilded bird cage that had brought so much pleasure was now a sad sight to behold. Though she was still dressed in bright feathers, it was clear that the canary hen had also gone into deep mourning: a dowager queen in an empty, grand palace. Anne put her finger through the bars and allowed her to peck at it. 'Poor little bird,' she whispered. 'Please don't be sad. We are both solitary now . . . One does get used to it.'

Anne had long been vexed that the adjective 'lonely' must always be put before the noun 'widow', when widowers were granted descriptive diversity. The latter came in all sorts: handsome, or wealthy or, at the very least, simply available. She picked up a cuttlefish and offered it up. 'We will find you another, and that is a promise.' She knew that if the cat had got the hen instead of her mate, he would have found a replacement already.

She stood up with a start. Is that what had become of

her father? Was he remarried? Could it be that he *had* received all of her letters and – She could hear crying. Oh, not Fanny again! Bustling off to investigate, Anne followed the sound . . . and was led to the door of the housekeeper's room.

'Mrs Salkeld?' Anne knocked gently. The sobbing was stifled. 'Mrs Salkeld. May I come in?'

The forbidding presence of the housekeeper was now a pitiful sight: crumpled into her chair with the cat in her lap and her face in its fur. Anne went to her side and put a hand on her shoulder.

Mrs Salkeld straightened up and reached for a hand-kerchief. Her thin, stern face was blotched, her cap damp at the edges. 'Forgive me, Miss Sharp. I fear I have let my emotions get the better of me. But' – she crumpled again – 'the Mistress has asked that I get rid of my Tom and I am not sure that I can go on.'

Anne looked down at the cat. With its mottled markings of black, white and orange and its unpleasant nature – she had never before seen a cat with a sneer – he was an unlikely love object. But was that not always the way? The choices of husbands and wives – the adoration of offspring with no visible charms – were so often a mystery.

'You see,' Mrs Salkeld snuffled, 'he's all that I've got.'

Anne had been at Godmersham Park for over a year, and the two women had barely exchanged a full sentence. Suddenly, they were confidantes. Anne took a moment to find her conversational feet, and then began. 'Come now. You are hardly stuck for company. The servants' hall is surely big enough for—'

'They don't like me there,' the housekeeper wailed. 'I've only got you, haven't I, Tom?'

Anne thought again. 'Did Mrs Austen say *when* she would like him gone?'

Mrs Salkeld shook her head, and cried a bit more.

'Then' – Anne lowered her voice – 'why not pretend that you are trying to find a new home, and see if the whole thing does not blow over? Events come thick and fast here in Godmersham. They may well forget . . .'

'Do you think . . . ?'

Anne patted her bony shoulder. 'It is worth trying. I will buy a lock for the bird cage, so that it doesn't happen again. And if I may offer a word of advice? The situation could be improved if' – she chose her words carefully – 'perhaps he were to spend more time in your room? And if he might be somehow encouraged to be a little more friendly when he is out of it?'

'But Tom's a sweet nature,' Mrs Salkeld protested. 'Deep down. It's just – well, he's proud, maybe. Yes, that's what it is. He is the *housekeeper's cat*, after all, miss. There is a dignity that comes with such a position.'

This, Anne reflected, was becoming most strange. 'Oh, we are all very mindful of that,' she assured her. 'On the other hand, nobody likes to be hissed at, do they now? They might be more friendly to him, if he was more friendly himself.' There seemed to have been some slip in the conversational footing. Were they still even talking of Mrs Salkeld's cat, or had they moved on to Mrs Salkeld herself?

Together, they agreed on the plan. Anne looked down and was surprised to see that she was now holding a hand – as if touching the Scylla! And yet she was not destroyed by it. This gorgon was harmless.

Anne slipped away quietly, and left the loved ones to comfort each other. As she pulled the door to, she smiled to herself. Whatever was to become of that wretched animal, she had formed a valuable alliance with its owner.

◈

As the month wore on and no word came, Anne began to believe that Henry Austen had forgotten his promise to somehow get her to London. She was greatly relieved. Agnes had now got a firm hold on the idea that they should hunt down her father. In her letters, Anne could issue her counter-instructions and sound perfectly firm. But she knew that, were she to be there in person, her powers would be greatly diminished. For all of Anne's strong will and obstinate streak, Agnes's were more so. She could never compete.

She continued to hope that nothing would come of it, and soon came to believe nothing would. The man had just lost his father. Not only must he grieve, he must as well surely be dealing with all the business that comes in death's wake. He was tending to the interests of his mother and sisters. There would be no time left over to worry about her. So by the day on which Mrs Austen called her into the parlour, Anne had quite forgotten the whole thing.

The Mistress was resplendent in her black bombazine. Mourning became her. 'Miss Sharp,' she began. 'First, I fear I must break some bad news.'

What was this? Was Mrs Austen now aware of the headaches? Did this herald dismissal? Anne could not breathe.

'Oh dear.' Mrs Austen looked dismayed. 'Please believe, I very much regret to say—'

Anne found no words. She had just started to feel more at home here . . . was so fond of Fanny . . . was doing so well . . .

'I am sorry to have to tell you,' Mrs Austen gulped, then continued, 'that, on this occasion—'

Anne closed her eyes. Would her papa take her back now? If it was a matter of her health then, surely, he would resume his paternal role . . .

Elizabeth, now close to tears, rushed out the sentence: 'Your-lottery-ticket-was-drawn-blank.'

'Oh!' Anne exclaimed and, in her relief, could not help laughing. 'Is that all? Madam, I assure you, I did not for a moment expect I would win.'

'Thank heavens that is over!' Elizabeth put a hand to

her breast. 'I feel so very responsible for wasting your money. I simply did have this *hunch* . . . And in fact' – she smiled happily – 'that hunch was correct. Godmersham *was* due some luck on this round. My husband won a magnificent twelve pounds!'

But of course! Money, Anne was starting to learn, is a curious substance, with properties unique to itself. It chose to flow only to the places where money was already established and, once there, liked to pool to a depth so very great that a person might drown in it. Rarely, if ever, would it cut some alternative course.

Anne offered her congratulations on this good fortune, and rose to leave.

But Mrs Austen was not yet finished. 'With that behind us, now on to the business of the day.' Her tone hinted at more difficulty ahead. 'It is not my intention for this to be an *uncomfortable* interview. Please know that I am happy with your work so far, and that Fanny seems very contented. She enjoys both your lessons and your company, so we are otherwise pleased.'

'Thank you, madam,' Anne replied, with some caution. 'Otherwise?'

'It is the matter of your health that concerns me. Please, do not think that Fanny *reports* on you, as such. But she does talk to me freely, as a daughter should to her mother, and I do hear of your poor eyes, and these headaches. It is *very* concerning.'

'I assure you, madam, that the trouble comes mostly

at night and I hope does not in any way affect my ability to perform my duties—'

'Indeed.' Mrs Austen did not seem entirely convinced. 'I must ask: did this condition ever strike *before* you took up this position?'

Anne lowered her eyes. She did not want to lie, but the truth was unfortunate. And the whole situation was made yet more awkward by their new, recent friendship.

'I see.' Mrs Austen's placid face was momentarily disturbed by a flicker of great irritation. 'Of course, I should have *preferred* to hear of it sooner.'

But then you would not have hired me, Anne dared not retort.

'Well. Now that you are here and Fanny so fond of you, we must endeavour to seek a solution. As it happens, I have heard lately from my brother, Mr Henry Austen, who knows of a specialist in the area and he has presented us with a plan, which pleases us. Next week, you will travel to London with my husband and little Henry to meet with that specialist for as many sessions as are required. Once cured,' Mrs Austen pronounced with great confidence, 'then you can take up your duties again.'

Anne was astonished. That Henry's mind should produce such a devious scheme! And that her own mind had come up with the same! Was that not strange?

'One *small* matter, Miss Sharp.' Elizabeth looked stern now. 'When individual members of my household are in difficulties *of any description*, I generally *prefer* it if they can come to *me* first, rather than *burden* my *entire* family circle.'

This was an injustice – Anne had mentioned the matter to no one except Fanny – but she swallowed it down, thanked her mistress profusely and left. Her head was spinning as her feet carried her back to the schoolroom. To be suddenly blessed by such kindness! It was so touching that Henry had not forgotten her plight; so generous of the Austens to permit her to travel. To live among people who cared for both her health and her happiness was a blessing indeed.

And yet, at the same time, she could not help but feel vexed to the most tremendous degree. For by these fine intentions, she was rendered powerless. Propelled by well-meaning and great magnanimity, she must now give up her duties, leave behind her the house where she had begun to feel settled and waste weeks in London . . . *where she did not want to go.*

CHAPTER XXIII

It was the end of Holy Week when Anne arrived back in Kent. She alighted from the stagecoach in Ospringe, exhausted by the distance, sick from the motion and suffering the first, tell-tale stabbings behind her tired eyes. Daniel was there waiting with the chair and together they set off for the last leg of her journey.

'Your visit went well, miss?' He tapped at the flank of the horse and they set off.

Anne bit her lip. This was a question she would often be asked, by so many people, in the upcoming days. How best to respond? For the most part, there was naught to report, save for weeks of ennui such as might crush her own spirit. And the worst of it – the last terrible day; that one moment of horror – was a matter of such great confusion it could never be mentioned.

'Quite as expected, thank you.' She had not the energy to say anything more.

As the chair rounded the bend and the Great House appeared, the horse quickened its step, relieved to be home to his paradise. Anne simply regretted that she had ever left.

For Anne had gone to London as bidden, arrived as arranged at the home of the Mercers. But no word ever reached her of any physician. And so, for several, long days, at the Mercers' she had sat.

Through the window, Anne watched as spring stirred in the city: green coloured the tips of the branches on Montague Square; crocus pushed through the earth where once she had played; the birds cleared their throats and found their new voices. But within those good, solid walls, an emotional winter persisted. The smell of must clung to her nostrils; dust swirled around in a blizzard. She had little to do, besides listen to the nurses recount their stories of what they would call 'the old days'.

Like a pendulum she swung – from low spirits to high irritation – reluctant even to go out, for fear of catching a glimpse of a top hat that might seem familiar. And overhanging it all was the issue that Mrs Austen sincerely believed Anne was receiving some form of treatment to improve her condition. Anne bore this pattern of diurnal unhappiness until her last day, upon which she surrendered. As it would very much help to return to Godmersham with some sort of medicine, she consented to try this new apothecary the nurses had found. A small bottle of nonsense, with a long Latin name on it, would give her something to show the Mistress, and should not break her bank.

London's streets were spring clean in sharp sunshine, inviting its citizens to come out for a stroll. Fearing some chance encounter, Anne insisted on travelling by hansom straight to the door. Despite its fine address, the low and narrow shop had only a toehold on the grand sweep of South Audley Street. Its modest exterior, pressed tightly as it was between Wedgwood's and Argyle the Jeweller's, did not promise miracles. Anne paid the driver, waited for the press of people to open up to a gap, and swiftly ran through to the door.

Its bell was indeed charming, the herbal scents overwhelming. All three walls, from floor to ceiling, were lined with so many glass jars that Dr Culpeper himself might stand back in awe. Anne felt improved from simply breathing the atmosphere. The nurses each took one half of the seat of the single chair that stood by the window, and the consultation began. The apothecary enquired after her condition, studied her over his spectacles as she began to describe it. He lifted the leaf in the counter, came round to examine her eyes. And Agnes let out a shriek.

Anne spun round, saw the nurses' shocked faces and knew at once she should never have come.

Nurse Mercer was pressed to the window. *'The fiend.'*

Much as she longed to, of course Anne could not resist. Swiftly, she moved to the side of the shop, pressed herself into shelving and looked out at the one man in the world in possession of the power to hurt her. He had met some acquaintance, stopped to lift that cursed top hat and exchange queries and compliments. At once, she judged him to be both well and happy. His strong face was smooth, his tall figure exquisitely dressed in a plum velvet frock coat which Anne had not seen before. So he could live with his conscience, and business was good, then. He was not horribly crippled by allowing her thirty-five pounds a year.

In their later years together, Anne had grown accustomed to the careworn and worried air which had hung about her father; attributed it to over-work, financial burdens and concern for the health of his wife. Now that wife was gone, her daughter banished, and to look at him now was to look at a man without a care in the world.

That entire assessment was, for a mind quick as Anne's, the work of mere seconds. And now she was free to move on to the company he was keeping: most particularly, the unknown woman on his arm. Anne had only the rear view of her: the narrow, trim back in its smart sapphire pelisse; the pale yellow skirt draped over slim hips. The quick, little movements and all-over petite frame suggested the lady to be some decades her father's junior.

As the shock at the sight of him finally hit her, bile rose in Anne's throat.

'May God strike him dead,' Agnes cursed at full volume.

'Surely,' Anne muttered, 'there must be some – some – rational explanation.' She spoke from the small part of her heart that still longed to find good in her father, and the section of her brain that was conscious the apothecary was listening, riveted.

Then the young female turned and Anne saw she was not much older than Fanny. Oh, the poor creature!

And now, in her mind's eye, she saw again the way Mr Jameson had once looked at her; her ears recalled her papa's inadequate response at the time. From her memory, she dredged up the young age of her mother at the time she was born. Was this . . . ? Surely, it could not be. Was this truly her father? How degraded had he become?

Yet the girl seemed to her not at all unrefined. Her fair skin was dimpled; her hair had a sheen to it; the clothing was fine. There was something about that smile . . . It seemed strangely familiar . . .

And, suddenly, all became horribly clear.

'Oh, my poor lamb!' Agnes turned and caught Anne as she crumpled. 'The Lord in his mercy, if that girl isn't the spit of you.'

CHAPTER XXIV

The Easter of 1805 came late, in the middle of April.
Anne found, in her absence, the mad winds of March
had mellowed to more like a whisper, a rumour of summer's approach. And that Fanny, after but a few weeks
free of the schoolroom, had caught the optimism of the
season as she would a contagion. French vocabulary was
flung away; the Stream of Time now a subject of total
indifference. Her young head had been turned towards
the themes of birth and renewal, and she was hungry
for fresh projects.

Anne, still reeling from her visit to London, was stol-
idly immune to spring's joy. The sight of her father, the
evidence of his child – the terrible, horrible truth of her
mother's debasement – spun around in her brain and
knocked at her balance. It would be quite enough to

completely derange her if she knew that sort of luxury but, somehow, it must be contained. To lose her mind would be to lose her position. Duty now beckoned. Work would distract.

So Anne suggested they create a small garden, that they might study the topic of Natural History from the leaves of a plant, rather than those of a book. Fanny jumped at the idea, begged her mother to allow them to plant in one little corner of that enormous great park. Not wanting to upset the groundsmen, Mrs Austen demurred. But when Fanny faithfully promised to do all the tending herself – 'simply *everything*, Mama. Truly, I *want* to. I *know* I shall *love* it!' – agreement was reached. They chose their seeds carefully and planted with care.

The second, grand scheme involved the poor, widowed canary. The subject here was Biology, and the hen was presented with a handsome new mate. The day he arrived, they held a wedding breakfast for the couple, with extra cuttlefish, sang little love songs through the bars of the cage and heaped blessings upon them. It was a quite lovely occasion.

As ever, in the matter of projects upon which one embarks with keen children, both were to become a source of regret. The first signs of trouble came with the lovebirds in the palace. The partnership was simply not working, and Fanny was mystified. Their accommodation was splendid, each canary a beauty and yet neither seemed happy. No eggs were laid, all issue unlikely. A definite chill hung over the cage, bringing to Anne's mind the Mayfair establishment of poor Hettie.

Fanny laid the blame on the beastly cat, brought in three eggs from another hen and insisted that the birds be moved to a quiet place for nesting. This operation, involving Anne, both footmen and a hovering, guilty Mrs Salkeld, was under way when a commotion began out in the hall.

'What now, is Godmersham Park turned into a ghost ship?' The strong voice rang round the marble. 'There was a time when a weary traveller might expect some sort of welcome. Brother! Have you mislaid all the servants?'

The cage was dropped and all moved in one body, like an outgoing tide. Anne held back and waited a little, before following at a respectable distance.

'This is more in the spirit.' Henry Austen was basking at the centre of attentions. His hat and coat were removed, his luggage attended to. Fanny hung from one arm. 'I do not expect bunting or marching band – though neither would be disagreeable – but to be denied even a greeting . . . Now tell me, what were you all busy with? It must be a matter of some consequence.'

Fanny gave details of the project as they moved through together and gathered at the cage.

'Hmm.' He peered through the bars, with the air of a distinguished ornithologist. 'I see . . .' He circled it.

'Yes!' Drawing himself to full height, he gave his prognosis: ''Tis as I suspected. Fanny, they simply do not get along.'

Though Anne could see no grounds to accept the opinion of this obvious layman, Fanny cried out in dismay. 'But this is a tragedy!' she wailed. 'We held a marriage and *everything*.'

Henry placed an avuncular arm around her. 'I am sorry, my dear. It is a cruel lesson we all have to learn, but better to learn sooner than later. Such an arrangement, made for them by others, amounts to no more than a house contract.' He was as confident on this as on all other subjects. 'Companionship and affection – love, even more so – take no direction. They simply land where they will, and must be obeyed.'

Anne listened, wide-eyed. Though, of course, she did not disagree with its substance, she was not convinced that Mrs Austen would approve such frank and uncompromising speech to her daughter.

'Then what are we to do?' Fanny begged to be told.

'Get rid of him!' Henry announced. 'Find her another! Why should a creature, as pretty as she, live without happiness?' He turned to the room, ignoring the fact that all faces gaped in astonishment, and begged for some tea in the library. Before leaving, he addressed Anne. 'Miss Sharp, how went your trip to London? Satisfactory, I hope.'

'Thank you, sir. It was – er – very informative.'

He smiled broadly, pleased to believe he had pleased her. 'And the physician treated you well? I hear he is the most excellent fellow.'

Anne glanced over at Fanny, saw her to be deeply involved with her birds, and shot Henry a quizzical look. He did not seem to register, and instead returned a smile all honesty and openness. So she opted for a simple and safe, 'As well as we could have hoped, sir.'

'Capital!' he cried. 'Now let us pray your cure is complete, and there will be no further trouble.'

Anne felt quite at sea. It was as if she were dealing with a madman. Did he not remember the whole thing was a ruse of his own design? Or was he so used to deceiving that he came to believe – even to live – in his own fantasy? If she had even a jot of self-interest in the moral status of Henry Austen, then either would be cause for concern. Fortunately, her only care was the enormous extent of the problems he had caused her. His 'good intentions' had tied her in such knots that even she, with her nimble fingers, could not begin to unravel them.

❧

The Tuesday after Easter, Anne went to church with her mistress. It was not a compulsory service and only lightly attended. But Elizabeth was a pious woman who happened to find herself in a particularly pious mood. Anne, too, felt the need for some spiritual solace as well as distraction, and also leaped at the chance to see her good friend, Mr Whitfield.

'We have all been quite cast down by your absence, Miss Sharp.' She and the vicar were walking together back to the vicarage, Elizabeth having taken the chair. 'It made us realise how much we do enjoy your visits. My wife values the company.' He opened the gate to the churchyard, and bade her go through. 'And I, the cakes. Cook makes more of an effort when she knows you are coming. It is a dark thought, and I should not even confess it, but, when baking for me' – he dropped his voice to a whisper – 'I suspect that she stints on the sugar.'

'Oh, Mr Whitfield!' Anne smiled. The morning sun hit the lane, a breeze danced through the daffodils and, as ever, the company of the vicar was a balm to her newly raging and turbulent soul. His was a splendid philosophy. He saw God in the small pleasures – the fine orange wine, the sponge cake at the fireside. He saw indulgence in them as a means by which he might worship the Almighty, and he did so devotedly. 'How you have suffered! Tell her my appearance was particularly wan, and I will visit tomorrow.'

Instead of complimenting Anne on her looks then, he said only: 'Our loss was London's gain . . .' and looked at her sideways. This seemed to both imply that she was, indeed, not looking her rosiest and offer an invitation to confide in him. How Anne longed to share her misery with someone, to unburden herself of its terrible weight. But it could not be done. If it was as she feared – and how could it not be? Had she not seen the evidence with her own eyes? – then the very fact of her birth was a matter of great shame. No one could know of it. She must bear it alone.

'And how do you find things on your return?' Mr Whitfield enquired. 'You must feel quite settled at the house now, I hope. It has been more than a year.'

Anne thought for a while. 'I suppose that I must. It is, of course, most pleasant to be back with my dear pupil, and here in this county for the best season of all. Perhaps there has been some sort of shift within me. Certainly, London no longer feels quite like home.' In fact, she would not mind if she never saw the capital again.

'And the rest of the household? It would be a comfort to hear that you have, at last, found friendship below stairs, and there has been no return of your earlier trouble.'

The mermaid which Fanny had given her had, inevitably, vanished during her absence, but that was too petty to mention. The disappearance of her thimble was more problematic, for it had taken a long while to wear down the metal to the perfect fit of her finger. But as she had so many more mental oppressions, Anne simply said nothing.

Mr Whitfield gave a deep and sorrowful sigh. 'To

steal at all . . . and to steal from one who herself has not much . . .' He shook his white head. 'I am shocked – shocked – that we should have such an errant living among us.' The thought did not seem to occur that he himself might act to bring the sinner back into the fold – he was the sort of shepherd who preferred to stick to the warmth of his hut. Still, the idea of the lost soul had left him a little cast down – so much so that he was forced to stop walking, and take comfort in the scent of the hawthorn. 'I am sorry, Miss Sharp, that you have had this experience. It has surprised me.'

With his back to her now, his head in the hedgerow, Anne felt moved to confide: 'I do not quite understand it myself. I do not see I am so much of a burden upon them. And I have tried so hard to be generous. The work I am doing down at the school is with their children and younger siblings, and going very well indeed.'

'But Miss Sharp' – he turned, held out his hands as if preaching – 'generosity comes with no guarantee of affection returned. Nor even gratitude.'

'Mr Whitfield!' Anne laughed. 'I did not have you down as a cynic.'

'Ha!' This new philosophical tone brought a return to his energy. He thrust out his cane and they continued their stroll. 'That is no cynical view, but rather empirical. Observation has taught me: to give generously to others more often provokes them to query that you failed to give more.'

'Yet I was under the impression that "God loveth a cheerful giver"?'

They had arrived at the door in the wall of the park.

'He does indeed, my dear.' He patted her arm. 'And that is why we givers continue to giveth. For our own spiritual improvement. Even though it might lead to a depreciation of popularity with our own fellow mortals.' He rubbed at the moss between stones and peered into a crevice. 'Our Lord himself was not rewarded on this earth . . .'

Anne bid him farewell, slipped into the park, into the lime avenue and found her favourite tree – the one with a kink in it, which was growing away from the clear line of its friends. Leaning against the bark, she took a deep draught of the blossom. While very much looking forward to St Peter's warm welcome, she would still like her things back. But how best to effect it? Clearly she could not expect this particular parson to waste precious energy on her behalf. Indeed, there was now no one whom she could trust to defend her personal interests, in matters trifling or large. Anne reached up, plucked a garish new leaf, ran her thumbnail along its thin, tender spine and awaited the familiar wash of self-pity. And instead was surprised by the sudden rush of something quite other.

After all, had she not always chafed against male control? Had she not craved independence since quitting her childhood? Well, now she had it and must make the best of it. Liberation! How absurd to have hoped that her father – that degenerate – might come to her rescue; ridiculous to let Henry Austen order her movements; pathetic to form some dependence on a man of the Church! This was her life now, and she alone would control it. From this day forward, she would anoint her mind with full power over her weak, foolish heart.

And, throwing the torn remnants of leaf over her shoulder, Anne marched back to the house.

CHAPTER XXV

My dear Fanny,

What a wretch of an Aunt I have been to you lately. And to think that I, of all Aunts, was your chosen correspondent! What <u>can</u> you have thought when I failed to write back? As I too was once a fanciful young Miss, I believe I can guess. You imagined me kidnapped or courted by Royalty or apprehended for larceny and thrown in a cell. Am I close? Then I must disappoint you again. My reasons are all of the tedious sort, I fear, and you will feel no sympathy when you hear of them. For example, we had to move into Gay Street with great work and upheaval, but that is of no interest to <u>you</u>. And your Aunt Cassandra has been away nursing the sick, leaving me with the charge of your dear Grandmama. And since you have not yet had to deal with joints of mutton or doses of rhubarb – and *long may you preserve your own innocence – you cannot know what it entails. You see, I am well aware that the <u>young</u> – like yourself – have little patience with <u>old</u>, and now nine-and-twenty, I find myself comfortably on the wrong side. For all that, my dear Fanny, I will not despair of you and your irredeemably sweet nature. Though my silence has been quite unforgiveable, I confidently expect you to forgive it at once.*

And in a few short weeks, my faith will be tested for we hope to arrive with you some time in June! We shall come via Hampshire, bringing you a playmate in the shape of your cousin Anna and then what fun we shall have! In the meantime, please have a word with the local weather on behalf of your Grandmama. She requires it neither too hot nor too cold.

Your loving,
Aunt Jane.

～❧

Once again, it was Elizabeth's birthday – the weather had blessed it and the family was out for the day – but this year, Anne would be afforded no leisure. For in a development that might not astonish all as much as she was astonished herself, it transpired that Fanny – though most keen on sowing and watching, loving and admiring – was found to suffer from a weak appetite for hard labour. Anne did not object. She was determined to keep as active as possible, so as to prevent any thinking. And that afternoon, in a thin blue linen dress, her head graced with a straw bonnet to keep off the sun, she was hard at work in the garden alone.

'Good day, Miss Sharp!' Once again, Henry was not with the family party though he was dressed for fine company: his frock coat was pale and impractical; the britches, Anne could not help but notice, exceedingly tight. 'And what now do I find? Is your ambition such that you have taken up yet more forms of employment?'

Anne could feel her own heartbeat; she put her mind firmly on guard. 'Sir.' She effected some sort of curtsey and then planted her hoe in the earth. 'My only ambition is to ensure that Fanny's sweet peas survive the onslaught of these horrible weeds. She does love them so.'

'And must it fall to me to point out, madam, that your role here is that of *governess* to my niece, rather than *slave*?' He thrust his cane in the soil, planted his boots in a wide stance of emphasis. The britches strained further. 'I am about to take a turn round the park. I beg you, do join me or—'

'Or you will be mournful as a catfish, sir?'

Though she knew him as a man to laugh often and readily, nevertheless Anne could not deny that she felt great gratification in provoking this loud laughter herself.

'Far beyond! For then, compared to my countenance, a catfish should appear as the sun's golden rays!'

Anne laughed too, then. Indeed, was this the first occasion on which they had both laughed in unison? 'Though the prospect is tempting . . .' She looked down again at the weeds.

'As my wife likes to say: There is only one cure for temptation, and that is to give in to it!'

His wife? Finally, she was mentioned! Now, Anne's curiosity was piqued. And so, led entirely by her own intellect and not – she was quite sure of it – by her wayward emotions, she chose to accept. Where was the harm? Peeling off her thick gloves and placing them on the hoe's handle, she said: 'That is the most estimable philosophy, sir.' And together they set off across the lawn. 'I hope it rewards her with a life of pure pleasure.'

'Not all the time, sadly.' He opened the small gate leading out into parkland. 'Though she continues to do as she pleases as often as allowed, she has had more than her fair share of afflictions.'

Anne replied quietly: 'Ah. I am sorry for that.' She longed to hear more, and cast a rod out to tempt him. 'Misfortune will never be dissuaded by something as simple as sweetness of temper.'

He laughed again. 'I believe she would be the first to own that *sweetness* is not one of her qualities. Rather . . .' He searched for the word. '. . . vivacity? Gaiety, certainly – those are the attributes more routinely assigned.' The land was starting to rise, and he struck at the spring of the turf with his cane. 'Or they *were*, perhaps . . .'

How old was this wife of his? Anne's curiosity

deepened. She went fishing again. 'Of course, if one does not know good health—'

'Her health cannot be relied upon. She has in the past struggled – and that is one burden.' Henry kept his face firmly forward, his eye on the brow of the hill. 'But sorrow is a heavier one. She was married before, you know, to a French nobleman who fell victim to the Terror. Then their only child, a son, who suffered a handicap, died soon after his father. He was but fifteen years of age, so you see . . .'

'Yes, indeed!' Anne gasped. 'A sequence of events that can only devastate!' This was even more detail and drama than she had quite bargained for.

As if out of nowhere, there appeared before them the figures of Sally and Becky, no doubt on their return from the gad. The maids' arms were linked, their heads pressed together in laughter; their spirits were high. On noticing the unexpected combination of Henry and Anne, they stopped and gawped, before falling into a curtsey. And when the two parties had crossed and gone off in their respective directions, the maids' giggles and whispers began.

For once, Anne was unbothered. Her only concern was to not lose the thread of the conversation: 'But if she suffers with her health too, then surely Godmersham is the ideal place for her?' Anne was in no position to make such an enquiry, yet she felt almost entitled. After all, Henry Austen had been so intrusive towards her, he could hardly object were she to intrude, for once, upon *his* private concerns.

Her assumption was correct. In the shadows of the copse, he began to truly confide. 'My choice of wife did not meet with universal approbation within the family. And here in Godmersham, she is considered a little—' He stopped – whether he was searching for his next words or regretting the previous, Anne was not sure.

They emerged from the trees into sunlight, and Anne spoke up again. She was developing a taste for it. 'Yours is a large family, sir and, if you do not object to the observation, an impressive one – a large collection of confident individuals. That can intimidate those who come from outside.'

'Oh, that was not the issue.' Henry stood still and turned his face upwards, studying the skylarks as they dipped and then soared. 'As we are first cousins, she was already one of us and they already most fond of her. Although . . .' He let out a sigh. 'But she does have *one* true friend and supporter.' He looked down and smiled at Anne. 'Your personal favourite, of course: dearest Aunt Jane.'

'Then that is enough for me.' Anne laughed. 'I can only presume she is a person of excellence!'

The Gothic seat was in sight now. Henry led them towards it while continuing his confession. 'I suppose it is an unconventional marriage, and that has somewhat surprised them. But as I have never before demonstrated a great fondness of convention . . .' He sensed Anne stiffen, and glanced at her sideways. 'Miss Sharp, you are offended?'

'Oh, sir, not at all!' Anne lied. 'I have always seen unconventionality as a badge of strong individualism.' Though since discovering the truth of her father, she now feared it was but a cloak for licentiousness. After all, her parents hardly enjoyed a conventional arrangement – and look at the damage that wrought. Could Henry be trusted at all? She must – *must* – remain wary when in his company.

And yet, nevertheless, she took the stone seat beside him. Despite all her strength and resolve, she proceeded to join him in admiring the vista. Though on her guard, she unguardedly partook in the sharing of their favourite aspects. She learned that, for Henry, these were the house itself – its size, space and grandeur – and the river which carried the world in and took it off to the sea. He learned that Anne preferred its more private spaces: the woods and walled gardens; the one lime in the avenue which she confessed that she talked to; the temple in which, on this day a year ago, she had let her heart sing.

In all her thirty-two years, Anne had never once known occasion to talk thus to a gentleman. Other than her father, she had never met one to give her good cause. As her tongue ran on unchecked – as they exposed private thoughts and together explored them; when each, in turn, gasped with delight at the sharp wit of the other – the thought rose up unbidden: it was no wonder that she had never before seen the advantage of marrying. For she had never before known the pleasures of a communion such as this.

'Ah.' Henry breathed in a draught of pure, Kentish air. ''Tis the season of optimism; do you not agree?'

Anne could not help but laugh. 'Forgive my impertinence, sir, but you strike me as one who finds optimism all the year round. Be the vistas so verdant or dulled, bare and brown, you seem unchanged.'

'And what of it?' he cried. 'What better approach to this short life of ours but to hope for the best from it? Smile upon fortune, and she will smile upon you.'

'In an already optimal life, then perhaps,' granted Anne. 'Though in the midst of all ruin, surely even you might find that less easy to maintain.'

Yet it seemed Henry's optimism was somehow contagious. Possibly it was no more than that previously elusive, simple spring joy. Anne had a kind sun on her back, all around her was beauty, she felt the stirrings of a sympathy quite close to friendship, so it could be nothing beyond simple happiness in the moment. But somehow, she could not shake a new sense of promise: a tingling sensation of the universe rearranging itself, so that her little life might somehow change.

And were that to happen – if fortune were one day to catch even Anne, from the corner of one munificent eye – then she would offer up no resistance but, as a dandelion seed must with a strong summer wind, she would surrender at once; give herself up to it; allow it to carry her off. And wait then, contentedly, to see where she might land.

⁓

When the family returned soon after dinner, Anne was back at work with the hoe, as if she had been out there all day. She saw them on the lawn, straightened then and gave a small wave. And heard one voice above all the others:

'Oh, *do* look at dear Sharpy! *So* sweet and simple. Now, is she not the very *essence* of the picturesque?'

CHAPTER XXVI

The following morning, Fanny began to show the symptoms of a slight summer cold and her mother decreed that she spend a quiet day indoors with her governess. This was met with some disappointment, as a fishing trip was planned and Fanny had been promised a rod. It was not easy to settle an almost perfectly well child when, through every window, a bright blue sky beckoned. The hours dragged on. Fanny's condition remained mild. And so, after dinner, Anne agreed to walk out with her, that she might catch up with the party.

Down on the riverbank, next to the bathing house, they found two couples engrossed in their sport, and the company of each other. Edward and Elizabeth were in their own aura of stolid contentment. Fishing with but half of their hearts; enjoying that gentle, conversational to-and-fro on the subject of shared interests that is the by-product of all happy marriages. Harriot and Henry, meanwhile, were in the midst of their own – highly refined – riot. At least, that is how it appeared to Anne. She selected a spot – a deferential distance between herself and the family, but, she made sure of it, well within earshot – and sat down on the grass.

'Dash it! My lady, are you determined to destroy all my concentration?'

'*Me*, Mr Austen?' Harriot widened her eyes, placing a delicate hand upon her innocent, exposed bosom. 'But *I* only have eyes for my *prey*! And by what possible means could *I* create a distraction?'

'You are simply being far too amusing, Miss Bridges!' the victim protested. 'How is a fellow to catch when he keeps laughing out loud? And as for your dress, madam—'

Miss Bridges gasped out in horror. 'Sir, you have *crushed* me! You do not like *my dress*?' Preferring beauty over good common sense, she had chosen to come out in a fine and pale muslin, trimmed with blue ribbons of silk. 'Oh do look!' Harriot called out in triumph. 'I seem to have pulled in a catch!'

Henry flung down his rod and attempted to seize hers. Harriot started, let out a sweet little scream and dropped it. And then, lifting her skirts – quite inadvertently displaying her fine ankles – she set off at a run up the hillside, with him following in energetic pursuit. Fanny clapped her hands with glee at the childish antics of adults. Edward and Elizabeth shook their heads and smiled as they watched on. Anne thoroughly disapproved.

Were her master and mistress to make no attempt to control their two wayward siblings? As they chased round her in circles, Anne stared into her lap and privately condemned all who were present. What did it matter that Henry's poor wife was old, and sick, and burdened with melancholy? The woman still lived, and this flirtation was wrong. It was quite clear that Henry and Harriot brought out the worst in each other. Anyone with their interests at heart would seek to keep them well separate, not thrust them together. No doubt many would say the governess had no right even to hold a view on the matter, yet how could she not? She was hardly a disinterested party.

Over the past year and a half, Anne had got to know Henry and Harriot better than she knew anyone at Godmersham, other than Fanny. Though each had his or her own faults, and discernible frailties, they had both shown her kindness and sought out her friendship – put themselves between Anne and the great, crushing force of loneliness. Thus indebted, she found that she cared for their happiness; so informed, she believed that – if or *when* he became free – they could never, in the end, be happy together.

Though Harriot might certainly pass as a flighty young miss – she was, at that moment, hiding behind the bathing house and stifling her giggles – within was the matron she had been bred to become. Anne had no doubt that, very soon, some landed gentleman would appear, plant her on his estate, cure her of silliness and ground her for good.

And then, Henry: oh, Henry! So long in virtues – sympathy, empathy, a mercurial brain and, yes, over-burdened with charm – and yet so short of self-mastery. Anne knew exactly the stature of woman he should have by his side. One who could match him in intelligence and learning, and so never bore him. One who had perhaps known some sort of misfortune which had brought her to wisdom. Who could weed out his weaknesses and so let his strengths flourish; stand ready to guide and per-suade him, should he be hit by the moment at which his luck finally ran out. With such a partner as that, well – then, he could astonish the world.

He sped past her now, his bellow bouncing off the hill of the parkland. And, in silence, Anne studied the exhibition he made of himself – no more refined than the maids gad-ding about at the tithe barn – and quite genuinely feared for his future. For, when his poor, old, infirm wife's time came, and if there was such a perfect, potential spouse out there, did he have the wisdom to notice?

'Miss Sharp?' Mrs Austen interrupted her musings. 'Perhaps you might take Fanny in now? She would, I think, benefit from an earlier night.'

꩜

'How do you feel now, my dear?' It was nowhere near dark, but they were in their nightclothes, the maid had now left and their prayers had been said. 'You seem much better.'

'I am well, Anny.' Fanny climbed into bed. 'Though I must confess, I do rather wish I was still with the party. It was such fun, was it not?'

'Indeed.' Anne tucked her in. 'But you do know that you are yet a child, and cannot be with the adults all of the time.'

Fanny sighed. 'Yes. But it is different when Uncle Henry is here.'

Anne got into her own bed, fiddled with the novel at her bedside and embarked on her sleuthing. All the questions she would never dare ask of the adults, she could ask of Fanny, and know that she would get the parroted version of the adult response. 'It is a pity that Mrs Henry Austen does not come with him, is it not? Perhaps her health does not permit it.'

'Her health.' Fanny paused to assemble a medley of opinions overheard and received. 'We do not believe her *health* to be much an issue, although we do often wonder if she is prone to *imagine*.'

'Oh.' Anne pondered that. 'Then her age, perhaps, makes her unfit for travel?'

'Her *age*?' Fanny laughed. 'Though *we* think her too old for my uncle, she is not in fact so very properly *old*. We think her to be a decade his senior, so now somewhere around four-and-forty.' She gave a moue of disgust. 'We do often wonder what led him *in*. Well, there was her *money*, of course, but it is hardly a *fortune*. And we feel, had he waited, he could have found a lady of his own age of equal worth. Of course, we cannot deny that she *was* terribly pretty, and is most handsome still. And the point *is*' – she sighed – 'each is simply most *fond* of the other. The strange arrangement seems to suit both of them. Love is a mystery, as we often say.'

Then that scene on the riverbank, and Henry's behaviour in general, was nothing more than innocent fun in the context of family. And this starched, fun-starved governess had simply misread it. Anne lay back on the pillow, and tried to digest the hard facts of Henry's conjugal happiness. Why should the idea of it create such discomfort? He had an arrangement to suit him, and that is all one could wish for. She resolved to feel pleased for him, while at the same time reminding herself this was all none of her business. Yet still, the discomfort persisted, developing into something more like a pain.

Oh – but of course! She sat bolt upright. These must be feelings of pity for Harriot! The girl was clearly in love; in too deep to pretend otherwise; too silly to see that it was all hopeless. Poor, dear Miss Bridges! Cruel Henry, for leading her on so. Anne lay back down again, sunk into sorrow on another's behalf.

'Anny! Are you quite well? You have gone a rather strange colour. Are you due one of your heads tonight?'

'Yes. Perhaps I am,' Anne replied quietly. 'I will do my

best not to disturb you.' Leaning across to the table, she snuffed out the candle. 'And Fanny, dear: there is no need to bother anyone else in the household with the details of my illness. If it does not cause you any difficulties, it is perhaps best not to inform your mama. I should not like her to worry. Let it be our little secret.'

Fanny adored keeping the secrets of the adult population. 'Oh yes! I *promise!*' She wriggled with pleasure. Then: 'Anny,' she whispered into the half-light, 'I too have a secret. May I share it with you? Something happened today while you were busy.'

Anne turned towards her.

'We candled the canary eggs and there was not a chick in them. I know that I should have simply thrown them away . . . But I am afraid that I let emotion get the better of me and, well, I violently smashed them! I am sorry. I know it was wrong of me. But I was *so* very hopeful.'

Anne replied, with some passion, that she quite understood. Disappointment was vicious. Even this governess well knew that feeling of wanting to smash something, sometimes.

She promised she would not tell a soul.

At three o'clock on the following afternoon, she and Fanny were due to take up their duties at the school in the village. Keen to set off at the quarter to the hour and seeing that she was neither in schoolroom nor nursery, Anne was forced downstairs in the search for her pupil. Finding no family at home in the parlour, she knocked and went into the library.

'Sharpy!' Miss Bridges turned around from her easel, a brush in one hand and her young face aglow. 'You have caught us right in the *act* of that which you so *disapprove*!'

'Disapprove, Miss Sharp?' Henry turned too, with a smile. 'Ever the governess! And to what do you object on this particular occasion? *Art* itself, perhaps. You despise it for not being *serious*.'

'Of course I do not,' Anne returned. '*Sir*.' She made to leave.

'You see our efforts as a waste of good paper, then?' He was beginning to enjoy himself, buoyed up further, no doubt, by Harriot's delighted response.

'Not at all,' Anne replied through gritted teeth. Though, from the distance of the doorway, she could judge the landscape-through-window, over which they both hovered, to be almost splendidly average. And that its composition seemed to demand an almost intimate proximity between artist and teacher.

'Then you have a loathing of the watercolour form.' He had already gone too far, but could find no restraint – quite lost in the cause of his own amusement. 'You prefer the oils of the Masters and subjects more sacred. The suffering of poor St Sebastian . . .'

The mirth of Miss Bridges inflated to a point close to

helplessness. Anne was now thoroughly bored by their antics. 'Sir, I am in no position to admit to my opinions, let alone offer them. Excuse me.' She turned her back on them. 'I have work to do.' She left the room.

She made it as far as the foot of the stairs, but such was her distress that she trembled all over. Clutching at the finial, she waited for it to subside. Did the man know no self-control? All was just sport to him, and the injury of feelings a mere part of the game. She could not help but feel pity for poor, silly Harriot – taking such risks with her own reputation; with her own heart, perhaps.

Nor could she not pity herself. To think that she had so recently felt that stirring of optimism! To think she had expected her fortunes to change! When, in truth, she was stuck like a beetle in amber. Locked into this ritual of offers of friendship, followed by some casual, swift rejection; offences repeatedly given, mute acceptance returned. The plaything of those who thought them-selves better.

The library door opened.

'Miss Sharp?'

She turned slowly towards him and paused, in wait of the apology she felt she was owed. None was forthcoming.

'I simply wanted to mention that I must leave this place in the next day or two.'

He then paused, too, so that she might express her regret at his departure. He was to be disappointed.

'But it may interest you to learn that my mother and

sisters are the next on the list of the Godmersham visitors. I thought the information might please you?'

As she would rather not speak to him, Anne gave a small nod of acknowledgement.

'It pleases *me* that you will at last have the opportunity to make the acquaintance of my sister, Miss Jane. For that will lead you to a true opinion of who indeed is your preferred Austen.'

Henry laughed; Anne stared back in wonder. This Jane would have to be the devil herself for him to win now.

'You can sit in judgement, like Paris at the wedding of Peleus and Thetis.' He chuckled. Anne could see that, yet again, he was in danger of straying into the long grass of comedy. 'When I return, I shall pluck an apple from the orchard; engrave upon it the one word: *kallistei*!' This pleased him greatly. 'As you know, 'tis the Greek word for—' He extended a pedagogic hand.

'The fairest one,' Anne cut in. 'Yes, sir. Thank you, sir, but there is no need to school me in the most *basic* Classics. I am well versed in Homer. I wish you a pleasant journey.' She turned to the stairs.

'Miss Sharp?' Henry took a few paces closer. 'Dash it! I fear that, yet again, I have offended you. I mean no harm, I assure you. 'Tis simply that I am too swift to seek the humour—'

Anne turned back to face him. 'Sir.' If her body would only stop shaking, she might then show more dignity.

'Forgive me for feeling the need to remind you that I am here in the family's employ. You look upon a mere governess. 'Tis not one of my duties to be the butt of your humour.'

He stopped her; came closer; crinkled his eyes. 'Then you must forgive *me*, madam, that I have previously mistaken you for something more like a friend.'

ACT THREE

CHAPTER XXVII

'Aunt Jane!'

Anne was conducting her last full lesson before the visitors descended and the disruptions of summer fell upon them; had hoped to spend a good hour with Fanny on a thorough revision of French vocabulary. But it was not even past noon when there had come a tap, the door had opened and a little, capped head peered shyly around it.

Fanny jumped up. The arrival covered the floor with quick, quirky movements, took the child in her arms, kissed her hair, and then pulled back at arm's length.

'Young lady, I fear you have the advantage of me. Indeed, I know I am Aunt Jane, for I never alter. But who, miss, are *you*? Please, introduce yourself.'

'I am Fanny!' she exclaimed. 'Your niece!'

'I refuse to accept it.' Jane held up a hand and turned her face away. 'My *niece* is but a child of so high. She has not yet your airs and your graces.'

'Aunt Jane, I am now *fourteen years of age!*'

'Well now.' Jane's highly pitched voice had laughter built into it. 'If you are indeed Miss Frances Austen of Godmersham Park – and I still struggle to believe it – then I must reprimand you. Though I cannot object to *some* developments during my absence, to change oneself utterly, beyond all recognition, is hardly polite to one's aunt.'

Having heard the noise from the usually quiet school-room, the smaller children escaped from the nursery and came to join in. Sackree and Jane embraced, as if the firmest of friends. Then the pattern continued.

'And *you* must be little Henry?'

'But I am *William!*'

'Then this is *certainly* Lizzie.'

''Tis Marianne!'

And on it went. Anne stood back, watching the sweet scene play out and assessed the newcomer. So this was Miss Jane Austen, the author of those letters – the stranger who could bewitch with the nib of her pen. Anne felt a spasm of dull disappointment. From all Henry had said, she had somehow expected someone quite different: his female equivalent, perhaps, in beauty and bearing. There were definite similarities: both had the same hazel eyes, though his were much brighter; they shared a facial resemblance, but her cheeks were a little too full. She, too, clearly had charm – the children certainly thought so – yet no trace of her brother's confident dazzle.

Were they side by side, anyone would note some familial connection, but not necessarily siblinghood. Henry could pass anywhere as a member of the upper classes. If anything, Jane would be presumed to be some poor relation – a first cousin, perhaps, from a less fortunate branch.

Sackree gathered up the smaller children, herded them back to the nursery and the schoolroom was quiet again. Jane's eyes met Anne's own.

'As you may by now have gathered, I am Aunt Jane. And you are Miss Sharp, I presume?' Miss Jane crossed to the work table and stood before Anne. 'From Fanny's *excellent* letters' – here she turned to her niece –'we *have* so enjoyed them, my dear – I feel we know you already! And my brother, Mr *Henry* that is, also speaks warmly and has instructed me to seek out your friendship.' She gave a nervous little hiccough of a giggle, cupped her hand to her mouth, whispered, 'Though I am not always so obedient as he should like,' and then raised her voice again, 'on this matter, I believe I can trust him. It is my pleasure to meet you.'

Anne could not help but be rather charmed, yet remained wary. She dropped into a curtsey. If she still could not quite trust Henry, then why trust his sister?

Nevertheless, she expressed all the correct sentiments and the two could share a smile.

'Aunt Jane,' Fanny cut in, 'where is my grandmama?'

'Still in the hall, my dear.' Jane patted the child's hair. 'Giving your poor papa chapter and verse on every step of our journey. As we all know, she has the fondest *attachment* to detail. I fancy he is pinned to the wall still, learning the biographies of every ostler we met on the way.' She turned back to Anne. 'Travel may be tedious, but talk about travel is quite simply intolerable. Do you not agree, Miss Sharp, or are we already in some dispute?'

'It is my view entirely,' Anne assured her at once.

'I am happy to hear it. Then let us go down and release them all.' She took Fanny's hand. 'Miss Sharp, I know the rest of the party is most keen to meet you. Please do come with us.'

❧

Please do come with us. It was not often, in Godmersham, that those magical words were thrown in the general direction of this particular governess. On this day though, Anne was bombarded.

"Will you not join us, my dear?' asked Grandmother Austen as she was finally seduced from the hall to the parlour.

'Sit between us,' Jane invited as she patted the space on the sofa between her and her sister.

'I hope you will come, too?' That sister, Cassandra, taller than Jane and definitely the more handsome, invited as they set off for a turn of the grounds.

For once, even Fanny had a friend her own age, for the Austen ladies had brought with them her cousin Anna. The two girls disappeared, leaving Anne bereft of all duties. In different company, she would feel obliged to make herself equally scarce. But the opportunity simply never arose. She was too busy being befriended herself.

This remarkable inclusivity continued even to dinner, where Anne – somehow caught in the slipstream of this infusion of visitors – found herself seated at the table with the family party.

'My dear Edward.' Grandmother Austen took another helping of veal. 'I cannot express my pleasure in being here again.' She reached for the potatoes. 'It seems a *very* long time has elapsed since our last visit. *Our* fault, I am sure of it.' She paused for some chewing and swallowing. 'I am a stranger to my own grandchildren!' She felt the need for yet more meat and indulged it. 'If only your dear father were here, too. How he would have loved to have seen you all one last time. Of course, you could not have known—'

'Mama,' Jane chided, nervously watching Elizabeth Austen, whose expression of tolerance did not quite mask the possibility of less tolerant thoughts. 'I know our father found great pride and delight in the happiness of the Godmersham family. And it is hardly Edward's fault that we chose to settle in Bath, of all places. We are the other end of the country entirely now.'

'Oh, it *is* a long journey,' Grandmother Austen agreed. 'When I was talking to that first coachman – I have not yet told you about him – let me think, what *was* his name? His wife has the most remarkable history—'

'And now we are here,' cut in Cassandra with firmness. 'And very mindful of our dear sister Elizabeth's generosity towards us.'

'Quite so,' replied Edward. 'And tell me, what have you ladies been reading of late? Anything to recommend?'

Anne caught the way Elizabeth stiffened, the newly firm grip on her cutlery. And Jane opening her mouth to reply, and then at once closing it.

Again, Cassandra climbed up to the driving seat: 'We are all thrilled with little Louisa. Another piece of perfection, Elizabeth. How clever you are!'

Anne looked on, intrigued. As always, when she was present, the room was bisected by an invisible boundary, but this time she did not seem to be alone on her side of it. The Austens, she now saw, were of the same family and yet two distinct classes. She was witnessing here both sides of the fairy tale: the before, represented here by the modest but respectably dressed womenfolk; the after, by Edward in his customary splendid attire.

❧

Anne refused to allow herself hope that such friendship would continue past the first day of their visit. She
had been here before with Austen relations; knew they
could blow both hot and cold, and did not want to be
burned again. And so after breakfast the next morning,
she opened the schoolroom and waited to see what
might happen.

There were now, in fact, three girl cousins in residence,
and each had their own sadness. Anna Austen's mother
had died when she was small and her stepmother, with
whom she did not get along, was expecting a baby and
wanted the stepdaughter out of the way. And then Elizabeth Austen's own nieces – Fanny and Sophia Cage – had
been recently, suddenly orphaned and brought here by
Harriot Bridges.

Anne had not yet been informed of her duties. Was
she now to keep to herself and out of the way? Or to
run a small school for children with confusingly similar
names and a background of tragedy? If the latter, then
she would, of course, welcome the challenge.

She was alone in her schoolroom for all of five minutes. The four girls came in first, chattering happily,
excited to be all together. Then in trooped their female
relations.

'Oof, those stairs are steep for me,' declared Grandmother Austen. 'Good morning, Miss Sharp! I hope you
can provide a comfortable seat for this bag of old bones.
There we are. This'll do.' She settled herself into the one

armchair. 'Well, now I am here, I shall not be moving, thank you very much.'

'Miss Sharp.' Jane put a hand on Anne's arm and spoke quietly. 'Please do not mistake our mother for some kind of invalid. She is a person of great strength' – here she dropped to a whisper – 'and a consummate actress.'

As this was Anne's territory, she thought it her place to welcome them all, and express her pleasure in having their company. 'I presumed you would be busy today with callers, or calling.'

'Oh, not I, Miss Sharp, though I will in due course,' the grandmother replied. 'We have many old friends and family in the county. There are Austens, of course – you must be aware my husband hailed from this very county – the Bridgeses – of whom I am remarkably fond—'

'I wonder, Mama,' Jane gently broke in, 'if Miss Sharp might better appreciate this inventory when she has the time to give it her fullest attention? Remember, we have come here to play with the children.'

'What a charming schoolroom you have made here, Miss Sharp,' Cassandra Austen exclaimed, drifting elegantly towards the bookshelves to examine their contents.

'Imagine, Sister, if we had known such a space, and the benefits of such an intelligent governess?' Jane put in. 'The learned young ladies we might then have become!'

That made their fond mother laugh. 'Do not listen to them, Miss Sharp. My daughters are both very clever, you know. Too clever by half, I often think them. Quite the match of their brothers.'

Little Sophia Cage, who was younger than the other girls, had found the box of old toys over in the corner from which she produced a fine doll.

'Come show me, child,' Grandmother Austen beckoned her over. 'Oh, what a lovely baby. Who does she belong to and what is she called?' And when Fanny – who fancied herself too grown to play with such things – admitted she had never got around to calling her anything, she was met with great outrage. Within minutes they were all consumed in the first of their many grand games.

The baby was to be christened, and given the fine name of Emma. A sombre ceremony must be performed; a grand celebration would follow. The dressing-up clothes were requisitioned. Aunt Jane, with a dog collar over her plain brown day dress, held the doll over a basin of water and assembled the godparents.

'Before I bring this blessed and beautiful child into the arms of the Church, I hereby invite you all to state your wishes for her future on her behalf.'

Cassandra, having – somewhat unimaginatively, in Anne's view – cast herself in the role of the aunt, wished her long life and health. Anna Austen hoped that she would always know the true love of good parents; Fanny Cage that those parents would stay alive. The mood having darkened significantly – old Mrs Austen seemed close to tears – Anne sought to lighten it. She stepped up to the bowl.

'I am the Duke of St Albans,' she boomed, feeling rather dashing in an old frock coat of Edward Austen's, 'and I wish to leave this child all my estate.'

Jane's face lit up with approval at Anne's committed performance, and raised her own. 'Then, your grace, I commend you.' She bowed deeply. 'To make such a bequest to a girl is the most formidable act of the imagination, and God blesses you for it. May she rule over your land—'

'My *lands*,' Anne interrupted with a convincing pomposity.

'—your *lands*, is it?' Jane covered the doll's ears and fell into a stage whisper. 'Tell me, your grace: how many thousands can this baby expect?'

'Ten thousand per annum!' The most fantastical amount Anne could produce.

'Oh dear, is that all? I was rather hoping – ah, never mind. I suppose it will do.' Jane shrugged and went on. 'May she rule with the wisdom and benevolence so natural to those of her sex. May she show to your tenants the love she would show her own children. May she remain forever true to her own womanly instincts. For with your great gesture she will know that rare freedom to choose any husband she wishes.'

'Or as I should prefer it' – Anne, as the Duke, stuck her nose in the air – 'no husband at all!'

The party spirit was returned. Grandmother Austen demanded that sweetmeats be begged from the kitchen to provide for a feast. An awkward silence ensued, during which nobody moved. Anne knew it was she who was expected to go, but as she was still – even now – persona non grata downstairs, remained pinned to the spot.

Aunt Jane came to her rescue. 'Fanny, please do go on the hunt for us, and take a cousin or two to assist you.'

Had she read Anne's situation, and seen through her predicament? Surely, that was not possible. Nonetheless, Anne was grateful.

Trays duly arrived, bearing large jugs of cordial and plates laden with slices of white gingerbread, and the feasting began. Anne stood alone, watching Sally, the maid, in natural and affectionate dialogue with Grandmother Austen, and felt a little jealous.

Aunt Jane came up beside her; her eyes followed Anne's gaze.

'It is not just the family my mother is so happy to see, but also the servants. They are so tolerant of we *poor* Austen ladies. Such a friendly, warm household, do you not find?'

Anne was taken aback by such a bold reference to their inferior station. 'Mrs Austen certainly seems to have a great appetite for friendship.'

'Quite insatiable.' There came again that hiccoughing giggle. 'She has an extraordinary interest in anyone she meets, which I can quite understand. The Human

Comedy, Miss Sharp. There is much of it to be found in Godmersham Park – tell me, do you enjoy it as much as I do?'

Anne agreed that she must.

'Then I *am* pleased. But where my mother leaves *me* behind is that she finds it within herself to *like* them all, too.' Jane grinned and shrugged. 'I wonder where *you* stand, Miss Sharp. In that I mean, as well as laughing *at* people, can you like them as much?'

Anne was aghast. It was as if she had been run through with a skewer. 'Miss Austen, I beg you forgive me! I hope I did not somehow convey the impression that I am in the habit of laughing *at*—'

'Dear Miss Sharp,' Jane put a hand on her arm. 'But of course! And if you had, I should not have believed it. Truly, I spoke only of myself.' She turned back to the study of Grandmother Austen. 'You see, that particular maid is quite new to us, and yet within minutes my mother will have discovered every detail about her, and never forget. Next time we come, you will hear her enquiring about the brother's digestion or the mother's lumbago . . . Miss Sharp, I hope, for your sake, that you have no secrets yourself, for she *will* find them out!'

'Then it is fortunate I have none at all!' Anne gave her best possible version of carefree laughter, and yet felt uneasy. Though she had tried very hard to say nothing of any personal interest, yet still it seemed that Jane Austen had gleaned a substantial amount.

'Well. What an amusing time we have had. The first of many, I hope.' Jane raised her glass to the room. 'Here's to our Emma!'

'To her fame and her fortune!'

The morning had left Anne with feelings of mild frustration. It could have proved an opportunity for a full exploration of the territories of friendship, yet she was sure they had penetrated no further than its delicate edges. Certainly, Miss Jane had made a particular point of talking mostly to Anne, and showing some warmth. And yet, with her speech, she seemed to warn against any warmth in return – to deflect it, before it was wasted upon her. How very different from Henry, who seemed to crave – he demanded! – affection from everyone.

Was Jane quite serious when she declared that she was not given to like people? That was too hard to tell. The effect upon Anne, though, was manifest: she was now determined to be one of the few lucky enough to win Miss Jane Austen's approval.

CHAPTER XXVIII

As luck would have it, the fates aligned to throw them together the next afternoon.

'Miss Sharp!' Jane Austen waved across the parkland and strode towards Anne. 'We are two solitary walkers. Shall we now walk together? Or perhaps solitude was what you came here to seek?' That way she had of tilting her head with sudden, sharp movements brought to Anne's mind a small bird who had spotted something delicious. For a fraction of a second, Anne saw herself as the worm.

'I am not so deprived of the pleasures of my own company that I wish to have more of it.' Anne smiled. They fell into step on the spring of the grass, and by mutual agreement aimed for the temple.

'You are often alone then?' For one slight of build, Jane walked at a very good pace. 'My sister is gone to

Canterbury for the day with our brother, so I am bereft of my most natural companion. Our *devotion*' – she looked at Anne sideways – 'to myriad family members means that we must live in the centre of a small, madding crowd. Fond as we are of them, one does sometimes yearn for more thought and less speech. Hence this habit we have formed of so *desperately* walking.'

Anne halted. 'Please, do feel free to continue alone! I shall not take offence and can easily . . .' She gestured to the opposite hill.

Jane grabbed her arm. 'Oh, I did not mean—' They fell back into step. 'It is the perfect day for it, is it not? Warm and yet breezy; a smattering of cloud. No need to hunker down into our clothing to avoid the worst of the elements – excellent conditions for good conversation. There is no better place to enjoy than my brother's estate. And you, Miss Sharp, are *fresh meat*. I cannot describe the joy that I find in the company of those particular strangers to whom I have not taken an instant dislike.'

Anne laughed. 'Miss Austen, that is now twice in my hearing you have denied your own amiability!' Again, so very different from Henry! 'I refuse to believe you such a curmudgeon.'

Jane giggled. 'I simply have very high standards, and those whom I come across do not always meet them. Oh dear.' She gave a pantomime sigh. 'I fear I am growing yet more intolerant with each passing year. What a frightful old spinster I shall become . . .'

Anne was struck that they were both now at the age at which marriage was so unlikely as to be almost impossible. One's thirtieth year – how quickly it came, how brutal its axe. While she felt pure relief to have that threat behind her, she could not be sure her companion did not. 'Surely, love can find one at any age, and one can yet be changed by it?'

'Love?' When amused, Jane crinkled her eyes in, Anne noticed, a Henry-like fashion. 'Miss Sharp, I assure you, I have love aplenty. Have you counted the sheer number of Austens? My heart is already *quite* full enough.'

They dropped into silence as Anne considered the opacity of that last reply. Had Jane once known hope, and since surrendered it? Or, like Anne, had she not hoped at all? They arrived at the temple.

'I do admire this place, for its bold incongruity,' said Jane as they studied it.

'A piece of civic Athenian majesty dropped into the Garden of England,' Anne proclaimed. Oh! the pleasure of having someone with whom to share her best thoughts.

Jane turned towards her, face lit with laughter. 'Miss Sharp, for all my tendencies towards the misanthrope, I find, to my horror, I rather like you.'

Anne felt a frisson of triumph as Jane took her by the hand and they walked up the steps.

'What a revelation you are! My brother was right.'

Oh why, thought Anne, must Henry intrude into all

conversation? She did wish Jane would stop bringing him in so, reminding her of one she had determined to forget. The very subject caused her some strange discomfort – as if a cloud had come over the sun. She would much rather put him out of her mind.

They went into the temple, and Anne changed the subject. 'It is a place made for fantasy, do you not agree?'

'Absolutely,' said Jane. 'It is magical. There could be such a ball, or a party up here. I wonder the thought has not occurred to Mr and Mrs Austen.'

'I have noticed,' Anne began with great caution, 'that they have not held such an evening since I have been here.'

'It is curious, I agree.' Jane studied the frieze at the top of the wall. 'They are entirely replete in their own company, and want for no one beyond family and neighbours. I suppose it is what is known as contentment.' She smiled. 'And all society is nonsense, in the end, is it not?'

'But of course,' agreed Anne. 'If this were mine, I should use it as a place for private theatricals.'

Jane's head gave a quick twitch at this titbit. 'Would you indeed?' Her eyes shone through the shade in the temple. 'My brothers used to put on plays in the barn of the rectory where we grew up!'

'We did the same!' This point of unity brought Anne close to ecstasy. 'My friends and I put on play after play for many years.'

'Of course! Miss Sharp, I see it now: you are an actress.'

Jane clapped her hands with delight. 'As one lucky enough to have caught your recent performance as the Duke of St Albans, may I declare myself your greatest admirer.' She fell into a curtsey; Anne, adopting her best ducal mannerisms, bowed in return.

They returned to the air, sat down on the steps and Jane turned her face to the view. 'And does your gift for performance help, do you think, in playing the part of the Governess?'

'I do not quite understand . . .' Anne replied haltingly. 'I am merely fulfilling my duties . . .' Such acuity was disconcerting. Anne had become used to invisibility, yet suddenly, it was as if she were naked.

Still, Jane probed a little deeper. 'I think you a brave woman indeed to take on this position in a family of which you can have known little.'

Anne deflected. 'Miss Austen, I am educating your dear niece, not taming a lion!'

'Of course.' Jane smiled. 'But the position of governess in general –'tis a hard one, is it not? I must admit to cowardice and the very thought of it has always struck fear into my heart. And yet you – you *appear* to perform it so very willingly.'

Anne brushed her skirts. 'You speak as if I have plucked one profession from a multitude of possible options.'

'Oh, please – forgive me.' Jane laid a hand on Anne's arm. 'That was horribly crass and I do *know* my own fortune in having such a kind family. But, since the death of my father I have had occasion to feel – well – a little less secure. Though I trust them entirely, the thought must sometimes occur: the kindness of brothers – all of whom have or will soon have their *wives* to consider – is a somewhat *flimsy* barrier between me and my sister and the rest of the world.'

Anne fell quiet. On first meeting Jane, she had compared her to Henry and now saw, in so doing, had committed an injustice. She took a moment to regret it, for all had become clear now: the sisters and brothers shared ancestry, background and blood; were bound together by undeniable affection. But opportunity did not see them as equals. The sons had been elevated by education and marriage, profession and fortune. And the daughters? Just left behind.

And then she caught herself. He had wormed his way back into her thoughts again! This would not do. She jumped up: 'Lead on, Macduff – in whichever direction you favour.'

Jane rose and turned towards the neighbouring Chilham estate and they walked then in a peaceful companionship; picked wild flowers on the way – bladder campion, forget-me-not – shared thoughtful silence and gentle conversation. It was upon arriving at the boundary between the two parks – the crenellations of Chilham Castle peeking out from the landscape, the deer grazing about it – that Jane had the idea.

'Why do we not put on a theatrical of our own at

Godmersham? I am quite sure I could obtain my brother's permission. It would be of great benefit to the dear children and, of course, the servants would love it!'

'Oh!' Anne exclaimed. 'I have wanted to do such a thing since the moment of my arrival.' She paused. 'And – well – if, Miss Austen, you do not already have some fixed idea, perhaps I could write something?'

'You are both actress *and* writer, Miss Sharp?' Jane stood stock still.

'I suppose, perhaps, I am.' Far too keen to impress, Anne flung off all ladylike modesty as she might an old bonnet. 'But of course, I pursue writing now more than acting, by simple virtue of opportunity, only to discover I enjoy it the more. I have always found great pleasure with my own pen and others have been kind enough to claim enjoyment in that which I have written.'

Jane led the walk again, back towards Godmersham. 'Then, Miss Sharp, you have my whole admiration. I have often thought it the most enviable skill – to amuse oneself and, in so doing, spread amusement to others. But oh – forgive me. I am being presumptuous. Perhaps this pen of yours cannot help but dwell upon other matters: *guilt*, say, or *misery*?'

'Certainly not!' Anne protested. 'Miss Austen, it is my firm belief that a light entertainment can carry the same moral weight, if 'tis well enough done.'

Jane seemed to find that argument most interesting, and proceeded to ask Anne many questions on the subject of literature and the craft of it. Anne held forth with her opinions for the rest of the walk and was delighted by the interest her listener showed. Jane was at least as intelligent as her brother Henry. But while *he* only seemed to want to give long explanations to others of that which he already knew, *she* showed a proper desire to learn. Somehow, her company was so much less troubling than his. Not that the comparison should even be made. Henry was a total irrelevance, and Anne made a firm mental note to remember it.

When they arrived back at the house, it was decided that Jane would take up the matter with Mr and Mrs Edward, and Anne would produce something suitable for all-comers.

'Miss Austen,' added Anne as they changed into their slippers, 'I hope you did not mind sharing your liberty.'

'Not at all,' Jane exclaimed. 'The company of one – sympathetic – fellow solitary must always be preferable to the company of one's simple self.' And at last they had cause to come together over dear Cowper. '*A friend . . . Whom I may whisper—*'

'*—solitude is sweet.*'

Anne had been careful not to catch any sun, so what could possibly account for this tingling sensation she felt all over her skin?

❧

'And, Miss Sharp, was *your* afternoon equally pleasant?' Fanny politely enquired over dinner in the schoolroom that evening. 'You look very well from it.'

'Very pleasant, thank you.' Anne tapped little Sophia's elbow, which looked in danger of straying on to the table. 'And I am so pleased you four all enjoyed yourselves.'

'I still cannot *recover* from the surprise of my canary laying three eggs!' Fanny had already described this small miracle at some considerable length. '*And* she is sitting! It is as if she has suddenly grown up, and realised who she is and what she's about. We could not *believe* it, could we, girls?'

Anne noticed that the cousins did not enjoy an equal share in Fanny's enthusiasm. Anna Austen, in particular, seemed rather off-colour.

'Anna, do you not have an appetite this afternoon?' the governess asked softly. 'You are not partial to fowl?'

Fanny replied for her: 'Anna heard today that she has a new sister, Miss Sharp, which *we* think is *delightful. Mama* says that *Anna's* papa sounded quite *joyful* in his letter. And yet *Anna* cannot seem to be happy.'

Miss Sharp addressed Anna directly: 'I am sorry to hear that, my dear. Is it that you enjoyed the position of only girl in the family?'

'Perhaps I did rather,' Anna admitted. 'If that is not so very wrong of me.'

'Well, I *love* it every time *my* mama has a little girl. Oh,

I love all the boys, of course, equally well. But a sister is a special thing, is it not?'

Miss Sharp winced at the insensitivity of that remark. For this baby was a half-sister; the mama just a stepmother.

Anna put down her fork. 'This is not – not – well, quite the *same*.'

'I cannot think why!' Fanny rejoined, going on to extol all the benefits of a very large family – to one motherless girl, and two little orphans.

Anne now felt deeply uncomfortable. Here, in a nut-shell, was why she preferred the company of those who had known some sort of misfortune. While she hoped – indeed, she prayed nightly – that Fanny would never know tragedy, that her life would continue to be blessed as it was, how then could the girl develop empathy? The work they did for the poor, the sewing and visiting, was not enough. Fanny could only pity them – oh, pity she had in abundance. But pity was not the same thing.

To distract the whole company from their conflicting emotions, Anne shared with them the idea of the play. Naturally, she dressed it all up as the project of Aunt Jane.

'Miss Sharp writes *all the time*, do you not, Miss Sharp? There really is *nobody* cleverer.'

Anne demurred slightly at that – and did wonder, fleet-ingly, if she should not have pushed herself forward so? Might there be someone who would rather enjoy some small share in her endeavour? She issued herself some reassurance. For while many a young lady could turn out a few pretty lines and fancy themselves writers, there were precious few like herself who were blessed with real talent. Besides which, she had been here long enough to establish that Godmersham was hardly a cradle of creative genius.

If an entertainment was called for, then who was more qualified than she to provide it?

CHAPTER XXIX

The next week was the happiest that Anne could remember. Indeed, until then, she had rather forgotten what happiness felt like at all. She rehearsed the cast in the mornings; in the evenings, she wrote alone – edited and revised. The work, to be known by the title *Virtue Rewarded*, she knew to be not one of her best. But then it was to be performed by the children, so that in itself was restrictive. And as she had set herself the task of including a morality lesson, specific to this particular household, her play was quite naturally robbed of a more universal appeal. She could take some comfort in knowing each member of her audience. Their gentle minds would be easily satisfied. There would be no savage, sharp critic out there in the seats.

Through great, mutual exertion, the production

seemed to come together with a remarkable ease. Since the unfortunate business with her cat and the canary, Mrs Salkeld had superseded Anne as Godmersham's Most Unpopular Figure. Desperate to make amends, she had taken it upon herself to organise all the costumes. An attic room was commandeered as the Wardrobe; Grandmother Austen was employed as the seamstress: and together they produced clothing that could shame the Drury, while enjoying an endless, merry consultation on their many medical complaints: 'And on top of all that, there's my knees. Do *you* suffer from knees, Mrs Salkeld? Well, then consider yourself a very fortunate woman. I must declare that by joints in general I am *severely* ill served . . .'

Harriot Bridges, who had by now joined the party, was set to work on the scenery. Anne wondered if this were not a joke being played by Jane, for she had heard of the 'art lesson', and the news had amused her. But, somewhat to Anne's surprise – though that of no other – it turned out that Harriot did indeed show some degree of true talent. For her, drawing was a little more than the usual – and meaningless – 'young lady's particular accomplishment'. The background to *Virtue* – as it came to be known in that closed, busy company – was pastoral: a castle from a dream, surrounded by meadows. Bustling past as she worked, Anne felt the prick of excitement, seeing her vision brought so well together. And noticing the energy which Miss Bridges put into creating – almost as much as went into her flirting – Anne found a whole new respect.

Cassandra, who had an excellent way with all children whatever their ages, stood off to the side, patiently rehearsing the lines with the actors. Jane, whose own 'particular accomplishment' appeared to centre around the pianoforte, provided the musical accompaniment, and, to Anne's ear at least, played prettily enough.

And there at the fulcrum – source of the answer to any question; ultimate arbiter of an array of decisions; mainspring of this whole, joyful enterprise – stood happy and busy Miss Sharp. She gave barely a thought to her father; Henry Austen was almost entirely forgotten. Yet dearly she wished that both could be there in the audience and forced to witness her undoubted success.

On the eve of the performance, the whole company came together for dinner. At the table, the nerves and excitement were palpable. *Virtue* was all they could speak of.

'Oh, but what if I *dry*?' cried Fanny in panic. 'Truly, the thought gives me nightmares. Imagine – out there on the stage, before all those people . . . And nothing comes out!'

'All actors dread it,' a cousin assured her. 'And yet it so rarely happens. Once you are *out there*, all eyes upon you,

you will find that you *become* your character. It will feel perfectly natural.'

'I have a tickle in my throat.' Anna clutched at her neck. 'Suppose I have no voice tomorrow? Then what will we do?'

'Trust to Dr Theatre!' Fanny Austen declared with a confident and knowledgeable air.

From his place at the head of the table came Edward's loud laughter. 'My love,' he called down to his wife. 'Do you hear them? They sound a lot less like young ladies, and more like travelling players who have been touring the houses for decades!'

'I do hope, Miss Sharp, that you will return them unchanged, when this drama is over?' Elizabeth smiled across at Anne. Mr and Mrs Austen were not involved in any part of the project, so that the performance would come to them as a lovely surprise. Indeed, no one had seen all of it through, besides the children and Anne.

'You must steel yourself, Mrs Austen!' This was from Jane. 'I fear their heads are quite turned. It is now more likely than not that they will run away to the circus. The day after tomorrow, we shall find four empty beds and four notes of farewell.'

In this now democratised dining room, all were united over the cause of the play. Anne talked often and openly; for the remainder, she was often and openly talked to. She was seated on one side of Harriot Bridges; Jane was put on the other. Together, the three women were getting on well. Even Harriot now treated the governess as her equal.

'Tell us, Miss Sharp' – her tone was all friendliness – 'as a dramatist yourself: which other dramatists do you most admire?'

This was Anne's opportunity to play down her own talents – to say 'Dramatist? *Me*? Miss Bridges, I assure you' and so on – but, sadly, she let it pass by. Instead, she cleared her throat and began a discussion on Shakespeare; Jane joined in with enthusiasm. Together, they rated the tragedies first, and then the comedies; compared the whole of the one to the whole of the other; briefly dismissed all the Histories, before moving on through the ages.

The longer that Harriot's silence went on, the more it merited its place in the category marked 'Stony'. Elizabeth Austen's eyebrows were risen so high as to be obscured by the roots of her hair. Though Anne did notice Jane was signalling some sort of warning, the message was too subtle for her to read. Besides which, she was enjoying herself greatly; had alighted upon the subject of Congreve, whom she so liked to discuss.

'*The Way of the World* was a particular favourite in my family.' Anne's brain did register the sudden lull in the dining room, but not quite in time to inform her own tongue. 'You see, my mother was an—' She stopped, appalled. What on earth was she thinking? To reveal such a fact at this table!

Grandmother Austen, who had seemed too intent on her dinner to be listening, suddenly spoke: 'Your mother was an—?' Bright eyes bored through Anne. 'Miss Sharp – you were saying?'

Anne's voice had shrunk. 'Great enthusiast. She was—'

'*An* great enthusiast,' echoed one of the children.

'I meant to say—' But Anne could not go on.

'Well!' Harriot spoke across to Elizabeth. 'How fortunate we *are*, Sister, to have received such a *lecture*. Perhaps we should start to carry a *tablet* and *pencil*, upon which to write down these *pearls* which are *scattered* before us. I should *hate* to forget even one *single* word.'

The conversation picked up then, moved on to matters of canaries and harvests and Anne had the good sense to keep quiet for the rest of the evening.

The next day passed at great speed, and suddenly the moment of performance was upon them. If they had been allowed to put up a curtain – Mr Austen had quashed that idea – then that curtain would be now twitching to rise.

The stage was set in the library. Harriot's charming background was erected in place. Jane was at the pianoforte, playing gentle dance music. The now-seated audience – quite a good crowd, made up as it was of family and servants and neighbours, the Reverend and Mrs Whitfield included – wriggled with anticipation.

264

Anne, out in the hall with the excitable children, peered through the door.

'Girls,' she whispered, 'I think the moment is now upon us. Marianne and Lizzie – you know what to do.'

Fanny kissed them both, saying: 'Good luck, little ones.' Though they were simply giving out programmes and announcing the play.

While they did so, Anne gave the cast an inspirational address – about conquering their fears, supporting each other and giving of their best – fit to create envy in the chest of Julius Caesar. Then they heard the words: 'Miss Sharp's . . . *Virtue Rewarded*!' The first loud applause. And Fanny was on.

'I am Serena, the Good Fairy, of the beautiful, exotic and faraway land known as' – she paused, as Anne had directed – 'St Albans!' The audience laughed. 'Here, there is no sadness. There is no hunger. Injustice is alien. 'Tis the happiest place on all of God's earth. For it alone knows the benefit of being ruled by' – another pause – 'a *woman*!'

Enter Anna, in full grand regalia. Standing downstage from the Fairy, she proceeded to bless the small children, all dressed as peasants and looking adorable.

'Our Duchess cares deeply for all of her subjects,' Fanny continued. 'She has banished all misery; will not tolerate poverty. With the great intuition of her sex, she has led her people on to the true path of righteousness.' The little villagers made the sign of the cross. 'And they love their Duchess for that, as they love her great munificence – for all she was given, she has given unto them. One small room in the castle, and the glorious jewels she wears on her person, are all she has left for herself. And yet – enjoying both the love of her subjects and the great satisfaction of knowing she does her best by them – she knows she is rich.

'Oh!' The Fairy looked around, startled. 'But what do I hear? The sound of *weeping*? Here in *St Albans*? This cannot be!' Fanny Cage, dressed in tatters, came on blowing her nose. 'I must away!'

The Duchess saw and went to kneel down by the pauper, asking the reasons for her distress. That was the point at which – at her position, hovering in the doorway – Anne should have begun to relax. The girls were giving their best possible performance, and had not dried once: the crowd was quite rapt. But with that fear behind her, there crashed in a greater one. How had she not noticed? What was she thinking? Was this not *the very worst play in the world*?

'So you have no home and no family.' The Duchess paced while she thought. 'Now, what can I do for you?'

'Oh, *anything,* your grace,' the pauper implored her.

And now Anne was certain. It was an abomination. No matter that the actors spoke each line to perfection: each line was an affront to Anne's ear.

'I have nothing more to give away but this one hovel,' the Duchess declared. 'Though small and though modest, here you will feel safe.'

'Oh, thank you, thank you, thank you,' the pauper cried. And as the Duchess turned to leave, swiped the crown from her head.

The audience gasped. Anne winced and grimaced. The way she had bragged about being *a writer*! The manner in which she had pushed herself forward! Only to produce this piece of stupidity. Thank heavens Henry was not here to see it.

At their next meeting, the Duchess presented the pauper with her own flock of sheep, so that she might learn the dignity of employment. All the little ones crawled in on all fours, wrapped in cotton wool, baaing. This should have been the great high point – they did look very sweet. But so loud was the love from the public that the lambs took fear and fled.

The audience – or, at least, the section of it come from below stairs – now found its voice. When the pauper stole the necklace, there were great shouts of 'Shame!' And when the earrings went too, some stood up out of their seats and started to boo. The Godmersham library was as noisy as the bawdiest of pantomime houses. Anne could not bear even to look at those in the front row – her master, her mistress, the man of the Church. Surely, they could not approve this base degradation. Oh, how was she to face them?

The pauper, once homeless, now sat at the door of her cottage; she was in the Duchess's dress and huge jewels; precious sheep – coaxed back on stage by Cassandra – flocked around her. The Fairy returned.

267

'You have taken so much, and yet still you weep! What now is the matter, girl?'

'I want more!' she wailed horribly. 'I want as much as that Duchess!'

Please, Anne silently implored, let this be over.

'But what more does she have? Do you mean you crave the great dignity that her grace so enjoys?'

'Pah! What use is *dignity*?'

'So then you want love?'

'I care nothing for love,' sneered the peasant.

'Then what else can we give you?'

'I want worldly riches! And I want *things*!'

Enter the Duchess, wearing Anne's drab day dress. She stood centre stage.

'And yet behold our Duchess! She has nothing left but her virtue. And with that she is happy!'

Her grace spun around and danced a little.

'For she knows she is virtuous, and nothing bad can befall her! And so I take back the jewels you have stolen.' The Fairy tore them from her person; the audience cheered. 'I take back your home and I confiscate your sheep.' The little lambs ran to Anna. 'The Duchess must have them all. And so much more!

'For Virtue' – Fanny spoke straight to the audience – 'is always rewarded!'

Such was her shame, so busy was she with grimacing and hunching and shrinking into the doorway, that, at first, Anne did not notice what was happening there in the library. Not until she could no longer hear herself think did she acknowledge that there rang all around her a deafening roar; only then did she look up and out and become newly appalled: the servants were cheering and clapping and stamping their feet. As they called out for 'More!' at the very tops of their voices, Anne slapped her hands to her cheeks. Mrs Austen was so particular about calm in the household! An hysterical Hall would be highly unwelcome! Housework would suffer, supper be ruined . . .

Much as she might long to, Anne could not flee – she had the children to think of. So instead, she pressed herself into the wall, hoping her brown dress would merge with the wainscot and make her invisible.

But as the applause died away, Elizabeth Austen was out of her seat and into the most prominent position at the main point of exit where, issuing a quick squeeze to Anne's hand, she then proceeded – with the greatest of grace and all that was modest – to receive every plaudit.

'*So* touched you should say so . . . Oh, sir, you *flatter* . . . Very much of a *team* . . . They were *rather* precious.' Anne, staring into the back of Elizabeth's taffeta gown, could not help but smile. 'The idea? Heavens, it has been such a *whirl* I cannot recall . . . Though not *too* clever, I hope?'

Virtue was no longer Anne's professional disgrace, but Elizabeth Austen's very own triumph.

At last the crowd was dispersed: the servants returned to their duties, the family to the drawing room. Anne stayed behind, needing a few moments to register all that had occurred. The evening had not gone quite as she expected. There came a small tap: the closing of the lid of the pianoforte.

'Miss Sharp?' Anne looked up to see Jane coming towards her. 'You are not floating on the clouds of your own success?' A small smile, a short tilt of the head but – Anne noted – no direct compliment. Was this one mind less gentle than all the rest?

'Any success is' – Anne put on a false smile – 'I assure you, down to the children. Were they not splendid?'

'Oh, but of course, they did very well,' Jane agreed. 'But it is you I admire. Miss Sharp, you have been *so* very clever.'

'You are kind.' Now too tired to pretend, Anne fell back on honesty. 'I fear it was not quite as clever as I had thought.' She gulped in some air and covered her eyes. 'In fact, it was perfectly dreadful.' In that moment, Anne hated herself.

'Miss Sharp, I do not know what magic you have, to make me say all these things I really should not. Please do not judge me as always disloyal, but . . .' She drew close and whispered, 'Have you learned nothing of Godmersham? All cleverness is met here with a general suspicion. Among *some* more than others; *one,* in particular. In *that* person, cleverness brings out a rash. And therein lies the proof of your genius! For *my own greatest* fear was that you might produce some sort of masterpiece – in which case, by now, we would find your bags packed and lined up in the hall.'

'Oh, Miss Austen.' Anne laughed. 'That is some comfort. Thank you. But still, I think perhaps I shall go up now.' She gestured towards the stairs. 'The evening proved tiring.'

'Fatigue must follow triumph, I suppose – though what do *I* know of triumph? But if I do try to *imagine* the experience, then I *believe* I am left with a feeling of *weariness*.' She took Anne's arm and led her through the great hall. 'Do at least join us for supper. We have the promise of blancmange *and* country dances.' She stopped at the entrance to the drawing room. 'Listen to that!' She put a hand to her ear. 'Such gaiety and happiness! The ambition of all art is to please its own audience. Please, Miss Sharp, do not be downhearted. So much joy in the household! Such *pride* in your mistress's bosom!

'And all of it created by your famous *pen*.'

CHAPTER XXX

Anne did not stay long at the party. She was still not in quite the right mood.

Fanny was sleeping with her cousins that night, so she was alone when there came a knock on the door.

'Good evening, miss.' Sally gave a nice curtsey. 'I was wondering if you'd like a fire this evening, or are you quite warm enough?'

This sudden and quite unexpected peace offering cheered Anne more than all Jane's fine words. It also amused her. A fire, in June? Oh, how she would have welcomed one back in February. She politely declined, while thanking profusely.

'Anything else I can do for you then, miss?' Sally continued to loiter.

'You are too kind, Sally, but I am perfectly content.'

Anne stifled a yawn. 'After all that excitement, I believe I am ready for bed.'

'As you wish, miss.' Sally turned. 'Oh. By the way . . .'

'Yes?'

'I keep forgetting to say. My ma says thank you ever so much for teaching our boys down at the school. She doesn't know where you get the patience. Says they're quite changed.'

❧

On Sunday morning, the household assembled around the front door to form the weekly parade down to church. The warmth of June blessed them: the church bells rang out; a clear, sunny day beckoned. Edward led the crocodile, his mother on his arm; Elizabeth selected her favourite, Cassandra, as that morning's companion. The children and servants all grouped together at the rear, leaving two women alone together in the centre.

They took the path around the house, crossed the lawn and, in stately procession, gained on the Lime Walk.

'I look forward to being back in the sanctity of St Lawrence's,' Jane began. 'I always prefer the smallest church to the largest cathedral, do not you? I suppose that is down to my background. Steventon – where we grew up – was almost a miniature, and my dear father such a big presence within it: one sat there in awe. Tell me, what are your views on the *illustrious spark* we have here in Godmersham?'

Anne smiled, to acknowledge this new reference to Cowper. 'Mr Whitfield has proved a great friend to me, and I am grateful to have him here in the village. I believe him an excellent gentleman in all possible ways, and the gentlest of souls. But "spark", I fear, is not a word that quite does him justice. Certainly, there is no danger of those sermons setting us on fire.'

They laughed together, their intimacy re-established. 'Miss Jane, I do hope you are enjoying your stay here?'

'Oh!' Jane exclaimed. 'So very much indeed.' She looked about her for listeners; dropped her voice in precaution. 'The contrast between *this* place and the life we now live is so great as to leave me quite reeling. Our latest home in Bath is so modest; here it is paradise. Everyone in Kent is so *rich* – have you noticed? – or it seems so to me. When here, I feel this constant struggle inside – a battle against my natural desire to *grasp* at every luxury which is dangled before me.' She gave that mischievous giggle. 'I *long* to eat too many ices, drink too much wine. In particular: to *outstay my welcome*! Though, of course, that would never do.'

'It is not easy,' Anne agreed with some feeling, 'when one is here, to recall the hard facts of the rest of the world. And do you yet know how long you are staying?'

'Madam, you want rid of us?' The creases appeared around her eyes.

'Quite the opposite, I assure you.' Anne spoke in earnest. 'The atmosphere is so much lighter with you here – or it seems so to me.'

'And you, Anne – if I may? – have enriched *our* visit. We have found more *animation* here this summer than previously. But as to the *length* of our stay: it is uncertain, and the final decision is – well – out of our hands. Certainly, we have a reprieve until the older boys have come home from school for the holidays. Then we must *cluck* for some days, exclaim over their growth, express astonishment at their genius, praise them to the heavens, whether we think them worthy or not. Once *that* is accomplished and the parents have had their fill of it, then my mother is set to return Anna to Hampshire. As for my sister and I – our plan is to *loiter*, as long as we can.'

'Do look, Miss Sharp!' The head of the company was passing through the door in the wall when Fanny broke out of formation and skipped to Anne's favourite lime. She reached down into the grass at the base of the trunk, plucked something and held it aloft. The sun caught its shine. 'Your thimble! I *saw* the *glint* of it from yards away. Are you not greatly delighted?' She turned it around in her fingers as she walked towards Anne. 'At least I *believe* it is yours. Though I do not *remember* it being so very shiny. 'Tis as if someone has polished it, but how can that *be*?'

Anne slipped it on to her finger and felt its grooves and good fit. 'It is mine, most certainly. How clever you are, Fanny! Thank you, my dear.' She would have liked to turn back to Jane then, for they had not many more minutes together alone. But, finding herself front and centre of such excitement, Fanny was not yet ready to leave it alone:

'What can have happened, do we suppose? What an *extraordinary* story!'

'And you are its heroine. Thank you, Fanny.' Oh, really, thought Anne, it is only a thimble, not the Crown Jewels. 'I suppose it must have fallen out of my apron some time or another, and has had a good wash from the rain.' Though, even as she spoke, another possible explanation occurred: could there be some connection to Sally's new friendliness since the night of her play?

It was clear that Jane's thoughts coincided with her own. 'Perhaps,' she smiled and said softly, 'this is *your* virtue's reward?'

As they went through the door, took to the lane and walked into the churchyard, Anne felt building within her a sense of great satisfaction.

And then, during the service, as Mr Whitfield ascended to the pulpit, Anne sat between Jane and the wall, bathed in the warmth of striped sunlight, one dear, narrow leg pressed tightly to hers. Prepared for a sermon to soothe, she saw that instead he had mustered some hitherto unknown, passionate force within his own bosom. Heard the new, thunderous tones; the command:

'*THOU SHALT NOT STEAL!*' Felt the thunderbolt strike through his shocked congregation . . .

Well, then, Anne was both touched that it was on her own behalf her mild-mannered friend had stirred himself up so – and triumphant that he had not needed to do so.

She had resolved the whole matter herself.

CHAPTER XXXI

'This is pleasant, ladies, is it not?' Grandmother Austen looked around her and smiled. 'An afternoon of good work, to be followed by strawberries for tea. I can forgive the weather its unfriendly turn, for it has brought us together into the family circle. I do like a circle, do I not, girls?'

'Famously, Mama, you are most fond of circles.' Jane reached over and took the scissors from her sister. 'Though I myself am more of a *triangle* person.'

'All those points and hard edges?' Her mother shook her head. 'Jane, I despair—'

Both daughters laughed. 'Mama, I do not believe my sister was being entirely serious. There!' Cassandra looked upon her work with some satisfaction. 'One small shift done. What is next in the basket?'

At once, Harriot laid down her own needle and took it upon herself to search through the pile. Anne looked up and watched her, thinking how she grabbed at any excuse not to sit still and concentrate. So doing, she pricked her own finger.

'Miss Sharp, you are wounded!' Grandmother Austen missed nothing. 'Do you not have a thimble, my dear?'

'Silly of me.' Anne mopped at herself with her handkerchief. 'I have lately got out of the habit of using it.'

'It was lost, Grandmama,' explained Fanny. 'So *many* of Miss Sharp's favourite possessions seem to go *missing*. *We* cannot understand it, can we, Miss Sharp? But then *I* discovered it out in the park!'

'I only thought they were missing, Fanny dear,' Anne put in. 'But, just very lately, I seem to have found everything. It is quite the mystery.'

In fact, there was nothing mysterious about it. To Anne, at least the explanation was clear. Since the evening of the play, which had brought such delight to all below stairs, her own fortunes had substantially changed. Not only had the petty thief gone into retirement, but the servants, once so very hostile, now approached her with friendliness. Even Cook dispatched cakes, still warm from the oven, as 'we can't have 'er looking half-starved.' Those little devilries which had plagued her existence for more than a year had been slain – by a few strokes of her inexpert pen. Anne had always had faith in the transformative powers of drama, but even she had not imagined a transformation such as this.

'Still,' she went on, keen to dispel any stirrings of fuss, 'all's well . . .'

Jane's eyes flicked up, but she passed no comment. Her all-seeing mother, on the other hand, had spotted some new thing of concern. 'Are you quite well, my dear? I have noticed you struggling over there with your eyes and now – am I correct? – I fancy your face and neck are a little engorged? Come here, Miss Sharp. Let me feel you all over.'

Anne thanked her, but resisted. Truly, she felt perfectly well, though would concede to resting her eyes, just for a moment.

Jane issued a warning: 'Miss Sharp, please do not excite my mother with symptoms, however mild they may be, for I fear you will not hear the end of it.'

'*I* believe Miss Sharp is getting one of her heads, Grandmama,' Fanny chipped in, all helpfulness.

'Her *heads*?' The information had an electric effect. 'You still *suffer*, Miss Sharp?'

Anne could feel Elizabeth's gaze and sense her displeasure. 'Only very occasionally,' she protested. 'Too rarely to mention.'

'Miss Sharp is being very brave, Grandmama. The truth is, her suffering is most *acute*.' And realising that, for once, she had in her own possession prized information of great interest to revered adults, Fanny sent her powers of description to new, soaring heights. ''Tis only *I* who am truly aware of it, for *I* am the unfortunate witness. They come at night, you know,' she said gleefully. 'In the *dead hours*. I should be asleep of course, for I am still *very* young and *growing* and sleep is essential, as we know, for one's complexion – or so Mama says. Do you not, dear Mama? And so I *should* like to sleep *more* – for one must care for one's *skin* – but with all the *writhing* and *screaming* provoked by the very *worst* sort of *agony*—'

Elizabeth gasped. 'Miss Sharp, is this true? This account goes much further than any I have heard previously.'

Before Anne could reply, Fanny did so for her. 'Perfectly true, Mama. Although we *thought* she was cured when in London.' She addressed the whole circle: 'Uncle Henry took great trouble to find for Miss Sharp the perfect physician – is he not kind and caring? And Mama let her go, which was altogether most generous – yet, sadly, all was in vain. For almost the minute she was home, it was *back* and, oh, we had a terrible bout of it then, did we not, poor, dear Miss Sharp?'

Anne could not assess the extent of her mistress's horror, for Grandmother Austen was upon her, and – as threatened – feeling all over. Anne's eyes, neck, tongue, even heart were now under scrutiny.

'Cass, dear,' the expert called over her shoulder. 'Fetch me the housekeeper. Ah, Mrs Salkeld. Thank you – how is Puss today, by the way? That ear repairing? – can you go to Cook for me please, and ask for snail milk? Poor

Miss Sharp is *horribly* unwell.' While they waited, Grandmother Austen plumped pillows and tucked them about Anne, then felt around her some more, saying, 'I do hope there is some potion all ready down there in the kitchen. We have not the time to pick thirty snails and pickle them before the attack gets into its stride. I fancy a large draught of this will avert it.'

The grey milk arrived and Anne drank it obediently, forcing the ingredients out of her mind. 'Thank you, Mrs Austen, for your excellent remedy and great concern. I feel better already.' She smiled to the room. 'Madam, if you will excuse me I might take a little air, then I have some letters to write . . .'

'Of course.' Elizabeth nodded. 'And perhaps, Miss Sharp, we might have a fuller discussion on this matter at some later date?'

❧

Outside, Anne turned her hot face up to the drizzle, took a few deep breaths and headed to the avenue and the sanctity of her favourite lime tree. Here, out of the gaze of any who passed, she put her arms about the trunk and feared for her future.

There was no doubt in her mind that this could put her position in jeopardy – and so soon after the triumph of her clever, or stupid – or cleverly stupid – private theatrical. That now counted for nothing in the wake of Fanny's dramatic testimony. Which mother would favour a governess of talent over one with sound health? Not Elizabeth Austen, that much was certain. Especially with the threat posed to Fanny's *growth* and *complexion*. Anne could be finished. She might well be done for. And she had nowhere to go.

Could she even hope for a reference? Even that much could not be relied upon. Elizabeth would not be so careless of her own reputation as to recommend this guardian to another mother of her class and acquaintance, and so endanger the priceless appearance of another well-bred young girl.

There had been a time when Anne should not have minded leaving this place, when she had still thought her father might well return. Now, though, that soft landing had been removed. If she could no longer teach . . . well, there remained but one more rung on this downward ladder: that of companion. And beneath that, there was nothing but the abyss. She must stay at Godmersham! Mrs Austen must keep her, or – Anne shuddered and silently wept.

'You have missed the strawberries.' Jane peered round the bark. 'I could pretend they were still green, or horribly squashed, but I fear they were quite *à la* Godmersham: that is, perfection.'

Anne wiped her sore and wet eyes, and smiled. 'I could not have done them justice.'

'Miss Sharp, you leave me quite baffled! Are you truly

suggesting, after being so graciously presented with the juices of a thousand soured snails – boiled in old milk, with smatterings of this and dashes of the other – that you still *refuse* to be cured?'

'I beg you, please – not the whole recipe! I feel quite sick enough.'

'Ungrateful wretch!' Jane moved around the trunk and now leaned beside her. 'I am sorry for my mother. She means well enough.'

'Oh – she has been very kind. I am touched that she seemed to care.'

'She does care, Anne – she cares very much. Indeed, you are in danger of being adopted as a new Austen daughter.'

'I cannot think of anything more pleasant. Can we sort the formalities at once, please – before I am out on the streets?'

'Come now,' Jane soothed. 'I am quite sure things are not as bad as all that. Clearly, Fanny is inordinately fond of you, and that counts for a lot. Her mama would not want to create any unhappiness in the breast of her eldest daughter.'

Jane enquired after her symptoms and, as there was now no point in pretending, Anne described them. Jane winced as she listened. 'Such an evil . . . And combined with all the responsibilities of your position . . .'

'That is the issue. The condition is not permanent – it comes and it goes – and was almost endurable when I was always at leisure, with a bedroom of my own.' Anne looked up and spoke to the lime tree's rich foliage. 'I must say, I had thought I was managing to work well enough around it, until my dear charge made her speech.' If only the girl had bridled her tongue.

'I take it, you do *have* to earn? There is no family or friend who . . . I see.' Jane fell silent. 'And you have tried every cure? Even sea-bathing has no effect?'

'Perhaps it *could* help. Certainly, I have heard all the talk of the benefits of the water, but I have not had the opportunity to try it myself. And now, of course, I do not enjoy the liberty or the financial resources . . . I should have liked to see the sea, once in my life. Do you go there, Jane? I never have.'

'*Never?* Well, Miss Sharp. That will not do. I wonder – yes!' Jane took Anne's hand. 'I do believe I can feel the stirrings of a lovely, grand scheme. Come, let us return. You must get to your bed.' She grinned. 'And *I* to my *plotting*.'

❧

'Miss – well, can I – can I ask you a question, miss?' Becky, the maid, was waiting on Anne at her solitary breakfast one morning. 'Please, do not think me impertinent, miss. Only, they did ask below stairs if I'd ask you.'

Anne was drained by yet another night of pain and would have preferred to be quiet. There had also arrived a troubling letter from Agnes, whose sleuthing had, at last, yielded result. Anne sighed, looking back with some fondness on those days when the servants had snubbed her. This new popularity was proving rather hard work. 'Of course, Becky. Do go on.'

'Thank you, miss. You're ever so kind, miss.' Really, thought Anne, there is no need to spread it so thick. I am still the governess, have not lost those airs and graces you once found so loathsome. 'It's not only me, the whole Hall wants to know: can we hope for another of your plays soon, miss? It's just, we did have such a good time.'

Anne began to explain that their master alone could make that decision, when the four girl cousins burst into the schoolroom.

'Miss Sharp, we have news! We are to play another Grand Game today!'

'And this time it is Schools. *We* are the pupils, and *we* have come up with all of the characters.'

'Even Mama is to join in,' cried Fanny. 'She is to play the part of the *Bathing Woman*! Is that not *a scream*? I cannot *wait* to see *her* acting so *vulgar*.'

'And *Aunt Harriot* is the *Housemaid*!'

While the girls collapsed in giggles at this preposterous idea, Anne shot a concerned glance over at Becky. The real maid had every right to take offence at all this, yet she too was giggling behind a polite hand.

'I fear, Miss Sharp, that you are left with all of the

masculine roles. I hope you do not mind it too much? Only, the *ladies* were a little reluctant.'

'Not at all!' What Anne did mind was being in the same room as her mistress, fearing that the events of the morning might open and yield some opportunity for their 'fuller discussion'. She had been avoiding her for days, in the hope that – like Mrs Salkeld's murderous cat – the matter of her illness might soon be forgotten.

Anne was given her parts, instructed to dress up in full costume and to present herself down in the drawing room.

Heading first for the clothes box in the schoolroom, she found what she needed and went to her own room to change. Undressing down to her linen shift, she pulled on a fine pair of britches – folding them over to fit her too-narrow waist – and the frock coat on top. Now at the glass, she scraped at her hair, tied it close to the back of her head, and quickly appraised her reflection.

She had worn this sort of garb before many a time, for the various roles she had played in her youth. And, now as then, she felt a little surprised at how well it became her. Strong, masculine colours brought out the best in her complexion; an emphasis of shoulders and the revelation of leg shape suited her figure. And, though it might be expected, she found she could not quite loathe the effect. While a lady's attire was made to convey delicacy, all this was designed to present an image of strength. It was no wonder that men should enjoy such levels of self-confidence. She felt the stirrings of something quite like it herself.

With long strides, she went down the stairs to the game. At the first turn of the stairs, she met Jane, whose own costume was a simple brown day dress.

'You must be the Dancing Master.' Jane fell into a curtsey.

Anne bowed. 'And Apothecary, and Sergeant – a man of multiple occupations. I have a busy morning ahead, it seems. And you, madam?'

'Miss Popham, the Teacher, of course.' Jane looked severe. 'I wonder you do not recognise me, sir, as it has been decreed we are to be wed by the end of the morning.'

The Game proved delightful, and the children were thrilled by it. In Anne's silent opinion, neither Elizabeth nor Harriot quite mastered their roles – vulgarity demanded some stretch of their talents and its achievement proved to be just out of their reach. Cassandra managed only a calm, quiet and sensible Governess, who rather put the real, complicated Miss Sharp to shame. But Grandmother Austen proved a highly credible Pie Woman, Jane a formidable Teacher. And Anne – who would have been wise to restrain herself – could not help but steal the whole show.

❧

'Oh, my! I am quite spent with laughter.' Grandmother Austen sank into the sofa with a plate of Cook's caraway biscuits. 'More of that, girls, and you will bring about my premature end.' She took a good draught of cordial. 'Well, I *say* premature, but at my age I cannot hope for many more summers. God will be calling me soon, there is no doubt on that score.'

'Oh, Mama!' chorused her daughters.

'Forgive me, my dears, you are quite right to chide me so.' She patted Cassandra. 'Of course, we must review all the amusements of our morning. Delightful indeed!' She chuckled, and then sank again. 'And yet, since my dear husband's passing, the shadow of death is never far from one's—'

'*Mama!*' Jane protested, and quickly addressed the whole room: 'Now what do you think, girls? Who played the best? I know whom I shall be choosing, but you children go first.'

Being so nicely raised, the girls were most particular to single out each player, and praise them all warmly. The privilege was then extended to their most senior member.

'Oh, simply no contest!' Grandmother Austen proclaimed. 'One in particular put the whole party to shame. What a rare talent we have here. Are we not lucky, Mrs Edward? Her improvisation, her mimicry – oh, *mimicry*, especially. If we did not know it already, we could tell it at once.'

'I am sorry,' Elizabeth looked confused. 'Of whom do we speak, and what is it we know?'

'Ah, perhaps you did not catch it at the time, dear. We had a very large table that evening – I do try to follow all that is said. At least my hearing has not yet deserted me – though the rest may be falling apart. My poor knees are particularly – I believe it was *then* that we heard her own *mother* was once an actress! Can you not see it now? Dear Miss Sharp, how very thrilling: it must run in your blood.'

A charge of shock ran through the drawing room. Anne's neck prickled and flushed. She saw Elizabeth, a sweetmeat poised at her lips, too frozen to nibble it; noticed Jane and Cassandra, out of their seats in an attempt to create some diversion.

'Dear, wondrous Sharpy.' Harriot gave a shake of her pretty little head. 'Did I not say so the moment we met? A *creature* of *secrets*. And how many *more* might you have up that sleeve?'

Anne felt herself teeter on the precipice of professional danger. For eighteen whole months, she had kept her true self under disguise: masqueraded as a prim and respectable mouse-like little creature; encouraged the idea of the Church in her background; pretended to the possession of great moral and physical strength. The Austen ladies had been here two weeks, and already Anne was revealed to be a consummate invalid begat from some showgirl. What would come next? It could only be her own legitimacy! Panic rose within her. Elizabeth would never put up with this . . .

And then, having done her best to propel Anne towards it, kind Grandmother Austen reached out and, with one small and deft movement, pulled her back from the edge.

Addressing Elizabeth, she went on: 'You astound me, my dear, with all you accomplish for the estate and your family. Your talent is quite unsurpassed. How is it you manage to employ the very best people for everything? I wish I had known a skill such as yours when I ran a large home.' She sighed. 'From butler – such good news about Johncock's boy, by the way – to scullery maid, all are quite *nonpareil*. But, of all your achievements, the finding of Miss Sharp must be one of the greatest. I do believe her the ideal companion and guide to dear Fanny and I might add – you are aware how I do like eavesdrop; 'tis one of my sins – all the neighbours are saying the same. Indeed, your good fortune in having Miss Sharp in your household is the talk of the county! I do hope you can persuade her to stay for the next girls in your pile. What an excellent choice she is proving to be. How clever you were to secure her.'

Elizabeth nibbled at her biscuit, gazed upon Anne with a look of proud ownership and happily preened.

CHAPTER XXXII

Having established that the Austen ladies could soon be sent away, and at some little notice, Anne's only desire was to seize as much time with them as might be permitted, and to cherish the moments that were allowed. She was also quite desperate to hear news of Jane's scheme, of which there had been no second mention.

Harriot Bridges had – mercifully – departed, taking with her the two little orphans. Miss Sharp was now expected to teach full daily lessons to Fanny and her cousin, Anna, and, in ordinary times, would have welcomed that opportunity. But this was proving to be an extraordinary summer. Though her body sat upright on the hard chair in the schoolroom, her mind was distracted.

'Very good, girls,' she said, though she had not heard a

word of it. 'So good, indeed, that you deserve a reward! The weather is so fine today that, much as I might prefer it, it would be wrong of me to keep you cooped up. Why do you not each choose a good romance and take it out into the park?'

The fact that Fanny no longer cared about *reading her goodness* – indeed, the wilder the story, now the greater her appetite – was perhaps Anne's greatest triumph to date. And, of course, her charges required no persuading. In an abundance of duty, Anne escorted them down to the garden door – making something of a performance out of issuing suggestions and directions, in the hope of attracting attention. It worked.

'Miss Sharp!' Jane appeared at the library door. 'I *thought* that was your voice I heard. You have deserted your schoolroom?' A small smile countered the idea that she might disapprove.

'The girls have taken their reading up to the Gothic seat. It is rare for Fanny to have at her disposal a friend of such similar sympathies . . .' This was so brazen, Anne's eyes cast down with the shame of it. 'So my day is now free.'

'And my own!' Jane's delight seemed unfeigned. 'My mother is up in the nursery, my sister out with our brother *again*.' She dropped her voice. 'Really, Anne, I do *wonder* at your master and mistress. They show not a jot of concern that my feelings might be a *little* hurt by these displays of such *particular* favouritism.'

'Oh, I am sorry—'

'My dear Anne.' Jane laughed. 'If we are to be *friends* it must be on the understanding that you refuse to believe nearly all that I say. I fear I am almost *entirely* unserious. And behold!' She opened the library door wider. 'This has been my own kingdom since breakfast! What do you suppose – would I *rather* sip cordial and discuss the health of the neighbours or . . . ? Quite so.'

Anne tried to hide her disappointment. 'Then let me leave you to your pleasures. I wish you a—'

'Oh, no! Anne, please do not leave me. If there is the possible prospect of another of our walks, then I should much prefer it.'

Anne held out her hands in a gesture of liberty.

'Then let us go.'

❧

'. . . where my dear parents *believed* us to be in the care of a refined Frenchwoman, Madame la Tournelle.' They were down on the riverbank comparing stories of their own educations. 'In reality, she was plain Sally Hackett, spoke no French whatsoever and hopped on a cork leg!'

They fell back on the grass. Once she had stopped laughing, Anne propped herself up on one elbow and studied Jane's face. 'I wonder that I did not see it at first, but your resemblance to your brother is quite remarkable. Not in looks so much, but the turn of your mind. If you do not mind me saying, there is a shared irreverence.'

Jane opened one eye and smiled. 'I have many brothers, Anne – too numerous to count – but I know at once
whom you mean. And yes – we are thought quite the
pair in our family. As are Cassandra and your master.
Though, I am sorry to say it, both boys eclipse us in *luck*.'
The smile dropped.

Anne lay back on the grass and hoped the mood would
repair. She was not forced to wait long.

'I do not wonder that my brother, Mr Henry, has taken
a liking to you, Anne. You provide exactly the sort of
company we both enjoy. And soon, we shall all three be
together. He will be down here in August!'

'Indeed?' Anne pretended the news to be more welcome than it actually was. The past week, she had not
spared a thought for him – well, perhaps one or two;
not an oppressive amount, she was sure of it. It was just
in odd, idle moments that he appeared as in a vision,
or his voice whispered into her ear. But certainly, Godmersham Park seemed more tranquil without him. His
absence was a delicious relief.

'Your pleasure seems less than I expected.' Jane sat up
and studied her, narrowing her eyes.

Anne protested the idea, but to no avail.

'Does his presence here create some awkwardness,
perhaps?'

The way Jane saw through her was really quite disconcerting. 'He has always been very friendly towards me,'
Anne managed to utter.

'*But . . . ?*'

'It is simply that – in my position – it is perhaps easier for *me* if people are not.'

'You speak of *gentlemen* in particular? I do hope, Miss Sharp, that we *ladies* are not causing you difficulties.'

'Not at all!' Anne exclaimed. 'Or at least, not as far as I know. This being my first time as a governess, I am still learning what is and is not correct.'

'Quite so.' Jane relaxed. 'And I can imagine my brother, with his great *bonhomie*, is a little prone to disregard such niceties.' She beamed with pride. 'He is simply incorrigible. Anyway, he is coming for the races and the Canterbury Ball. So we will be quite the crowd then.'

'I see.' Anne found this new intelligence equally unwelcome. The last time there was such a crowd, she was entirely cut out. Though it was not her place to ask such a thing, Anne could not resist it: 'And will Miss Bridges be of the party in August?'

Jane cocked her head to one side while she plundered this innocent question for its deeper meaning.

'Do not worry yourself on Miss Bridges' account, Anne, nor on my brother's. Each is more sensitive – and sensible – than they appear here, to you. Godmersham offers release to them – a holiday from harsh reality. Miss Harriot enjoys it because it is the only chance she gets to be out of the sight of her fond but *assiduous* mama; Mr Henry likes it because here he leaves behind himself all of life's cares. I assure you, they are both well aware what the world requires of them. But here, in this Palace of Pleasure, they are not quite their true selves, and who can be, I wonder, when transplanted into the Garden of Eden? *I* am certainly altered . . .'

Anne could see where Jane was leading, and had no intention of sharing any more of her personal make-up or history. Much as she would like to change the subject to scheming and plotting, she stood and said: 'Dinner approaches.' Brushed down her skirts and straightened her bonnet. 'I must see to the girls.'

They arrived back at the house at the same time as Cassandra. Anne watched on as the two sisters embraced. Such warmth between them! It was as if they had been separated for more than a year. Cassandra gave the briefest report of her outing with Edward – a visit with a bailiff; an inspection of a farm; a call upon a neighbour for a discussion of the building dispute around pigs and acorns. To Anne's ears, it all sounded remarkably dull – she was quite sure that, had Miss Jane endured such a day, then her account would have held some note of wickedness. But Cassandra laid claim to great pleasure in it all.

'Meanwhile, *we* have been idling, have we not, Miss Sharp?' Jane gaily began. 'While *you* have been engaged in the maintenance of peace and prosperity throughout the county, *we* have been lying on the riverbank and laughing like schoolgirls.'

'So yet another day in each other's company?' There was a sudden coolness in Cassandra's tone, Anne could not help but notice.

Jane put her arm through her sister's. 'We should have so much preferred it if you had been with us, would we not, Miss Sharp? Three is much more amusing. Let us aim to do something tomorrow – all ladies together. Come, Sister, we must change and prepare for another delightful dinner.' She led Cassandra to the stairs, calling over her shoulder: 'The morrow, Miss Sharp! Do try and be free for us.'

Alone in the hall, Anne watched them leave.

The weather was not so kind the next day, but the irresponsible governess chose to ignore it. Announcing a surprise holiday, she helped while her charges packed bread, cheese and water, and provided them with pencils and paper.

'So, girls, the whole day is yours to spend in the park and do as you please. Enjoy yourselves!'

'But what will you do, Miss Sharp?' Fanny asked as they walked down the stairs. 'We should not like to think of you being too lonely.'

A fine time to ask! Anne had been lonely for most of one year and a half, and – at last – she had a companion.

'Oh, I shall find something to occupy myself.' She opened the garden door and stepped back for them. 'Now, shoo, and enjoy!'

Jane emerged from the library. 'You have rid yourself of them sooner than I had hoped. Excellent! I fear it is just me *again*. Poor Anne, how bored you must be! My sister is much easier company, but today, she has been claimed by your *mistress*.' She shrugged. 'Truly, could they be any less subtle?'

'I am sorry indeed to lose the opportunity to spend time with Miss Austen,' said Anne. 'And even sorrier if it leaves you feeling slighted. Do you mind very much?'

'Not a jot!' Jane cried happily. 'But I fear we are in for a storm, so let us walk in the morning and stay close to the house. 'Twould be wrong to catch cold – my mother's nerves could not stand it.'

Having been told of the weather threat, Anne should then have run after the girls and demanded that they not go too far. But, as she gathered her hooded cloak for her better protection, her thoughts were all for herself, and her own pleasures.

'Does Godmersham feel like a home to you yet, Anne?'

A bright sun battled with building dark clouds as they turned round the rose garden.

'With each month that passes, I become more accustomed to being here, I suppose. Though that is not quite the same thing.' Anne was not sure how far she should go with this answer. 'The truth is I do not have the luxury of ever thinking myself *settled*. My place here is entirely in the gift of the family, until the moment I am no longer wanted or needed and so I must remain wary. To let it feel like a home would only make my inevitable departure even more painful.'

Jane sighed, and gave her arm a squeeze of compassion. 'Oh, insecurity! How wretched it is. I do believe it is the shape of the devil himself. 'Tis how he chooses to visit and test all blameless, good women. I am quite sure that *I* could be tempted to commit any sin, if it were to lead to a home of my own.'

Anne laughed. 'And *I* am quite sure you would not! You are too good a daughter, Jane, as well as sister and aunt.'

'Oh, Miss Sharp.' Jane grinned wickedly. 'You have no idea of the depths to which I am willing to sink.'

'I know what they would entail, and think too highly of you to believe you are capable.'

'Scandalous Anne!' gasped Jane. 'You have met with temptation! Tell me, did you *resist* or are you *fallen* already?'

'I resisted many an offer that would have brought me much material comfort.'

'*Riveting!* And I am too riveted to put one foot in front of the other.' She sat down on the bench with a thud. 'Miss Sharp, the Adventuress!'

'Hardly!' Anne took a seat. 'I have already said that I resisted. And have no regrets. I was not born with a yearning for the conventional life.'

'And yet, here we are.' Jane was gentle now. 'In the conventional garden of a conventional estate, lived in by the most conventional family ever created. And do my eyes deceive me, or are you not the very *model* of the traditional governess? You certainly act the part, and we are all taken in by you.'

Anne held up both hands in submission. 'I grant that is not without irony and nor is it the outcome I had expected. For men, there is so much *choice*, variety and opportunity. For we poor ladies, the unconventional path is not easy to find.' Then she became serious: 'It took me a while to get over the shock of finding myself here and in this position. But now that I have, I find I can excuse it – in my own mind at least. I have discovered I enjoy teaching, for example, and I could not have known that before.'

'And, clearly, you have a gift for it!' Jane cut in. 'Fanny has made such progress under your tutelage.'

'Thank you.' Anne smiled, and went on. 'And there is a pride – a certain dignity – in the fact that I am now able to earn my own living.' She omitted to mention her father's pittance – it rather undermined her own argument. 'I live under my own control, am not the prisoner of some *man* to use as he pleases . . . and that last was, once upon a time – in easier days – my greatest fear.'

'Quite so.' Jane was thoughtful. 'Although there is my brother, of course. Did you not earlier mention he has the power to evict you whenever he pleases . . . In which case, is *he* not the arbiter of your situation?' Seeing Anne's shoulders sink, she put out an arm to embrace her. 'I am sorry, dear Anne. Sometimes, I simply forget to command my own tongue. And these issues, of how we might live and what we can do and who will protect us – let us wrap the whole thing together and call it the Female Conundrum – has lately become a *preoccupation* of mine.

'I must shake it off – no point in worrying at it. The more time I waste upon it, the more firm my conclusion: there is no correct answer. We must rely on ourselves.'

'And I intend to,' declared Anne. She stood and held out her hand. 'Was that the first drop? Come, let us find a quiet corner of that Great House, and put it all out of our minds.'

CHAPTER XXXIII

Anne watched the rain course down the window pane and welcomed each splash. For it was thanks to the weather that Cassandra had come home so early, and that the three women were now enjoying the coze of the library, and delights of a card game. That Anne was discovering the pleasure of being with the sisters together, whom she was, even now, soundly beating at whist.

'On our walk earlier, we were discussing the notion of "home",' Jane was saying. 'Miss Sharp is like us, Sister: *of no fixed abode.*'

'Oh, dearest' – Cassandra picked up a card and gave Jane a look – 'I hope you have not been exaggerating our situation. Miss Sharp, I assure you, we can expect good enough lodgings in Bath over the winter, and are quite spoilt by our kind brothers. We have much to be thankful for.'

'And yet where is it we *belong*?' Jane demanded. 'Certainly not—'

'Miss Sharp,' Cassandra swept in, determined to prevent her sister's outpouring. 'You have transferred happily from London to Kent, I hope? My brother was telling me of the excellent work you have been doing down at the school.'

The conversation moved on to the joys and amusements of village life: Anne sharing her perspective as an incomer; the Austen ladies reminiscing of their old Steventon home.

'And there is always a wise, elderly woman. *She who knows everything*. Each place must have one; without, it is anarchy.' Jane put down a row of threes. 'You know, Sister, I think it is my ambition to be such a person. Let us find a small place in which we can grow *horribly* old – and *I* quite *terrifyingly* ugly – and you can do *good*, while I *rule* by my *wits*.'

Anne found such comfort in this society that at no point did she wonder: had the girls yet come in? Their existence had – temporarily – slipped her happy, diverted mind. And the fact that she was in charge of their welfare – that, indeed, she was employed to that very purpose – was entirely forgotten, until they appeared at the window, wet through to the skin.

Fanny started to cough soon after dinner. The first time, Anne could ignore it; the second brought the first twinge of unease. But after a third burst – long, uninterrupted, going on for some minutes – then Anne too was struck down, with a case of such guilt as to bring on the nausea. In an effort to forestall any later recrimination, she went to Elizabeth and informed her at once, while forbearing to mention her own culpability.

'Madam, may I suggest Fanny sleeps with me tonight? She is starting a chest, and I should very much like to keep her under my eye.'

'A *chest*?' Elizabeth was at once on high alert. 'How bad does she sound? Please, bring her to me at once!'

Anne waited in the hall, until Fanny emerged with her report.

'*We* believe you worry unduly, dear Anny. We think me *perfectly* well and it somewhat of a *shame* to sleep with my *governess* when I could be with my *cousin* – for *we* think I do not see enough of girls my own age.'

The next day, Fanny was worse. Anne tried again. 'May I have Fanny tonight, madam? I put my ear to her chest and did not like the sound of it. If she is infectious, 'twould be better that I caught it.' To half die of a fever might go some way to restore Anne's reputation.

'If she *is* as bad as you say, then she should sleep in with me. Miss Sharp, *I* am her *mother*.'

Soon, both daughter and mother were too ill to come down the stairs. The whole family was only mildly concerned; Anne was beside herself. Through her own selfish behaviour, she had brought risk upon both the beloved eldest daughter and fond mother of nine.

It made her feel even worse that, the longer their sickness went on, the more it brought her material benefit. Whole days were now spent in the company of the Austen ladies. Mornings were passed in the park with the children; afternoons, while Cassandra helped in the nursery, were spent in the drawing room, working. Without the natural inhabitants of Godmersham there to control it, their conversation ranged – wide, loose and unbuttoned. Anne's contentment would be entirely complete, but for her fears for the invalids.

'Ah, good,' Grandmother Austen cocked her head at the sounds out in the hall. 'There goes Dr Wilmot now.' She chuckled as she stitched. 'No doubt, the patients will be back down with us tomorrow.'

Anne looked up from her darning. 'Madam, you believe he can cure them so easily? Oh, I pray it is true!'

'My dear.' The lady looked at Anne over the rim of her spectacles. 'You seem quite overwrought.'

'Indeed, I am worried. Most certainly worried.' What mystified Anne was why this most health-conscious of women appeared so untroubled.

'But it is only a small summer chill! I have examined her myself and assure you her condition could not be milder.'

'I do not quite understand.' Anne put her work in her lap. 'Yesterday, you issued Fanny with an emetic! Surely, that suggests—'

Mrs Austen chuckled again, leaned towards Anne and

confided: 'The potion served no *medical* purpose. 'Twas more for the *mind*. Both mother and child seemed to require *reassurance* that their condition be treated as serious. I chose an emetic for its particular *unpleasantness* – a little reminder of the horrors of *true* illness.'

'But what of my mistress? If it is only a chill, then how could she have caught it? From what does *she* suffer?'

'Allow me to translate.' Jane put down her sewing, stood up and began a turn around the room. 'Mama, Miss Sharp blames herself. The poor thing is convinced it is through her own negligence that Fanny and Mrs Edward are now at death's door. She feels her position here is most precarious, sees the threat of dismissal around every corner and believes she will never be forgiven for this episode.'

Mrs Austen tutted in sympathy. Anne, who had confided none of this to anybody – who had kept her fears secret and pretended insouciance – sat quite dumbfounded.

'And, Miss Sharp, as you have noticed, my mother has a great preoccupation with all matters of health and *can*' – Jane held up a hand to staunch any protest – 'I only say *can*, be a little too dramatic on occasion. *However*, from her position as matriarch, she has become something of an *expert* in the business of *malingering*. We, her children, have been raised in the knowledge that such nonsense can never be tolerated. *Godmersham*, however, operates on *quite* different principles: the imagination is – just occasionally, mind – let off the *reins*. My mother spotted at once that *this* is one such example.'

'Then I shall take comfort in your diagnosis, madam,' Anne replied. 'Thank you, both, for putting my mind at rest. But I still do not quite understand why. Why should they pretend? It makes no sense to me. Fanny was so enjoying spending time with her cousin.'

'Fanny is, I believe, merely grasping the opportunity to have time alone with her mama.'

'Which leaves the Mistress . . .' Anne prompted.

Jane sat down beside Anne, and sighed. 'I fear it is that which I had earlier mentioned.'

'Now, Jane,' her mother cautioned.

'Really, Mother, we can talk freely to Miss Sharp, I assure you. She is our friend.' She turned back to Anne. 'Your mistress is tiring of us already. We can pray that, with a few days confined to her own chamber, Mrs Austen may find some new appetite for our *excellent* company, but we cannot rely on it. It is possible that our days here are numbered, and fewer than we might have reasonably hoped.'

This was worse than the thought of the illness! 'Oh, then I shall miss you all. Very much indeed.' Anne wanted to cry.

Mrs Austen held up a finger. 'Hear that! Dr Wilmot is leaving. It does not take long to examine two patients in excellent health. Tomorrow, the elder boys are being brought home from school and Miss Bridges returns. We shall be back then to normal and' – a pointed glance here towards Jane – 'on our best behaviour.

'Do not panic, Miss Sharp. We are becoming quite *wily* now that we are three single ladies. I fancy we can stretch it out yet. I am more concerned about you now, my dear. Precarious, you say . . . That poor head of yours . . . No home or family . . .

'Jane, we must endeavour to help. We cannot abandon Miss Sharp by the wayside.'

The resurrections of both Fanny and Elizabeth came exactly as predicted and all were pleased to see that their convalescence did not impair, in any meaningful way, their full enjoyment of the next picnic.

The entire family was assembled down on the river-bank, but this was not like previous outings. The atmosphere was altered by the older boys' presence, who had assumed what seemed to be considered their natural place at the centre of things. Anne thought them a sorry addition. Good money was being thrown at a school that seemed to make them less civilised rather than more, and they imported their rough manners back home.

Sports and games dominated. Jane, Cassandra and Harriot were amusing their nephews with a loud game of shuttlecock. Fanny and Anna splashed and shrieked in the river. The grandmother sat with her daughter-in-law and listed the virtues of every child there on parade. 'Young Edward is become most handsome and tall . . .

Quite *struck* by young Henry's intellect . . . *Marianne* is the beauty.' Anne listened with her back to them and smiled at this expert performance. Surely that should mollify Elizabeth, and increase her disposition towards her husband's relations.

But what was Anne doing to support her own case? Everyone was happily occupied in their own pursuits, yet she sat alone. While spectating was pleasant, she must not appear idle. So it was to her good fortune that little Charles split away from the games, crying and clutching his doll. Anne made a great show of running to his side.

'Charles, dearest.' She bent down and gathered him into her skirts. Of all the younger children, she was fondest of this one. Such a sweet, delicate nature. May he never know the benefits of a public-school education.

'They won't let me play and they're being horrid and beastly.'

'I am sorry to hear that. Here, come sit with me.' She bundled him into her lap, wrapped her arms round and rocked him. 'What are they saying to you?' Though she could guess at the problem.

Charles looked meaningfully down at the doll in his arms; fat tears formed between long, thick lashes.

'Ah, I see.' When Charles was in the nursery with his littlest sisters, then he felt secure and the doll – which he called 'his wife' – was less in evidence, much to his parents' relief. They were never quite at ease with the idea, and it always provoked a little, gentle teasing. Now he was unsettled by his big brothers' return, the 'wife' went with him everywhere and of course the big boys would be merciless. Only Anne thought the boy's habit enchanting.

Anne was stroking his silky curls and making comforting murmurs, when Jane broke away from her game and sat down beside them.

'Oof. Charles – your brothers! Were they always such brutes? I cannot play with them one second longer. But what is the matter, my sweet one?' She caught sight of the doll. 'And who is this? Your *wife*, indeed! Then may I congratulate you on your choice, and her astonishing beauty. I wish you both every happiness.'

And in that moment, Anne loved her completely.

'But, oh! Mrs Charles, do my eyes deceive me or are you not very happy?'

Anne lifted the doll to her ear. 'Why, she is feeling too hot! I believe this strong sun must disagree with her. Charles, what think you, shall we take her to bathe?'

Down at the river's edge, they began bathing the doll, all the time chattering their nonsense. Charles was delighted and the two women were enjoying themselves hugely. What a pretty spectacle they made, the three all together – sunbeams on the water; a breeze in the bulrush – colluding in their own little fantasy. Who could look upon such a scene and not be touched by it?

'Miss Sharp?' Elizabeth Austen had risen and was

sedately transporting herself in the river's direction. 'May I have a word?'

Anne wrenched herself out of her make-believe and jumped to attention. The Mistress led her uphill, away from the river and into the shade of a poplar. 'I may have been *absent*, but I am *always* on duty. Even while I was *sickening*, my thoughts were *all* for the *comfort* and good *management* of my family and staff. And it occurred to me as I *lay* there – too *ill* to raise my poor head from the pillow – that you are now owed some holiday.'

So it was she who was to be sent away! Anne could not bear it. 'Oh, madam. Please. This is a particularly busy summer; I should hate not to be here to help you with all the children. I am more than happy to waive it for this year.'

'No, no!' Elizabeth had the saintly air of a model employer. 'I will not hear of it. We do not have a *monopoly* on you, and I must be mindful of that. Shall we say three weeks? And that you may leave as soon as is possible?'

Three weeks? Then she might never see her newest and dearest friends ever again! They would be banished by the time she returned. She thought quickly.

'In fact, madam, three weeks would present something of a problem as I cannot find accommodation for that length of time. The people I stay with—'

'Could they manage a fortnight?' Mrs Austen had never been quite so amenable.

'One week,' Anne replied. 'Six nights in fact. I believe that would be the maximum.'

Elizabeth let out a sigh that was perhaps meant to sound sorrowful, though Anne only heard irritation. 'Then I must agree to it. But if you find you *can* stay away a bit longer, do not *hesitate*—'

'Thank you, madam.' Anne dropped a quick curtsey and ran back to the game.

'What was that?' Jane mouthed over Charles's head.

But before she could explain, Elizabeth was calling again.

'Ah,' Jane whispered. 'It seems it is now my turn. We are being picked off one by one, as if by an archer. I wonder – will it be only a flesh wound, or am I to be horribly slain?'

❧

There was a large dinner downstairs that evening and Anne was not included. She did not mind in the least. The long list of guests – all landed neighbours – was not enticing, and she had been lately so spoiled for good entertainment that she rather welcomed the break. Her plan was to catch up on her reading, yet she found she could not easily concentrate. Instead, she sat in the schoolroom, evening sun on her hair: drugged with the pleasure of the past, happy weeks.

'Anne! Are you *dozing*?' Jane stood in the doorway.

'Oh!' Anne started. 'I am not quite sure where I was. I feel rather dazed.'

'If 'tis the arms of Morpheus you seek, you would have been better off down in the library. A few minutes of our *conversation*, and my dear mother was drifting away happily.'

'Your dinner was not entertaining then?'

Jane pulled a face. 'They came; they sat; they went – and other than that, there is not much to report. I should have had more fun up here, with a tray in the schoolroom and your superior company.' Anne's heart gave a quick flip of joy. 'Especially now, as it appears we are to be split up. Had you heard? I am come to discuss it.'

'I am told I am to go to London and, in truth, I do have important business to attend to, so it is no inconvenience. But only for six nights – on that, I was most emphatic.'

'And my mother is to take Anna home – Elizabeth feels it *very* important that both now meet the baby at the earliest opportunity. Then, the moment you return here, I am to be sent off to the Bridgeses at Goodnestone, while Cassandra stays here. And once they tire of me there, then I return and my sister replaces me. It is a most *masterful* plan, when one studies it hard.'

'But this is a great disappointment!' Anne cried. 'What can explain the thinking behind it? Jane, is it my fault, do you suppose? We have become too friendly and—' Anne bit her lip. From her reading, she had learned it was wrong to attract any gentleman. But what of sisters and mothers – did they, too, fall under the same protocol? She had not seen it written.

Jane took the chair across the table. 'My sister-in-law prefers spinsters to come at her as single spies, and not in whole battalions.'

'And yet you are no trouble at all!' Anne insisted. 'You play with the children and stay close to your mother and are kind – so kind! – to the servants—'

'My *sister* is no trouble, that is true. So good with the sick and the infant; a kind tongue that never gets in the way. I believe they would happily give her a perma-nent home here, but then what would they do with my mother and me? It is hard not to think that we two are the problem.'

They sat in silence, each mindful of their own, particu-lar frustrations, before Jane broke the bad spell.

'We have one day left to us, which we should enjoy to the utmost. And, of course, we *shall* meet again, when you get back. All is not lost. And remember: I still have great hopes of my *scheme*.'

CHAPTER XXXIV

'So this is it, you say?' Anne stood, her back pressed to the railings that edged the gardens of Chester Square. Though still before noon, the London streets shimmered with thick August heat.

'Number Six,' Agnes replied. 'And very pleasant, I'm sure,' she added with a sniff.

'And you have seen him go in there?' Anne turned a stern face towards her. 'You do promise me? This *is* his, you are sure of it?'

'I most certainly am.' Agnes was all indignation at this absence of faith in her labours. 'I've worked hard, I have. *Nurse* says I'm *dogged*. "Nurse," she says, "you're *dogged*, that's what you are. And I *hope* you're appreciated."'

Anne turned back to the house, and studied it. Tallish – four floors – and kept in excellent order, it was very pleasant indeed. Her father always did like the finer things. How very contented he must be.

'Now tell me exactly: how did you discover he lives here? It seems quite the stroke of good chance that you should come across it.'

'Well.' Agnes grinned. 'I knew that, sooner or later, he'd go and visit that Jameson – birds of a feather, those two. So I loitered!'

'Agnes! You *loitered*? In *Mount Street*? Oh, dearest: really . . .'

'No need to come all hoity-toity with me,' Agnes shot back. '*Someone* had to do something, so – yes – I loitered, what of it? Then I followed him home.' She began to relish her own narrative. 'And – oh! – my heart, it wasn't half thumping. I said to Nurse after, I said—'

'But dearest,' Anne interrupted, 'he may just have been visiting?'

'Oh no.' Agnes was now in full triumph. 'This was weeks ago. I come here a lot, you know. Stand back here in the shadows and watch him. Seems he lives on his own. No wife in residence. I can't wait to see his face when—' As happened so often, Agnes lost her own drift then, turned and fingered Anne's frock. 'Don't know why you had to come out looking so drab, Anny. Suppose he comes out? He *did* like it when you were dressed up all nice.'

'You'll see, dearest.' Anne stared at the shine on the imposing front door and mustered her courage. 'Come on.' She grabbed Agnes's arm, while setting her chin up in defiance. 'No need to say anything. I will deal with this.'

She waited for a carriage to pass and the cloud of dust raised by the horses to settle, then dragged a protesting Agnes across the cobbles, down the steps to the basement and rang at the bell.

'Have you quite lost your mind, madam?' Agnes demanded in her deafening whisper. 'We can't do—'

The door opened, and there stood a uniformed maid.

'Good day to you.' Anne, still the consummate actress, adopted the voice and demeanour of one of the honest-but-poor. 'Begging your pardon, miss, but is the housekeeper available? My cousin here' – she indicated Agnes – 'is such a wonder with a needle and keen to work, miss.'

The household, it turned out, was desperate. They were admitted at once, begged to take a seat at the scrubbed kitchen table and offered a beer.

'If your work is good enough, then you might just save my bacon.' As Anne had hoped, the housekeeper was of the voluble sort. 'Honestly, this family – the mending required!' She shook her head fondly. 'That busy enjoying themselves, they just forget to take care. So you do a lot of work then, do you?'

This was directed to Agnes who, for once, sat silent and stupefied.

'Don't mind her, miss,' Anne cut in. 'She doesn't say

much. I can see you run an excellent kitchen.' Anne studied the gleaming array of copper pans on the wall.

'No option, with my master! He's a one for his food and drink, is Sir St John.'

Sir St John? Not plain Johnny Sharp? Anne gave a twitch and then collected herself. 'Got the family at home now, have you?'

'They go down to the estate in August – that all comes from her ladyship's side. Between you and me, it's *her* with the money.'

But of course, thought Anne. Does not everything come down to the money? She gulped. The taste in her mouth was bitter as snail's milk.

'The Master's still here, though,' the housekeeper chatted on. 'But don't worry about him. Spends all day at his *club*, of course. Gents and their clubs, eh?' They shared a knowing chuckle. 'Honestly, can't fathom why he stays up here. Doesn't *work* for a living, that much is certain. And, I always fancy, the light goes out of him with the children away. Never known such a fond father. "It's we four, Mrs Brown," he says to me, regular. "We four against the whole world." Bless him. We won't see him now until well past his dinner. I could show you the place if you want?'

Though Anne's insides were churning, her exterior was quite natural as she rose and was led from the room. It seemed her skills as an actress were better than even she had believed.

They moved down the corridor, passed the house-keeper's quarters, to the door of a small room where a pale girl sat sewing. 'This here is Jen,' said the house-keeper. 'She does most of the sewing, but she'll wel-come the help. So much to do at this time of year, what with getting the Mistress's wardrobe all ready for winter.'

Anne walked in and fingered the garment on which Jen was working. 'I don't envy you this, miss. Such a thick green velvet. See that, dearest?' Anne held it up, so that Agnes could not fail to recognize it. 'A cape, is it? Tsk, all those folds. Still, very lovely, I'm sure. Must be a favourite – one of those that comes out year after year? Well, I wish you good luck with it.'

After the gloaming of the basement, the glare of the ground floor was quite overwhelming. Bright August sun flooded through the long, generous windows and bathed the vast space with a celestial light. When Anne's vision recovered, she was facing the fireplace.

'Now, that's what I call a fine portrait,' she murmured as she approached it. 'Who is this pretty young lady, then?'

'Charming, is it not?' The housekeeper beamed proudly. 'That'll be the Mistress, the year they were mar-ried. Now when would that be? Seventeen hundred and eighty or thereabouts. Oil, mind you – not one of those sketches. I always take care to clean that one myself. Don't ask me why, but it just brings such pleasure.'

'By that painter, oh, what is his name? Famous, I'm sure, though I'd forget my own leg if it wasn't screwed on—'

'Reynolds?' Mrs Brown put in. 'Sir Joshua. Yes, that's the one. And this' – they processed to the second mantel – 'is by Lawrence. That's our Miss Jemima. Now, is she not a beauty? Apple of the Master's eye, of course. Not spoiled though, mind you. Unlike her brother . . .'

'Oh, so there is a son,' said Anne. 'I did wonder. They do like a boy, do those gentlemen.'

'And this one is doted on. Took them a while, mind you. We weren't blessed with him until . . . now, when was he born . . . do you find the years just run away with you? . . . It must have been the summer of '92. Oh! Is your cousin quite well?'

Agnes was white of face and shaking all over. All at once, common agreement was reached that fresh air was needed, and the housekeeper had to get on. Anne issued thanks and farewells – promised that Agnes would return soon to pick up those linens – and they departed.

While Anne longed to collapse on the steps, she suspected the servants of watching and so somehow gathered the strength to take Agnes's arm and hold herself upright. From somewhere, there came to her a distant echo of 'Flagpole!' She sighed. Of all the counsel her mother might have supplied – the warnings that should have been issued, the preparations laid down – Margaret

Sharp had chosen to concentrate on the one issue of posture.

Anne shook her head in despair and, pulling Agnes along with her, strode off into the morning.

∾

'You may have this, if you would like it?' Anne was clearing through the possessions she had left piled up in Agnes's room. They had been lovingly preserved for the moment when her life turned back to normal. Now, she wanted rid of all of them. 'I certainly do not.'

'The painting?' Agnes gasped.

'It is not a painting, my dear.' She studied the Reynolds. It must have been done at the same time as the oil – paid for, no doubt, with his wife's money. How very sensible of her father to kill two birds with one commission. Anne did hope he'd negotiated a fair price. 'Full portraits were reserved for the other family, remember? 'Tis only a sketch, and means nothing to me.'

Four days had passed since that morning in Chester Square, when truth – hard, cruel facts – had so viciously assaulted her. Though the wounds were still fresh and, no doubt, would scar her forever, Anne found, somewhat to her surprise, that she was not actually crippled. There was still life in and ahead of her, and she intended to live it.

'I shall always treasure it.' Agnes started crying again.

Anne sighed, got up from her knees and proceeded to issue comfort. 'There, there. Let it out, dear, and then let us get on.' Her own head was clear, her eyes perfectly dry now and she was finding this grief-by-proxy a cause of some irritation.

Blowing her nose on her apron, Agnes looked up. 'So?' Her eyes searched Anne's face. 'When is it to be then? I'm not sure I can take the not knowing much longer. When will you confront him?'

'Confront?' Anne sighed, closed her eyes and took the seat by the wall. 'Oh, Agnes.' She twisted her hands in her lap now as she garnered her patience. 'Do you not see? I can never confront him!' She leaned over and asked, with some urgency: 'What powers do I have?'

'You're his precious girl, Anny! Remember, he *doted*.'

'Dearest, I am the natural – that is to say *illegitimate* – child of a man with unnatural habits. He owes me nothing.' Anne's voice cracked. 'I have no rights at all! Indeed . . .' She let her head loll back against the chair and rubbed at her neck. 'Indeed, it occurs to me now, my allowance is, in fact, generous. He was not obliged to provide me with a farthing. Suppose I were to create difficulty? He may well withdraw it, and then where would we be?'

'So you're telling me', Agnes wailed, 'that, just like that, *he gets off scot-free*?'

'Oh, that happened years ago,' Anne replied bitterly. 'When my foolish mama agreed to live as his mistress.'

'Anny! Don't you *dare* use that language about your dear mother!'

'Even though it is the truth?' Anne cried back. 'I shall not carry on with the pretence you all concocted around me!'

'We did no such thing!' Agnes was up now, and shouting. 'I thought they were respectable! They never let on to *me*!'

Anne stood then, too. 'And why did you never suspect him? He did not live with us, he vanished for weeks upon end.'

Agnes slumped again. 'It just never occurred to me.' The crying returned. 'He had such a way with him, you see. So convincing. That *charm*.'

'Ah, yes.' Anne bit her lip. 'The charm of the devil.'

'Anny?' Nurse Mercer put her head round the door, then. 'Anny! Visitor for you. *And he's a gentleman!*' She leaned in further. 'A Mr Austen, *or so he claims.*'

A Mr Austen? How much more drama was to be inflicted upon her weary form? Anne took a deep breath, wiped at her face and pretended to cool. 'If that is who he claims to be, I do not think it our right to doubt him.'

But *which* Mr Austen? And why would he call on the *governess*? All distress fled the room, as both nurses attacked dress, face and hair to make Anne look her best. Should they change her into the aqua? The way it brought out her eyes . . . But then that lilac *was* fetching . . .

Anne shrugged them off with impatience. 'I am quite

certain his purpose can be nothing more than the relaying of some household business, so my dress does not matter.' Besides which, she had always thought this lilac particularly flattering.

Before making her entrance, Anne stood in the hall and peered into the parlour. *Henry!* Startled, she pulled back again and flattened her back to the wall. Her heart thumped at her bosom. What on earth could he want with her? Was it truly him? It could not be him. She craned her neck and peered in again. It was Henry, most certainly – but quite out of context.

He appeared entirely at home there upon the threadbare chair amidst the dust of the old schoolroom. He did not stare at the curtains, half off their pole, or the wall paint that flaked as one watched it, like snow. He was blithe in the presence of the rubble of five long-lost childhoods. Anne studied him, and could not help but admire his great gift for feeling at ease: oh, Henry, she thought, with a fond shake of her head, you make it so hard to hate you for long.

❧

Giving no hint as to his business, instead Henry gave every impression of having come only to converse with the nurses. Nothing, it seemed, could be more delightful! And, having had such a treasure delivered into their clutches, the nurses were unlikely to ever let him go.

He could be imprisoned here for life, if Anne did not do something. She stood and insisted they should all take some fresh air; gathered bonnet and parasol. And in some short order, the curious party of four – two behind two at a respectable distance – were on their way to Hyde Park.

Society had fled from the heat of the capital; the paths were quite clear. Horses idled in the shade, muzzled in their nose bags: all rides were abandoned. The green swathe was parched to pale brown; the bright flowers in the beds wilted and drooped. Beneath every branch was a nurse close to fainting, rocking a small charge to sleep.

'Perhaps this is a foolish idea?' Henry turned towards her, concerned. 'I should not like this torpor to cause you a headache.'

Still no explanation of why he had come! 'Sir, I am not an invalid, and the heat does not affect me.' Anne had no intention of once more sitting enclosed with her chaperones. 'I enjoy being in Town when it is so empty. I always summered here as a child, and have happy memories.' She smiled. 'I presume your own views are quite the opposite, knowing your great fondness for the company of people in general. No doubt you have the sense there is some splendid party going on elsewhere, to which you have not been invited.'

'Then I fear I must correct you, madam. Without the great crowds, one sees more of the *place*, and its beauties. Though my brothers and sisters will mock me for it, I appreciate wonders man-made as well as God-given. The city is a marvel to my inexpert eye. 'Tis the *nursery of the arts*, after all.' He paused, as if to gather new strength. 'Besides which, I am not exactly alone, for—'

Anne, a little nervous of where this sentence was leading, cut him off with a little, hard laugh and an inarticulate: 'Ah!'

'I am now with a particular person, whose company—'

'Mr Austen, perhaps you were right: it is most frightfully hot. Should we turn, do you think?'

At that moment, a bench beneath a horse chestnut became suddenly vacant and – all courtly concern – Henry steered the nurses towards it.

'There was a stroke of luck. Ladies, I insist you rest here until the sun starts to drop a little. I assure you, we will not go far from your sight.'

Anne anxiously studied the sky. The nurses would be happy to sit there for hours, and she fated to walk around in tight circles.

'So I gather you have – as I predicted – made firm friends with my sister,' said Henry. 'We conduct a regular correspondence, she and I, and are quite open with each other on any number of subjects. For example, she was most amused to hear herself selected as your favourite Austen.'

'Sir!' Anne stopped, flushed with outrage. 'I am mortified! I had no idea that you would – Then you put me at great disadvantage – She cannot think I was serious?'

'Miss Sharp, please make for the shade! And do not distress yourself. Even the slightest acquaintance with *that* Miss Austen should tell you that she too finds the humour in everything.'

'Then you are both equally vexing.' She turned away and set her eyes to the pond. 'I resent—'

'Oh, dear Miss Sharp,' Henry chuckled, 'what a fine gift you have for finding resentment! Truly, I admire you for it. No doubt there must be some enjoyment to be had in taking great umbrage. I am a sad creature indeed for having been denied that particular pleasure all my long life.'

'Perhaps, sir,' Anne replied with some tartness, 'the world has not given you reason for it.'

'You are no doubt correct, madam. It seems that instead *I* have been cast as its cause, and must spend my days in the act of apology. And so, *once again*, Miss Sharp, may I beg your forgiveness? Now, that behind us, I long to be told: have you decided? Which of us is your favourite?'

'Sir, I find the question absurd and your insistence on continuing with nonsense is becoming upsetting. I—' She turned, and saw he was now leaning against a tree, studying her and smiling.

'You—?' His long legs were crossed at the ankles; those britches were straining again. 'Do go on, Miss Sharp.' He crinkled.

And suddenly, Anne was tired of it. Tired of minding the social difference between them. Of expressing her resentment and receiving his apologies. Of acting the servant when a fair world would deem them as equals. Of all the time protecting the small scraps of dignity afforded by her position, when really she could not care less.

'I have decided the matter. The winner is your sister, and by some considerable distance.'

He guffawed. 'Then this is an outrage!'

'Is it, sir?' She spun the handle of her parasol between her long fingers. 'And do you claim cause for *resentment*? If so, pray do *forgive* me.'

'*Touché*, madam!'

Together they strolled again, and – at last free of restraint – began a quite natural dialogue. The hot weather came up, as did the war; books were discussed and gossip was shared. It was a conversation between equals and, now emboldened, Anne asked him: 'Sir, am I to be told the purpose of this meeting today? Your call *cannot* be purely social.'

'Can it not?' Henry seemed genuinely surprised by this news. 'I do not see why . . . But, if you *insist* on it, let me give you a good explanation. The first is that I am told by my sister you are due back to Kent on the twelfth of August. And as I am due to go on the fourteenth, it occurred that it might spare you the cost and unpleasantness of the stage to share my coach?'

Anne imagined the faces of the household if she were to alight in such company from such a vehicle, the questions that would then arise. The idea was simply impossible. 'That is a very kind offer, sir, but I fear I cannot accept it. I must leave on the day arranged, and my fare is already paid.'

'And I cannot persuade you? My stay at Godmersham will be brief and quite hectic, so we shall not be much in each other's company . . .'

'No, sir. Thank you, but no.'

He did not try to press it or take over arrangements. Was it possible he was learning a new respect for her – even some modicum of self-control?

'And the second matter: my sister has had some success with the scheme she has been cooking.'

'Has she indeed? I wonder that Miss Austen did not tell me herself, as I received a kind letter only yesterday. Am I to be made party to the details, as I gather it concerns me in some way?'

'Sadly not,' he said cheerfully. 'It is all a great secret, and I should not have spilled it. But there it is: when secrets *do* have some particular interest, it seems somehow *unjust* and *ungenerous* to keep them from others. I shall say no more for the moment, other than that I most thoroughly approve it.'

Though Anne protested at this, he was implacable. 'My sister is a politician of particular skill – they could do with her now in the Houses of Parliament – and she has, very sensibly, convinced your mistress that *she* will be the one to tell you herself.

'But, Miss Sharp: I promise it will prove to be to your benefit. And, indeed, to my own. For, when all goes to plan, I too am to be included in some small part of it – if you should not *resent* me too much.'

On their homeward return, Anne's step was light; her heart held itself high in her breast. She caught herself laughing at all Henry said, even though it was not that amusing, and issued a stern reprimand to herself: What a very perverse creature you are, madam.

For when Henry interfered in her plans, she was prey to such rage and resentment. Yet when Jane did the same – making schemes and keeping them secret – she found the very idea of it simply delicious.

ACT FOUR

CHAPTER XXXV

Anne screamed. The freezing water lapped at her neck. Would it now rise up and take her? She looked down as if to gauge its intentions, saw only impenetrable blackness. A wave came and rendered her out of her depth. Screaming again, she flailed at the steps, but her fingers could not grasp them. Was she to die here? Surely, she could not survive this. Then so be it. Her days ended with this one. Beneath a blue Sussex sky, Anne raised her eyes to the neat, puffball clouds and surrendered.

Fully expectant that the next voice to come through to her would be that of her Maker, she was taken aback to hear the words 'You all right in there, madam?' in a deep, coastal brogue. The dipper's interest in her welfare sounded purely professional and remarkably mild.

Anne began to reply that she certainly was not. That

the distance between herself and 'all right' was, in fact, considerable. That, indeed, she had been plunged into a danger most mortal. Before it dawned that all feeing had returned to her body. She was quite whole again. Strangely, the water was suddenly warmer and the experience of being in it not entirely unpleasant.

'Always like that the first time,' the dipper went on. 'No one knows quite what to expect. Let's get you back in the machine now. I reckon that's enough for today.'

Anne removed the sopping muslin shift, rubbed herself down, was dressed again and returned to the sands as Mrs Austen emerged from her own hut.

'Miss Sharp, what luck that you should begin your bathing *career* with such perfect conditions! Did you not find it *delightful*? You look better already; I am convinced of it.'

'Thank you, madam.' Anne gazed back at the sea with a new sense of wonder. 'It is the most extraordinary thing! I can feel the heat of my own blood beneath my skin.' She looked down at her hands – bleached shell-like nails in rosy-pink fingers – and could not quite recognise them.

They began walking together, past the fish merchants and their nets spread out on the beach, in the direction of the new Colonnade.

'Some weeks of this – mind, we expect you to dip as often as possible. Bad weather is *not* an acceptable excuse – and, Miss Sharp, you will return to us *transformed*.'

'Madam, are you quite sure? It is the most remarkably kind offer, and I am, of course, grateful. But to be away from Godmersham for so long; to neglect Fanny's lessons and not be on hand to help with the children . . . Well, I cannot help but feel guilty to put you out to such an extent.'

They reached South Street, upon which the non-bathers were beginning their morning promenade.

'Nonsense, Miss Sharp. I am quite convinced of the plan. No doubt more than a month here does *err* on the side of the *generous*' – Elizabeth gave a pleased little smile – 'but, please be reassured, we see it as an *investment*. Fanny is so *fond* of you, and has so come on under your tutelage. I feel it *behoves* me to do all I can to enable you to continue with us for as *long* as is possible.'

'Then I thank—'

'And, as it happens, the arrangement has proved to be a most *economical* one, with the family here anyway, and the cottage already rented. Four bedrooms for four ladies seemed more than *ample*. It seems to us *sensible* to fit in one more. And though, as a *party*, it might seem a trifle *eccentric*, I hope you will be happy enough.

'Worthing is no Brighton, as you can see. 'Tis a quiet little place, as yet. You might not find it *lively*, but then it is for the best that there is not much to *distract* you. Your whole mind can be centred on your complete *cure*.'

Edward, Elizabeth and Fanny stayed in Worthing for just a few days. The remaining ladies – the Austen grandmother and sisters, and their close friend Martha Lloyd – were dug in through the autumn and into the new year. That Anne should join them had been Jane's private scheme, and as Jane's private scheme, then it was doomed to sure failure. To demand such inconvenience of the Godmersham family: it was simply too much! But, somehow, Jane had transformed it into Elizabeth's own brainchild. And, thus blessed with an extra weight of importance, it had come together with ease.

At first, Anne could scarcely believe her own luck. To enjoy long weeks of *freedom*, among *friends*, at the *seaside*? Surely, this could not be real? There must be some trick at play. No – neither Jane nor her mother would condone such a thing. More likely – yes, this would be it – there would be some domestic emergency and she would be summoned to sort it. In fact, that was inevitable. Much as her mistress might claim to enjoy the idea of showing compassion to a governess, the reality was bound to have limited appeal. And so, armed against all disappointment, she determined to enjoy herself while she was here and to always appear grateful – though that last came easily.

Certainly, the idea to bring Anne right here was, as Henry would say, 'Capital!' The wonders of the sea rendered Anne awestruck. Her only knowledge of it came from books of geography and gallery walls, and she could now say with some certainty that no artist or wordsmith who ever lived had quite done it justice. The way it played with colour and light, the shadows skipping on its surface: it was a perpetual drama of epic scale that could never be captured by one, small static image.

When she was not in the water – how she did love her dips now – Anne simply stared at it. For as many hours in the day as her companions and the weather allowed her, she stood alone, above the beach. Her pale, care-worn, governess face caressed by the breezes; her sore eyes bathed with celestial light; pure air cleansing her mind of all troubles: she felt the first twitching of life, as sensation began its return to that afflicted heart.

Every aspect of these seaside days was a pleasure, but Anne's favourite moment by far was that of their ending. And that evening, as all evenings, with dinner accomplished, she was out again, watching. The ladies chose not to come with her, preferring to spend that time in the parlour together. But they never minded her leaving them; in fact, they encouraged it.

'Are you off out, my dear?' Mrs Austen studied her over her spectacles. 'Do not stay in on our account. Go, Miss Sharp, while opportunity favours you.'

But the temperature was dropping now – and she could not help but worry that these solitary trips might appear anti-social – and so Anne stayed just long enough to witness the sun begin its reluctant descent, and then turned away. Behind her, the sea danced alone against a rose-coloured sky. Ahead, was Stanford's Cottage and the dear Austen ladies. She crossed the fields, took the twitten on to Warwick Street, saw the candlelight glow through the bow-window; crossed the courtyard, ducked under the walnut tree and let herself in.

Hanging up her bonnet in the hall, Anne heard Jane's voice. From the rhythm of it, and the absence of any conversation, she deduced that some novel was being read aloud. Was that why they preferred to stay in of an evening? Yet Anne enjoyed novels! What had she been missing?

As they had not heard her arrival, Anne, somewhat guiltily, listened in at the door, heard the names Elinor and Marianne, and tried to place them. Being so well read herself, she did enjoy a literary puzzle. It appeared the characters were sisters, their personalities quite opposite. But what could the book be? Anne wondered that she did not already know it.

She heard: ' "*What am I to imagine, Willoughby, by your behaviour last night?*" ' And: ' "*It would grieve me indeed to be obliged to think ill of you.*" ' There was a quality to the style, an intelligence at work. So this was not some cheap thing that Anne might have avoided. The intrigue was too much to bear. Quietly, she slipped into the parlour and took her seat slightly apart from the circle, hoping to go there unnoticed. But Jane paused, and looked up. Anne saw glances of enquiry shoot across the room – raised eyebrows, slight nodding – before Jane tilted her head in a gesture of acceptance, and then carried on.

'. . . *though it did not give much sweetness to the manners of one sister, was of advantage in governing those of the other.* And there' – Jane put down the pages – 'I think that is enough for one evening.'

Mrs Austen took her eyes away from the fireside and looked around with a look of amusement. 'And what think you of that, Miss Sharp? Have you come to a judgement?'

'I enjoyed it enormously!' Anne exclaimed with great fervour. 'There is a fluidity to the prose . . . a depth to the characters . . . an amusing, ironic tone . . . And yet, try as I may, I simply cannot place it. Please, put me out of my misery, for I should like to hear more of this work and its author.'

'The work is called *Elinor and Marianne*.' Jane gave her nervy giggle.

'And the author' – Mrs Austen gestured towards her youngest daughter – 'is sitting there by the fireside.'

'Miss Sharp! You appear shocked.' Cassandra looked up from her embroidery and smiled.

'I hope not by the *content*.' Jane, blushing, looked through the pages. 'My Willoughby is not too much of a scoundrel for your tender mind?'

Anne was simply too mortified to form a coherent sentence. 'Miss Jane – I cannot begin – I do not know – Your talent – I fear I now owe you the most abject apology—'

'You apologise for my *talent*?' laughed Jane. 'Please, do

not trouble yourself. 'Tis *I* who must apologise for the want of it and, believe me, do so often enough.'

'For the way – the over-bearing manner – when I took the play over – when you are – I simply had no idea that – Oh!' Anne buried her face in her hands. 'I look back and see my own behaviour as quite monstrous!'

'Anne, please!' Jane crossed the room and put an arm around Anne's shoulder. 'You were quite right to do so. *Virtue Rewarded* was a delightful production and we all enjoyed it very much.'

Anne struggled on: 'You have been so kind to me and I – in my ignorance – Oh! Arrogance, rank arrogance—'

Jane sat then on the arm rest. 'Stop now, I beg. If you think we are but being *kind*, please let me reassure: you are here for our *pleasure*. We enjoy your company. And I feel greatly relieved that my squalid *secret* is now out. I fear I had let it become too much of a *barrier* in what I hope is our friendship.'

Anne could not shed her sense of embarrassment. 'To think I assumed the position of superior talent, when you—'

'Anne, enough! You were quite right in your thinking. Let us settle the matter by saying *I* am the prose writer, and *you* are the dramatist. Believe me, the literary world is so large as to give us both *equal* stature – that is, they will take no notice of either: turn their smart heads away and applaud all the *men*.'

❦

Once Anne had recovered from her own shame, it turned out the disclosure had the effect of deepening the friendship between them. Anne learned that Jane had produced two other such novels and, once she was made privy to their contents, they enjoyed long conversations on the manner and tricks of their composition.

Jane was still bruised by her first, unsuccessful encounter with the professional world. A rogue publisher, who had paid ten splendid pounds for her *Susan*, chose simply never to print it. So discouraged, she was considering whether to lay down her pen.

They were crossing the fields behind the house, in the direction of the Downs, when Jane confessed this humiliation.

'Unthinkable cruelty,' Anne gasped. 'How I detest these acts of violence against us! Will we ever be free from the tyranny of the caprice of men?'

Jane stopped, and looked somewhat surprised. ''Tis not *all* men, dear Anne. Just this one Mr Crosby.'

'Oh, but of course.' Anne reined in her display of emotion and examined her own violent response. This must be the legacy of her own father's behaviour. So, still he controlled her . . . She must throw it off, at once. She was no longer his creature. She would accept no legacy from him of any description! Other than those thirty-five pounds . . .

But there was now a deep chill in that October air, and they could not stand still for long. Now walking again,

Jane continued the thought. 'Most gentlemen are *good* people, in my experience. Often too proud, perhaps . . . flawed by their upbringings . . . too conscious of that *superiority* the world seems to ascribe to them . . .' They achieved the brow of the hill and turned to look back at the light on the sea. 'Not as well-schooled as us, in the Great Arts of *Patience*!'

'Ah, patience!' sighed Anne. 'Sadly, I was not born with that virtue – though, lately, have received quite the education in it. I am almost proficient, but—'

'Yes?' Jane peered round the brim of her bonnet into Anne's face.

'I cannot help but harbour some trace of resentment.' A wave crested the horizon and crashed towards the shore. 'Do not let this man Crosby destroy all your confidence! Though he has behaved unjustly towards you, that injustice does not give you licence to punish yourself. Write, Jane! Carry on, at all costs! Are we to take ourselves at *their* estimation? No!' she cried into the wind. 'We must prove them *wrong*.'

And from then on, a new mutual activity entered the fixed pattern of their days. Around the bathing, the walking – the trips to the library and visits to market – they made sure to spend an hour or two together in the parlour, each with their pen.

Anne worked on *Virtue*, determined to cure it of its silliness and bring it back to the play she had once intended. The idea of a woman, with title and lands, was not a bad one. It should be more political, and less fairy-tale non-sense. And in the light of Anne's outburst on the matter of proving men wrong, Jane chose to revise her novel, *First Impressions*. The partnership suited each writer well, though one found it more instructive, perhaps, than the other. Reading Jane's words as they were written, Anne had to confront the plain truth: her own work was sadly inferior.

Naturally, this arrangement entailed that the two women were almost always together – to the exclusion of the rest of the party. When Cassandra put her head round the door to announce her departure on some household errand, or when Martha came in to report that she was taking Mrs Austen for her constitutional, the writers merely lifted their heads and bid them enjoyment.

With each passing day, Anne's feelings for Jane deepened to something like ardour. The understanding between them – their almost common endeavour – loosened the stays on her passionate nature. For the first time in years, Anne was no longer lonely, no more alone, and she found it exhilarating. She was reminded of that phrase she had once used to Hetty: 'closer than sisters: twin halves of one soul'.

Anne gave no thought to the past, nor considered the future. If only the world would forget her existence, and leave her just here.

CHAPTER XXXVI

'I cannot believe I have but ten days here left to me.' It was a crisp and clear day. Anne and Jane were on their short way to the Colonnade Library. 'The weeks seemed eternal in prospect, yet they have sped . . . Perhaps Time behaves differently here by the coast.'

'But have you not noticed? *Everything* is different with the sea in the picture,' Jane replied with great certainty. 'We are all so much *freer* – those *restraints* by which we are bound when in society: they are undone. With one leap, we become something more like our own selves – have you not found it so?'

In her every conversation with Jane, Anne found some cause for astonishment. The way her friend's mind worked; that ability to take apart the mundane and produce some profundity: seeing the world through her eyes was to peer through a microscope. Yet again, she had pierced through to Anne's centre.

'I am sure you are right . . .' she said as they alighted on Warwick Street.

'But of *course!*' Jane cut in. 'Have you not noticed that either? I generally am.'

They passed a couple, arm in arm – handsome heads pressed together in laughter.

'What do you think?' Jane whispered. 'Respectable or *illicit*? Newly wed, or *not*?'

Anne looked back at them again, over her shoulder. 'Well, they look deeply in love, so I say – illicit!'

'Madam, you shock me!' Jane flung her head back and laughed. 'Listen to your own logic: they cannot be married because *they are clearly in love.*'

Anne shrugged. 'If I had ever seen such romantic attachment between two who were legally enjoined, then I might change my view of it.' Another twisted legacy from her own dear papa. How she wished she could confess the whole story to Jane. Now, there would be freedom. 'True love always seems to come with more complications.'

They had arrived at their destination. From within came the bubbling sounds of social activity. People gathering to check out the newcomers, to shop or to gossip – some even come for the books. Jane stopped by the steps to the entrance, turned and took Anne's hand. '*You*, my dear Anne, are certainly altered here. I believe you have stopped *acting* at last. I see a quite different side to you.'

'I—!' Anne stared. Was she being too much herself? Was her heart now on show? Perhaps the Austen ladies preferred that prim little governess to this passionate woman, with her liberal ideas and disdain of convention? Perhaps she should put on that cloak again, hide beneath the respectability of her chosen profession? Then she looked out at that mischievous sea, glittering, playful. And determined to revel in this liberation while it was on offer.

~&

Battle done at the subscription desk, the two ladies emerged again into bright, late-autumn sunlight, and were forced to stop for a crocodile of uniformed schoolgirls.

'Poor wretches,' Jane muttered. 'It brings it all back to me. They should abolish this terrible practice.'

'Abolish the education of girls?' Anne demanded. 'Jane, I am shocked!'

'Not the *teaching* of them – of course not! But these absurd little academies. They learn nothing in them, you know.'

'Perhaps not in most, I agree.' Anne studied the figure of one young girl, walking alone and surreptitiously reading. 'Though that is not the fault of schools in general, but of each in particular. So many pupils get nothing at home. Surely 'tis better that they learn *something*

348

rather than be left in complete ignorance. I will forever be grateful for my sound education. Without it, what would have become of me when—' She broke off. 'I shudder to think.'

Jane took Anne's arm. 'You are wasted on dear Fanny, you know! You should be educating whole swathes of the feminine population. Prepare them for revolution!'

Anne grinned back at her. 'And perhaps one day I shall! Then I will expect you beside me, up on the battlements, waving your musket.'

'Oh dear.' Jane giggled. 'My mama would not like *that* idea one little bit. It *might* ruin my chances.'

The crocodile had now passed; they moved off the steps and Jane looked down at her copy of Charlotte Lennox's *The Female Quixote* with no small satisfaction. That season, Worthing had more readers than good books. 'I am pleased to have secured this. We shall enjoy it together.'

'It is such a joy to read in a circle,' said Anne as they began their beachside stroll. 'Not a pleasure I have ever before known . . .'

'Have you not?' Jane was aghast. 'Then I am sorry for you. We have done it all our lives. My father believed it promoted strengths in the individual, as well as family unity.'

'And you are certainly the most united of families,' Anne had to agree. 'There must be great security in that.'

'Indeed, that is my fortune. If I were alone . . .' She

shot a quick look at Anne. 'Well, let me just say it again, Anne: I admire your great fortitude.'

'Can I pretend to great fortitude?' Anne mused back over her life: those firm refusals of inadequate marriages; nursing her mother alone, day and night. Becoming a governess, indeed, and finding some success in it. 'Obstinacy, certainly . . . My occasional fortitude seems to chime with those occasions at which I am met with little or no choice.'

'Then I hope I might know strength such as yours when I am called upon. For the moment, at least, I have some protection.'

They stood for a while, and watched the bathing: the machines trundling out to the water and back to the sands.

'What are your plans after this?' Anne asked. 'Have you a firm destination?'

Jane shook her head. 'There is no evidence of a *firmness* in our immediate future, I fear.' She sighed. 'For the moment, we four are pledged to form one household – my mother and sister, and Martha, that is.'

Oh, lucky Martha, thought Anne. Although she knew the woman to have little to be thankful for – no money, two married sisters who only took her in when it suited them – to be picked up by these ladies was fortune, indeed.

'After this, it is back to Bath.' Jane gave a small shudder. 'And then, who knows? There is talk of a large house in Southampton, to share with one of my sailor brothers. Though that will also be temporary. Perhaps we will always live like this – a strange little caravan, a motley collection. Ah dear, here we are again, Anne: the Female Conundrum. If we cannot take root in some established position, then where must we put ourselves?' She gave a sly look towards Anne, took her arm and then squeezed it. 'I do believe I am hatching another great *scheme.*'

CHAPTER XXXVII

Of all the many advertised benefits brought by daily sea-bathing, Anne had privately noticed one other: almost all thoughts of Henry were washed clean away and out of a young lady's head. His face swam up before her less often; his voice did not constantly echo: truly, she considered him . . . well, hardly at all. Of course, he was still frequently mentioned by his mother and sisters and, in those moments, it was truly as if he had appeared in the room. But, on the whole, she could declare herself near healed of that low thrum of obsession which had bedevilled her. It came as an enormous relief.

Towards the end of Anne's stay, though, this peace had – needs must – to be ruptured. Henry was due to arrive at the beginning of her final week. In the days leading up to this august event, the Austen ladies talked of little other than him – his route and conveyance; his room and his dinners – and Anne's pretence at neutrality was taxing enough upon all her resources. But, for the moment of his entrance, she was filled with great dread.

Her nightly prayers, which should have been filled with the health of others and the war with the French, were, instead, all on the subject of Henry. *Please*, force him to stay longer in London. Or, if he must come, then *please*, let him not single her out. If he persistently flirted, then his mother or sisters might start objecting. She would hate to be the cause of some family conflict, when they had all been so kind. So, please *God*, do not let Henry be Henry.

Her prayers were ignored. Henry duly arrived and was received with an immense outpouring of feminine rapture. Anne stood back a little while homage was given, and there followed a review of his superior looks; his excellent health; the graciousness he showed them by simply coming at all, with such demands on his time. Astonishment was expressed; praises were sung. The ladies were like cultists in the presence of the Supreme Being. Even Anne had to admit she felt, unaccountably, lighter: perhaps his presence was not quite as bad as she had feared.

Having embraced all his kin, Henry turned to the friends. First, bowing to Miss Lloyd – who flushed while she curtseyed – and then to Anne.

'Miss Sharp!' He bent; she dipped. 'What happy chance that I still find you here.'

And at once, he was up to some subterfuge! They

had discussed the dates of her visit on their last, fleeting meeting in Kent. Cassandra had been there as their witness. What was the point of these games?

'But I see you are restored by the holiday. Your looks are quite—' He broke off and turned back to his mother, gently hinted at an Odyssean journey, murderous hunger and dangerous thirst, and set forth a chain of great feminine busyness which occupied them all for some time.

❧

At the end of a loud, happy dinner – during which Henry delighted the company with a fine-tuned and unceasing monologue – Anne stood and declared it time for her last walk of the day.

'Can I tempt you to join me this evening, Miss Lloyd?' The company of this adored son and brother was such a precious commodity, it might be appreciated if the non-family made itself scarce. And she, too, could do with a break.

Martha blinked and seemed flustered. It was true that these two women had not yet spent any time alone. Anne was not sure what they might find to talk about, but nevertheless she pressed her. And Martha – whose great role in this world was that of agreeable helpmeet – established that Mrs Austen would not require her services, and then meekly agreed. They were heading for the cloak pegs when Henry stood, too.

'May I join you, ladies? I would welcome the air and a first glance of the sea.'

'Oh!' Anne turned back to the room. 'Well, there is not much light left now . . . But of course, sir. Perhaps we might all walk out together then?'

But Mrs Austen could not possibly, citing age, joints, sundry other disorders – up to and including the threat of imminent demise. In which case, Cassandra was duly obliged to sit with her mother. And Jane, it turned out, preferred to be alone with *The Female Quixote*. So it was the unlikeliest of all trios that set out into the evening.

Henry knew nothing of Worthing or its geography, but nevertheless – with the purposeful stride of one who had lived there for centuries – he at once assumed the role of their leader, and led. Though they found themselves taking a long route of some inconvenience, the ladies followed politely.

Amused, Anne stole a glance over at Martha, hoping to share a small smile. But, instead, saw a flushed face of pure terror and thought: Oh, the poor woman! Surely, Anne herself could not be the cause of it? She looked ahead, at the broad shoulders packed into the seams of a frock coat. No, it was Henry. She let out a sigh. What sort of world was it, in which one sex could so easily intimidate the other?

She longed to reach out, grab Martha's arm and encourage her: he is no better than we are! Merely bigger, and louder . . . But she was not given the chance.

355

Martha remembered an errand to be run. Anne insisted on accompanying, but Martha resisted: it was in a poor part of town, away from the sea. And, on top of that, there was an invalid to visit, and an elderly lady to look in on and – The pile of excuses now so high it was in danger of toppling over and smothering them both, Anne surrendered. Martha vanished in an instant.

'Ah, Miss Sharp.' Henry had observed the panicked exchange with wry amusement. 'It appears we are alone.'

'So it does, sir.' A result some distance from her original intention. She did hope the ladies did not come to hear of it.

'May I give you my arm?'

Anne looked up at his face – those wicked eyes, that infernal crinkle – and then all around her. She saw a few couples still *en promenade*, a pink edge to the sky, a wave cresting on the horizon, foam caressing blue water. Thought: What would it matter? Said, 'Thank you, how kind.'

They reached the edge of the sands, where the bathing machines slumbered, and stood there together, bewitched by that view.

'And you have taken to bathing?' Henry enquired.

'Very much indeed, thank you. I have been in every day, and would go more often. But your mother is very firm on the subject: one dip is healing; two, certain death.'

He laughed. 'That sounds like my favourite physician – enormously caring, though not always quite rational.'

He looked down at her then. 'It clearly suits you, Miss Sharp. You seem altogether – well – *different*, somehow.'

'I feel very much better, sir.' She did not wish to share any more detail. It was not just that her mind had become clear and more tranquil, or the bright eyes and fresh bloom that she saw in the glass of an evening. It was now in the tingle on the skin of her chest and her stomach. She would suspect some disorder if it were not so very pleasant. The new rhythm to her heart; the new response at the touch of another – as if her whole being were somehow electrified.

'And you are sleeping well, I take it?'

'Now who is the physician?' Anne laughed at him. 'Yes, thank you, sir. No immediate need to drug me with laudanum.'

In fact, her nights were strange. She found it harder to get to sleep here, for some reason. Considering the exertion of her days – not just the cold bathing, but the long walks with Jane – she had expected the opposite. But the further they walked, the more restless the evening. Some wild sort of energy seemed to course through her blood. Then when she did sleep, her dreams were peculiar – though come morning, no details remained.

And indeed, were those the words to describe this alteration, then Anne could hardly say them aloud. Nor could she explain them. She cast her eyes up to the pink, mackerel sky and examined the cloud flecks as she might the pieces of a puzzle. Was it—? Could it be—? Well, it was rather . . . almost as if she was in love. But that could not be the answer. Of course it was not! She shook her head, turned to Henry, smiled and turned back to the cottage.

For, if this was love, then who was its object?

CHAPTER XXXVIII

'So we have made a new plan,' announced Mrs Austen one evening.

Jane held three slim volumes aloft. 'For once, the library has come up trumps.' She rose to distribute them. 'Not one each, I am afraid. That would be too much to ask from dear little Worthing. But we shall manage well enough, I dare say.'

'*Twelfth Night!*' Henry turned over the copy he was to share with his mother. 'Not one of my favourites, dear Sister. Surely, you remember my Hamlet? I—'

'My dear sir.' Jane was all primness. 'Our purpose is not merely to marvel at your *talent*, but to find pleasure *together*. Now, then. How shall we cast it?'

Mrs Austen spoke up: 'Well, *I* am Malvolio, that much is clear.'

'Are you, Mama?' Cassandra smiled over at her. 'And why would that be?'

'For his face has upon it *more lines than is in the new map!*'

'Very good, Mama.' Jane laughed. 'Then I should be Olivia, burdened by a debt of love, *but to a brother.*' She made eyes at Henry, who blew her a kiss. 'And I believe our best performer should take Viola.'

'But dash it!' Henry slapped his knee with his copy. 'I beg you rethink. I am not made for Viola.'

'And nor,' replied Jane, 'are you our best performer, so worry yourself not. That honour is reserved for Miss Sharp, and I have no doubt she will deliver. You, Mr Austen, will be our Orsino. And perhaps Sir Toby Belch is in you somewhere, is he not? Come now.' Jane held up her hand. 'No more protestation. We are a *company,* Henry – all equals in our endeavour.'

Anne, who had been a trifle disappointed in the supplication Jane had shown at the beginning of Henry's visit, was delighted to see this new control. She was also much pleased with the choice of the play, and her own part in it. Having been Viola back in her youth, she knew the lines almost by heart. She was only sorry that there would be no costumes.

The reading began.

If music be the food of love . . . Henry, as Orsino, wallows in the melancholy of romantic frustration.

What country, friends, is this? Anne, as Viola, alights in Illyria, is told of Orsino and determines to trap him. To enter his court, she dresses as a manservant: *Disguise, I see thou art a wickedness.* Orsino is fascinated by this girlish man, who can *sing high and low.*

He sends Viola as manservant to pledge his case to his great love Olivia. Viola says enough to create a great sense of mystery – *I am not that I play* – and Jane, as Olivia, is also entranced: *Even so quickly may one catch the plague?*

So well did each of the three principal actors play off the others that the rest of the cast had some justification to feel a little put out. Anne, Jane and Henry could hardly have noticed: the limelight was theirs; they gave no thought to the shade. But as Orsino declared of Viola: *One face, one voice, one habit and two persons. A natural perspective that is and is not!*

Mrs Austen took the book from his hands and firmly closed it.

'There we are!' she said, all brightness. 'Enough for this evening. And how very delightful it has been.'

'Indeed.' Cassandra put her own copy down. 'So many lines for Miss Sharp. Poor Miss Sharp! To entrance not one but *two* persons . . . horribly draining. We must take care not to tire you out at the *end* of the holiday. It would not do to bring on the *headache.*'

The excitement of performance – even a private play reading – had left Anne in an excitable mood. She took a few minutes out in the courtyard, stared at the stars and filled her lungs with sea air, before going up to her room. Holding her candle, she trod lightly on the stair so as to not disturb the sleep of the others. But on the landing, she heard talking from within the room that the two sisters shared.

Anne's motive was not to listen in on their private conversation. The attraction was simply its quality, its tone, which drew her to stand at their doorway. So deep was the shared intimacy that they had only to murmur in fragments of sentences. One needed to hear but a few words from the other to glean understanding. Anne could hear smiles in low voices, and the explosions of fondness: 'Oh, *Jane!*'; 'But, Cass, dear . . .'

She stood there for a while, enjoying it as she might enjoy listening to fine music. The text of it – 'I *beg* you, Cass, to show some feelings of sisterhood. Mama has agreed . . . We have our *brothers* to support us, our *mother* to look after: *we have each other*. But imagine for a moment if we did *not*. There but for the grace' – quite passed her by. All she picked up was the sweet sound of love.

And oh! Anne thought, as she studied the flickering light of the candle. Oh, to enjoy such a life-long relationship! Oh, to know and receive such depths of emotion!

So why should her own heart feel so thoroughly crushed?

❧

The following morning, Anne and Jane blew into the cottage – rosy of face, bright of eye – fresh from the brisk bathe of the morning. They found the rest of the party snug in the parlour.

'Look at the glow on you, girls!' Mrs Austen said with approval. 'It makes me feel old just to bask in your bloom.'

Henry looked up from his newspaper. 'Very well, indeed.' Did Cassandra give him one of those glances? '*Both* ladies, that is.' He returned to his reading.

'Oh, Mrs Austen, it was perfect this morning.' Anne moved to the fire and stole a few seconds' warmth for her hands. 'Cold – oh, so very cold – and yet calm as a mill pond.'

'Mama, I *do* wish you would come with us.' Jane flopped into an armchair and sighed. 'I feel after this morning, I shall now live forever.'

'Live forever?' Her mother scoffed. 'What on earth should I want with such nonsense? I have an appointment to keep with your dear papa.' She pointed to the ceiling. 'And the sooner I make it the better. No doubt he is wondering what keeps me so long.'

'Excellent health, Mama.' Cassandra smiled over at her. 'That is the cause of it. And long may it continue.'

'And, while it does, then may you enjoy it,' chided Jane. 'However long it takes you to get there, eternity will not expire.'

Though the conversation presented Mrs Austen with a

splendid opportunity to relate all her symptoms, just this once she let it pass by untaken. 'The post boy came in your absence. Miss Sharp, it is none of my business, but I could not help but notice dear Fanny has written again.'

Anne rose and went to the hall to collect it.

'You make us all jealous, Miss Sharp, with this great correspondence,' Jane called after her. 'Fanny is *ours* – do you know? – and yet she writes to *you* more.'

Anne shrugged. 'And she is spending my absence in making some gift. Cuffs, I believe . . .'

'Like Penelope, she sews through her *tears*. Well, *read* it then, and – pray! – share with us the news.'

Anne began – the dear, familiar writing. She felt a great swell of pride. How Fanny's hand had improved.

'Miss Sharp?' Cassandra must have been watching her as she read. 'You look worried. Not illness in Godmersham, I hope?'

Anne looked up. 'No, no. Not at all! They are all perfectly well.'

'And yet something concerns you?'

Anne put the page down. 'It is – oh! – I am sure I am just being silly. It is just that, as you know, my mistress has brought back Fanny's old teacher, Mrs Chapman, to cover in my absence. And Fanny describes it as such a happy arrangement. I wonder if it was not foolish of me to take over a month here with you.'

Henry's newspaper lowered again. 'But it was your mistress's idea. You have come at her behest.'

'Ye-es. That is true . . .' But the thought did not comfort her. For she had an insight which these good friends did not: employers could not be trusted to behave in a rational manner. They gave not a fig for the literal truth, trusting more as they did to gut feeling and whim – especially in the arena of the education of daughters. But this could not be explained to Elizabeth's own family. And yet, if her parents were to somehow believe Mrs Chapman the most suitable companion for Fanny . . . Dash it, she thought: then what will I do?

Anne bit her lip as she looked around the room. Saw Henry's long legs stretched out on the carpet; three ladies working with an air of contentment; the calm sea through the bay window; the sparkle in Jane's kind, friendly eyes. What a tight group they formed.

'And if you *were* forced to seek a new post,' Henry's voice was quite casual, 'which locality would you choose?'

'Choose?' Anne looked over at him with wonder. As if one simply found a new position, as one might fall from a log. Oh, to be a great Man of the World, and know that protection from all the world's wicked ways. 'I expect I would have to go wherever I might find myself wanted.'

'London, I fancy? London would suit you. Close to your friends . . .'

'Miss Sharp's friends?' Cassandra's head remained down as she measured her cotton.

'Yes, Miss Sharp does have very kind friends, whom I—' Cassandra looked up and narrowed her eyes.

'I am so pleased to hear that,' Martha cut in. 'We do need our friends, do we not? Without these dear ladies, I know not where I would be. I do hope, Miss Sharp, that you one day find yourself the beneficiary of such generosity.'

Though Martha spoke only with kindness, Anne felt herself bristle. Somewhere in those words, she sensed the assumption that they were both some sort of stray animal, desperate for shelter and the odd saucer of milk. Perhaps that was indeed how Martha had seen herself. Well, *she* had not yet sunk that low.

Meanwhile, Cassandra had put down her work, stridden to the table and was taking up paper and pen.

'I will write to Mrs Austen now, on Miss Sharp's behalf, reiterating all that we have said to her before: an excellent governess . . . such a fine influence . . . the considerable benefits apparent in Fanny . . . how lucky the Mistress . . .' She looked over at Anne. 'After all, we have gone to such trouble to cure that poor head. It would be the most terrible pity to see our good work undone.'

'Do you truly worry about Godmersham?' Jane asked as they set out across the fields.

'You cannot be surprised by it: I have said so before. It would be a mistake to give in to feelings of security . . .'

'Well, perhaps change might be a good thing,' Jane

began. 'And I think *now* might be the time to present my new *scheme*.'

'Oh?' Anne stood still by the last of the cottages, heart thudding against ribs.

Jane turned towards her and smiled. 'You have already heard me talk of our *caravan* and our motley *collection*. Anne' – she smiled – 'why do you not come and live with us? My mother *quite* sees the benefits, and Martha would never complain—'

'And your sister?' Anne enquired, though she well knew the answer.

'I believe she *can* be persuaded, in *time*.'

Anne stood in silence while every piece of that infernal puzzle fell into its place. Then, at last, she spoke up: 'Jane, you are kind and I do appreciate all you have done for me. There is nothing I would like more than to spend every day with you.'

If those last words were too passionate, Jane made no acknowledgement. 'So you accept?' she asked cheerfully.

'With the greatest of gratitude, I respectfully decline.' Anne sighed, thought how ardently she loved this dear woman, and said: 'I have become very fond of you.' If only it could be just the two of them. 'But I am not used to – or suited to – living in a large party.' She would not put up with the periphery, as poor Martha did. 'Large families are a foreign country to me.' And nor could she share Jane. 'And if your sister requires strong persuasion, I would much rather not.'

'Oh!' For a moment, Jane seemed a little discomfited. 'You are sure? I thought it the *perfect* solution. And my sister, I am sure, will—'

'No,' Anne said with some firmness. Her composure slightly recovered, she led them to walk again. 'It would indeed be the perfect solution for all sorts of women but, sadly, not me. I am now used to my way of existence. I like to earn my own living. For as long as I stay at God-mersham, then we shall meet often.'

If Jane felt disappointment, then she dealt with it easily. 'You are an excellent governess, after all. And, if you *are* forced to leave, then you can be sure of finding another post quickly.' Jane grabbed at Anne's arm to pull her along – her legs still felt somewhat weak – and adopted an affected narrative voice: 'I dream of you in a household with some *spare man* attached to it . . . He finds you bewitching . . .' She paused, then added, 'Truly, Anne, you do have the potential to be *extremely* bewitching . . .'

This flight of fancy was too much for Anne. 'Miss Austen, please!' she protested, too loudly. 'I am not the bland heroine of romantic fiction. I have no interest in men, spare or otherwise.'

'Come now, Anne! I was not being serious. And – by the by – *my* heroines are not *bland*!'

'Forgive me,' Anne murmured, now thoroughly deflated. 'I was not referring to your own, of course.'

'Of course! But to return to my *plot*: such things *do* happen. A widower, perhaps, with no need of a fortune, and offspring – few only, mind; just the one would be the ideal – who require a good, steady hand. And, after all, there is still *plenty* of time for you to furnish such a good gentleman with yet more children, if he were so inclined.'

'Then heaven forbid,' Anne said crossly. 'I shall seek work in a nunnery!'

Jane laughed, delighted. 'Then you do not long for your own progeny?'

'Oh, I like children certainly. I love Fanny. And of course, little Charles.'

'Ah, Charles is *delicious*. How he must miss us!'

'But somehow I have never imagined myself as a mother. And the *having* of it' – Anne pulled a face – 'the whole process . . .'

'And *there*, we agree. The *process* is a *deeply* unfortunate business,' Jane replied with some fervour. 'It *does* put one off, rather. And besides' – she took Anne's arm once more – 'we have our own offspring: your plays and my novels!'

At that, Anne let out a laugh with her head back. 'I am not convinced that *Virtue Rewarded*, or anything else I could write, will ever be good enough for professional production.' She took Jane's hands in hers. 'But *you*, my dear, you *could* have a future.'

Pursue him, and entreat him to a peace.
He hath not told us of the captain yet;
When that is known, and golden time convents,
A solemn combination shall be made
Of our dear souls. Meantime, sweet sister,
We will not part from hence. Cesario, come –
For so you shall be while you are a man;
But when in other habits you are seen,
Orsino's mistress and his fancy's queen.

They had come to the end of *Twelfth Night*, and Anne felt quite drained by it. She put her book in her lap and rubbed at her eyes. Having to play both Viola as well as her twin Sebastian – so successfully wooing both Henry *and* Jane – had proved rather hard labour. Though for the rest of the company, the evening had provided nothing but pleasure.

'Capital entertainment!' cried Henry, slapping his thighs. 'I think we all acquitted ourselves admirably.'

'We did well enough, Brother.' Jane stretched and moved in her seat. 'But you have to admit it: Miss Sharp *is* the superior performer.'

Henry smiled bravely. Anne watched through her lashes. He did not speak out in disagreement but nor, it was clear, could he find any pleasure in the position of second best.

'Miss Sharp is a tremendous asset on these occasions. We have had such fun together these past months. And now, 'tis your last night! The pity of it.' Mrs Austen felt down the side of her chair in search of her spectacles. 'I have particularly enjoyed the enlargement of our little circle. It has felt quite like the old days.'

Cassandra rose, crossed over to her mother, and reached into the cushions. 'Do you not remember, Mama? Jane does prefer *triangles.*'

Anne stood. 'I think I might take a last breath of air.'

'There we are, Mama!' Cassandra produced the spectacles and put them back on for her mother. 'All better! Now you can see.'

Alone in the courtyard, Anne buried into her shawl to keep out the chill; she found the little sweet chestnut, and leaned on the bark. From there, by craning her neck just a little, she could see the indigo water, the silver path spread by the full moon.

And, after tomorrow, would she see it again? That was impossible to answer. She had been led here by such a curious chain of chance and event that could never be replicated. And now she was in love with so many different elements: the sea, the sands, the skies here; these dear, dearest of characters and their extraordinary minds. She shivered. The emotions of the day, the stress of performance, had bequeathed in her that strange restless energy. Brimful of a desire that she could neither identify, nor knew how to fulfil.

Tears of frustration formed then, and spilled. How she longed to feel a presence at her shoulder; a touch on the arm; some whispered word in her ear. She would not even mind who it was. Just one other person, who might offer some kindness . . .

Instead, she stood there alone and patiently counted each wave as it rushed from the vastness and home to the shore.

CHAPTER XXXIX

'Welcome, Miss Sharp.' Elizabeth crossed the hall smiling, stretching out both hands to Anne. 'We are *so* pleased to have you home with us again. Now, let me look at you.' She drew back. 'The most extraordinary change! One can see it at once! Miss Sharp, you are *cured*.'

Anne agreed that she felt so.

'And is that not a *miracle*?'

Anne replied that it might be, or something quite close. Again, she offered up grateful thanks for the generosity shown to her, remarked on the wisdom of her mistress's plan; saw from the tilt of Elizabeth's head that yet more of the same might be expected; went on and supplied it, adding, for good measure, a few extra superlatives. Achieving sufficiency, she then turned to the others who were lined up to greet her.

She was pleased to find Fanny, and delighted – relieved – at the warmth of her welcome. Touched, too, by the staff: Mrs Salkeld, most affectionate; Johncock the butler, respectful and proper. Sally and Becky, wrangling in whispers over who was to have the honour of unpacking her things.

Apprehension had travelled with Anne on every step of her journey. Was she still wanted? Might Mrs Chapman still be in residence? Would they all have forgotten her? Had she been mad to turn down Jane's offer? Those dismal thoughts could now be banished. Dear Godmersham Park, where all were so kind.

Anne, Fanny and the servants began the process of gathering her possessions – Elizabeth was on her way back to the drawing room – when the noise of a serious argument assaulted their ears. Phrases such as '*Stupid boy!*' and '*Then I call you A DAMNABLE FOOL!*', shouted at such volume as to penetrate the solid front door.

Elizabeth turned back with a look of sheer horror. 'What on *earth* can be happening?'

Mr Johncock opened the door. The women drew closer to get a good look. Anne saw a gentleman, aged between thirty and forty, perhaps; handsome of dress, but not so of feature. His face was built on the coarse side, and made significantly uglier by the rage he was in. A craven servant hunched, as if fearing a blow, by the side of a grand carriage.

The spectators in the hall were agog. They gathered

there had been some confusion of clocks. The gentleman's said one thing, his man's quite another: they were out by a good half an hour. Whether they were early or late was never made clear. Either way, the master could not be placated. Mr Johncock closed the door again, and looked to his mistress.

'Ahem.' Elizabeth gathered herself. 'It appears our dinner guest has arrived. Johncock?' She sounded most apprehensive. 'Perhaps let him – er – finish his – er – *discussion*, and then we will receive him. I am quite sure it is merely a matter of the simplest misunderstanding and not at all as it seems. Off you all go.'

What dramas, thought Anne as she made her way up the stairs. And what a gift! She had promised to write to Jane as soon as she arrived, and was loath to bore her with the details of the journey. Now, she had something choice to report.

She arrived in her room, followed by servants and trunk, to find Miss Harriot Bridges was already there.

'What do you think?' Harriot, bedecked in a midnight-blue silk threaded with silver, spun between the two beds, and adopted a few poses from the page of a pocket book.

'Enchanting,' Anne said with some feeling. 'Truly.' She crossed over and fingered the fabric. 'One of the loveliest visions I have ever beheld.' And a bit much for dinner in Godmersham, surely? 'Is there some special occasion? Oh, and good day, by the way.'

'Sharpy! Forgive me, such is my excitement at having you returned to us, the niceties quite eluded me. How *are* you?' She took both Anne's hands in hers and looked into her face. 'I have missed you *so much*!'

Oh, Harriot! Anne smiled back at her. Always the dearest of friends when Henry was absent.

'You look very well. Quite remarkably so, indeed. Sharpy, you little pickle, you have your bloom back! What have you been up to? Do not tell me, you are *in love*?'

'Miss Bridges, *please*,' Anne scolded. 'I have merely discovered sea-bathing and found it rather agreed with me.' She then remembered the maid, who was watching them rapt, as if in the pit at a drawing-room comedy. 'Thank you, Sally. Perhaps we will unpack a little later?'

They watched her reluctant departure.

'So, pray – may I know what is behind all this splendour?' Anne gestured back at the costume; its owner delivered a twirl. 'Is the King come to dinner?'

Harriot giggled and blushed. 'Not quite the *King*, Sharpy. But . . .' She bit her lip. '. . . one who may soon be *my prince*.' She took the one chair, looking down at her skirts as she smoothed them. 'A *gentleman* whom *they* have in mind for me!'

'Miss Bridges, that is thrilling!' Anne busied herself with her trunk. 'I am happy for you. Tell me all that you know. You have met him already, I take it?'

'Not *exactly*,' Harriot was forced to admit. 'Once, years

ago, I am told, but then I was almost a *child*.' She wriggled in her seat. 'And as to the *facts* of him, they are all *very* promising. His father is Archbishop of *Canterbury* – is that grand enough for you, Miss Sharp? – and he is himself a *churchman*, of course. But I must not mind that, for he has the diocese of *Wrotham* – have you *seen* it? One of the best houses around.'

Anne unpacked her books while she heard the rest of his background. He was a widower – 'Not *ideal*, I agree. Or perhaps it is *better*, do you think? Oh' – a sigh – 'I do not know. But a widower he is, so one must simply get on with it.' Harriot paused in thought, then went on: 'Just the *one* child, which is a relief. One would not like to take over a *team*, after all. And it's only a *girl*, so *that* leaves me at some advantage.'

Anne arranged her writing things back on her desk. 'It sounds to me as if your mind is already made up. But, Miss Bridges, what if you find him disagreeable? I hope you would not do anything rash.'

Harriot stood up. 'Oh, do not worry, I am *determined* to like him. *They* have convinced me. The time is now come. No more of my *picking* and *choosing*. Sharpy, I am now off to meet *Destiny*! Wish me good luck.'

'Miss Bridges, I wish you all the luck in the world.' Anne meant as she said. 'I hope he is perfect. What time does he arrive? I might spy from the landing window and see if he is worthy of my approval.'

Harriot gave a little shiver. 'I *gather* he is come already!

A full half-hour early! But that is no *bad* thing – better *early* than *late*, I always say.' She flitted through the door.

As Anne watched her go, urgent pity tugged at her breast. When the great forces of the marriage market choose to conspire around us, they prove hard to resist. That girl did not stand a chance.

CHAPTER XL

My dear Anne,

So prompt was your letter that my mother had not nearly finished her list of the disasters you had most likely met on your journey, when her fun was quite spoiled by the news of your safe arrival. <u>She</u> then felt robbed of a full day of pleasant anxiety, whereas <u>we</u> were delighted.

And as for the stuff of your letter – we are all stunned! What can I say but poor Harriot. I cannot think this Mr Moore is her <u>one</u> possibility, and only hope that he shows the kindness to his wife that he withholds from the servants – although is there any better judge of a man than such rudeness to <u>those</u> quarters. Fond of Harriot as I am, I am determined <u>never</u> to like <u>him</u>. My good opinion, once lost, is rarely regained and I am quite sure he will not endeavour to try it. Well – may he *make Harriot happy – or may she make* <u>*herself*</u> *happy, as that is so often the way with us women.*

You are right to picture us before our warm fire in our usual fashion, but wrong that I have managed to bathe yet in your absence. Without you, my dear friend, I have not the heart for it. And speaking of hearts, my Brother has left us already! A restlessness set into him soon after you left – for which we cannot account – but, there – Gone he is. And much missed already, as you are, dear Anne.

Please keep us up with all the latest instalments of this Romantic Saga, and do take good care. You were so well when you left us and we beg you remain so.

Fondest love to you and all at Godmersham,
J. Austen.

❧

'Miss Sharp, please! If you *could* look at me.'

Anne's mind jumped back from its reverie. 'Forgive me, Miss Crow. My eye was drawn to something happening outside.' She got back into position. 'There. I promise I will not move again.'

'Thank you, I'm sure.' The artist adjusted her pencil and stared at her subject. 'I will not keep you long. That's why they hire me, you know.' She dashed off a few strokes. 'The fastest work in all the east of England. That is my gift.'

Anne, who had not been led to believe that the measure of fine art was in the speed of its completion, tried not to smile. From her vague memories of sitting for Reynolds, she knew that he took his time. No doubt, Miss Crow would like to hear how the methods of the master were so inferior to hers. Sadly, Anne's instructions were to keep her mouth closed, in a prim, governess manner.

Much to her surprise, Anne's popularity in Godmersham had deepened in the fortnight since her return from the sea. She had been prepared for the opposite; had expected that, once life got back to normal, she would become, once again, another piece of the attic furniture. But it appeared that the many testimonials to Anne's excellence from the wider family had made a deep and lasting impression. Her mistress continued to heap favours upon her. Anne was included in more dinners, invited to cards, spoken of to neighbours as a 'veritable treasure'. The lengths gone to for her cure were quite often mentioned. And when Miss Crow was engaged to take the likeness of all the daughters, Elizabeth Austen asked Anne if she would sit, too.

Anne found it all rather startling. 'Are you quite sure, madam? I do not expect it and would most happily not—'

'Nonsense, Miss Sharp!' Elizabeth had returned with that disarming, new warmth. 'You are a much-valued *member* of the Godmersham family. When the children are all grown and your work here is finished, then we shall have something of *you* to remind us.'

And so Anne sat in the library, posing this way and that, rather wishing she had been spared this great honour. There was so much to do. She ought to be teaching down at the school that afternoon – those boys had fallen back in her absence. Darning had piled up; it was laundry day tomorrow. Holding this position was increasingly uncomfortable. And, most importantly, Harriot was out walking in the gardens with the Reverend George Moore. Anne would much rather be looking at them than this tiresome woman.

'Do you have enough yet, Miss Crow?' she enquired through closed lips. 'I am quite pressed for time.'

Miss Crow furrowed her brow. 'I ought to be done now, it's true. But you're a difficult study, miss.' She cocked her head to one side. 'It's as if you've changed the shape of your face, just since you've been sitting there.' She looked at the paper again. 'All most peculiar. I had you as oval, and now you're all round.'

'Peculiar, indeed.' The significance of the observation sailed past Anne completely. 'Perhaps you might simply plump for one shape and continue accordingly?' She really did have to get on.

At last released, Anne thanked Miss Crow, glanced at the sketch – nothing like her, of course – and went to the window. Miss Bridges and the Reverend had turned and were walking in the direction of the house, through the shrubbery. Anne gave their figures her fullest attention: he was opining; she was listening, rapt. His gait was sedate which, with his figure, came as little surprise. He bore a heavy load at the front there, carried a great sphere

before him. It was as if that stomach was a general leading the way, and the couple his troops, following behind.

More unexpected was the manner of Harriot. Anne
stood for some minutes, yet did not see her laugh, or even
smile: she seemed only to nod, and deeply agree. She had
only once before seen Miss Bridges so serious, and that
was when she feared for her dear sister's life. Where was
that gaiety, that flighty young miss? Anne remembered
the sun-dappled riverbank: the young woman chasing
with Henry, her joy and abandon.

Of course, she had disapproved of it at the time, but now
Anne found she mourned its sad passing, and was taken
aback by the speed of it. A few dinners, the odd walk – the
committed attentions of one, landed churchman – and
Harriot was transformed. It was a natural progression,
but, to Anne's mind, played out in an unnatural order: like
watching a beautiful butterfly becoming a grub.

With a sigh, Anne turned from the window. She could
not look any longer. The sad sight hurt her eyes. Indeed,
was she crying? Surely not. She put a finger to her cheek,
checking for damp. All dry, yet her vision seemed a little
distorted . . .

Her heart dropped with a thud. No, please, let it not
be – and yet, she was suddenly certain. Miss Crow had
noticed her face swell. She was irritable and fidgety. The
eyes were the final, irrefutable proof.

The headache was back.

CHAPTER XLI

'Ah, good. Miss Sharp.' Elizabeth looked up from a letter and gestured to a chair. 'Thank you for coming. Pray, do take a seat.'

Anne sat.

'Now then. As I am sure you expected, Fanny has reported to me on this unfortunate business.'

'Of course, madam.' In fact, Anne had not completely expected it. Having so strenuously begged Fanny to – just this once – keep one, single secret, she had harboured some small hope of success. 'And please, let me apologise. I had taken such care to not disturb her . . .'

This much was true. Despite the pain, Anne had resisted that primeval urge to pace up and down; had instead curled up in the one chair, biting her own hand to stop herself crying. Yet still, Fanny had picked up on something, got out of her bed, taken Anne into her arms, and rocked her like a mother. It was a reversal which should have left Anne humiliated, but for one shaft of light in that darkest of hours. For, even in the throes of her agony, she could feel within Fanny the stirrings of a simple, pure empathy. And with that she was pleased.

'I believe you,' Elizabeth said, kindness in those blue eyes. 'I *believe* the pain to be such that you cannot conceal it.' She sighed, placing a pale hand to pale bosom. 'Oh, Miss Sharp! It is so *very* disappointing. After all—'

'I quite understand, madam.' Anne hung her head in sorrow and shame. 'You have made such effort on my behalf, been enormously generous.'

Elizabeth tilted her head; Anne praised a bit more, again condemned her own absence of worthiness. And then, in an attempt to speed up the uncomfortable process, added: 'So I quite understand that we are now at the end of—'

'*The end?*' Elizabeth's eyebrows shot up. 'Oh, dear me: no! Miss Sharp, *please* do not think *me* a woman who *gives up* so *easily*.' She laughed prettily. 'I believe I have one more *trick* up my *resourceful* sleeve.'

❧

Mr Lascelles turned up at Godmersham the following week. Mrs Austen, who could hardly contain the joy and pride caused by his securement, introduced him to Anne as 'a physician of *eminence*'. From the depths of her curt-sey, Anne looked up into those saturnine eyes and knew, at once, Mr Lascelles was a quack.

'Sir, this is your patient.' Elizabeth spoke from the sofa. 'Miss Sharp, we have, at last, come into some *luck*. Mr Lascelles has developed his own *technique* for the treatment of your very condition! Is that not extraordinary? Do not even *ask* how I discovered him. Let us just say, wheels within *wheels*, letter upon *letter*, friend unto friend . . . When I *determine* on a thing . . . And, Mr Lascelles, what is your assessment?'

While Mrs Austen was speaking, the 'physician' – hands at lapels – walked around Anne in circles, study-ing her head. 'If you would not mind?' He stretched out long fingers and pointed at her neck. Anne pulled hair and cap up to expose it. 'Ah, yes.' He probed the valley at her nape. 'An excellent candidate. Madam, I am will-ing to give you a verbal guarantee of complete success.'

And thus he proved all Anne's darkest suspicions. No serious doctor would make such a claim! Human beings were not some manufactured product, always set to behave in a uniform way. Anne's head was unique – as was the rest of her: she had her own set of quirks, condi-tions and reactions. Mr Lascelles could have no earthly idea what went on in its interior.

'The most *splendid* news.' Elizabeth beamed. 'And, Mr Lascelles, you are happy to start straight away?'

'My bags are outside with my manservant.' He rubbed

his hands together – as well he might. Anne had to presume that his services did not come free.

'Mr Lascelles, if I may ask a question?' Anne pulled down her cap to cover her neck. 'I wondered how long this procedure might take? I am expected to teach at the school this afternoon and—'

'Ah, no. Miss – er?' Mr Lascelles looked to the sofa. 'Yes, Miss Sharp. Perhaps you are not yet in possession of all the facts. Though the *operation* itself—'

Operation? So not a procedure . . . Anne's panic began.

'The operation will be over in less than an hour, the *effect* of it lasts a good week. Though, fear not, Miss – er, I shall attend to you personally for the next seven days. My diary is clear, and my instructions' – another nod to the sofa – 'are to stay until the cure is complete. Now, if you will excuse me, I shall go and prepare.'

Anne stood, mute, on the carpet. Was she to be given no say in the matter? A whole week out of action was simply impossible! She did not want that man's hands anywhere near her; had no trust whatsoever in his expertise. He was as likely to kill as he might be to cure. Now alone with her mistress, she began to protest.

'Madam, this is truly too much. The sheer cost of it: the imposition! If you have come to believe that my condition so affects my performance, then please, allow me to leave. I would be happy to stay until you find a replacement. I really cannot accept any more of your—'

'Dear Miss Sharp!' Mrs Austen stood up and took Anne's hands in hers. 'I am afraid we are not letting go of *you*. You are too perfect, my dear – I find myself the *envy* of the whole neighbourhood, as well as the wider family – and Fanny has become simply too *fond*. Yes, I am aware that to bring in a special physician – I do approve the *manner* of the gentleman, don't you? – is to go *above* and *beyond*, but so be it! If this is what it costs us to keep you, then we are all too willing to pay.'

❧

Up in her attic room, Anne sat at her desk, laid her face into the pillow, like Charles I on the scaffold. '*Remember!*' she whispered as she exposed the nape of her neck. Sally sat beside her, clutching her hand, while behind them Mr Lascelles mixed his magic potion.

'Sir.' Anne spoke into the pillow. 'Am I permitted to know what is happening?'

'But of course!' He had given up trying to recall her apparently impossible surname. 'So, first, I must grind all I need in the mortar: mustard seeds, Spanish fly and so on.'

'And so on . . . ?' Anne would like to know the full recipe.

'And now' – there was a tapping, the sounds of stirring – 'I mix it with clay to form a good paste. There! Be still. I must get this in place before it has started to set . . .'

Anne smelt something bitter; felt something cold and damp spread over her neck. And then caught the stench and the sizzle of melting flesh.

'Do not move!' he commanded. 'Maid, hold her in place! We are at the crucial – there! Cometh the blister, then cometh the needle. Pin her down, girl!'

Anne tried to sit up; their force was too much for her.

Sally started shrieking, for she could see what was happening. Anne, blinded by pillow, had but sensation to go on: the sensation of being run through with a sword.

'Perfect!' exclaimed Mr Lascelles, while Anne slumped.

'Lord!' Human interest had now got the better of Sally. 'That is a very long needle, sir. Did it go all the way into her brain?'

'A simple piercing through the neck for the release of the pressure which has built up behind the eyes . . . Now here, girl, I need you while I perform the suture.' There was a pause for some busyness. 'If you could just pinch the skin together . . . The tighter the better.' More needles; more stabbing; a sharp tug that lifted Anne up by the neck.

This new pain was different, but no less violent than the pain of the headache. Gingerly, she tried to sit up. Kindly, Sally assisted her. The blue trellised wallpaper danced and spun . . . Somehow, with the active assistance of both doctor and maid, she managed to cover the room. Anne lowered herself down to the bed and attempted to get comfortable.

Mr Lascelles washed his hands in the basin and cast over his professional eye. 'It will not be painless for some hours – I would not pretend otherwise. However, I can state with some confidence, the operation was a resounding success.'

❧

Six long days, Anne lay in the darkness; six long nights she tossed and she turned. Alone with the pain, her sole stimulation and comfort were the now dear, familiar room and the objects within it. Those precious books and the desk; the small, glowing fireplace and that print of the parable which still hung above it. *For nothing is secret, that shall not be made manifest; neither anything hid, that shall not be known and come abroad.* Those words ran round her thoughts, burned their way through to her soul. And was she deranged now with fever, or did the Lord's lamp illuminate something deep down within her? She was sure that in her poor, damaged head there had come a new clarity.

On the seventh day, Mr Lascelles appeared in her room for the last consultation, bringing with him the Mistress.

'Miss Sharp, have you become a nocturnal *creature*? It is no longer the night-time!' Anne heard a note of laughter in Elizabeth's voice. 'Sally, do draw the curtains please. There, is that not better?'

Anne winced at the light on her eyelids. The wallpaper pattern shifted and dizzied her. She turned her face away to the wall.

'Oh dear, Miss Sharp.' Elizabeth approached the bed and peered at the patient. 'Is something the matter? Are you *ailing* in some other way?'

With no small struggle, Anne sat up, opened her eyes and attempted a small smile. 'Not at all, Mrs Austen. Thank you for coming . . . Forgive my déshabillé . . . You are quite right to say so. I have let things slip rather . . .'

Elizabeth held up her hand. 'Please, do not apologise. Mr Lascelles *did* warn me that there might be a *little* discomfort. 'Tis only to be expected, after such an *elaborate* business. But a price worth paying, I believe. Is that not so, doctor?'

'Oh, I should hope so.' He spoke with such fervour it led Anne to wonder which 'price' he referred to: his fee, or the toll upon her? 'Now, Miss – er—'

A week! Resentment bubbled within her. A whole week of stabbing and prodding and interference with her person, and still this great medical mind could not master her name.

'Let me examine you for the last time, prior to your discharge. Sit forward, pray . . . Excellent . . . You see, madam, this bruising here . . .' He prodded Anne's neck. 'Though it may still appear as *livid* and swollen as ever, we must take that as a good sign. The sutures have held fast and the tighter the hold, the less room for pressure to build in – er – our patient's head. So my advice is to keep them in place for as long as is possible – months, even years would be most efficacious.'

So she was to carry this protrusion of coarse thread for the rest of her life?

Mrs Austen was bestowing upon Anne a proud, happy smile. 'Then all is good news!'

Mr Lascelles was already at the table, clicking his case closed. 'Madam, it is, and I say that with some considerable satisfaction. The headache is an accursed business and it is the pride of my career that 'tis I who have found this ingenious solution.' He looked over to Anne. 'And may I say, miss, how fortunate you are to have such a *generous* employer, so *open* of mind.'

As Elizabeth basked in his testimonial, Anne felt beholden to speak: 'Thank you, sir – and madam, for all you have done. I am grateful for such extraordinary kindness.'

CHAPTER XLII

My dear Anne,

First of all, I beg of you – never think of yourself as a burden. Who among us has <u>not</u> burdened at some time or another – that is, apart from my sister, who nobly carries all upon her strong back. We were <u>most</u> cast down to hear that your affliction is upon you again, but only my mother was <u>fully</u> surprised. She will put such faith in those who call themselves medical men – despite all the contrary evidence put before her own eyes – and the very idea that an <u>operation</u> was <u>paid</u> for was enough to give her every hope of a cure. Alas, <u>I</u> expected much less from your <u>doctor</u>, but am for once devastated to have been proved right. That you had to endure the business in the first place, and then that it left you unchanged – Oh, my poor Anne. I – indeed all of us – feel for you keenly.

You failed to mention how your mistress has reacted to this latest sorry development, and <u>that</u> we are most keen to hear. You say you led the household through Mr and Mrs Austen's recent absence, which must surely speak in your favour. But then if Fanny is back in your room, and your poor eyes are struggling . . . <u>Please</u> write at once and tell us the outcome – or at least what you think it will be.

Another Godmersham Christmas must have come as a welcome delight – they do everything so well there and, no doubt, the children were as enchanting as ever. Fanny tells me you were the wonder of charades, and sang very beautifully – none of which came as a <u>shock</u>. Though pray do remember my earlier injunction – do not <u>parade</u> your great cleverness to all and sundry. Ration it! The smallest of portions will go a long way.

Our own Christmas, being the first since the sad death of our father, was suitably quiet. In truth, we did not know quite where to put ourselves, without that great guiding light. But that is the trick of life, I now see – to meet the changes with fortitude, and rearrange oneself neatly. Which brings me to the nub of this letter.

If you <u>do</u> find you are no longer needed at G'mersham, I now speak with full authority on behalf of <u>all</u> in my household: you would be most welcome with us.

Your loving friend,
J. Austen.

❧

'Miss – Madam! Good heavens! What on earth has been done to you?'

Anne, bare-headed – the cap did chafe on her scar so – started, and pulled her head up from the table in the schoolroom.

'Mr Austen!' she cried. And – oh! – she might have shed genuine tears at the sweet sight of his person. 'You were not expected till the evening.'

'My dear lady.' Henry crossed the room and took the chair opposite. ''Tis evening already. How long have you been sleeping?'

Mind still muddled, she looked to the window and the darkness beyond. The candles were lit, so a servant must have been in. She had slept through it entirely. Really, it was high time she pulled herself back together.

'Tell me, immediately: that wound on your neck.' For once, those bright eyes were not laughing, but shot through with concern. 'This *cannot* be to do with the *doctor* of whom I have heard. I refuse to believe it! It is *weeks* since—'

''Tis my own fault, sir – I am sure of it. Mr Lascelles was quite adamant I should be better by now.' Anne was careful to say nothing that might hint at complaint. 'In fact, I *am* better. I am sure I am better – indeed, perfectly well. Certainly, there are signs of a considerable improvement.'

Henry leaned back in his chair to study her; stretched

out those long legs, one foot brushing hers. Anne stayed very still, calmed by the contact – warmed by his touch.

'Miss Sharp, I do detect' – Henry studied her keenly – 'that, for the very first time, you are not *un*pleased to see me.'

Anne made no reply.

'Dash it – I am right!' He sat upright and called out in triumph: 'Won over at last!' He lolled back again with a swagger. 'Do you know, I had seriously come to believe that it might never happen? Ha!' He slapped the school table.

'Sir, you speak as if we had been engaged in some sport of which you are the victor.'

'That is because, madam, it has seemed so to me. An eternal game! The most ingenious quarry! Tell me' – he crinkled his eyes – 'what has occurred to make your mind change?'

'I am so shocked by this schoolboy behaviour that I now cannot recall,' Anne replied primly.

Though she knew. She knew deep in her soul. Her mind had not ever changed from the moment she met him.

'Ah, Miss Sharp, 'tis a pleasure to spar with you again, and to be back here in Godmersham for the start of the year. Tell me first all that has happened, and what is ahead.'

'We have been very quiet, sir. Let me think: what is our news?' Anne tried to think of more cheerful subjects than her medical drama. 'Oh, you have, of course, heard of Miss Bridges' happy engagement?'

'Word had reached me.' Henry raised both his brows. 'And what do we know of this Reverend Moore? I hope there is *some* love there. Is he attractive?'

That was not for Anne to say. '*She* finds him so, I believe.'

'Easy of manner?'

To speak the truth here might dampen the spirits. 'Miss Bridges seems very content.'

'A decent match, then, you say – all that a friend of the lady could hope for?'

'Oh, I have no doubts on that score.' Anne met his eye. 'His house at Wrotham is said to be one of the finest around.'

'Ha!' he barked with delight, and then grew more serious. 'Poor, dear Miss Bridges. Still, I am sure she will make the best of things. She is due to join us here, I am told – one final hurrah before she is married.'

'I am not sure how much *hurrah* you will find in her, sir,' Anne cautioned. 'She is very much changed.'

'Hm.' He turned his mouth down. ''Twas inevitable, looking back on it.' He nodded acceptance. 'A pity all the same. We did have some fun, she and I . . . So' – any regret was quickly processed and roundly dispatched – 'what then *can* I anticipate?'

Anne put her arms on the table, leaned in towards him and told him her secret.

❧

The past weeks of Christmas had not run smoothly. It was increasingly clear Anne had lost the status of treasure, and was now a dragging disappointment: an ingrate who, when blessed with a cure, refused to get well; a servant who cost a small fortune, and gave less in return.

With every day passing, Anne found her mistress became increasingly cool. She did her best, of course – acted restored; pretended at wellness – yet Elizabeth saw all, and was dissatisfied. Mrs Austen recoiled from the wound on Anne's neck. The manner in which Anne now had to squint when training her poor vision upon distant objects was judged to be less than genteel.

She kept to the attic as much as was possible. But at the unavoidable events where Elizabeth could not but catch sight of her, Anne noticed the once so fond mistress now turned her head away, and let out a sigh.

There was nothing for it but to employ all her powers and win Godmersham round.

Anne admitted but three accomplices into her scheme. Mrs Salkeld, the housekeeper, and Sackree, the nurse – firm allies, both of them – took on the costumes. When not out shooting or riding, or playing at cards and amusing the neighbours, Henry undertook to rehearse all the children. For the rest, the responsibility of the entire production fell upon Anne. No corners could be cut, no risks would be taken: the performance had to be stunning, to save her professional life.

In this new version, *Virtue* was considerably changed. There were no girl cousins to play female parts, and, with the older boys back home for the holidays, Anne had added new characters so she could include them. They needed the civilising influence of a private theatrical; they would find benefit in the odd break from killing things. The local wildlife could have a reprieve.

The text itself Anne had changed when back in Worthing working with Jane and, this time, she had total confidence in what she had written. It was not, she well knew, a work of great genius but, as a rank amateur, she had acquitted herself well. The Duchess of St Albans – this was Fanny's big moment – was still the heroine but now she had men – dastardly men – to contend with, who were desperate to get their hands on her estate. Paying no heed to Jane's warnings, she had let in a small dash of cleverness, allowed it to run and play through the text. But what of it? Anne *was* clever, so why pretend otherwise? All her gifts must be out there, on show.

Fanny found much of it hard to believe. '*Monstrous regiment?*' She wrinkled her neat nose. 'But Anny, *why* would a fine gentleman refer to *ladies* as *monstrous*? That seems to me *odd*.'

Reluctant to impart bad news to the innocent, Anne merely replied: 'Last time, Fanny, *you* were a fairy – as you no doubt recall – who granted wild wishes, and vanished in a puff, and got up to all sorts of nonsense. Was that more credible, do you suppose?' She took Fanny back into position. 'Mind, this is pure fiction. We are here to entertain, that is all. Now again: from the top of this scene.'

So different was the result that Anne changed the title. On the fourth day of January 1806, *Pride Punished* had its premiere in the Godmersham library.

❧

As before, Anne watched, shrunk, in the doorway. This time, though, she enjoyed every second. The servants seemed to appreciate this more muscular work as much as the flab that had preceded it. Perhaps their interest lay more in the evening off than the content, but the great shouts of 'Ooh', 'Ah' and 'For shame!' were all that mattered to Anne. Neighbours and guests were in the front rows, with Henry right at their centre. From time to time, she must admit, she did occasionally move a little, to judge his reaction. Of course – dearest Henry – his delight was equal to that of Sally and Becky. It was only Elizabeth whom Anne could not see. She had graciously agreed to provide the musical accompaniment, and her face was obscured by the piano.

Whether or not the performance was received as a triumph, Anne had already determined to claim all the credit for everyone to see. This time she needed acknowledgement. And so, as the final scene played out and the applause began, little Charles – as rehearsed – came over and dragged Anne on to the stage. She played at resisting, before modestly curtseying to the front, then sidestepping to offer her applause to the children.

And now we are arrived, she thought, at the moment of truth. Dipping again, she stole a glance to the piano to judge the face of her mistress. Could she read pleasure upon it? Had this done the trick? Might she be saved? Mrs Austen was standing, hands certainly clapping – a smile on her face. But her eyes, slightly narrowed, were fixed on the front row.

Anne followed her gaze, to see what had caught her attention. And – oh, the calamity! Elizabeth was looking at Henry. And Henry – handsome face ignited to radiance by the pure light of deep admiration – was looking only at Anne.

And suddenly, that brightly lit stage became the dock of a courtroom; the rapturous applause rang in her ears as the baying of a mob. She could almost hear an imaginary judge list the charges against her. The crime of poor health! Of unnecessary cleverness! And, the worst above all of them: the attraction of a masculine eye. Anne stood there, frozen: three times a criminal.

Now, would she be punished, or reprieved yet again?

❧

The events of the following morning played out like a drama.

In Act the First: Fanny burst into the schoolroom. She had tears in her eyes, clutched their portraits to her breast. Handing to Anne the sketch of herself, she choked out the words: 'Dear Anny. *Promise* me, *please*, to keep this likeness of me by your side – for ever and *ever*?'

Anne looked down at the sketch of a face that might have belonged to any young girl. Shaking her head – really, Miss Crow was an uncommonly poor artist – she handed it back.

'Surely, its rightful owner is your dear mama!' she protested. 'It was commissioned by her, to make a collection of all her darling girls. Fanny, I could not possibly . . .'

Fanny sobbed and ran out of the room.

Her next visitor was Sally, who first embraced and then told her the Mistress awaited her down in the parlour. Once in the hall, Mrs Salkeld walked by her, and pronounced things 'a shame'.

And then came the denouement. Anne was shown into her mistress's presence. She was not offered a seat, and nor did she require one. Regrets were expressed; disappointment admitted; best wishes extended.

And, within a matter of moments, Miss Sharp was back out on those black-and-white tiles – dismissed, with immediate effect.

CHAPTER XLIII

'Well, Miss Sharp, it seems that Cook has chosen to mark this sombre occasion with the most exquisite cake yet.' Mr Whitfield's sorrows seemed quite becalmed by the iced splendour before him. 'There!' He salivated as he cut Anne a slice. 'If we cannot indulge ourselves at a time such as *this*, then when will the Good Lord permit us at all?'

'Thank you, Mr Whitfield.' Anne took the plate and sank back into the commodious chair. 'Is it not wonderful how He tends to provide just what one needs?'

'Indeed, indeed.' Mr Whitfield brushed the crumbs from his chin and served himself to a second helping. 'And yet, there is one thing that puzzles me. I *had* believed that *you*, my dear, had been brought to us in the interests of some Higher Purpose . . .'

'Me, Mr Whitfield?' Anne laughed. 'I think you, perhaps,

are reading too much into the random events of we *very* small mortals. I cannot see myself as the rod of divine intervention.'

'Forgive me, Miss Sharp, but, politely, I must disagree. Just two nights ago, after your *excellent* play, I said to my wife: "Are we not lucky, my dear, to have Miss Sharp come among us?" Your theatricals brought us together, as a *village*. Of course, one likes to think that one's church does the same but the process is, necessarily, different. To see all and sundry united in merriment! Truly, it was a wondrous event.'

Well, thought Anne, at least they all enjoyed it. If only Mrs Austen had taken the same view.

'And then your work in the school.' Mr Whitfield reached over and took yet another slice. Was that his third or his fourth? 'The place is transformed, those children now literate. Your gifts as a teacher are quite . . . Oh!' Sorrow overcame him at last, and he put down his plate. 'What a great pity it is for us all. I do hope you intend to continue your teaching?'

'Oh, yes, indeed,' Anne replied with some force. 'I have found I am good at it. And, after all, what greater privilege is there than to teach a young mind?'

And what could be more important? Anne had pledged in future, to take on as many young girls as she could possibly handle. She would make it her mission. Arm them, not with muskets, but a strong education. So that when they, too, were hit by disappointments and heartbreaks – or poor, feckless fathers – then they, too, might have some means to survive.

After the fondest of farewells, Anne left the warm, yellow light of the rectory for the very last time, and went out into the gloaming. Following the thread of the lane – past the cottages, the school, the hump-backed bridge over the river – she kept her head down and pressed on to the house.

Once through the front door, she hung her cloak on her peg for the very last time – Stop it! Anne commanded herself. Enough with this maudlin nonsense! – ignored the gay sounds of the family behind the big library doors, ran up to her room and pressed the door shut. Sanctuary! For a moment, she leaned her shoulder upon it and gathered her strength. Though emotionally spent, she still had packing to do and was determined to do it alone.

Almost at once, there came a tap at the door, and Anne's heart sank further. No more sentimental partings – she had not the stomach for it.

'Miss *Sharp*.' Harriot stood patiently awaiting the respect of a welcome. Anne curtseyed and bade her come in. Harriot gave a curt nod. 'I am come to say my goodbyes. I am sorry you have to leave Godmersham, but there we are.' This brisk formality was quite disconcerting. 'These things cannot be helped.' A small smile contained no discernible sympathy. 'I wish you well.'

'And I you,' Anne returned and curtseyed once more. 'Every possible happiness and good fortune in your married life.'

'Oh, *Sharpy!*' For a solitary moment, Harriot enjoyed one last flirtation with her original self – Anne feared an outpouring and possibly tears – and then she summoned restraint. 'Thank you. That is kind.'

And in that moment, Anne finally surrendered all hope for her. 'Farewell. I shall miss you, Miss Bridges.'

This was true: she would remember that lively young woman with great affection. And for that other poor creature, the future Mrs George Moore? For her, she could only pray.

CHAPTER XLIV

Shortly before dawn, on 18 January 1806, Anne stood in the hall and began her last Godmersham ceremony. Two footmen fussed with her trunk as Mrs Salkeld bundled her into warm clothing. The servants lined up on the marble, and Anne kissed each in turn.

Cook had risen at five to make caraway biscuits, and hoped Anne would eat them while they were warm. Sackree clucked, stroked Anne's hair and chucked at her chin. Mrs Salkeld offered her cat up for a petting. Becky, then Sally, both wept on her shoulder. And throughout, Charles clung to her skirts as if he could never let go.

'My dear, dearest girl.' Anne held out her arms, and Fanny flung herself into them. Anne winced with pain.

'Oh, Miss Sharp,' she sobbed. '*Anny!* I am so terribly

sorry . . . Thank you for everything. You have taught me so much.'

Anne pulled away from her embrace and studied her face. 'And you me, dear Fanny: you, me. But we will write?' She put a hand to the young cheek.

'Oh, for ever and *ever*!'

Mrs Austen came between them. Anne dropped into a curtsey. 'Thank you, madam. You have been very kind.'

Elizabeth sighed. 'I am only sorry that—'

'But of course.' She looked around her and smiled. 'I shall never forget you all. Come now, Charles.' She took his hot hand in hers. 'Will you be a kind gentleman, and escort me to the coach?'

Henry followed them out, issuing good tips to the servants, warm goodbyes to the children. But between him and Elizabeth there was a new, marked *froideur*. As she was the cause, Anne hated to see it. She turned to the carriage in order to miss the cold peck to the cheek and resolved to urge peace in the matter, when they were alone.

Mr Johncock shut the carriage door, called to the coachman, and the journey began. Anne looked at the serried ranks of the household, lined up now outside as if for a dignitary. The horses – their breath turned to steam on the cold winter's air – whinnied on the gravel, and prepared for departure. Anne issued one final wave to the friends gathered on the doorstep, before, by mouthing and mime through the glass of the carriage, insisting they now go back in. Fighting the desire to express their true sorrow at her leaving – the battle was short: it was still early morning; there was much to be done and the chill of that wind from the east was notorious – they did as was bidden. The interior swallowed them up; the front door closed to the world. The gait of the horses rose to a trot.

Through her tears, Anne watched the Great House recede from her view. In her mind's eye, she could see the beginnings of a new Godmersham day. Fires must be lit and breakfast prepared. Babies roused from their sweet, milky sleeps and adults dressed to high standards. The routine would grind into life without her assistance. As if Anne had never been there.

'That cannot have been easy.' Henry, beside her, covered her gloved hand with his own.

The lump in her throat prevented immediate reply. Instead, she drank in her last view of the parkland. They were on the long drive now, approaching the gatehouse. An almost full moon dipped towards white, crystalline fields. They passed the small, hump-backed bridge, over which she once skipped. The river, where they fished – beside which they had picnicked – was now glassy with ice. As the carriage picked up speed and rocked, she turned away from the window and sat back in the seat.

'There,' she declared. 'We are now on the Canterbury Road.' She became wistful again. 'Out of the village. Two years I have spent here . . .'

'Only two years,' Henry agreed. '"Twas not much, in the end.'

'And yet, long enough.' Anne felt a gentle squeeze to her hand. 'Long enough to change every pore of one's skin and every feeling of one's mind.'

'It was certainly a most splendid send-off,' Henry said with some bitterness. 'For a governess, relieved of her duties.'

'And an equally splendid conveyance,' Anne returned. She stroked the blanket on her knees, looked around at the well-upholstered interior and settled back on to the leather. 'You are so kind to take me, and I am very grateful. Though I fear some raised their eyebrows at our odd pairing.'

'Then let them!' he retorted. 'I would not have you going by stage, after all you've endured.' He softened his voice. 'And besides which, I value your company.' At that, Anne shifted and looked out of the window. He spoke the rest to her profile. 'Tell me, Miss Sharp, though I have no right to ask it. Might I hope to believe that, in some small measure, you value mine, too?'

She gave a sad shake of her head and then turned back to face him.

'I see.' The bright light in his eyes spluttered and died. 'So that is no.'

'Oh, Mr Austen!' Anne cried. 'You know full well that I . . . But indeed, no! No, you have no right to ask it!'

The light flickered again; the crinkles appeared.

'Indeed.' He cleared his throat here. 'Then perhaps you have now given me the courage with which to speak my true mind: Miss Sharp, I have to declare it, I have become very fond of you.'

And at last, in the privacy of these closed, narrow quarters – no longer in the employ of the wide Austen family – Anne, too, felt free to admit: 'As I have of you, sir.'

But only to herself could she acknowledge the real cause of the turmoil within her.

In that long week of illness, through the strange, festive season and the shock of dismissal, Anne had found that clarity, confronted her own feelings and solved her own puzzle. She was in love, certainly. Oh! she was madly in love. But only now could she acknowledge love's object and, in so doing, explain away her own unsettling derangement. Those astonishing siblings, Henry *and* Jane: so similar, she could not choose between them; each so individual, she had not the power to resist. In the space of those two, wonderful years – within the walls of that splendid, unforgettable park – her heart had been captured by both. She could hold no hope it would ever know release.

Henry's whole being relaxed now. The pure force of his smile struck at Anne like a blow. 'Then, may I enquire if it might please you to continue our friendship?'

She had been expecting this moment; had guarded against it. 'That would be most unconventional . . .'

And yet still, despite it – Oh! Wicked temptation rose up within her, suffusing her whole being. Somehow, she summoned all her strong will to fight it back down. You cannot, she urged herself. You will not be his mistress. You must not give in. *Remember your mother!*

While battle continued to rage around and within her, Anne pulled away from him, leaned into the corner and forced her eyes on the rain as it coursed down the glass.

'I am afraid not, sir.' At last, she spoke to the sunless, gunmetal sky. 'It would not please me at all.'

For there was the other truth – and this one more bitter. She could not – she would not – share, or pretend, or hide in full sight. And yet that is what would be expected. However ardent her feelings, Anne could never have licence to love Henry, *or* Jane. The world would insist, or it would be no sort of a friend to her. Nor would the world's law.

She felt Henry slump then, beside her; heard him let out a sigh. 'You are quite correct, of course. And I beg you forget that I asked it.'

''Tis forgotten.' Anne tried not to cry.

For a while, they travelled in silence; they were held up in a town that was crowded for market, forced to divert before they were through to the country beyond. The delay was not serious – perhaps twenty minutes? No more. But time enough, noticed Anne, for Henry to regain his composure completely. He would, she thought wryly, survive.

'Well,' he went on, 'I shall be sad not to hear all your news . . . Never know how you are, or where life has taken you.'

Anne sniffed, rubbed at her face and endeavoured to match her demeanour to his. 'You can be sure that, wherever I am, I will still be a teacher. That much is certain,' she said as she mustered her spirits. 'And as for the rest: if you would like it, I am sure your sister will keep you informed.'

For she might not be allowed much – could never hope for the blissful fulfilment of all she desired – but there was one, unimpeachable role Anne would still be permitted to play. Indeed, the world would smile kindly upon this one. 'She has been kind enough to suggest that she values the relationship between us. We will continue to write and have pledged to meet up, as often as my duties allow it.' She turned to Henry and smiled then, her heart brimful with new confidence. 'I am quite sure that, with such a warm intimacy established between us, we will never lose touch now.

'I will *always* be a close friend to Jane.'

AUTHOR'S NOTE

'Poor thing,' Jane wrote once of Anne. 'She is born to struggle with evil.' It is frustrating that she did not give an inventory of all Anne's afflictions, beyond the problem of her health, and that we have no idea why she was forced into employment in the first place. We know nothing at all of Anne's life before her arrival at Godmersham Park. So the story of her early years here is a fiction, fashioned out of the biographies of other, contemporary genteel ladies who found themselves working as governesses. For a few it was a vocation, but the majority were all condemned to it by the failures of their menfolk – fathers, brothers or suitors who had let them down.

However, the period which Anne spent working for the Austen family was meticulously recorded by Fanny in her diaries, and the plot of this novel closely follows her account: from Anne's arrival, through the canaries and parties and vile operation, up to the day she departed with Henry beside her.

And what happened to her next? Fortunately, the trail does not then completely go cold. Through Fanny's occasional mentions and the extant Austen letters, we can map Anne Sharp's journey for the rest of her days. Though they were rarely to meet again – geography and poverty kept them apart – Jane and Anne continued to correspond.

So we know that, within two months of her dismissal from Godmersham, Anne was working again, still as a governess, to the six-year-old daughter of a Mrs Raikes. Again, this wasn't to last long – perhaps she was still troubled by her 'heads' and not thought quite up to it? – and, yet again, her employers did not quite want to let her go. Unfortunately for Anne, though, their solution was almost worse than another dismissal. She was re-located to Hinckley, in the Midlands, to work as companion to Mrs Raikes's difficult, frail, unmarried sister.

Anne was there for four years, and they were not happy ones. Her own health was not good, her new employer's was worse and Anne was stuck there performing onerous, unpleasant, intimate duties for a woman with whom she did not get on. Now in some desperation, she consented to a new cure for her headache, which seems to have involved a primitive, early form of electrotherapy. As Fanny reported, she had all her hair cut off and electrodes applied to her head. She got 'continual blisters, and all to no purpose'.

Meanwhile, Jane's own luck was improving. In 1809, Edward Austen gave the now famous cottage in Chawton to his mother and sisters. Jane was, at last, able to write properly and, the following year, *Sense and Sensibility* was sold to a publisher. Now secure in her living arrangements and in full creative flow, she felt an urge to share a portion of her own happiness with her friend.

In May 1811, she came up with a 'magnificent project' to enable Anne to come and stay with her at Chawton. Anne got the requisite leave, and all that was required was for Cassandra and Martha to alter their own travel plans by a few days to bring her to Hampshire. It appeared neither was willing to put themselves out for her, and the whole plan fell apart. Anne's disappointment must have been bitter. So it is interesting that she was finally able to visit that same autumn. Could it be, as she had just been appointed to the role of governess by a Lady Pilkington of Chevet Hall in Yorkshire – someone even higher on the social scale than Edward Austen – that Anne was suddenly considered to be more acceptable?

Anne visited Chawton once more, in 1815, and, as Jane's success grew, cheered her friend on from afar. She read each novel as it was published and delivered her views to the author, who kept a note of them all.

On 22 May 1817, Jane wrote to her friend – *My dear Anne* – detailing the news of her illness and her hopes of recovery. It was the final communication between them, and the last words Jane would write in the cottage at Chawton. The next letter, in July, came from Cassandra in Winchester, with the terrible news of Jane's death. Anne's reply seems to have been, characteristically, emotional; Cassandra was, characteristically, brisk in return: *What I have lost no one but myself can know*, she wrote tartly. And closed with one final barb: *I am much more tranquil than you with your ardent feelings could suppose possible.*

'Ardent feelings' . . . Such a loaded expression. Clearly, the relationship between Anne and Cassandra was not an easy one. Each seemed to resent the other's closeness to Jane. Nevertheless, the two women never lost touch. And from her regular correspondence with Jane and then, after her death, with her sister, Anne would have been able to keep up with the news of the whole wide Austen family.

So, in 1808, she would have heard that Elizabeth Austen died shortly after giving birth to her eleventh child. She would know that Fanny then had to step up, as supporter to her father and surrogate mother to her ten younger siblings. That Fanny then did not marry until her twenty-eighth year – late for those days – when she became Lady Knatchbull, took on six difficult stepchildren and produced nine more of her own.

This large family did not come without a good deal of trouble and heartache, but still, Fanny enjoyed a long and comfortable life. And, as she had started at the beginning of 1804, so she continued to record its daily events in those little leather-bound pocket books for almost seventy more years, when she became too frail to continue.

Harriot Bridges was wed to the Reverend George Moore in 1806, became the fond mother of three and – although the rest of the world continued to find him disagreeable – gave every impression of contentment with her choice of husband.

Of Henry Austen, the news had, as Anne might have expected, more twists and turns. His wife, Eliza, died in 1813, and he took at once to the carefree existence of the handsome, wealthy and sociable widower until his good luck finally ran out. In 1815, his bank and business suddenly collapsed and he was ruined. Henry had lost not only his good name and all of his money, but also all the substantial investments of his uncle and brothers. It was a shocking blow to the whole family; Jane took it particularly hard. Only Henry seemed to walk away with his spirits unbroken. Within weeks, he had happily reverted to his father's original plan for him and become a man of the Church. He was ordained in Salisbury in 1816, and thereafter lived as a curate; embraced the evangelical tradition; married a Miss Eleanor Jackson and was hard up, childless but perennially cheerful until his death in 1850.

While all this was happening to Henry, Anne went from strength to strength. She left Lady Pilkington with a sound reputation and, it appears, some money. Her health must have improved because, in 1823, she set up her own boarding school, on York Terrace in Liverpool, where she taught generations of girls, ran her own fleet of servants and lived as a highly respected member of the local community. What a pity it is that Jane didn't live to see her eventual triumph.

Anne was able to retire in some comfort, and died peacefully in 1855. She was buried, on her own instructions, in a 'plain and decent' fashion, on the south side of Everton church.

We learn as much from wills as we do from letters. In fact, perhaps we learn more, as there is no dissembling at play. The value of Anne's estate came close to two thousand pounds, including cash, shares, fine jewellery and good furniture, and was distributed among an astonishing forty-three 'very dear' friends. So not only must she have been a great professional success, she had made a good, happy life for herself: had loved and was loved.

And it is significant that Cassandra, before her death from a stroke in 1845, took the trouble to bequeath thirty pounds to her sister's old friend. After the initial animosity, some warm feeling must have grown up between them. No doubt what later bound them together was the same force that had once thrust them apart: their love for Jane Austen. For Anne, like Cassandra, was one of the very few people who, when Jane's work was forgotten, still believed in her genius. And we know that for a fact.

In 2008, at Bonham's auction house in London, a rare first edition of *Emma* came up for sale. One of only twelve presentation copies sent by Austen's publishers to friends and family on her instruction, it bore a handwritten inscription: 'Anne Sharp, from the author'. Anne knew its worth. She had entrusted it to a Mr Richard Withers, whose family kept it safe for three generations. It is now a treasure for bibliophiles – and sold again recently for over £200,000 – but it has a value to us, too.

Its very existence is proof of the enormous personal affection between Anne Sharp and Jane Austen.

ACKNOWLEDGEMENTS

I embarked on this novel just as we went into lockdown, and the libraries were closed. Research had become almost impossible until Rebecca Lilley, of the Godmersham Heritage Centre, put me in touch with local historian Margaret Smyth. Margaret just happened to have photocopied all of Fanny Austen's journals from the years that I needed, and was generous enough to share them in my hour of need. For that, and her enormous, enthusiastic support, I will always be grateful.

Once travel was allowed and at last I could visit, Fiona Sunley was a welcoming host, and Margaret and Rebecca gave up their days to guide me around the estate. Everyone I have encountered at Godmersham Park has been kind and helpful and I thank them all.

Yet again, the work of the late Deirdre le Faye proved invaluable, as did her encouragement. Even in her last weeks of illness, she somehow found the strength to share with me her thoughts about Anne. She was an extraordinary scholar of huge generosity, and is much missed. *A Secret Sisterhood*, by Emily Midorikawa and Emma Claire Sweeney, has a fascinating section on Jane Austen and Anne Sharp; *Almost Another Sister* by Margaret Wilson is an excellent biography of Fanny, and Hazel Jones' *The Other Knight Boys* is an evocative work about the Godmersham children. Giles Smith shared his knowledge of the 'cluster headaches' which bedevilled poor Anne.

Grateful thanks as well, to my wonderful agent, Caroline Wood, and to the great team of: Laura Brooke, Sophie Whitehead, Emma Grey Gelder and, most importantly, Selina Walker, who has been the perfect midwife – a wise, patient source of strength through my labours.